TEYSHA W.L.

A BOND BEYOND MAGIC

K Corp Novel Book 1

First edition

ISBN: 979-8-218-55444-6

This book was professionally typeset on Reedsy.
Find out more at reedsy.com

To my beautiful family, who have stood by me through years of wild ideas and endless stories. Thank you for your patience, love, and unwavering support.

To Jennifer Wheeler, my steadfast reader and most honest critic—thank you for always being there to help me find my way, especially when I felt uncertain. Your friendship and insight mean the world to me.

And to my eldest daughter, Maria, for helping me sift through countless ideas and for simply being your amazing self.

Preface

I started this book over three years ago. It began as a spark of an idea—a world that I could escape to, filled with magic and challenges that felt strangely familiar. But as life got busy, this story stayed quietly in the background, a world waiting to be fully formed.

Fantasy and fiction have always been my escape and my passion, so I decided to create a world with its own unique trials, not unlike the ones I've faced. Through writing this story, I found myself confronting parts of my past, working through old wounds, and even discovering a path toward healing. This book became a place to explore, to grow, and to begin again.

I wrote the story I wanted to read, and I have read it countless times. Over the years, it changed and evolved, just as I have during this journey. Today, as I share it with you, I hope it brings you the same comfort, adventure, and magic that it's brought me. Thank you for stepping into this world with me—one built from resilience, dreams, and a touch of enchantment.

Linktree QR for easy to find links

Prologue

Everything was going according to plan until I fell in love. I didn't just fall; I tumbled headlong into oblivion. I clung to him like he was my lifeline in an endless void. He became all I saw. But as we built a life together, he slowly changed. The man who once respected and supported me started to morph into someone I barely recognized. He yelled more, expected more, and isolated me from the people I cared about.

Josh always thought he deserved more than life gave him. He was an account rep for an advertising company. Being "just a rep", was a blow to his ego, he acted big and powerful when he was home to make up for his lack of power at work. His business meetings were especially stressful for me. If they didn't work out in his favor, I'd pay the price. One time he messed up a pitch to a large corporation and lost the account for his company. The dinner I spent all day making paid the price. The baking dish that had roasted chicken and vegetables in it ended up on the floor in pieces after it was thrown into the dining room wall, leaving a 9 inch gash in the drywall as a reminder of his temper that day. I knew better than to say anything. I waited out the tantrum in silence, wincing at every loud crash, hoping that day it wouldn't be directed towards me.

That was just one occasion- my marriage was full of stories like that. All of them ending in him gas-lighting me into thinking it was my fault and with me picking up the pieces of our life that he broke.

I tried to get a job to get out of the house more, but he wouldn't allow it. He was afraid if I experienced freedom, I'd leave him, but he feared that I'd get a better job than him in turn making him feel more insecure. He didn't say those things out loud, he would say he needed me to keep the house up for him, he had a standard to keep, he made up all sorts of excuses why I had to be home. His mother would be mad if there wasn't dinner ready for him when he got home, and whatever made his mom upset, would make him upset. So, I cleaned up the house, and the mess he left in our life on a daily basis.

The loneliness was suffocating. Josh would say he was okay with me seeing my friends, but once he found out that my friends didn't like him and encouraged me to leave him, he made it very difficult for me to see them. The mounting pressure made me back away from those friendships. One by one, my friends stopped calling after I repeatedly canceled plans. I didn't blame them. I was ashamed of the life I'd let myself fall into the very life I swore I'd never live.

When Josh was away for work, I was relieved. His absences became the only moments I could breathe. I began sneaking away to a local coffee shop with a free lending library. That's where I found little sparks of life again. I'd lose myself in books about art, studying the pages up close, marveling at the colors and forms. The art called to me, stirring something deep inside. I wondered if I had the ability to create something as beautiful as what I was seeing. I didn't have access to painting supplies, so I got creative.

There were scraps of drywall in the garage from patching up the holes in the walls he made on a regular basis. Josh would never notice them missing. I wasn't allowed to have a bank account or carry cash, so it was almost impossible to purchase painting supplies, but I found ways. I'd draw out extra cash at the grocery store check out, then hide the receipt so he wouldn't know. I saved up enough to buy a cheap set of brushes from the small home improvement store next to the market I shopped at. I could only buy the cheap sets, and they didn't hold up long, I'd resort to using my hands when my brushes dropped their bristles. I was determined to create a beautiful world of my own to live in, even if it was just a secret world for me.

The paint I used wasn't anything of quality, just regular house paint that we had left over. Luckily Josh's mom wanted each room in our house to have a 'focus wall' of a different color so we had gallons of partially used paint leftover, not being used.

When I was painting, I felt like a different person. The paintbrush moved as if guided by an unseen hand. It glided and tapped across the board, creating something beyond me. Stepping back, I was breathless. At close range, it was a mess of brushstrokes and drips, but from a distance, a woman emerged soft, curvy, sitting naked with one leg drawn up, covering herself. Her body, marked in lines and splashes of paint cutting across her but still so beautiful. I sat on the cold garage floor for what felt like hours, stunned by what I had created. I dreamed I was her, hidden away somewhere beautiful, somewhere Josh couldn't get to me.

Art became my secret escape. I hid about a dozen paintings in various sizes of scrap boards behind a shelf in the garage, far from Josh's eyes. I'd take pictures of them on my phone, so on the darkest nights, when Josh's rage boiled over, or when I felt utterly invisible.

One day, while Josh was out of town, I escaped to the coffee shop again. I was scrolling through pictures of my paintings, holding back tears of grief at the loss of them when a woman gasped behind me. Startled, I turned around.

"Oh, my goodness," she said, her hand over her heart. "Who made that stunning piece of art you were just looking at? I didn't mean to peek, but it's the most beautiful thing I've ever seen! I have to know the artist."

I blinked, stunned. "I… I made it."

Her jaw dropped. She slid in beside me without an invitation, her eyes wide with admiration. "Darling, you're incredibly talented! Do you sell them? I'd love one for my studio. I'm a photographer and do boudoir shoots, so your work would fit perfectly in my studio."

"Oh, I don't sell them. I just paint for fun."

"Honey!" she exclaimed. "You could make real money selling those! Would you ever consider it?"

I hesitated. Selling them? I'd never considered that. They were my therapy, my way of surviving. "No, sorry". I couldn't risk Josh finding out and getting mad again.

"I can feel the pain in these," she whispered. "I have a friend who owns a gallery. I bet she'd love to show your work. If you'd ever consider it. These are mesmerizing."

"My husband wouldn't like that. They're just for me to have a hobby. Sorry" I tried to look busy on my phone to deter any future conversation.

"What does your husband have to do with anything, honey?" She paused, and realization dawned on her face. "Oh… I see." she paused, digging through her purse to find a pen. She picked up the napkin my coffee cup was sitting on and wrote something as she spoke, "I don't know what you've been through, but I want to help you get out of it. I have a friend who runs the women's shelter in Saginaw, and my sister is a divorce lawyer who often does pro-Bono cases for the shelter from time to time. If that's something you'd be interested in, here's my number." she paused, resting her hand on mine, making me look up at her, "Let me help. Please."

"You don't even know me. Why are you being so kind?"

"Because, honey," she said softly, "I've been there. I had an abusive husband, too. I hit rock bottom, just like you are now. But you can come back from it, I promise. You don't have to do this alone. My name is Susan by the way." She said, reaching out her hand for me to shake it.

I reluctantly took it, and responded, "Aoife, I'm Aoife"

"What a beautiful name. Irish, right?"

"Yeah, I think so." Trying to cut the conversations short, I just wanted to have a few seconds of peace to decompress from the stress of my home… if you can call that hellhole a home.

She sensed my unease, "Well, if you change your mind about those paintings, let me know. And about the other stuff too, I'm happy to help connect you with people that can help."

I nodded silently, unsure of what to say. She gave me a small smile that didn't reach her eyes. How could I ever leave him? My life wasn't great, but he was gone a lot, and I had my art. It wasn't so bad. I could live like this…I had my art, even if it was a secret. It helped make my life bearable.

I hid myself away in the garage as often as I could when Josh was away. I hadn't planned on him coming home from his trip early, he'd lost another account. As the garage door slowly opened, revealing his SUV sitting outside, idling, waiting to fill up the garage with its presence, he saw me. I was caught red handed, literally. Red paint dripped through my fingers as I stood frozen in fear. I couldn't move as Josh slowly walked into the garage, while looking between me and the paintings. He strode up to me, stopping inches from my face, he ripped the paint can away from my hand and threw it across the room. It hit one of my paintings with a thud, splashing red across it, sending it toppling to the ground. He went over to another and cracked it in half over his knee, then smashed another with the broken pieces of the last. He continued until there was nothing left but rubble, overflowing with red paint, leaving a crime scene of art destruction in his wake.

He went in the house, I jumped at more crashing sounds that echoed through the walls. I was left to clean up the devastation in the garage. My heart felt like my art looked; broken into hundreds of pieces. Ruined. Shattered. Unfixable. My life was at the lowest I could ever imagine. How would I ever get out of this hole? The weight of life felt so unbearable, like I was being smothered by darkness, unable to see any light from the deep hole I fell into, or rather was pushed into with force by the one person who should have been helping raise me up in life.

Josh was on the lookout after that for any sign of me doing anything fun. He even sent his mom over almost daily now to 'check up on me'. She wasn't very sly with her snooping to make sure I was staying in line. I didn't dare attempt making art again. I went through the routine of cleaning and cooking. Wash, rinse and repeat. I did nothing that brought me joy. I was a Stepford wife robot. Not alive anymore.

Josh took his mom out to dinner, I wasn't invited, they said I brought their mood down. I was grateful that I didn't have to endure dinner with those two. They deserved each other. I was looking for a mint in my purse when I found a wadded up napkin. The napkin that the kind stranger wrote on weeks before. It had been lost in my mind, just like the napkin was in my purse, buried deep. The conversation replayed in my head. She wanted to help me. She said she had ways to help me get out of this so-called marriage. But what if Josh found out? Would it just make things even worse? How much worse could they get? I didn't see how life could get worse, he could kill me, but then it would just put me out of my misery, so he'd be doing me a favor. I had nothing to lose at this point. I was already lost.

With shaky hands I smoothed out the napkin, brushing off small crumbs that accumulated in my purse and dialed the number written in blue pen. I recognized the voice on the other end. "This is Susan." She said cheerfully.

I paused, debating if I should just hang up. But I reminded myself I had nothing left to lose. I quietly responded, "Hi Susan, you probably don't remember me. We met at a coffee shop a few weeks ago. We were talking about art."

"Oh yes dear! Aoife, right? Your beautiful name is easy to remember. How are you?"

"I um…I think I need help. He found out I was painting, and he destroyed them all. I have nothing left." I stumbled out.

"Oh honey, are *you* safe?" she asked in a concerned tone.

"I, um, I'm safe, I'm just… I don't know what I am. I can't live like this anymore." My resolve broke, I couldn't contain my emotions any longer.

"Tell me where you are. I'll come get you and take you to the shelter. One step at a time. We need to get you out of that place first. Get you safe."

"Okay" I said between gasping breaths.

"I'll be on my way in a few minutes." I gave her my address and she quickly hung up as I heard the rattling of keys in the background.

I was really doing this. I was leaving. But should I leave? Doubt began to creep in. I was gaslit for too many years, I was made to believe everything was my fault. But I never did anything wrong, I was the perfect wife. I wasn't the problem. I *knew* I wasn't the problem in our marriage. This is the right thing to do. My heart beat so fast it felt like any second it would break out of my chest. I steeled my nerves just as Susan pulled into the driveway.

I climbed in the car with a small backpack of essentials, I didn't bring many clothes because all mine were chosen by Josh and his mother. All of them weren't my style, weren't an expression of me. All of them were a facade they wanted me to put on. I had to leave that life behind. I didn't want any reminders of that life.

Pulling up to the women's shelter was surreal. I never thought I'd be in one of these. I was at my lowest of low. I couldn't get any lower. The first night was the worst. I cried as quietly as possible so I wouldn't wake up the rest of the women that were looking for a safe place to sleep too. My tears soaked the rough pillow case and seeped into the worn out pillow.

Susan came by the next day to check on me. "So, I know you have a lot going on right now, but I wanted to offer my studio for you to paint in. That is, if you want to paint again. I have an extra room there that's not being used right now. You could have the whole room to work in."

"Oh, I couldn't. That was very nice of you though. I already feel bad enough about all this, I couldn't ask for more from you." I hated needing handouts from strangers.

"If you'd like to paint me a picture for my studio in exchange, we could call it a rent payment. I'd love one of your paintings".

That got me thinking. It would feel better not just taking a handout, I could paint whenever I wanted, I wouldn't have to hide it. The empty spot in my soul, that dark place where I felt like I'd fallen in a black hole, I was beginning to see some light. Giving me hope to be able to climb out and find myself again felt so good. I almost couldn't believe it. It felt too good to be true. Good things didn't happen to me anymore, I kept waiting for the other shoe to drop.

I couldn't stop the tears from falling. I shook my head in silent agreement.

She held her hand out, I shook it, "We have a deal! I get one of your amazing pieces of art, and you get to create your art. My friend has an art studio just down the block from my place. I mentioned your art to her after we first met. She said she'd be willing to see your work and talk about a possible show if you'd be open to the idea. I know it's a little 'cart before the horse' scenario right now but think about it. It could help bring some money in so you could start over.

That's how a complete stranger had saved me. She took a risk on me, and I took a risk on her. It was the best decision I ever made, along with finally filing for divorce. I began to see more, feel more, be… more. I began to truly live.

That was the beginning of me finding out what made me happy. I worked extremely hard to make myself a life that represented me. A life of predictability and stability but full of art and creativity. But nothing prepared me for what came next.

Chapter 1

I tried not to think about my old life too often. But small memories crept in every now and then. Sometimes, I'd spot a man with a similar build to Josh walking ahead of me, and my heart would race in panic. I'd hear the ringtone he loved so much, and I couldn't help but scan the room, making sure it wasn't him. Or I'd notice a woman cowering from her husband for just asking a simple question. Moving cities was supposed to stop most of this, but the worry lingered, ever a distant thought in my mind.

It had been years since the divorce, but I still wasn't ready to date. I loved my life as it was. My friends disagreed, but I was content with my adorable studio apartment, my art, and the comfortable life I'd built. Dating just wasn't on my radar.

I had gallery exhibitions almost every weekend. I was on a great schedule of creating my art every day and showing it every weekend. My life was like clockwork. I liked that, it was predictable.

After weeks of relentless nagging, they finally convinced me to go to an afterparty after one of my shows. They were convinced I'd find "the man of my dreams" in a dark, hot, loud place that reeked of sweat, alcohol, and vomit. I knew better, but one night of discomfort for a few weeks of peace seemed like a fair trade. Our friendship has always pushed me out of my comfort zone, and I needed that. They kept me in check when I got too complacent.

The woman in the mirror felt like a stranger. I normally wore overalls that had layers of paint caked on them, well-worn clogs, with my curly red hair pinned up in a messy bun by a paintbrush. But tonight? A sparkly dress, way too much makeup that covered up my freckles, and a headache-inducing tight hairstyle, courtesy of my friends. "You look so hot," they insisted. I didn't feel hot, I felt like a walking disco ball. "It's good for you to get out of this apartment. You're going to turn into a hermit or a single old, crazy cat lady if you don't start getting out more, Aoife."

"I get out, I go to my shows every weekend." I argued.

"That's work, not fun. You need fun too. I know it's been hard dating since Josh, but not all men are like him. But you definitely won't find one sitting in your apartment!" She paused, and chewed on her lip before continuing, clearly unsure if she wanted to tell me what she really wanted, but I knew she was going to, they always did. I appreciated that about them. "We're worried about you." They shared glances between them and nodded in agreement, "we know you're fine living on your own, you're an independent woman, and that's fantastic, girl power and all, but you need someone, other than us to force you out of your comfort zone. You know we'll always be here for you, but we want you to have someone to share your life with. Someone to create beautiful art with." she winked, "Someone who loves your quirks as much as we do but won't let you settle, because you deserve the best life has to offer, girl."

I let out a defeated sigh. Deep down I knew they were right. I was hiding myself away because it felt safe. But I was running from any possible relationships because I was scared, they'd turn out to be just like Josh. I had to stop projecting my fears. Easier said than done. I silently cursed my friends for being right… again. They always told me what I needed to hear, not just what I wanted to hear.

Tears threatened to ruin the layers of makeup coating my face, all I could do was nod. They both rushed up to me. They're hug kept me together. They were my glue when my body and mind felt like they were broken beyond possible repair. I pulled myself together, determined to have a good night, for them, and hopefully for me. I didn't have much faith that I'd actually meet someone though, most men at art shows were rich snobs with no taste, and the ones that went to the afterparties were just horny and annoying.

I reassured myself that Axel would be there. They were good friends, but Axel was the first person in my new city that I really opened up to. We met at an art gallery, bonded over how we didn't understand the weird art and our appreciation of the female forms of my art. He was constantly trying to sneak into my painting sessions to 'help make my models more comfortable' by fanning them or getting them water. Even with his ridiculous ways, we've been inseparable ever since. He's like a brother to me, always there as moral support and a safety net if men got too weird. I could always count on him being there for me. Always.

Unlike my other friends, Axel never pressured me to date. In fact, he worried that if I found someone, they wouldn't let me be friends with him anymore. He knew me inside and out, not literally, we were strictly friends, he's like a brother to me. I didn't think I could trust another man after my last explosive relationship, but Axel defied the odds. He saw the happy, positive Aoife, and the depressed, ugly crying Aoife. I'm so grateful that he's stubborn and refuses to give up because I'd be lost without him. That's why I think I was partially scared to date again. I imagined falling for someone but then having to make the choice between Axel or him. I worried about that scenario but pushed it in the back of my mind because giving up Axel as a friend would never happen.

As expected, the party smelled awful, an overwhelming mix of cologne, sweat, alcohol, and vomit. I reminded myself I was doing this for my friends. Scanning the room, I spotted Axel on the dance floor with his arms around a girl, her short dress riding up with every move. He waved at me, then made a gross face as he licked his lips at her. Men are disgusting, I thought. But I knew Axel would be there if I needed him, gross behavior or not.

I left Axel to his antics and headed to the bar for a drink, hoping it would help with the overstimulation. Just as the bartender placed my drink down, a man behind me pressed into my back and handed the bartender cash.

"I've got her drink," he yelled over me to the bartender.

I nearly spat out my sip. "No, thanks," I replied, "I can buy my own drinks." He pressed into me harder, clearly expecting something in return.

I drove my elbow into his stomach. He backed off, gasping. "I said I can buy my own drinks. Thanks. This way, you won't think I owe you anything." I turned back to the bar. The bartender gave me a knowing smile as she took my money. When I glanced back, the man was already sidling up to another woman with cash in hand. My skin crawled.

I started toward the wall, but on the way, a few men brushed my lower back, one even blew hot breath into my ear as he leaned in to speak. That's when I tapped out. I couldn't handle the constant objectification.

Axel was nearby, spinning his dance partner toward me. "You okay? I saw that creep at the bar, but you looked like you handled it."

"Yeah, just another day in the life of a woman."

"I feel bad for y'all. It must be exhausting." That was one thing I loved about Axel: he knew men were pigs, and he knew he was one, but at least he respected women.

"I'm heading out. If you see the girls, let them know I'll call them tomorrow?"

"They'll probably slap me, but sure. Want me to walk you to your car?" His dance partner groaned in disapproval.

"I'll be fine, thanks though." We bumped fists, I smiled, it made me happy to see him happy, even if it was fleeting for him.

My friends hated it when I drove separately, but it gave me a sense of control. I could leave whenever I wanted without waiting for anyone. My car wasn't far, just down the block, but as I walked, that familiar tingle crept up my neck, that feeling that women inherently born with, we just knew when someone was watching, we could feel it.

My heart began to race before I gathered up the courage to glance over my shoulder, trying to be discreet. A shadowy figure trailed behind me, it was a good distance away so I couldn't see much other than darkness moving with me. My first thought, of course, was Josh. I kept glancing back every few steps to figure out how fast it was following me. As it started to get closer and closer, I strained my eyes, but I still could not make out any discerning features or markings. The figure was tall though, too tall to be Josh. It was picking up pace, gaining on me, too close for comfort.

I regretted not taking Axel's offer to walk me. I sped up, though the heels made running impossible. I couldn't risk taking the time to stop and take them off. My heart pounded faster in my chest as I tried listening for footsteps to judge how close they were without having to look over my shoulder, but the figure moved silently, leaving no hint of their proximity. I glanced back once more, now they were getting closer, into reaching distance, still shrouded in shadows, revealing nothing about who they were.

I tried to focus on my self-defense training, but my mind was racing in directions that weren't helpful. I should have stayed at the club. Did I leave wet clothes in the washer? Was I about to die? I should have brought my purse that fit pepper spray in it. My thoughts spiraled, and I felt lightheaded. My vision blurred, and I struggled to breathe. My chest tightened as if I were drowning, and just before everything went black, one final thought flickered through my mind: someone must have drugged me.

My eyes felt heavy, and it took an immense effort to force them open. For a moment, I feared I had been beaten, maybe my eyes were swollen shut. But as my vision slowly returned, the world seemed to spin. No, it wasn't the world itself, but something in the air, swirling around me, like the air itself encapsulated me. I pushed myself up off the cool pavement, so I was crouching. I gasped as I took in my surroundings. I was in the middle of some kind of cyclone. Stray hairs had come loose from my bun, whipping across my face in the wind, making me blink through the flurry of movement. But I wasn't being flung around like I would expect if you were inside a tornado. I feeling the tiny pebbles embedded in the cement beneath my hands, I could still smell the Chinese restaurant, just past where I parked my car. I knew where I was, I just didn't know what was happening.

The air wasn't just wind moving past me, it shimmered with gold, glittery dust. I didn't understand why the wind was gold, mid-thought, the swirling air eventually tugged the rest of my hair free from its bun, sending it flying around my face. The gold dust didn't feel the stinging assault of particles like it would in a sandstorm. I squinted through the wind and my hair trying to cover my face. The wind itself felt like nothing was in it making it look gold, it just felt like wind. As I was trying to figure out my thoughts I spotted the dark figure again on the other side of the cyclone's spiral walls, I had forgotten about the person following me until that moment. Awe was replaced by panic. Whoever it was, they seemed to be moving around the whirlwind, as if searching for a way inside to reach me. They didn't seem able to get in through the wind barrier. A small victory in that weird situation. I shook my head recapping what I knew; I was in a cyclone of some sort, it didn't do anything to me though, I was not being thrashed about by the intense wind, I was unharmed, I was still in Flint, but I had been followed but the shadow of the man had disappeared. None of that made sense to me.

Maybe I had a concussion, or I was drugged, and they were messing with my mind, making me hallucinate. I had no idea what happened, but I felt a warmth seep through my body, building, filling me until blackness swallowed me whole.

Chapter 2

There was nothing. It was as if I had ceased to exist. I woke in a daze, unsure of what just happened. My first thought was that I would find myself safe in my bed, wrapped in warm blankets, realizing that all was a nightmare. But as my head cleared, it became clear that I was not where I hoped. I no longer recognized my surroundings. There were no tall buildings, no cars lining the streets, no bright streetlights, no smells of the city or the Chinese restaurant. All I saw was forests and barren spots of land lit by the bright moon. I smelled only pine trees, wet earth and cold, crisp air that stung my lungs. The chill in the air quickly bit through my thin dress, seeping into my bones. I was definitely not in Flint anymore. I was so confused, if I didn't feel the stinging of the cold on me, I would have thought I was still dreaming.

I pressed my back against a large boulder nearby, hugging its shadow trying to get my bearings. A small, fairy-tale-like building, pale yellow with colorful, intricate details that decorated the eaves and a cedar roof, illuminated by the bright, full moon above. For a second, I thought I might have died and gone to some strange afterlife. Nothing else made sense.

My ears strained for any sound, footsteps, voices, anything that might show I was being followed. Silence. I knew I had to move, if I stayed where I was, I'd surely freeze to death. My body and mind were fighting. My body screamed to find someplace warm, my mind was struggling to understand what happened and wanted to run away from this new place. There was no place to go except the building, I knew if I stayed out there, I'd fall into hypothermia very quickly. I needed to get out of this bitter cold, or I'd lose my toes; I was rather fond of my toes. I didn't like the idea of going inside a strange building in an unknown place, but standing exposed felt worse. I kicked off my heels to move more quietly, the partially frozen ground beneath my feet cracked with each step.

Reaching the building, I cautiously slipped inside. The heavy door creaked slightly, making me pause in fear momentarily. I managed to squeeze in without needing to open it any wider. The first thing I saw was a large wooden crate near the door. I ducked down behind it, trying to make myself as small as possible. My feet were caked in wet cool earth along with the cold cement floor, it was beginning to numb my toes. My body shivered uncontrollably as the cold set into me. I clenched my jaw trying to keep my teeth from chattering too loudly.

I took a second to scan the building. The inside of the building was nothing like what I expected. Large industrial lights hung from the rafters, casting harsh shadows across the room. It looked like a warehouse stacked with plastic containers, wooden pallets, and tangled roller carts in the center of the room. The space was much larger than the fairy-tale exterior suggested. I strained my ears, listening for any sign of movement.

A figure moving across the room. My breath caught in my throat, and I crouched down lower behind the crate. Was this the same person who had followed me? I couldn't be sure, but the man didn't seem to notice me. I sank further into the small space between the pallets, heart racing as I silently observed him. He wasn't Josh, but that didn't mean he wasn't dangerous. He could have been hired by Josh. I considered the worst possibilities.

He began walking in my direction. I ducked as low as I could, hoping my wild, red curls would stay hidden in the shadows. His heavy boots clapped against the cement, stopping just in front of my hiding spot. I watched through a crack in the storage container as he reached into the bin revealing a heavily tattooed, muscular arm as he pulled out something small, dropped it into a large velvet bag he was carrying. Then he moved to another container, adding more items to the same bag.

I thought I'd managed to not be seen, as my adrenaline was finally starting to let up, he froze in place, mid-step. He slowly turned, now looking in my direction. My heart skipped a beat, or ten. "It's safe here," he said in a deep, gentle voice with a slight accent I couldn't place. "You won't be harmed. Please come out." He'd seen me. He knew I was there, I fought with my body to not make a run for the door. There was no place to go outside, I'd freeze to death.

I hesitated, fear still clutching at my chest. I wasn't ready to trust anyone, not in a place like this. Was this man part of some trap? I prepared to run, even though I knew I couldn't outrun him. I could fight, kickboxing might give me a slim chance. I didn't know where I'd run to though. I was in a strange, frozen place and I wasn't exactly dressed for the weather. But something in his voice, a calm reassurance, made me pause.

When I didn't come out, he repeated, his tone was even softer, "It's safe here. I swear, you're not in danger." thinking maybe I didn't hear him the first time.

I stayed crouched, edging toward the door while remaining in the shadows. I didn't want to trust him, but I also didn't have many options. Slowly, I stepped out from my hiding place, pushing my fly away hair out of my face, shoulders back, trying to look bigger and more confident than I felt.

"Who are you? Where am I?" I demanded, my voice steady despite the fear gnawing at me.

The man's wide, muscular shoulders relaxed visibly when he saw me, as if my appearance put him at ease. His face visibly relaxed, releasing the tension lines between his brows. He ran his hand through his silver streaked hair. "My name is Nick. You're in my warehouse," he said, his voice calm, almost soothing. "How did you get in here?"

I didn't respond at first, still trying to gauge his intentions. His large frame loomed in the dim light, but his body language was nonthreatening. He gestured to a padded chair near the door. "Please, sit. Let's talk." He must have seen my body trembling with child chills rapidly taking over my firm stance.

My instincts were conflicted. He didn't seem dangerous despite the tattoos, he looked more like a businessman, but that didn't mean he wasn't dangerous. I cautiously moved toward the chair, closer to the door, in case I needed to bolt. As I sank carefully onto the edge of the chair, every muscle in my body was still on high alert.

"You're in Canada," Nick said as if reading my mind. "Northwest Territories, to be precise. I run a factory here. Where are you from?" There was no way I was in Canada. None of what was happening made sense. I was just at a party in Michigan for goodness sake.

"Michigan," I said through the chattering of my teeth. "How the hell did I end up here? Was it you who followed me?" I felt the need to call him out, if he was the stalker in the alley.

Nick chuckled softly, shaking his head. "No, ma'am. I've been here all night working. No reason to follow anyone around."

He held an arm out in the direction of another door. "Come, let's get you checked out by our doctor, just to make sure you're okay. Then we'll see to getting you back home. I would feel better making sure you're not injured first though. If that's okay with you"

I took a few minutes to have an internal debate with myself. I did know how to fight so I stood a chance if he attacked me. I didn't know what was on the other side of that door though. It could be a house of horrors, or his house, which could be one in the same. I could still run, but where to, there was no place even around this building. I wouldn't survive long out there. I reluctantly nodded in agreement, knowing I didn't have many options. My purse with my phone and wallet went missing… somewhere. I had no way to get home if I was where he said. Not knowing how I got so far north in Canada had me worried. As I walked to the next door, Nick motioned to the jacket that was hanging on the knob, I nodded. He gently laid jacket on my shoulders. It was large, someone with strong shoulders owned this jacket, it smelled like cinnamon and something else I couldn't place. I was grateful for the warmth. I reluctantly followed Nick through the room to the next door.

As I entered the room, I wrapped myself tighter in the jacket attempting to comfort myself as I took stock of my surroundings again. There was another door on the far side of this new room, a kitchen-like setup, and two round tables with four people seated around them. But something about the people seemed off. I questioned if I had indeed hit my head during the cyclone, or was I really seeing them as they were? I couldn't tell if they were men or women; their appearance was fluid, as though they could be either. As an artist I was drawn to their beauty but as a person I was wondering if I was hallucinating. People didn't look like that.

I rubbed my eyes, trying to clear my vision. Their skin shimmered, pale and almost iridescent, reflecting soft pastel rainbows under the ceiling lights. Their lavender eyes felt like they were right out of a dream, maybe I was dreaming after all.

I hesitated by the door, unsure if I should move further into the room. Nervous, I waited for someone else to speak first. Finally, one broke the silence, their voices carrying the same unique accent as Nick's. "Who do we have here? I didn't know we were expecting visitors." The person's lavender eyes glanced down at my bare, mud-caked feet.

Nick answered for me, shifting his weight slightly, slipping his thumbs under his red leather suspenders, attempting to hide his slight nervousness. "She doesn't know how she got here. She's from Michigan. No visible injuries, but we should have the doc check her over, just to be safe." The four slim built figures with varying shades of pastel hair, exchanged looks of surprise at the mention of Michigan. One of them, with pastel blue wavy hair, slid their chair back with a loud squeak and stood. They were tall, not as tall as Nick but towering over me. Their slender frame was less imposing than Nick's bulk, but they still moved with confidence.

The blue-haired figure strode across the room to a phone on the wall, taking just a few long strides that would've taken me ten steps. They dialed a number and spoke in a hushed tone, the language unfamiliar to me. After a brief conversation, they hung up and gave Nick a nod before returning to their seat. I was left questioning what I just saw. They looked like they weren't human, but they had to be, maybe they were like the mountain people who ate too much colloidal silver and turned blue. I ran all sorts of illogical reasons for what I saw through my head. None of which explained what I experienced. I was left questioning even more. I didn't know what reality was anymore, I felt like Alice in Wonderland.

Chapter 3

Without a word, Nick gestured toward the next door. This time, the silence felt oddly comforting. I stepped forward and opened the door myself, determined to show I wasn't some helpless girl. I squared my shoulders, walking confidently into the next room. It was a vast contrast from the last, a sleek, modern reception area that resembled a hotel lobby. Shiny white granite floors gleamed underfoot, and large, ornate Christmas trees filled every available corner and wall space. Poinsettias and wreaths decorated the tables and doors, adding to the festive atmosphere. Across from us, a sturdy desk with computers faced a set of revolving glass doors. Outside, it was still dark, but I couldn't tell what time it was. I vaguely remembered that this far north, the winters had only a few hours of sunlight. The cold outside was bitter, though there was no snow.

As I walked across the lobby, I became acutely aware of how out of place I felt, especially as I left a trail of drying mud behind me. I cringed inwardly at the mess.

Behind the desk sat a slender, strikingly beautiful woman with long, sleek black hair. Her nails clicked rhythmically on the keyboard as she typed. Eventually, she looked up and smiled casually at Nick. "Oh hey, Nick. Who's this?" she asked, her voice friendly.

Nick turned to me, realizing I hadn't yet introduced myself. He paused, waiting.

"Aoife," I said, filling in the gap. "My name's Aoife, pronounced EE-fa."

The receptionist smiled brightly at Nick, as if sharing some inside joke, then turned back to me. "Nice to meet you, Aoife. I'm Huyen. The doc will be down in just a moment." She gestured toward a nearby seating area with plush couches and a glass-enclosed fireplace. "You can have a seat while you wait."

I made my way over to the seating area, choosing a corner spot where I could see the entire room. The warmth of the fire soothed my feet, but as the feeling returned, it brought with it sharp, stinging pain. I bit my lip to stifle a grimace. Nick took a seat in a chair beside me, not blocking my view of the room, which made me feel a little less trapped. He gave me a small half-smile, which, embarrassingly, made me blush. Luckily, before I could make a fool of myself, a short stocky man in a white dress shirt and gray slacks approached us.

"Iz zis zee guest zat needs meh zoo vuk on?" he asked in a thick German accent.

"I'm fine, just a bit confused," I said, my arms crossing defensively.

Nick noticed my discomfort and turned to me. "I know you can take care of yourself, Aoife, but I'd feel better knowing you're okay. Once the doc checks you over, we'll figure out how to get you home." His voice was calm and reasonable, and I realized I didn't really have any other option.

The doctor led us toward an elevator and pressed the down button. Instinctively, I tensed. I wasn't about to go into a basement. That's always where bad things happened in movies. I didn't see a tall building from the outside, I would have noticed that. Sensing my hesitation, Nick explained, "The building's built into the ground. It's an eco-building. It helps with heating, and the city doesn't restrict the number of underground floors."

I gave him a questioning look, but I relaxed slightly as I peeked inside the elevator. The mirrored walls showed the reflection of dozens of buttons, just as Nick had said this building was definitely not built upward. Reluctantly, I stepped in. Nick, keeping his distance, giving me space, which I appreciated. The elevator chimed softly with classical music, adding an odd sense of calm as we descended. I took the few seconds of calm to take in the men in front of me. The doctor was unremarkable, except for two odd bald spots on either side of his head. It looked like he may have cysts or something growing there. I tried to not stare but it left a lot to my imagination, which was going wild lately. Nick on the other hand, looked remarkable in every way. His crisp button up shirt and fitted slacks fit his muscular body in all the right places. I mentally slapped myself for even thinking that. *Head in the game Aoife! We're trying to survive here, not pretend we're on the Bachelor.*

We exited on floor 22, and the doctor led us down a sterile hallway lined with nameplates: D.D.S., E.N.T., M.B.S., OB/GYN. The diversity of doctors piqued my curiosity. Was this a medical facility or something else entirely? I had so many questions and I wasn't sure who to ask.

Finally, we reached a room marked "M.D." Inside, the setup was familiar: an examination table, a couple of chairs, a computer on a small desk and a rolling stool. The doctor motioned for me to sit on the table, removing the folded gown and placing it aside. I was grateful he didn't ask me to change into that, because there was no way that was happening. I climbed awkwardly onto the bed, letting out a small "umph". I caught Nick smirking out of the corner of my eye and ignored him, focusing instead on the doctor, who was now sanitizing his hands.

His hands were cold but gentle as he checked my neck, searching for any signs of injury. He worked his way up to my head, carefully parting my tangled curls as he examined me. He checked my still mud coated feet, making sure I could feel all my toes. I did my best to not stare at the bumps on his head. I failed, when he bent down, I got a clearer view of them, they looked like horns almost, broken off horns. It was the oddest thing. Lastly, he pulled out a small light, asking me to follow his finger with my eyes. I complied without hesitation. As unnerving as this all was, part of me needed to know if something was wrong if there was an explanation for what had happened.

The doctor returned to the computer, tapping away. "I zee no obvious injury," he said. "No signs of concussion. You zay you just blacked out, zen found yourself here? Anyzing else happen zat might be… unuzual?" He air-quoted the word "unusual."

I hesitated, my fingers nervously playing with the sparkles on my dress. I didn't want to sound crazy. "I thought I was being followed," I began slowly. "I felt dizzy, like everything was spinning. Then there was this…golden wind. I think I was drugged, or maybe I hit my head."

The doctor exchanged a glance with Nick before replying. "Hm, zis iz unuzual indeed, but I zink it's not a medical izzue. You're perfectly healthy." He pulled out a phone and whispered a few words into it before hanging up.

Nick stood on the wall, stoic and confident. "We'll figure this out, Aoife. I'm sorry you're going through this. We have the best team here though. You won't be alone through it." he smiled, a feeble attempt to give me some of his overconfidence.

The doctor returned his attention to me, "Zis iz a zituation for my colleague. If you'll follow me, I zink zee can help you more. If you'd follow me?" He walked briskly, his short legs working fast to keep up a brick pace.

I followed the men back out of the room, down the hallway, to another door labeled "M.B.S." A petite woman with silvery purple hair greeted us. She extended a hand adorned with rings, bracelets jangling as she moved. "I'm Dr. Finn. Head of Magical Being Services here at K Corp. You've had quite the journey, haven't you?" She said as she pushed her large framed glasses up on her nose higher.

Her gentle tone set me at ease, but her words left me reeling. Magical Being Services? I must have misheard.

"I'm sorry, did you say…Magical Being Services?" I asked cautiously.

She looked at Nick, "Nick, could you please wait outside, Aoife and I have a lot to talk about and it may be less intrusive if it's just her and I. Is that okay with you Aoife?" She then looked at me.

I had no idea how intrusive this would be, but I trusted her for some reason. I nodded. Nick looked at me, his green eyes with specks of gold bore through me, he smiled and nodded. I don't know why but I felt like I didn't want him to leave my side. He was almost comforting to have near me. Maybe it was Stockholm syndrome, maybe it was something else, but it gave me anxiety thinking he wouldn't be there.

Dr. Finn smiled and nodded, leading me into her office. I sat across from her in well-worn leather chairs. She laced her fingers together and rested them on the solid wooden desk, her bracelets jingling as did. "The good news is, you're perfectly healthy according to doc." She smiled, trying to ease my tension. "I know this is all very new to you but unfortunately we have to jump right into it in order to figure this out," she paused, giving me a second to breathe. "This is a safe space, so feel free to ask anything. What's said here won't leave this room." Her words about confidentiality were comforting, at least. I had a million questions but didn't know where to begin. Instead, I waited for her to guide the conversation. "Let's start from the beginning. Can you tell me what happened right before you arrived here? Don't leave anything out, any detail could help."

I took a deep breath. "Well, I had an art show then I went to an afterparty in Flint with my friends. I left around midnight or 1:00 AM. I was walking to the parking lot to get my car when I realized someone was following me. As they got closer, I panicked and fell. Then this… tornado-like thing made of…" I paused, feeling ridiculous for even thinking it. "…glitter-looking stuff surrounded me. When I woke up, I was outside this building in the cold. Please tell me that didn't really happen and that I'm just in a coma somewhere, dreaming all this up. There can't be glitter tornados, right?" My words tumbled out in a rush, adrenaline spiking as I relived the fear.

Dr. Finn listened intently. "The dark figure, did they look normal to you? Or did they seem unusually tall, thin, smoky, or wavy?"

I blinked at the question. It hadn't occurred to me until now, but the figures had seemed off. "Now that I think about it, they were kind of smoky, like their outlines weren't solid. That's why I couldn't make out any details about them."

She nodded knowingly. "Ah, I see. Did you know anyone here before you arrived? Or have you felt a connection to anyone you've met so far?"

I frowned, considering the question. "No, I don't know anyone here.

Michigan is close to Canada, but it's still a bit of a distance from here. I don't even know anyone this far in Canada. As far as people I've met here, they've all been nice, but I guess, um, Nick… he seemed to calm me down. I'm usually on edge most of the time, but somehow, he makes me feel… more at ease." I hurriedly added, "You're not going to tell him any of this, right?"

"That's completely understandable," she said, her tone reassuring. "So, you didn't know anything about magic before you arrived here?"

Magic? My mind raced. Magic isn't real. Was she serious? "Uh, no. I mean, I know about pulling a rabbit out of a hat, but that's the extent of it. It's all a bit confusing." I didn't want to say it out loud, but I was starting to think she might be a little… unhinged.

"Here's the truth Aoife, it may be difficult to take in, but this is your new reality. You seemed to have developed abilities. If abilities don't develop in childhood, it usually happens after a traumatic event in one's life, after you've healed emotionally from it. It opens up a kind of gateway to the magic locked inside you from past generations." Dr. Finn continued, "It is a beautiful thing but can be upsetting for those it happens to. We'll help you understand and control them, but we'll need to run some tests. The tests aren't invasive and won't hurt. They're not medical. There's nothing wrong with you. We just need to figure out how to help you from here."

I didn't understand. It sounded like a foreign language. How could I have magic? I was no one special. I didn't have ambitions of gaining power or popularity, I just wanted a quiet, normal life. What did this mean for my future now? I didn't want this. Any of this! I just wanted to be back home.

Dr. Finn gave me a few minutes to calm down as much as I could in that situation, then continued, "I'm sorry my dear but there's a downside to magic too. There are creatures that can sense it and will try to take it from you. And to make bad news worse, Nick may be connected to you somehow.

My head spun, and I couldn't form words. This felt like something out of a movie, not real life. I barely nodded, my mind too overwhelmed to process it all. She talked as if it was all normal things. I couldn't wrap my head around anything she was saying.

"You may have to figure out how connected you truly are. Not knowing could put you both in danger." Dr. Finn leaned back in her chair, crossing her arms thoughtfully. "Not everyone learns to control their powers, and without guidance, they can be dangerous. There are creatures out there like the dark figures you saw that gain power by consuming others' magic."

I froze. "By 'consume,' you mean… kill?"

"Yes, they must kill to access the soul and release the magic within it." Dr. Finn's voice softened. It was clear that she felt the weight of what she was telling me. "But there are ways to stay safe. We'll teach you how to protect yourself."

"This is a lot to take in," I admitted, my voice rising in panic. I started pacing the room to let off some anxiety that threatened to explode. "I have powers because my parents were magical, something they never told me about and now I'm somehow connected to a man I've just met. And these magical beings are trying to kill me for powers I didn't even know I had?" The words tumbled out in a frantic rush.

"Your parents may not have known either," she explained gently. "The magical gene often lays dormant. Some are born with magic, some it manifests later in life. It's possible the stories were lost along the way. It's not uncommon. Sadly, so few people have powers these days that those who do often end up ostracized or misunderstood, and many don't even know what's happening to them. That's why we have offices around the world to help people understand and control their magic. Your particular kind of magic isn't a common one though. I am not sure what you are exactly, but Njeri will help you discover all your abilities. From what I can gather, you can create a kind of portal with your mind, and it can transport you to different places. I've never seen your magic before, but I'll start digging, you have me very curious what you are." She said biting the end of a pencil.

I sat there, silent, trying to process everything. I have powers, but she's never heard of mine. It made me wonder how many powers there were and why mine were so unique. Maybe I'd never get answers if my so-called abilities were so rare. "Can I just get rid of the powers? Or if I don't use them, will I be safe?"

Dr. Finn's expression was compassionate. "I'll have to look into that for you. Most inherited magic can be detected once it's activated, even if you're not actively using it, it's a part of you, in your genetics. Your past traumatic event triggered yours. It will only emerge once you've healed emotionally and mentally from it. Magic can take time to grow inside you. Which is why you've only now started noticing it. Your magic saved you. It knew what to do, before you even did. You'll learn to know your magic so you can control it. Being inside this building will protect you, the barrier spell surrounding it cloaks all magical beings inside, so you don't have to worry about being safe while you're here. We have people who can teach you how to mask your powers so once you leave here too".

She paused, watching me closely, seeing the tears trickling over my cheeks. My entire life had just changed in a matter of minutes. I was now a part of some crazy world with magic apparently and I was in danger, I was so overwhelmed. She saw my need for reassurance, "There may be a small chance we can break the magical line. It will take some research though. You'll have to give me time on that. Do you have any questions right now? I know you wish you could have more time to rest and adjust, but if you want to return to your life, you need to learn to wield your magic safely. You'll do just fine. I can tell you're strong-willed. You'll adjust quicker than you think." She smiled, patting my hand reassuringly. "I'll set you up with Njeri tomorrow. She's our resident MM, Magical Master. She's the best at what she does and will teach you everything you need to know to protect yourself. She's intense, but you're in good hands with her. Meanwhile, I'll keep looking for answers."

I shook my head, too overwhelmed to speak. I felt like a zombie, I was numb to everything. I silently watched her stand, and barely heard her say, "I can leave a note at reception for you if I find any information for you. Huyen can relay any questions that may come up too."

She opened the door, Nick was waiting outside for me. I blinked blankly at him, tears still staining my cheeks. He attempted to put on a brave face, but his expression showed worry. He was worried I couldn't handle this. I didn't know if I could either, to be honest.

"I had them get a room ready for you. I'm sure you could use a good night's sleep after your day. I'm sorry we can't get you back home just yet. I promise we'll get you back as soon as it's safe for you."

I could only nod, saying any words would break the dam inside me holding back a flood of emotions. I followed him silently in a daze. I nearly bumped into him when he stopped in front of a door and opened it. He pushed it open and held it for me, not walking into the room himself made me feel more comfortable.

"I'm down in room 400 if you need anything, or you can reach the concierge on line 1. Let us know if you need anything else. We'll figure out the next steps in the morning." Nick always sounded so calm and confident with a whisper of sympathy. I was glad someone was being brave, because I was freaking out inside. "The team brought up some pajamas and clothes for tomorrow," Nick explained, glancing at my still mud-streaked feet. "They're usually pretty good at guessing sizes but let us know if anything doesn't fit. I thought you might want to get out of that dress, it looks lovely on you, but a shower might feel nice after the day you've had."

"Thanks Nick, for everything."

"It's no problem. We have a large network, we do this a lot actually."

"You do?"

He leaned against the doorframe. "Yeah, my parents started to rescue creatures in need, I just kind of took up the reins. I'm just glad we could help you, and glad you're safe." He gave a small smile.

As he turned to walk away, I remembered, "Oh Nick, here's your jacket back." shrugging it off my shoulders.

He stopped me, "Keep it for now. Get it back to me later. I'd hate for you to turn into a popsicle again." He left me with a beautiful smile and a warm jacket. I nodded, grateful for the thoughtfulness. He was most definitely not like Josh. I couldn't remember a time when Josh put my needs before his. I quickly shut down that thought. I can't let him take over my mind again. I had bigger worries to think about.

Chapter 4

The room was not what the bland outside suggested. The word "grandeur" didn't do the space justice. Dark-stained wood paneled the walls, and vintage, heavy drapes covered what I assumed was a window, though, being underground, I wasn't sure what it actually concealed. Too tired to investigate, I left that mystery for another day. A carved, four-poster bed dominated the room, opposite a fireplace with a small seating area. A neat stack of clothes lay folded on the bed.

I made a beeline for the bathroom, deciding a shower was the best way to wash off the grime of the day. The hot water felt like heaven, but as it washed the mud away, it also drained the last bit of emotional strength I had left. I broke down, sobbing under the stream of water. I was in a strange place, with no idea how I got there. I had no clue if anyone was looking for me, or if my friends thought I was dead in a ditch somewhere. My mom, was she beside herself with worry? How was I going to get home? Though I didn't feel unsafe, there was something about this place that made me anxious, like something was off; not bad or scary, but different, I couldn't pinpoint what.

The smooth tile under me, I sat, letting the water wash over my face. I needed to feel something, I felt like a zombie, unable to think clearly, wanting one thing, to get home. But that wasn't a possibility, at least until I learned how to control my magic. Would I ever get used to saying that? *I have magic.* I felt so alone, more alone than in my marriage, I had no one I trusted here to talk to. Everyone seemed fine, I just didn't know them, I got thrown into this crazy world and I didn't know if I could accept the answers that I was given. I felt like I was drowning, the water rushing over my face was just a physical representation of how I felt inside.

After what felt like hours, the tears stopped. I pulled myself together, dried off, and slipped into the soft flannel pajamas waiting for me on the bed. Exhausted, I checked to make sure the door was locked then sank into the pillowy mattress, welcoming the dark as I drifted quickly into sleep.

When I woke the next morning, for a moment, I thought it had all been a dream, rather hoped it was a dream. Surely none of that could have happened. But as I blinked awake, I took in the elegant wooden room and the rolling table beside the bed, topped with a covered plate. My heart shattered, it was real, all of that really happened. I'm in a strange building with even stranger people, with no way home. The fact that they were able to bring food into my room without me knowing made me uneasy. I pulled off the plate cover to find a steaming omelet, toast, fruit, orange juice, and coffee. At least they brought good food. It looked fresh, as if it had just been delivered. I wondered how much this little stay was going to cost me.

I picked at my breakfast for a while, unable to find my appetite. The butterflies took up too much room in my stomach, leaving no room for food. I decided to explore my room. I opened drawers and cabinets, but they were mostly empty, save for a notepad stamped with the letter "K" in a fancy script and a Christmas book where you'd usually find a Bible, the back had an embossed 'Klaus' on the back cover. Odd, but given the love of Christmas I'd seen around here, it wasn't surprising. I wanted to learn more about this place, but it wasn't giving me much, maybe Dr. Finn had more luck. I got dressed into some clothes they left for me and dialed the number for the concierge. A familiar voice answered. "Good morning, Miss Aoife. What can

I do for you this morning?"

"Hi, Huyen, right? I was hoping Dr. Finn left some information for me."

The sound of nails clicking on the keyboard started right away, "Hm, let me check." After a second, she said, "Oh yes, looks like she's set you up with Njeri. I can walk you down there if you'd like. It's a bit of a maze. Hate for you to get lost on your first day."

I am glad she offered to walk me, this whole building is like a giant maze to me. I went down… er up to the lobby to meet her.

When I arrived, Huyen was at the elevator when I arrived, her soft smile greeted me, making me a bit more at ease. The ride was silent except for the soft cello music playing through the speaker, maybe she knew I was too in my own head for a conversation. When we reached our floor, she stepped out first and called out for Njeri. The sudden yell startled me, making me jump. While we waited, I glanced around the floor, noticing it was filled with what looked like an obstacle course, like something you'd see at a Quantico training field. In the corners, a few glass-walled rooms stood out, adding an even more intense atmosphere to the space.

An imposing woman strode up to us with long, purposeful steps. She had beautiful dark, smooth skin and dreadlocked hair that framed her strong, confident features. Her outfit was a mix of functionality and style: a perfectly fitted t-shirt, a leather jacket, baggy pants, and combat boots. She exuded an air of authority, her gaze sharp and assessing.

"Hey, I'm Njeri. I'm here to keep you alive," she said with a firm handshake that nearly crushed my fingers. My stomach dropped, knowing this woman meant business. Before I could respond, she pulled me along, leading me into one of the glass rooms. Huyen spoke to Njeri in that same unfamiliar language I had heard before, and it was starting to irk me. They knew I couldn't understand, and yet they kept using it. Were they talking about me? Of course, they were.

She waved goodbye and returned to the elevator, leaving me alone with the intense trainer.

I could only hope Njeri was as capable as she seemed. Though intimidating, I was relieved she was a woman, I wasn't comfortable with men, especially if it involves physical contact, PTSD my therapist diagnosed it. Still, the sheer force of her presence made me question how in shape I actually was, despite my self-defense training.

She motioned for me to go to a room in the corner. Inside the glass room, Njeri motioned to one of the folding chairs. I sat down as she shut the door behind us. "Alright, let's see what you've got," she said, her eyes fixed on me.

"I have no idea what I'm supposed to do," I admitted sheepishly.

"I want you to show me your powers."

I stared at her blankly. "I don't know what my powers are… or even how to use them. The woman said something about creating portals? I still don't fully understand it".

Njeri sighed. "Dr. Finn wasn't much help with that, huh? Alright, we'll start with some basic tests. Don't worry, they shouldn't hurt… much." She said the last part in a whisper that didn't exactly inspire confidence. With a huff, "Okay, the basics, you have a power, we'll figure out the details later. But you also have the power to cloak yourself, it's like a magical bubble you put around yourself to prevent your magic from being sensed. That will keep you safe while you live your life. It will become second nature for you. But first, let's figure out your power."

I sunk lower into the chair, already feeling defeated, so not only did I have to learn what exactly my magic does, but also learn how to control a freaking magic bubble to protect myself? I had been up for two hours, and I already wanted that day to be over. She laid out a few objects on the table: an apple, a butter knife, a candle, and a child's wooden toy airplane.

"Concentrate on each item, one at a time, and see what you can make happen."

I focused on the apple first, imagining it floating, growing, or even exploding. After several long minutes of staring at it, nothing happened. I moved on to the butter knife, feeling nervous. Even though it was blunt, I didn't want it flying through the air and hurting anyone. But again, nothing.

The candle came next. I groaned internally, squinting and even waving my hands dramatically, like I'd seen people do in movies. I heard Njeri chuckle in the corner, but still, nothing.

Finally, the toy airplane. I stared at it, completely unsure of what I was supposed to make it do. Once again nothing. I was about to give up when suddenly, Njeri shouted, "Boo!"

I jumped in my chair, startled, and then, out of nowhere, a small, golden tornado appeared in the room. It was much smaller than the one I'd experienced before, only about the size of a person. It whipped the air around me, sending my hair flying into my face. I squinted through the gusts, trying to see through the chaos, and then, just as quickly as it had appeared, the tornado vanished.

The toy airplane was gone, too.

I spun around, looking for it, but it was nowhere in sight.

Njeri stood frozen in shock, her mouth hanging open. "You… you did it!" she exclaimed, running over to hug me. Her grip was too tight, I could barely breathe. I squirmed out of her grasp, still confused.

"What the hell just happened?" I asked, catching my breath.

"You, my dear, are magnificent! There hasn't been a materialist found in over 200 years!" she said, practically beaming. "You can create and manipulate objects out of thin air! This is incredible!"

I blinked, still lost. "What does that mean?"

Njeri composed herself. "I'm sorry, I didn't mean to overwhelm you. It's just… this is a huge deal for us. We pride ourselves on having a variety of magical members, but materialists are incredibly rare. It would be an honor to help you develop your abilities." She placed her fist over her chest and gave a respectful bow. "In history there have only been a few materialists, their powers varied, some could only portal small objects, but some of them… man, they were powerful. They were often recruited by governments to go into battle with them, they helped win many wars. I'm not saying you're going to have to join the marines or anything." She laughed, "but they were highly regarded. You can obviously move small objects, and yourself, but we'll have to figure out exactly how much you can move and how far. Some could move things to and from different dimensions."

As exciting as it was to accomplish moving an item with my magic, Njeri left me with even more questions. So, I was a 'materialist', whatever that meant, she said a bunch of words, but I barely heard any of them after battle. I didn't want to battle, I didn't want to learn this new thing, I just wanted my old, boring life. But I had to come to terms with this, I saw the proof that I had magic, it wasn't some weird dream. I don't want this magic, but I had no choice but to learn how to use it so I could go home and pretend I didn't have it. So, I'd do her lessons, if only to leave there sooner.

I was still reeling from everything. "So, where did the toy go?"

She giggled, clearly thrilled by the mystery. "I have no idea! But you are very special. Your power is rare and strong. You have no idea how much potential you have."

She led me out of the glass room and into the large obstacle course area. Picking up a few small foam balls, she chucked one at me without warning. I screamed, trying to shield myself with my arms, but another small golden tornado appeared and sucked up the foam balls. Just as quickly as the wind had started, it stopped, and the balls were gone.

Njeri beamed. "See? You're stronger than you think."

Before she could throw another ball, the elevator dinged. Nick stepped out, looking as calm as ever, dressed in jeans and a flannel shirt. He held out the wooden toy airplane, flipping it over to reveal the name "Njeri" written on the bottom.

"I think this belongs to you," he said with a grin.

Njeri turned to me, then back to Nick, but before she could say anything, foam balls rained down on him from a small golden hole in the ceiling. He didn't even flinch. They bounced off his head and shoulders, rolling across the floor. Njeri couldn't hold back her laughter.

"You," she said, pointing at me, "are connected to Nick somehow. That's why you were transported here." I couldn't believe she said that out loud, she connected the dots. I was not prepared to even consider that when the doctor mentioned it. Now that she's made it public, it created a pit in my stomach. I did not want to be connected to anybody, anywhere right now.

I blinked, trying to wrap my head around it. "Wait… what?"

Njeri continued, "Have you heard of soul mates or fate? For some reason, you and Nick are linked. That's why you ended up here, you were drawn to him." I shook my head in denial. There was no way Nick was my 'soulmate', we came from two very different worlds. And soulmate isn't a real thing. I didn't know why Nick seemed to be involved in everything, but it sure wasn't because we were *supposed to be together.*

Nick looked just as stunned as I felt. "Um… well, that's interesting," he stammered. He pinched the back of his neck with his head nervously, "how would you feel about it, if it were true?" he looked at me with puppy dog eyes, almost pleading for me to be okay with that scenario.

"I, um, I don't know. I don't really believe in soulmates. I think we all just hope to find one person that can put up with all our crap, ya know."

"I've seen true love, my parents had it. They respected each other's strengths and helped with their weaknesses, balancing each other out. Maybe my parents were the anomaly, but I have enough faith for the both of us."

I on the other hand didn't believe in true love, I married my Prince Charming, and he turned out to be the Beast. I had lost faith in a healthy relationship, and lost faith in finding love altogether. I didn't want to be forced to be with someone. If I was to fall in love someday, I would have liked it to be organic, a bond formed over time on its own. How could I trust that this was the right man, the right relationship? I was just supposed to go along with that?

I didn't know what to say, if he wanted to hold onto some fantasy about true love, so be it. I'd be the realist. I'd keep an open mind, okay, not completely open, but partially, to the crazy world of possibilities there.

"After you're done here, would you like to grab a bite. We have a great restaurant and I'm sure you could use some food after Njeri is done with you. She's relentless." He said making a face at Njeri then smiled at me.

I was getting hungry, I regretted not eating the breakfast they brought for me, and the whole magic thing was exhausting, it really zapped my energy. I nodded. He left me with a toy lane and a smile.

Njeri wasn't done with me yet, she spent another few hours throwing things at me. She seemed to be enjoying it far too much. Luckily, I was getting better at controlling my magic tornado thing, so I rarely got hit then. She set me free for the day as long as I promised to practice my magic more on my own.

She tossed one more ball at me, this one I caught and practiced 'portalling', that's what Njeri called it, the ball back to me. Sometimes it ended up at the end of the hall, but always in sight then so I was improving.

I wandered through the building, practicing my new skill, all the while keeping Njeri's advice in mind, *don't kill anyone*. The foam balls were landing in my hand after disappearing in a whoosh of gold. It was beginning to become easier, though it was still hard to wrap my head around what I was doing.

Chapter 5

I found myself a quiet hallway and practiced my new skill. I was getting pretty good at the whole 'portaling' thing, my mind started to wander. I didn't want to be there, but my stupid magic brought me there, to Nick, my supposed *soulmate*. Even thinking that made my head spin. Nick, my soulmate. He was a GQ cover model material, and I was a hot mess of an artist. I was no one, and he was definitely a someone.

I zoned out overthinking what was happening, while still practicing the portaling with my golden tornado. The next attempt, the ball didn't come back to me. I was left in an empty hallway, confused. I was opening doors in the hallway, trying to find my lost ball when the elevator dinged, Nick stepped out holding a grin and a foam ball.

"Yours I'm assuming?" he said with a chuckle.

"Guilty. Sorry, I don't know why it keeps going to you." I felt my cheeks starting to redden. He tossed the ball back to me. I knew, because I was thinking about him. Why did I find my mind wandering back to him, his green eyes, his very muscular body… I kicked myself for letting those thoughts linger in my mind. I wasn't staying. We wouldn't be together. We couldn't be together. I couldn't let his magnetic looks take hold of me.

"You hungry?"

"Famished!"

"Let's find a solution to that issue as well. Shall we?" he said, pointing his hand towards the elevator.

We rode down in silence, and when the doors opened, he led me through the lobby to a restaurant with a large "K" on the door. The aromas inside were heavenly. The hostess greeted Nick warmly and led us to a reserved table near the kitchen. Apparently, Nick was a regular.

I sat my foam ball on the table as we glanced at the menu. The chef burst through the kitchen doors, dramatic, like most chefs are, I thought. "Good afternoon, Nick and Aoife! May I make something special for you both? I have a feeling I know exactly what you'd like."

Who could say no to that? A chef making a custom meal, Axel will be so jealous when I tell him this crazy story. I dealt with a lot of people in the service industry with my art shows and after parties, I was very comfortable around the high energy personalities. I had no doubt the chef would make something to show off his skills. The chef disappeared back into the kitchen with a wide grin, leaving us to talk. The silence was excruciating, Nick must have been waiting for me to start the conversation. I wasn't great at casual conversation.

"So, what do you do here?" I asked awkwardly, trying to fill the silence but also hoping to learn more about Nick.

Before he could answer, the server arrived with drinks, lingering a little too long with her smile aimed at Nick. I couldn't help but watch the interaction, Nick clearly ignoring her efforts to gain his attention, and her practically throwing herself on him. He cleared his throat, bringing my attention back to him. "I help run the day-to-day operations here". The waitress took the hint and walked away in a huff, giving me a glare over her shoulder.

"So, you run the whole place?" I asked again, I had a feeling he would try to dodge my questions. He seemed to be evasive when it came to talking about himself.

"Not really. Everyone here is pretty self-sufficient. I just make sure things run smoothly and everyone has everything they need to do that." He handed me a dinner roll from the basket.

"You seem to do more than just supervise, you're the go to guy. I see how everyone respects you. You must do more than stand around and watch people, you said your parents helped people?"

"Yeah, they made it a big part of K Corp to help people and creatures in need. My mom, especially, dad was busy with the factory and making sure orders went out in time. It was very time consuming and stressful, it kind of took over his life. But my mom, she filled in, she was like a mom to everyone here."

"She sounds wonderful Nick," I knew I didn't want to push him too fast for personal information, I'd settle for snippets of his past, hoping it'll add up overtime and I got to see the whole Nick he tried to hide with his brave facade. I changed the topic before it got too deep, I was too mentally exhausted from learning about my magic for deep emotion. I fiddled with it, thinking about my life back home, it was never far from my mind. "So, how long am I staying here?"

"That depends on how quickly you learn. Some people stay for days, others for months. It's up to you, we just want to make sure you're safe."

I sighed, days was one thing but months? I couldn't be gone for months, I worked so hard to have a stable life in Flint, I would go back to nothing. I'd lose my studio space, my manager may not hold my job for me which meant I couldn't pay my rent. Stress began to sink in again, I had to find the drive to learn my magic, fast. I had a life to get back to. I was not about to get complacent and stay longer than was necessary. "I appreciate the offer, but I have a life to get back to. I have a job, friends, and family. I can't stay here forever. What do I need to learn to be safe? I know self-defense."

Nick grinned, attempting to hide his disappointment but failing, I saw the slight sadness in his eyes. "It's more than self-defense, darlin'. You need to learn how to cloak your magic so you're not traceable. And you'll need to control your powers so you don't transport here every time you get upset... though I wouldn't mind that," he said with a wink.

"Does that wink work on all the ladies?" I shot back.

Nick chuckled. "Just lightening the mood. We're just getting to know each other better, that's all. Don't you want to know why we're connected?" He danced around the subject of relationships. It made me wonder if he was hiding one, perhaps with the waitress he tried so hard to ignore. If that was how he treated his significant others, I wanted no part of that.

I had forgotten about him being my supposed soulmate for a second, but it didn't matter. "I'm fine not knowing. I'm not staying here long enough for it to matter."

His expression fell slightly, but he nodded. "Alright then. Let's finish lunch and get you back to your day. I'm sure you have a lot going on." I could tell there was still some awkwardness between us. I hoped he wasn't upset about my lack of enthusiasm over the whole soulmate thing. It wasn't anything against him, any woman would be lucky to have him. He was a real catch, from what he showed me at least. He made it hard to see the real him, I could tell he hid a lot from people, only letting snippets of his true self out. It made me wonder if he truly wanted to have a soulmate, or if he was content with the life he made like I was. No matter what someone told me, I had to find out for myself what I truly wanted and right then, I just wasn't looking for a relationship. I liked my life the way it was, career-focused and relatively simple.

"Thanks for lunch Nick. I really appreciate it. You taste good, I mean the food tasted good." Heat sprung in my cheeks as I quickly corrected my stupid brain thinking about how hot he was instead of forming an actual sentence.

He chuckled in a deep, rumbling sound that did things to me- I wished it didn't. "Any time." He turned away and added, "Oh, I almost forgot. Dr Finn talked to our magical genealogist in our Ireland office, they found some information they think you'd be interested in. just ask at the front desk, and they'll set it up."

He continued down the hall, leaving me with yet another overwhelming piece of information to process. A genealogist? I wondered who was magical in my family. Did they know? Did they keep it a secret? Curiosity piqued, I made my way to the front desk.

Huyen was still there. Did she ever take a day off? "Hi again, Huyen. Nick mentioned I could set up an appointment with Dr Finn about the genealogist?" I left the 'magical' part off as it still felt too weird to say out loud.

"Of course! Is there a time that works best for you?"

"It's not like I have much going on here," I said with a light laugh. "Whenever she's available is fine."

Huyen smiled at me then typed quickly, "She has an opening in ten minutes or one in an hour. Which would you prefer?"

"I'll take the one in ten minutes."

"You remember where you're going?"

"I think so, if I get lost, I'll just portal an SOS to Nick" I joked.

I made my way back to Dr. Finn's office, hoping I remembered the way and I wouldn't end up in some weird lab and be experimented on. I was beginning to think I had watched too many horror movies, but weird scenarios kept popping in my head. I could not predict what would happen next in that place. I smiled as I reached the doctor's door. At least something was going right.

"Greetings again Aoife. You've had quite the whirlwind of a time, pun intended," she said with a small chuckle, pushing her glasses higher on her nose.

I couldn't help but smile back. Her quirky energy was contagious. "Yeah, it's been an experience for sure. Thanks for helping with this."

"My pleasure dear. I found some interesting things about your family. Would you like to hear what I discovered?" She typed quickly, soft clicks on her keyboard, and after a few moments, a soft click on her desk activated a light that projected a glowing family tree onto the ceiling. The sight was mesmerizing, like something out of a sci-fi movie. She pulled out a thick leather-bound book, flipped to a marked page, and ran her finger down a list of names. "Ah, here we are." She clicked a few more times on her keyboard, and two names on the tree lit up in red.

"These two," she said, pointing with a laser pen, "are the originators of magic in your family, on your mother's side. It seems they made a deal with a witch to gain magical powers. That deal has been passed down through generations since. Once a spell is linked to genetics, it's hard to break. It quite literally intertwines in your DNA. It will continue on through the generations. Sometimes past traumas can open up a bridge to that magic. Healing from an even lowers that drawbridge to allow the magic to be freed."

"This takes generational curses to the next level," I nervously joked. A deal with a witch? That sounded like something out of a fairy tale, or a nightmare. "Why would they make a deal like that? Didn't they care how it would affect anyone else?" I shouted, my frustration bubbled over. My ancestors caused this, caused me so much pain and upset.

"I'm afraid I can't answer that, but love is a powerful motivator," she responded gently. "The details are lost to time, at least from what I can find. But I can tell you this: it wasn't black magic. Your family isn't cursed. If they were, you'd see a pattern of bad luck, illness, or tragedy, and it would be well-documented in our system." It still felt like a curse to me though.

That news brought a small relief though. At least we weren't cursed. But something else bothered me. "My aunt always claimed she was psychic, but we all thought she was just… eccentric or schizophrenic. Turns out, she might've been telling the truth. I'm not psychic, why are my powers different?"

"She quite possibly might be magic," Dr Finn said with a nod. "Many who carry a magical gene may experience things like déjà vu or minor psychic abilities. But only those who have allowed that magical gateway in their brain to open will experience stronger abilities. Powers manifest differently in everyone, just because your family has a gene doesn't mean you'll have the same abilities."

I kind of wished we shared abilities, that way I'd have someone to talk to about everything. Instead, I'm left with more questions and feeling even more alone. I thought about my family. They had never spoken about magic. I wondered if they hid that side of our family, not wanting to be ostracized. "Do you think my family had any idea about this?" I hoped they didn't know instead of just hiding this huge fact about our family.

"It's possible they didn't. Magic only opens up itself to people who are ready and strong enough to handle it. Some don't even realize they have magic, it can be so subtle, like dreams that come true or being good at guessing people's names. When the magic isn't obvious or the signs are ignored, it's often forgotten about overtime. That can make it difficult on the next person who inherits magic and has powerful magic. I don't know much about your specific situation, just about your close family and none have registered powers with us. It seems the lore of magic has been lost with time in your family. However, if you'd like, I can look into the witch who made the deal. Her lineage might still exist. That may give you some answers. I can't guarantee anything, bloodlines are lost overtime, but it may still be active."

"I'd appreciate that. Do you think they could do anything about it?" Hoping they could maybe break the magical gene or something. Free me of this burden.

She smiled and said, "I'll contact my colleagues in Ireland and see what they can find. Give me a few hours, and I'll leave a note at the front desk with any updates."

I thanked her, my mind swirling with new information. Witches, magic, deals, it was all so much to process. How was I supposed to bring this up with my family? 'Hey, so who else here has magical powers? No one? Just me? Yeah, that would go over well at Thanksgiving.

Chapter 6

I headed back to my room, hoping to rest my weary mind. I opened the door, I found my bed neatly made, breakfast dishes gone, and a one-piece swimsuit with a plush terry robe draped across the comforter. There was also a note in elegant calligraphy: "Meet me at the pool if you feel up to it. The water is very rejuvenating. —N.K."

The thought of seeing Nick half-naked by the pool made my heart race, but the promise of a relaxing swim was too tempting to pass up, I wouldn't allow myself to get attached. I had a life to get back to and I was not about to give it all up for a few nights of fun with some mystery man. I slipped into the swimsuit, thankful it wasn't some tiny bikini, and wrapped myself in the robe before heading down to the pool.

Opening the glass door, I saw Nick lounging in the hot tub, the steam rising around him made him look like a god appearing from the clouds. His muscular chest glistened above the water, showcasing a few tattoos I hadn't noticed before. I wondered where else he had tattoos, then I quickly shut down that thought. I could not get invested with Nick, frustratingly my mind kept defying my orders to not think about how he looks.

"Come on in. The water's perfect," he said, patting the wet tile next to him.

I dropped the robe on a beach chair, trying to avoid making eye contact with Nick. Which was difficult because I noticed his quick glances in my direction. I slid into the hot tub, careful to keep a bit of distance from his body. He was right, the water was warm and inviting, it instantly relaxed my muscles but my mind kept racing back to Nick. If he'd stop looking at me with those green eyes maybe it would have been easier to ignore him.

"Our wardrobe specialists really know their stuff because you look amazing," Nick said with a playful grin.

I felt my cheeks heat up, not from the warm water. "Thanks," I muttered, I've never been great at receiving compliments. I awkwardly shifted the conversation. "Okay so I'm dying to know, how do the windows work here? Most of the floors are underground right? So how are there windows?"

"Oh, I forget that it's even like that. The windows are actual windows but there's a series of mirrors that are in a channel that runs the entire height of the building. The mirrors reflect the light and view from the top of the channel."

My jaw must have dropped open.

He chuckled, making my body react again. I really needed to have a talk with myself about this whole attraction thing. "We have some great minds that pass through here. Some want to give back as a thank you, so they help us with projects from time to time. That was the brilliant work of one of our friends who passed through."

"That's actually really neat. I don't fully understand it, but it sounds fascinating."

"Anything else you're wondering about?"

"Lots! But for now, that's good. Let's limit the information so my brain doesn't explode."

"We wouldn't want that. I'd like to get to know that mind more. If or when you're ready."

"This place seems like an anomaly. It seems like it's a large company, obviously making good money, but it also helps people? I didn't think rich people cared about helping people, other than using their fake goodness as a tax write-off."

"We have done well in business, it's true. It's been in the family for generations, my parents saw the need growing so they built K Corp to be able to expand and make more things. But the helping people aspect has always been a part of us too. As far back as I know my family has helped creatures. It started with small things like giving them food, tools or weapons they need to protect themselves, then it grew from there. Now we are a safe harbor for many, like yourself. Those in the magical community know about us, but we have tried to remain a secret from the outside world, we're just a toy factory." He ended with a wink.

I knew deep down that I wasn't going to stay so I didn't want to get attached. He was making it hard though with his talk about helping people in need. It brought back memories of Susan and how she helped me out of a bad situation and all the people who helped me get back on my feet during all that. I didn't want to hurt myself by getting attached but I especially didn't want to hurt Nick. I couldn't be responsible for that, he put on a hard exterior, but I sensed there was a soft, sensitive center to him. "There are so many odd offices… and people. I've been trying to figure that part out."

He leaned back, a genuine smile crossing his face. "I've been waiting for you to ask. I try not to just announce it, it tends to overwhelm people. But since you asked, this place helps magical beings of all kinds, witches, fairies, you name it, and some I can't even name…like I literally can't pronounce it."

"Creatures, huh?" I raised an eyebrow.

"Yeah, we've got a little bit of everything here. There're so many different creatures out there, almost as many different kinds of insects in the world. It's pretty amazing really. We help those in need, whether it's teaching them to control their powers, providing shelter, or relocating them to safety."

I was in disbelief to hear creatures. I mean I've seen some things that weren't quite… normal but it never occurred to me that most would not be human. I started questioning everyone I saw, recapping in my mind who I'd met and trying to figure out if they were human or… something else. It wouldn't matter if they weren't human I guess. I just don't like the unknown.

Josh ruined future surprises for me. His surprises usually ended up with me in tears. I wasn't scared of anyone there so far. In fact, everyone I had met were the nicest people…er creature's I'd ever met. I wouldn't judge them any differently.

I tried to refocus and stop my mind from overthinking who may not be human. "That's… incredible," I said, sinking deeper into the warmth, letting the water calm my mind like it did my body. "So, is this what you do all the time? Not the hot tub, but helping people find their way?"

Nick chuckled. "No, not exactly. Normally, I just help run the factory and oversee the day-to-day stuff. But you're a special case."

I wasn't sure how to feel about that. I was no one special.

"My mom did most of the saving, I just try to step in now when I can."

He moved to the pool before I had a chance to ask about his mom, it seemed he wanted to avoid that topic, so I let it slide for now. I remained soaking in the hot water a bit longer, while I enjoyed the view of Nick swimming laps. I can't get attached to him, it didn't mean I couldn't enjoy the view in the meantime.

I stayed until I was feeling much better about my situation. Maybe it was the water, maybe I was just starting to wrap my mind around this whole other world I had no idea existed, but I was starting to feel better. I was thoroughly puny, before leaving, Nick offered to give me a tour of the factory. I accepted, curious about what kind of things they made. As I dried off, I found myself wondering more about Nick, his family, his past, and why he seemed so guarded. There was more to him than just the flirty facade, I just had to decide if I wanted to get to know that part. I didn't want to risk getting attached. I had a life to get back to, and it didn't have room for another person. I couldn't get attached, because that could lead to getting hurt. I wasn't sure if I could survive that again.

I found a note from Dr. Finn waiting for me at the front desk. The witch's name was Helga Eiris, and her descendants still lived in Ireland. This was the moment I'd been waiting for. Answers. And hopefully freedom from magic after I got the answers. I knew people I'd met in K Corp so far were excited that I had magic, and the particular kind of magic apparently was rare. But I wasn't part of that world. I lived in Flint, Michigan for goodness sake. I was not meant to have magic, save people, or whatever else these people did. I wanted nothing more than to blend into the background and live my quiet life.

I started wondering if they could undo the deal? Break the magic that has hurt so many people in our family. What if they refused? How long would this continue and who else would it hurt? The possibility of being stuck with this magic forever started to sink in, I clung desperately to hope that I could get rid of it somehow, but good things didn't happen often in my life. Thought lingered in my mind as I went upstairs to change, unsure of what lay ahead. There seemed to be nothing but change happening lately. I liked stability, the unknown is terrifying.

I took some time for myself to breathe and process what had happened so far. I couldn't wrap my head around all of it being real. How did people not know about magic and creatures? How did they keep it such a secret? I had so many questions I was burning to ask someone, Nick felt like someone I could ask but I needed to bide my time for the right moment. I sensed that if I pushed Nick before he was ready, he would just shut down. I didn't know how long I'd be there, my goal was to leave as soon as possible, so I had to tread carefully with my questions.

I changed out of my wet swimsuit, back into the leggings and sweatshirt I had on earlier and tried to put my wet curls into a bun. Making my way back down to the warehouse, I then noticed the staff. Some appeared human, others had certain features that I recognized were most certainly not human. Small spots on people's heads where horns should have been, tails peeking out from under dresses, and eyes with slits instead of round pupils. How did I miss all that on the first day? I must have been in such a fog coming in because it's so obvious to me then. My mind was still trying to convince me I wasn't really seeing what I knew I saw. My world wasn't the same. Could I go back to normal life after knowing all these unique creatures existed? I added that worry to my long list of things to overthink later.

Walking through that break room door was surreal. It felt like an eternity since I'd first stepped through it. I'd been exposed to an entirely new world.

It seemed that it was a secret world that not many were privy to know of.

I made my way to the large storage area where I first met Nick. So much had happened since then, it felt like weeks, not mere hours. Learning about my magic, my family's deal with a witch, and finding out I had a soulmate, it was almost too much to think about. I pushed my worry deeper inside me, I was curious about what Nick wanted to show me. I could not guess what it would be at that point. There were only empty chairs scattered around the tables in the breakroom. I followed the voices and sounds into the next room, the first room I stepped in from the bitter cold of this new place.

The room, now filled with soft moonlight filtering through large windows at the top of the walls, along with the lights that hung from the ceiling, felt less intimidating than it had before. It was the same space, with plastic and wooden crates lining the walls, but now I noticed the little details, like the crates that were filled to the brim with toys, everything from soft dolls to plastic robots. It felt like a wholesome family toy factory. The thought of seeing little Nick playing with the toys when he was a kid made me smile.

I spotted Nick in the far corner, loading the familiar red velvet bag, just like when I first saw him. This time, he also had a clipboard in hand, methodically marking items off a list. He waved me over, a genuine smile lighting up his face.

I tried to stay casual as I approached, hoping I wouldn't trip over my own feet. "So, show me what you do here big man." I said with immediate regret and embarrassment.

His chest rumbled with a chuckle. "Well, it's not just me, we have a great team here, and we do this together," he said with a grin. His humility caught me off guard. I had been half-expecting him to take full credit, as some guys would. Maybe I had misjudged him. Sure, he was smooth and sexy, probably rich too, but he wasn't giving off that arrogant, entitled vibe I'd assumed he might. A flicker of trust crept in, even though I tried to stay guarded. Too much had happened too fast to fully trust anyone. Trust had to be earned with me.

"Where is everyone? Are you here alone?" I asked, not wanting to be alone with him for too long. The chemistry between us was undeniable, and I wasn't sure how long I could keep denying it. But I sure would try my hardest to!

"They're in the back," Nick replied. "We run 24 hours here, and I'm just checking inventory for a big order. Want to see where the magic happens?"

I wasn't sure if he meant *actual* magic or was just using a figure of speech. But I nodded, curiously.

He dropped the red bag and held out his hand for me to take. I hesitated, so he started to pull away, but I quickly laced my fingers in his, igniting a fire in my palm. The skin to skin contact felt like we completed an electrical current when we touched. Nick must have felt it too, he looked at me, wide eyed, then smiled.

He led me through another carved wooden door into a bustling factory. The clattering sounds of machinery filled the air. Workers, all tall and slender with the translucent, iridescent skin and shades of blue and purple hair, moved swiftly between stations. They were mesmerizing, like living works of art. I tried my best to not stare at them, I settled for little glances as they walked by.

My attention finally shifted to where Nick was leading me. "Do you have more machines hidden away somewhere?" I asked, glancing at the dozen or so machines but doubting those few machines could make the massive number of bins full of items they had piled high. "How do these make all the toys?"

Nick looked at me with a mischievous grin. "Do you really want to know? It's a bit unconventional."

I nodded, both nervous and excited. I wondered If I could accept the answer I was about to be shown.

"We have a family friend, a witch, who consecrated these machines. We just program what we need, and they do the rest. Simple as that."

"That sounds a little like cheating," I teased, nudging him lightly in the ribs.

"Not cheating just using what we've got," he said with a wink. "We all use what's available to us."

I couldn't argue with that. "Can you show me how it works?"

He reluctantly unlaced our hands and let mine slide through his. My hand immediately felt cold and empty. But his eyes lit up like a kid's, "Of course! What do you want to make? Name anything!"

I gave him a questioning look, "anything?"

"Anything."

I thought for a moment, I considered art supplies, but I had loads of them back at home, I didn't really need more, and then it hit me. "Roller skates. Old-school, purple ones. I'd like to get into roller derby, so I'd love to have them to practice."

Nick laughed, clearly enjoying my excitement. He punched a series of buttons on the control panel, then stepped back. "Wait for it…"

After a few minutes, the machine whirled to life, clanking and whirring before finally spitting out a pair of purple roller skates with stripes of varying shades of purple. Nick inspected them, spinning the wheels and checking the trucks underneath before handing them to me.

I couldn't help myself. I jumped up and down, thrilled, and before I knew it, I threw my arms around his shoulders, hugging him tightly. He wrapped his arms around my waist in return, holding me to him, and for a few moments, we stood there, breathing in each other's presence. It was brief, but something about our hug felt… electric. The world stilled for just a second, and then reality returned, and we both pulled back, stepping away from each other. The air between us felt charged, like something had changed. I had enough change though. I needed to get out of that situation, slow it down at least. I was barely holding onto my thread of sanity with everything I'd learned but I refused to fall for a man that, well he just didn't fit in my world, and I didn't fit in his.

I was sure my face was on fire from blushing. "Thanks," I mumbled, clutching the skates to my chest as if they could shield me from my embarrassment. I tried to retreat to the safety of my room, but Nick caught my arm.

His touch sent a shiver through me. "You're leaving already? The tour's just getting started."

"I, um, I'm really tired. I think I'll finish the tour another day, if that's okay." I made up an excuse, I needed some space, being that close to Nick was starting to make my body react how I didn't want it to. I needed to have a serious talk with her later about her betrayal.

His grin faded slightly, as he let go of my arm. In that moment, I realized I didn't want him to, I wanted him to touch my arm, trace his fingers down my neck, gently touch my…*get a hold of yourself girl! You're acting like a teenager. Your hormones are being stupid, ignore them!* "Yeah, that's fine," he said. "I get it. You've had a lot thrown at you." He said he was fine, but his expression told a different story. I couldn't worry about him right now, I felt bad, but I had to put myself first.

Holding my new skates tightly, I hurried away, my heart racing from more than just excitement. As I left, I could hear Nick speaking with the workers in that strange language again, and though I couldn't understand the words, I knew they were talking about me. The workers kept glancing in my direction, nodding and smiling. I hated being the center of attention, but I really hated not understanding what they were saying about me. I hoped they didn't hate me, it's never a good idea to piss off the people you're stuck with.

A few moments later, I heard footsteps behind me. I glanced over my shoulder and saw Nick, his usual grin in place.

"Mind if I walk you back? I need to head to the lobby anyway." His workers stood smiling in our direction, I guessed they pressured him to do this. I was okay with it though, as long as I didn't make a fool of myself again. I was at my limit of embarrassment for the day.

I nodded, grateful for the company, even if it did make my emotions more complicated. We walked side by side, making small talk about the factory, though my mind kept drifting back to the hug, to how comforting it had felt to be in his arms. It had been years since I'd let anyone get that close to me.

Nick broke the silence. "So, what do you think of everything? I know it's a lot to take in."

I shrugged, unsure how to answer. "It's… overwhelming. There's just so much I had no idea about. I feel like a baby learning about the world for the first time." I took a deep, calming breath, "but I think I'm handling it okay."

"You're doing better than okay, much better than most with all this," he said with a warm smile. "But how are you *really* doing with all of this?"

I hesitated, surprised by his concern, I felt like he truly wanted to know so I let myself be a little vulnerable. "Honestly, it's a lot. Yesterday was rough, but today I'm starting to feel more settled. Having some answers helps."

He nodded, his expression thoughtful. "If there's anything you need, I'm here. I want to help you through this."

His hand slid over mine, gently squeezing. The warmth of his touch sent jolts of electricity through me, and when he let go, I felt…vacant.

I shifted the conversation, trying to ignore the pull I felt toward him. "I was thinking… is there any way to talk to the family of the witch who made the deal with my ancestors? I want to understand more about where this magic comes from."

Nick seemed caught off guard by my question, but he quickly recovered. "I'll make some calls and see what I can find out. How about we talk more over dinner? If you're too tired, I can just leave a note at reception with the details."

Despite my exhaustion, I knew I couldn't pass up the opportunity to learn more. "Dinner sounds good. Where should I meet you?"

"I'll pick you up at eight. The shop will send up some dress options."

My eyes widened at that. A fancy dinner? "Uh, okay," I stammered, trying to hide my surprise.

"If you'd rather rest, that's fine too," Nick offered.

"No, I think a distraction would do me good," I admitted. "I tend to overthink when I'm stressed and alone with my thoughts."

He smiled, and with a nod, we parted ways. He walked down a hallway past the reception desk. I was left with more questions. And not enough answers. I wanted to learn more about that man before we had dinner together. Normally Axel would do some cyber stalking for me, but he wasn't here, I hadn't talked to him in days which felt weird. I missed my best friend. I channeled my inner Axel and decided to do some cyber stalking myself.

The business center of the lobby was filled with sleek computers, ergonomic chairs, and even a hot cocoa machine on a Victorian-style tea table. I settled into a computer in the corner, craving some privacy. I typed in "Nick Klaus" in the social media I had. It pulled up no results. I assumed his last name was Klaus because of the Christmas book in the bedroom, maybe I had it wrong. I moved onto searching "Northwest Territories businesses," hoping for answers. But the results were just the usual, grocery stores and local shops.

My last option was to put "Klaus/K Corp" into the search engine. Most of the results didn't seem to match the building, so I switched to the image tab. That's when I found a picture that stopped me cold. It showed an older man, solidly built, with white hair and a gray wool sweater, standing beside a classy-looking woman in a flannel dress. Behind them was the building I was in, and the letter "K" was prominently displayed on the front. Finally, a clue! It was a start. I zoomed in on the older man in the picture, he had the same green eyes Nick had, I'd never seen a color of eyes so striking, it would be an odd coincidence. They had to be related. They looked so happy, embracing each other. It made me wonder why there wasn't much information about the building, Nick's parents or even Nick at all. It made me wonder if they were hiding something or if their secret world kept things off the internet. He had opened up a little about his parents and the past business. I hoped the dinner would help him settle in and open up more to me about his past and hopefully about the witches because I was dying to know.

Chapter 7

Back in my room, I barely had time to sit down before there was a knock at the door. "Room service," a voice called.

I opened it to find a young man holding a tray with a steaming cup of coffee. "Mr. K thought you might enjoy this. It's his favorite, a secret recipe."

I took the cup, thanking him as he left. The first sip was divine. Fruity notes, strong but smooth. *Nick sure knew his coffee,* I thought with a smile.

Just as I was settling in, another knock startled me. This time, it was a beautiful woman with pastel hair pushing a rack of dresses, followed by another woman with a cart full of makeup and hair tools.

"I'm Elena, and this is Trina," the first woman said cheerfully. "We're here to get you ready for your big night!"

I wasn't sure I was ready for all this attention, but I went along with it. The evening was shaping up to be far more than I had expected. Part of me regretted agreeing to dinner, the other part was excited to see how the other half lives. Just glancing at the dresses, they rolled by me, I would have never been able to afford any of those, maybe if I saved up my whole life, how beautiful would I be at 80 in one of these? I laughed to myself. I tried to just enjoy this short, weird moment in my life.

I had never fully understood what people meant when they found "the dress" until now. Even on my wedding day, I said 'yes' to the dress Josh's mom liked. This was different, they wanted a dress I liked. I tried on the first dress they handed me, it was a nice dress but it was itchy and uncomfortable. Plus, both women shook their heads at it. So, I moved on to the next one. This one cut into me in weird places, I kept fidgeting with it to try and readjust it. I shook my head, and they agreed. No since on keeping it on longer than necessary.

The next one…just felt different. The other dresses didn't make me feel the way this forest-green velvet gown did. For the first time, I felt like my soul was dancing inside me. The dress hugged my curves perfectly, the fabric cascaded elegantly while still letting me feel like myself. Both Elena and Trina exchanged a knowing look, a smile passed between them. They knew they'd nailed it. I never wanted to try on another dress for the rest of my life after that one. It's a feeling that's hard to describe, I just felt pretty.

Trina took over from there, starting on my makeup. She applied a light nude eye, which I appreciated since I wasn't used to wearing much makeup. Somehow, she managed to make my skin glow without covering my freckles thankfully, because I loved them, and not many redheads did. With a dusty nude lipstick, the look was natural but polished. When I caught my reflection in the mirror, I almost didn't recognize myself. I looked… different. Beautiful even but still *me*.

When Trina moved on to my hair, the challenge was real. But instead of trying to completely change my hair, she worked with my curls, enhancing their natural wildness without making them look overdone. My hair remained free, vibrant, and real. I looked in the mirror at the finished result, and for the first time in forever, I felt like I had truly transformed. It wasn't just the makeup or the hair, it was something deeper, something that made me feel more alive.

The girls packed up, and I thanked them profusely. They had worked miracles. Slipping on the black heels they left for me, I grabbed the clutch filled with makeup essentials for touch ups and headed down the elevator to meet Nick. The heels clicked as I walked on the smooth tile of the lobby, drawing Huyen's attention to me. She gave me an encouraging smile as I made my way to the rotating doors. I spotted him waiting outside, leaning casually against a sleek Ford GT. He was wearing a gray suit that accentuated his strong arms with dark green accents that matched my dress, and I figured the beauty team must have tipped him off.

I couldn't wait to tell Axel about Nick's car. I only knew it was a Ford GT because Axel was obsessed with muscle cars and made me watch too many car shows with him. He was going to be so mad at me for not taking a picture of it, a little hard to take a picture without my phone though.

"You... look... amazing!" Nick stammered, his eyes wide with appreciation. "Thanks for having dinner with me."

"Thank you," I said softly, glancing down and smoothing the dress nervously. "When you mentioned dinner, I assumed it would be back at the restaurant in the building. I'm not used to all this dressing up, but it's kind of fun. Is it... safe, though? I mean, I'm still learning how to shield myself." I regretfully have been forgetting to practice my magic, Nick is a great distraction. I hated that I allowed him to become a distraction.

"You're safe with me. I'll protect you," he said with a smug grin, clearly knowing how much I hated needing protection. He was always antagonizing me, but in a way that made me smirk instead of snap.

Nick opened the car door for me, those dramatic Lamborghini-style ones that lifted up rather than out. I slid into the luxurious dark blue leather seat as gracefully as I could manage in heels and a gown, hoping I didn't look too awkward. Nick hopped into the driver's seat, and with the push of a button, the engine roared to life. As we sped off into the night, the car seemed to hug the road, and I couldn't help but grin. The speed was exhilarating, though I fought the urge to grab the door handle.

We eventually pulled up to a building under a large canopy, and Nick hurried around to open my door. He offered me his hand to help me out, which I gratefully accepted this time, especially as the rounded cobblestones underfoot made it tricky to walk in heels. Not three steps later, I misjudged the ground, and my heel slid off one of the uneven pavers. I nearly fell, Nick caught me effortlessly, his arm wrapping around my waist to hold me steady. For a second, we stood frozen in a dip position, staring at each other. I could feel his breath, just inches away from my face. For a moment, I thought he was going to kiss me. For a moment I would have let him.

Instead, Nick smirked, inches from my lips, and gracefully brought me back upright. My heart pounded as if I had run a mile. It all felt so cinematic, too perfect, like a scene from a rom-com. But I reminded myself this wasn't my real life. I wasn't staying. Still, I decided to enjoy the moment, just for now. *Don't get attached. Don't get attached. Don't get attached.* I repeated my mantra for the night.

I slid my hand along his bent arm as we walked inside, feeling the warmth and strength of his bicep under his suit jacket. I allowed myself a small indulgence, relishing in the closeness. Why not, just for tonight…because I wasn't going to get attached.

We were greeted by a hostess who immediately led us to a private room filled with lush greenery, delicate twinkling lights, and wooden accents. It was a dark, intimate space, stunning, magical one could say.

The chef himself soon came out to greet us, speaking to me in what sounded like French before turning to Nick and exchanging pleasantries. The two spoke for a few moments, their conversation quick and familiar, before the chef retreated to the kitchen. Nick sat back in his chair, looking far too smug.

"What are you up to?" I asked, crossing my arms playfully, sensing some hidden agenda.

Nick just laughed, crossing his arms as if to mimic me. He didn't answer, though. Instead, a waitress soon brought us drinks. In front of me was a Blue Cheese Martini, my all-time favorite. Nick had a short glass of something dark, probably whiskey or old-fashioned.

"How did you know?" I asked, narrowing my eyes at him. "How did you know I loved Blue Cheese Martinis?"

Nick's grin grew wider. "I have my ways."

"What ways?" I pressed, still curious, but also a little freaked out. "Are you stalking me or something?"

Nick chuckled, holding up his hands as if to surrender, his eyes twinkling with mischief. "The stalker accusation again? I'm starting to wonder if you wouldn't mind if I was your stalker." He laughed, "No stalking required, I promise. I'll explain later. For now, let's just enjoy the evening."

Though I wasn't thrilled by his cryptic response, I decided to let it go, for now. I took a sip of my drink, savoring the salty tang of the blue cheese olives. It was perfect. I had to admit, Nick was good at impressing me. I wondered how it would be dating in the real world after this. Would I expect extravagance like this, or would I be okay with sidewalk hot dogs as a 'good date' again?

To break the tension, Nick suggested a game. "Let's take turns asking each other questions," he said. "It'll help us get to know each other better."

I was hesitant, but it seemed harmless. "Okay, but I get to go first," I insisted. "Why are you helping me so much? What's in it for you?"

He leaned forward slightly, his smile softening. "Because I like you, Aoife. I want you to be safe, and I want you to be happy." His answer seemed guarded, like he wasn't fully saying what he wanted to.

I couldn't argue with that. His sincerity caught me off guard. Now it was his turn. "Why are you so afraid of getting close to people?"

I hesitated, the memories rushing back. "I was married," I admitted. "It started off great, but after the wedding, he changed. He wasn't... a good person. I was such a fool for not seeing it sooner."

Nick's gaze softened. "You're not a fool. He was the one who was a fool, he didn't deserve you." While I appreciated his kindness, he didn't really know me. I'd only been with him a few days, maybe the longer I spent with him, the more he'd realize I did deserve to be treated that way. Maybe he'd change his view on me. Maybe I was the broken one, not Josh. All the gaslighting Josh did to me was a hard habit to break. Words cut deep, it rewires you somehow into thinking maybe they were right after all.

It was my turn again. Since he had gone deep, I decided to return the favor. "Did they ever catch your parents' killer?" Tit for tat and all.

Nick's expression darkened, and I immediately regretted asking. "No," he said quietly. "We don't have many clues. It was a Wiijigoo that got them. We just don't know which one."

My heart sank. *The same monsters that were after me.* Dread brewed in my stomach, would I suffer the same fate I wondered… I could barely get a response. "I'm so sorry."

Nick sighed. "It's okay. It's just… frustrating not having answers, I won't stop looking though. They will pay for what they did." He looked down for a moment, lost in thought. Then he smiled, though it didn't reach his eyes. "I understand the stress of not knowing."

I felt like he was being genuine. He did understand my frustration. I didn't want to be another name in someone's memory. I wasn't ready to give up and cease to exist. I fought hard for the life I made, and I wasn't about to let some shadow creature take it from me. I needed more information, I decided to try and push Nick for more information, hoping he wouldn't shut down.

"Nick?" His attention was brought back to me, his mouth slightly turning up almost into a smile. "Do you think I'll end up like your parents? They had to be better at protecting themselves than I am, how am I supposed to survive if they couldn't?"

His smile faded, I could tell he was also worried about the same thing. "We won't let anything happen to you. You'll master your magic just like you do with everything you try, you'll be able to protect yourself. I know you aren't a quitter, so I imagine you'll give anyone a run for their money in this building in no time." He paused, clearly thinking about what he was going to say, or how much he was willing to share. "The Wiijigoo are sly creatures, but they're dumb, driven by desire. That leaves them vulnerable. If it comes down to it, we can defeat them, we just have to get close enough to one."

The thought of being close to another one made a chill go down my spine. "Nick, how did it get your parents? I know you don't like talking about it, but I need to know. I need to know what to look out for."

I knew he didn't want to answer but he knew I wouldn't stop asking until I had the answers. "They got a call, someone wanted to make an appointment to meet with them about needing their help. They left the building for this urgent meeting when they were attacked. It seemed like a set up, but we could never find a connection. The investigators labeled it a freak coincidence. I don't believe that. They were set up." His eyes filled with tears but didn't overflow. He took a deep breath and stilled his emotions.

"Nick, you don't have to put on this tough guy facade with me. I won't think any less of you if you actually had emotions."

"I…I don't know how. I want to show you all my sides, but I've been alone for so long. I'm the CEO, I'm the hero, I'm so many important things but I don't know how to be what you need."

"I don't know what will happen after this, but I do know, if you don't show me who you really are, I could never fall for that. I didn't fully know my ex-husband, it was a painful learning experience when he finally showed me all his sides. I won't go through that again. So, I'm not saying I am staying or anything, but if you even wanted to truly be my friend, you'd open up to me. I know it's hard but you're so guarded, I can tell you're hiding things from me."

"I'm sorry Aoife. You do deserve to know all the sides of me. I have been guarded. I can't expect you to even want to be near me when I'm not being honest with myself. I promise I'll work on it. Can you give me the time I need to figure out how to open up?"

"I don't know how long I'll be here Nick so I can't guarantee anything. But if you'll work on opening up, I promise to give you the time I have with an open mind."

"And open heart?" he added with a smile, always trying to lighten the mood.

"I can't guarantee that one either. That one is earned by honesty and actions."

"Fair enough. I want to be a better man for you," he said. I immediately started blushing, no one had ever said that to me. Men said it in movies, but it was only to try and get into a woman's pants. Call me naive but I believed him.

Before I could respond, the waiter arrived with our meal, an assortment of tiny, artfully presented dishes. Each bite was a burst of flavor, and soon the heavy mood lifted as we both savored the food. Nick ordered me a local beer, and we laughed as I tried to pronounce its name. We talked for what felt like hours, in a good way. He started relaxing, being the real Nick, not CEO Nick.

I stretched out my legs under the table, unknowingly grazing his leg with my feet. The thought immediately sent small bolts of lightning through my body. Nick must have felt the same thing because his eyes went from laughter to deep longing, like I hit a button of sexiness in him.

I bit my lip stifling a small moan from the physical contact, however small it was. That made Nick smirk, he knew how he affected me, and it made me so mad. I didn't want him to have that power over me. But the attraction was hard to ignore, it was far more than just a fling. There was a curiosity of something deeper. It scared me.

I gave him an apologetic look and drew my legs back closer to my body. I needed to avoid contact. He sensed the night was coming to an end. I could tell he wasn't ready to say goodbye, he asked "Fancy a dip in the hot tub?"

It sounded like the perfect way to end the night, though it would break my heart a little to have to take that dress off, I bet it would be frowned upon to swim in it though. While I would just like to go back and go to sleep, I was beginning to really love swimming too. There was something special about those waters, and seeing Nick in swim trunks wasn't too bad either. "Sure, why not?" *But no physical contact Aoife! Keep your distance!*

Back in my room, I found a bouquet of lilies on the dresser, my favorite flower, along with a toy airplane and a note from Nick: *Thank you for the best night I've had in a long time. XO, Nick.* I smiled at the thoughtful gesture.

After changing into my swimsuit, I made my way down to the hot tub. The warm, salty water was heaven after such a long day. A few minutes later, Nick strolled in, carrying a pizza box.

"You, sir, are a genius, the food was great but why are the portions always so damn small!," I said, laughing. "Thanks for the flowers by the way."

"I'm glad you liked them." he said with a proud grin.

Nick sank into the warm water, relaxing his head back with a sigh. I took him in, he was so handsome and seemed like a genuinely good person. So why was I holding back my feelings? Josh really did a number on me, my therapist would be so mad that I wasn't opening myself up to the chance of love. But I hate to admit it, I was scared. It's so easy to hurt someone, and impossible to take that hurt away once it's created.

I had to be okay with baby steps. I'd learn to trust him a little bit at a time. His actions will prove if he's authentic. I needed proof he was different. I hoped he was different, but that would make this situation so much harder. I couldn't stay. I had to get back to the life I worked so hard to make. I wasn't ready to just give that up. That was a worry for another time. That night, I tried to unwind, and take a break from possible love, from magic, from the world and just be with a friend.

The two of us sat there, eating pizza and talking late into the night. For the first time in a long while, I felt truly relaxed, even if I was trying to deny the growing connection between us. But for tonight, I let myself enjoy the moment…while also doing everything in my power to avoid physical contact with him. I thought of it as window shopping, look but don't touch.

Chapter 8

A new day, a new start. Despite the fog that lingered from yesterday's overwhelming events and not enough sleep, I had hoped that today would bring more clarity and, hopefully, answers that could end this wild magic saga. I woke up early, craving coffee before anything else, I also wanted to try out my new roller skates. Two birds, one stone. I strapped on my new skates and spun my way down the halls to the restaurant in hopes of grabbing a cup to go. Maybe, if I was lucky, I could convince them to brew up Nick's special coffee. While there, I stopped by to see Huyen, who greeted me with a smile as she spotted my roller skates.

"I hope it's okay I'm wearing these here. You don't think Nick will be mad?"

"Nick mad at you? I doubt that could ever happen. He's been playing grown up far too long. Maybe you'll bring out the fun in him again. I approve of this." she said as she waved towards my skates.

She handed me two notes. One was a thick piece of paper sealed with wax, and the other was a smaller note and I spun around bowing towards her as I left, coffee in one hand, notes in the other. I resisted the temptation to open them right away but waited until I was comfortably back in my room.

I'd have to ask Nick about his secret coffee later, it seemed a bit weird it was such a secret, but being allowed to have it felt like I was in his secret group. Once I was safely in my room and getting caffeinated, I broke the seal on the letter and carefully unfolded the papers, taking a deep breath. The first note read: "Dear Aoife, I have discovered some information, and Nick has taken the liberty of sharing the news with you. Hope this helps. Let me know if you have any questions, dear. Dr. Finn."

The smaller note, which was unmistakably from Nick, simply said:

"Clear your schedule for today. I have a surprise. XO Nick."

Nick and his surprises. I was both intrigued and nervous. I had no clue what he had in mind, so I layered my clothes prepared for anything and made my way downstairs to meet him. As I stepped into the lobby, Nick was already there, holding two leather duffle bags and showing off his sexy smirk.

"I took the liberty of having a bag packed for you," he said, holding up one of the bags with a grin, clearly pleased with himself.

"Um, thanks… but what do I need a bag for?" I asked, both curious and apprehensive.

"It's called a surprise for a reason," he teased, gently ushering me toward the door.

While I was beginning to like Nick's surprises, I still wasn't fond of not knowing. Planning things and knowing exactly what will happen gave me peace of mind. I could control the variables. Nick was nothing but one big, sexy variable. I tried to reassure myself that he had my best interest in mind, and he wouldn't let anything happen to me. I knew I was a control freak, my friends told me that all the time, after my past, making sure I had control of my future was a big part of every decision I made. Nick was tossing all that on its head. I took a deep breath and tried to let go of the need for control. *I could be easy going... I think.*

His usual sleek gray car wasn't outside this time. Instead, a blacked-out luxury car was waiting, with a driver standing by. Nick opened the door for me, I slid inside, attempting to be graceful. Either he had rented this, or he owned multiple cars, neither of which would surprise me at this point.

We drove for a while, the silence between us comfortable, though my mind buzzed with questions. Soon, we turned onto a winding road that led to a small private airport. The planes and buildings all bore the same fancy "K" emblem I'd seen before.

"Wait, do you own these too?" I asked, incredulous.

Nick was trying to play it cool. "The company owns the airport and planes, not me, per se."

Not him, *per se*. The fact that he casually owned a fleet of planes, and an airport left me speechless. We pulled up to a sleek, small jet, the stairs already down. The driver opened the door for us, and I followed Nick onto the plane. The flight attendants smiled and greeted us warmly, though I felt incredibly out of place. I sat across the aisle from Nick, my curiosity at its peak.

"So… are you going to tell me where we're going now?" I asked, practically begging.

Nick handed me a brochure. I unfolded it, and my eyes widened when I saw the cover. *Ireland.* "Shut up, we are NOT going to Ireland!" I exclaimed, half laughing, half disbelieving.

Nick grinned, his excitement contagious. "Yes, we are. Aba set up a meeting with the coven that cast the original spell on your family and Axel sent me your passport." He flipped it open to look at my picture and smiled.

"Stop, it was a humid day, curls and humidity don't mix well okay." I said defensively.

He held up his hands in a surrender pose, "I didn't say anything." with his stupid cute grin.

"You were thinking it." I scowled at him.

He tried to smooth over the situation holding the Ireland brochure again, "But Ireland! Have you ever been? Your passport says you haven't yet."

I tried to put a nice face on for him and let go of my hatred of my picture, "I have not been. I got the passport hoping to travel for our honeymoon, but Josh didn't want to leave his mom. So, I haven't used it yet, I kind of gave up on going anywhere. This will be my first stamp. Do you think they can break the spell? I would do anything to get back to my normal life to not have to deal with all of this magic."

As soon as the words left my mouth, I saw Nick's expression shift. He grew quiet, and I realized I had said the wrong thing. I didn't mean to offend him, but it was clear that I had. Magic was a huge part of his life, it was his *normal*. But for me, it was an unwanted intrusion into the life I had worked so hard to create. I didn't want magic. I didn't want soul mates or adventure or unknown creatures. I just wanted my old, stable, boring life back.

"I'm sorry," I stammered. "I didn't mean that I didn't want to be with you, or never wanted to see you again. I was just…"

Nick winced, cutting me off. "It's fine. I'm a big boy. I know what you meant. This is a whole new world for you, I'm sure it's a big adjustment."

His voice was subdued, and though he tried to downplay it, I could see I'd hurt him. The rest of the plane ride was quiet, filled only with the soft hum of the engines. Nick was absorbed in his laptop, and I tried to nap, though guilt gnawed at me. I hadn't meant to hurt him, but my future was on the line, I had to worry about this one decision completely changing my future. Still, I hadn't realized how deeply Nick cared until then, and it started to sink in how my decision would also affect Nick. He usually kept his emotions in check, always cool and composed, and I hadn't seen the depth of his feelings.

When we landed, another car was waiting for us. The hour-long drive to our destination was marked by heavy silence, neither of us wanting to address the growing tension. Eventually, we arrived at what looked like an old castle.

"Is this where the witch is?" I asked.

"No," Nick replied, his tone still a bit distant. "This is where we're staying. We'll meet the coven tonight."

His avoidance of eye contact was making my heart ache more than I expected. I wasn't used to wanting someone's attention like this, but with Nick, it felt different, more personal.

The castle staff greeted us warmly, their thick Irish accents filling the air as they addressed Nick as "Mr. K." Inside, the castle was every bit as grand and medieval as I had imagined. Tapestries adorned the stone walls, and a roaring fire warmed the great hall. The bellboys escorted us to our rooms, which were across the hall from each other. I followed the one assigned to me into my room as he began unpacking my bag for me, placing my clothes into the drawers and lined up bathroom essentials. It felt strange but oddly luxurious like something out of a fairy tale.

Nick, however, had barely looked at me before shutting the door to his room. The cold shoulder was evident, and it stung more than I wanted to admit. I sighed, sitting down on the bed in my room, wondering how I was going to fix it. I didn't want to hurt him, but I couldn't lead him on either. I wasn't staying. That wasn't my life. But it didn't mean he deserved to be treated poorly. I had to find a way to make things right.

It wasn't the same situation as with Josh. With Josh I had to be careful how I said things, or he'd get angry and violent. But Nick wasn't like that, he didn't have any of the same signs. He just felt so deeply about me, I feel it too, but I can't give into it. I would love a world where I could just fall madly in love with my soulmate and live happily forever, but this isn't a fairy tale, this is my life. My decisions have consequences. I don't fear Nick, I fear losing him.

I didn't know when we'd be meeting the coven, but in the meantime, I used the moment of stillness to lie down, attempting to reconcile the storm inside me. Exhausted, I flopped back onto the bed, staring at the ornate ceiling, trying to shake the heaviness that had settled between us. I didn't know what that night would bring with the coven, but I hoped for some clarity for both of us. It wasn't just the magic or the mystery surrounding my family, it was Nick, too. His silence gnawed at me. I needed to make things right with him, but the weight of everything else pressed harder on my chest.

Right now, meeting the coven took priority. I needed to know why my family had done this. What had we been hiding for so long? And would this magic, this curse, as it felt to me be something I could ever escape?

The ringing phone jolted me out of my restless thoughts.

"Miss Aoife, Mr. K requests that you meet him in the lobby at 8:30 PM."

"Thanks for letting me know," I replied, but the realization hit harder than I'd expected. Nick didn't want to talk to me directly. A simple phone call, a buffer between us. I let that sink in as I sat up, the knot in my stomach tightening. Hopefully, the night would bring some peace both for my family's history and for the complicated feelings swirling between Nick and me.

Pulling myself together, I ran a hand through my hair, trying to tame the unruly curls, but they were as stubborn as my emotions. I had so much on my mind, so much was unknown. I had to worry about my own emotions, decisions and future but also Nicks. I wasn't used to worrying about someone else's emotions anymore. I wasn't worried about making him mad, I knew Nick would understand, eventually, I was worried about my decisions affecting him. I could leave him alone, his parents gone, if I go away too, what would that do to him? I didn't know him really well yet, but I knew he didn't deserve to be alone. He deserved happiness, if not more than the average person does.

My feet felt heavy as I walked through the old stone hallways, each step echoing in the silence. It was strange how a place could feel so welcoming, yet so cold at the same time, much like how I felt with Nick. There was warmth between us, but also something unspoken, lingering, unsolved.

When I stepped into the lobby, Nick was already there, sitting in one of those worn leather chairs that seemed as old as the stones around us. He stood as soon as he saw me, his expression softer than I'd expected. I had prepared myself for tension, for the cold distance of earlier, but before I could say anything, he beat me to it.

"I'm sorry about earlier," he said, his voice low and sincere. "I took it personally. I know the past few days have been overwhelming for you. You just want answers, and I wasn't being fair. I had this idea that you'd just fall for me, and we'd just be happy together. When things didn't work out that way, I realized I was being selfish. I fully believe in free will. If this world, if I am not what you want, I will accept it. I apologize for being so self-centered and just assuming you'd want to be a part of it."

His words disarmed me, and I realized I'd been holding onto more than just the need for an apology. I was carrying the fear that I'd pushed him too far.

"I was hoping to apologize, too," I admitted, feeling the weight lift slightly. "I didn't mean for it to come out like that. I've loved every moment we've spent together, Nick, but everything in my life has been turned upside down. I thought I knew where I was headed, and now… I'm just trying to understand my future." I looked down, feeling the vulnerability of my own words. "I'm so grateful for your help, but I need to know what this all means. I know my decision will affect you as well, but I need the choice. I can't just accept it without trying to understand it better."

As the words left my mouth, I realized it wasn't just about the magic. It wasn't even just about my family. It was about everything I thought I had control over slipping through my fingers. My future, my choices, what if none of them had ever really been mine to make? What if our future was already predetermined? That thought terrified me, what if I was fighting so hard for nothing? After our apologies, he held his arms out to welcome me into a hug. We embraced, reconciling our differences, even if just temporarily.

When we hugged, it felt different than before, so much more was said in that embrace than in our words. The way he held me, strong and certain, grounding me in a way I hadn't realized I needed. His warmth melted away the fear, at least for a moment, but the fear of losing this, losing him, lingered at the edges of my thoughts. When our heads awkwardly tilted in the same direction and our faces came dangerously close, I pulled back just enough to avoid it, but the tension of that almost-kiss hung between us.

I don't want to let go first. I needed him to know that I was still there and that despite everything pulling me in different directions, I wasn't running. I needed information, I needed answers before I could make any decision.

The hug lasted longer than it probably should have, but I clung to it, to him, for as long as I could. When we finally broke apart, the sense of loss hit me immediately, like the cold air rushing back in after stepping away from a fire.

He led me toward the door, his hand resting gently on my lower back a small gesture, but one that reassured me more than any words could. He opened the passenger door for me, and I climbed in, feeling the strangeness of being on the opposite side from what I was used to. Everything was backward lately, even the small things.

The drive was silent, but the tension had eased. The narrow, twisting roads blurred past in the dark, the outside world becoming nothing more than shapes and shadows. But inside the car, it felt safe. I glance at Nick now and then, wondering if he was as tangled up in all of it as I was. Did he feel the same pull between us? Or was it just me holding onto something that wasn't really there?

When we finally turned down a dirt road, lined with tall pines and crumbling stone walls, my stomach tightened again. The road seemed to stretch on forever, each twist and turn making me feel further from everything familiar. And then, we stopped in front of what I could only describe as a house pulled from the pages of a fantasy novel. The entire structure was buried in the earth, with a roof of moss and grass, and only a round wooden door and two small windows peeking out. Flowers cascaded from the ground surrounding the windows, their vibrant colors muted by the night.

I couldn't shake the feeling that it was a threshold, once we stepped out of the car, nothing would be the same.

It might have been my nerves, but I quickly began shivering as I met Nick in front of the car. He draped his jacket over my shoulders, and I pulled it closer, grateful for the warmth and the comfort. His scent clung to the fabric, that familiar mix of spices and something distinctly him. It made me feel connected to him, even when words failed us.

An older woman greeted us, her gray hair braided down her back, her presence commanding but gentle. "You must be Nick and Aoife," she said, her thick Irish accent rolling over her words like a lullaby. "I'm Fiona. Dr. Finn has spoken to me about your situation. Come, I'll introduce you to our High Priestess, Hilde."

I followed her, but my mind was elsewhere. The moment I'd been waiting for that might answer all the questions that had been swirling in my mind. And yet, all I could think about was Nick, and how tightly he was holding my hand as we walked. His touch anchored me, and I wasn't sure if I wanted to let go. He was my buoy in the storm that was my life, guiding me, protecting me, I knew he'd keep me safe.

We walked down a long dark path, plants brushed my legs as we walked by. Fiona led us to a dead end. A wall of ivy blocked the path ahead, I almost didn't see it. The leaves blended so perfectly into the night that it was only when she began to speak in a language I didn't understand that the wall parted, revealing the rest of the path, a hidden path beyond the ivy. A fire beyond it flickered in the distance, casting eerie shadows that made the hair on my arms stand up.

Nick leaned in close and whispered, "That was a ward. It only lets in those with pure intentions. This is sacred ground." A shiver ran down my spine. What if my intentions weren't pure? What if my heart was too full of fear, of doubt?

Fiona repeated the words, and the ivy merged back together, completely blocking the entrance. There was no way out. I hope that it went well because I was feeling a little trapped.

As we approached the fire, I saw her. The High Priestess. She sat cross-legged on the ground, her long white hair pooling around her like a veil. She didn't look up as we approached, but when she did, her smile was kind, through her eyes held something deeper, something ancient.

"My dear," she began, her voice soft but heavy with meaning, "I hear you've come a long way. Let's see if we can find the answers you seek. But first, clear your mind. You must let go of everything, your fears, your doubts, your past. Only then will you be ready."

Nick's hand left mine, and immediately, the cold seeped in again. Without him, I felt exposed, and vulnerable. What if I'm not ready to face whatever was coming? What if I'm not strong enough?

She reached into a small bag next to her, with a handful of the contents she spit on it, then threw it onto the fire. The scent of rosemary and sweet cherry smoke filled the air, it didn't assault my lungs, it smelled herby and aromatic, calming my frayed nerves. The fire burst to life radiating heat far beyond what a small campfire should, the embers began to dance around us like fireflies, but never burning us. At that moment, I realized this was bigger than me. Bigger than my fears, bigger than my uncertainties. It felt like I was being shown a secret ancient wonder. Something not many people got to witness. I felt honored to be a part of it.

She closed her eyes, hummed a long low note, the other women around the fire joined in humming low, soothing notes, then Hilde chanted in what sounded like Latin to me.

'Maledicam cunctae familiae tuae
amor dici aeternum terrorem.

Tuum sequere cor ut excutias

Insidens iuramenti huius benedicat.'

The intensity of everything that had happened settled over me like a heavy blanket, suffocating me as I tried to process the enormity of it all. Hilde motioned to me to look at the fire. I studied the embers trying to figure out what she wanted me to see. I steeled myself and slowed my breathing, giving the fire my full attention.

The sounds of low chanting and humming echoed through the woods, reverberating through me, through my soul. As the embers shot up high into the air, they began to dance and swirl around chaotically until they got closer together, starting to form shapes through the collecting embers floating in the air. Eventually, I could make out three distinct figures, two of them handing something to the third. I didn't understand. What were they giving the person? What was this all supposed to mean? I wanted answers, but instead, I was left with more questions. The embers lost their form and then, in a sudden rush, they were drawn back into the fire like a reverse explosion, leaving the air with just the normal, low gentle flickering flames.

I looked over at Hilde, hoping for some kind of explanation. Her eyes were closed, her expression serene, as if she were waiting for something. A moment passed, and then she opened them, her gaze settling on me with a weight that made me feel small.

"Your ancestors' village was under attack," she began, her voice deep and measured, as though she was recalling the story from some ancient, hidden place. "Your great-great-great-great-grandmother was taken by a neighboring village. Desperate, her husband, your three times great grandfather made a deal with the local coven to bring her back. He loved her so deeply that he couldn't imagine life without her. To find her, to always have the power to reach each other, he struck a deal that tied magic to your family. But there was a price. That bond, the power they were given, passed down through generations. And now it falls to you. You will be drawn to your soulmate, the fates have chosen him for you because you two balance weather out. The universe always has to have a balance. To allow the magic to take hold and guide you together, you must give into your heart. Stop fighting it and let your magic guide you. You must trust in it."

Her words washed over me, but I couldn't fully grasp them. Magic, love, desperation. My ancestors' choices now rested on my shoulders. I'm not sure I'm ready for that. I'm ready for any of this. I was supposed to just blindly trust this magic that put me in danger? I just found out about magic, and it wants me to just give into it, give up everything I'd worked so hard for? It felt like I was supposed to give up being…me.

"Can I get rid of the magic?" I asked, holding onto faith that it would be possible so I could get back to my life, the life I carefully sculpted.

She took a deep cleansing breath in, steadily exhaling before responding. "To break the bond, you must find the talisman your ancestor received, it holds the power of the magic. You must hold it in your hand, your blood will break the bond of the spell. You have a choice. Keep the magic or return it to the coven. But know this: should you choose to break the magic, you will lose your true love forever."

Her eyes flickered briefly to Nick, and then back to me. My heart stopped beating for a second.

"So will I ever find love if I give up my magic?"

"Your soul is tied to one, if you choose to break the bond, you will lose your chance at love, so will your mate. No person will fit your heart like your soulmate. You cannot give up one without giving up the other. Choose wisely lass for it's not just your future at stake," she finished, her voice final.

I felt like the ground was shifting beneath my feet. I wrapped my arms tightly around myself, trying to create a barrier against the overwhelming tide of emotions. It was too much. Hilde's words echoed in my mind. *You will lose your true love forever.* Was love really supposed to feel like this? Like a burden, a price too high to pay? My ancestors had risked everything for love, had tied their entire bloodline to magic for it. And now I had to decide if I was willing to do the same. I wasn't even sure if I wanted magic, and yet the thought of losing Nick tore at me.

Hilde invited us to watch the rest of their rituals. As we watched the coven as they began to chant, their voices rising in beautiful, otherworldly harmony. They danced and spun, their bodies moving with such joy and freedom, so connected to something larger than themselves. I envied them. I had grown up with Christianity, but it had never filled me like this. I had never felt that sense of belonging, of certainty. Instead, I had drifted through life, searching for something, but never quite finding it. I wondered what it would be like to belong to something like that, something bigger than myself. Nick had that, he had K Corp, he had a whole community of people who supported him. I envied that. The thought lingered that I could have that possibly, if I chose to keep my magic, and Nick. I could be a part of something amazing. But it meant giving up so much to have it. Is love meant to be this selfish, this dangerous? My ancestors had been willing to risk everything for it. But am I?

Nick and I sat next to each other in silence as the coven's chanting continued, the night around us filled with the sound of ancient words I didn't understand but felt deep within myself. The silence between us isn't cold or angry, but it's heavy, weighted with the knowledge of what we had just learned. I could tell he clung to the possibility of me giving up my magic and along with it, him. He would be alone. With his parents gone he was orphaned. If I gave him up, how would it affect him? I didn't want to break his spirit, he deserved love, I just wasn't sure if I could be everything he needed or deserved.

Maybe a safer, steadier strong-like would be enough. Something that didn't come with so much risk, so much pain. I could settle for 'like' if it meant going back to my normal life… I think.

The drive back to the castle was quiet, but that time, it wasn't the kind of silence that left me uneasy. We were both thinking, processing. If I give up my magic, I lose Nick. It was as simple and as complicated as that. And yet, nothing about it felt simple. Was this what true love looked like? I had to be willing to sacrifice everything, no matter the consequences? A part of me isn't sure I wanted that kind of love, the kind that demanded so much, that asked you to give up the world for someone else.

We sat by the large fireplace that dominated the central room. The concierge quickly brought us warm drinks, noticing how chilled we were. I was grateful for the warmth of the drink in my hands, but my thoughts continue to spiral.

After a while, I finally broke the silence, my brain tired of going over the same information and coming to no conclusion. "So, if you're my 'true love'…" I said, the words feeling heavy on my tongue, "if I choose to break the magic bond, you'll lose your true love too." I stared into the fire, not able to meet his eyes. "That's a lot of pressure. I'm not sure I can handle that kind of weight."

"Don't decide for me," his voice soft but steady. "You have to do what's right for you. I'll be okay, no matter what you choose. I just want you to be safe and happy."

But his words didn't convince me. He said he'd be okay, but the way his voice caught at the end tells me otherwise. He looked away from me, attempting to hide the wetness gathering in his eyes. He said one thing, but his heart was screaming for something else. I had no idea what to do.

He gathered himself, "First things first, don't stress about things that aren't even an option yet." His words stung a little, leaving a hint in my mind that it won't be possible to break the magic but also being rational. It may not be an option, ever.

"I don't even know where to begin," I said after a long pause. "How am I supposed to find this talisman? How do I even start? It could be lost forever." I let out a long sigh, the weight of it all pressing down on me again. "I appreciate you bringing me here, though. I know you've got the factory to deal with, so if you need to leave…" I trailed off, giving him an out. Maybe he didn't want to be tangled up in this anymore. Maybe it was better if he didn't have to deal with me and my cursed family drama.

"The factory can wait," Nick said, cutting off my thoughts. "I want to help you, Aoife. I want to help you find peace with all of this. But if you'd rather go through it alone, I can have someone cast a protection spell on you, just in case the Wiijigoo shows up."

I was shaking my head before he even finished. "No. I don't want to do this alone. I can't. You… you help keep me grounded, Nick. I need that. I need you." I paused, my words stumbling out faster than I intended. "But that's not the only reason I want you around," I added quickly. "I mean, I enjoy your company too. Not just for the help. I…"

I was rambling, and I knew it, but I couldn't stop. The stress, the emotions, it was all pouring out in awkward fragments. Nick gave me a strained smile, his eyes soft with understanding, but he didn't say anything.

I'm not sure if that made me feel better or worse.

I couldn't deal with it anymore. The exhaustion, physical, emotional, mental, is too much. "Well," I said, standing up slowly, "I'm exhausted. I think I need to get some rest." I paused, glancing over at Nick. "Do we need to pay for the drinks?"

He chuckled softly, the sound light but tired. "Aoife, I own the castle. We don't have to pay for anything."

That caught me off guard. Of course, he owned the castle. Why wouldn't he?

I laughed, shaking my head. "Right. Well, goodnight then." I paused, "Hey, Nick, thanks. For everything. I really do appreciate everything you've done for me." He gave a small smile as a response.

I waved goodbye and headed down the long, cold hallways to my room. The stone walls felt colder than before, or maybe it was just the chill in my heart, the uncertainty, the fear of what I had to face, of the decisions looming ahead. I crawled into bed, grateful for the warmth of the flannel pajamas and the comfort of the thick blankets. The hot water bottle at the foot of the bed was an unexpected but welcome surprise to help warm my chilled bones. For now, I allowed myself to rest. Tomorrow would bring more questions, more decisions.

Chapter 9

I woke to the soft blinking of the phone light, pulling me out of a deep, dreamless sleep. A message from Nick invited me to join him for breakfast. It was a good sign he left the message himself instead of using a messenger. It gave me hope it would be better than the last. I hurried through my morning routine, pulling on one of the prepacked outfits and running my fingers through my hair in a futile attempt to tame my curls. It would have to do. Heading downstairs, I followed my nose towards the food.

The mouthwatering scent of sausages, pancakes, and sweet syrup filled the air in a large room with stone walls and wooden rafters exposed on the ceiling. It felt overkill for breakfast. Nick was already seated at a table with several plates spread out in front of him. He waved me over with a smile, and soon, a waiter brought me a steaming cup of coffee.

I took a sip, closing my eyes as the rich, warm flavor soothed my tired mind. When I opened them, I noticed Nick staring at me, quickly averting his gaze when I caught him.

"Is this your special coffee?" I asked, raising an eyebrow.

He grinned. "It is. Do you like it?"

"Very much." I let the warmth of the coffee seep into my bones, already feeling more awake.

"I'm glad. I like making you feel good." His voice held a teasing edge, and I shot him a side-eye, unsure how to take the comment. He smiled knowingly and uncovered the plates in front of us, revealing fluffy pancakes topped with strawberries and sausage on the side.

Without any pretenses, I dug in, the sweet and savory flavors a much-needed comfort. Nick smirked as I devoured my food, his amusement obvious. I couldn't help but wonder what he thought of me. His world seemed to be one of sophistication, probably filled with polished socialites. Meanwhile, here I was, a mess of wild curls and unfiltered thoughts, barely holding it together in the middle of an ancestral curse. He'd have to be crazy to accept me as I was, maybe that was why he was still single? *Maybe he is crazy, maybe he's my kind of crazy.* I wasn't sure if I wanted him to walk away or stay. Either way, he'd need to see me as I really was.

"What are you thinking?" he asked softly.

"I can't believe you did all of this," I said, my voice barely above a whisper. "You've only known me for a few days, and yet you've gone to all this trouble. I'm basically a stranger."

He smiled warmly. "You're not a stranger, Aoife. I knew from the moment I met you. A long time ago, my mother, she had the gift of sight, told me I'd meet my soulmate, and it would be a whirlwind romance. And, well… here you are. My whirlwind." He chuckled, his grin boyish and genuine. "She wasn't always clear on details, but the moment I saw you, I knew."

I stared at him, half in disbelief. "You knew this whole time?" I asked, trying to keep the frustration from bubbling up. "Why didn't you say anything?"

"You've had a lot on your plate," he said gently. "You just found out about your magic, and creatures are trying to kill you. I didn't think you needed one more thing to worry about."

Maybe he was right. Would I have even believed him if he'd told me I was his destined soulmate? Probably not. Taking a deep breath, I leaned back in my chair, trying to let go of the lingering annoyance. Thinking more about it, "wait so what else do you know about me. Did your mom tell you all my secrets?" I laughed nervously, hoping she didn't.

"She didn't mention anything in particular, but she did keep having visions of tacos and blue cheese martinis. She mentioned them often when we'd talk about her visions, but She never knew who it was connected to."

I gasped, "So that's how you knew about the martini!"

He shrugged, "I didn't know for sure it was connected to you, I took a gamble with it. By any chance you don't have a taco business or anything do you?" he ended laughing.

I laughed back, "No taco business, but my friend Axel and I have Taco Tuesday every week."

"Then that makes sense too. I wish she was here to see all this. She'd get a kick out of her random visions actually making sense." He said in a sad tone.

"I'm sorry about your mom." I reached over and gently touched his hand. His eyes connected with mine, melting my heart. He had so much pain hidden behind them.

"Thanks. She would have loved you. You don't let me get away with anything. She would have approved of your spiciness."

"Oh, you think I'm spicy huh?"

"Si, Muy Caliente"

We both laughed, he did know how to lighten the mood, but I knew it was a facade, a camouflage to hide his inner thoughts. He was just as lost as I was. Maybe this journey would also help him find the lost parts of himself. I hoped so. He deserved peace as much as anyone else, if not more.

Wanting to change the subject to keep Nick from getting sad, it broke my heart to see him so down, "So, what's next? How do I find the amulet? Any grand ideas on that one?"

Nick smiled, seemingly relieved at the change of subject. "I've scheduled a meeting with the curator at the National Library of Dublin. They might have more records, and we can trace if your family still owns any property here."

My jaw dropped slightly. "How did you get an appointment with the curator on such short notice?"

He grinned. "I have my ways. Let's just say, he owed me a favor."

I couldn't help but laugh. The man was full of surprises.

The drive to Dublin felt long but beautiful. The rolling green hills, dotted with ancient ruins and random stones, made my heart ache with a strange kind of joy. As an artist, moments like these filled my soul. I lost myself in the landscape, grateful for the quiet.

When we arrived at the grand stone building, a man in a black cap was waiting to take the car. Nick tossed him the keys, and we made our way inside the library. The halls were lined with endless shelves of books, and the air smelled of dust and old pages, a scent I hadn't realized I loved so much until that moment.

Nick led me down a hallway to a large, polished door. Behind it, the curator, a stout, older gentleman with white hair, rushed up to hug Nick. His enthusiasm caught me off guard, but I found it endearing. He turned to me and hugged me gently, his warmth surprising.

"I'm Tom," he said in a thick Irish accent. "Nick told me you might need some help. Let's see what we can find, shall we?"

He led us down a set of ancient stairs carved out of the natural stone in the earth. They were worn with age, uneven and cracked, I had to be careful where I stepped so I didn't tumble down them and take out Nick and Tom along with me. The air grew colder the deeper we descended, the cold bit into me, I was grateful for my blazer at that moment. As we went lower into the tunnel of stairs, the natural light disappeared. Tom pushed on old buttons along the wall, making fluorescent lights flicker above our heads, giving us light to see the uneven steps.

Eventually, we arrived at an intricately carved wooden door, which Tom unlocked with an old skeleton key he pulled out of his pocket. He pushed open the heavy door, it groaned in protest, as if it hadn't been opened in some time. The room we entered was more like a cavern than a room, dusty, dimly lit, and filled with ancient books whose leather bindings were tattered and worn that lined the walls on old wooden shelves.

Tom walked to one of the shelves, he ran his fiver over the spines of the books, wiping off the dust so he could see the names on the side. The smell of dust filled the air, I fought back a sneeze, afraid to disrupt even more dist. He carefully selected one, blowing off the dust before laying it on a large wooden table in the center of the room. The top was covered in dents and scrapes showing its age and hard use. With reverence, he flipped through its pages; dust wafted from them with every movement, finally stopping at one that he beckoned me to read.

The book appeared to be in Latin at first, but as I stepped closer, the words shifted into English; maybe I had just thought it was in Latin from far away. It was a census of sorts, detailing names, dates, and descriptions of events. My heart raced as I spotted my family name: Wallace. The entry read, *Sorche Wallace, descendant of Jon Wallace and Gabrielle O'Brien. Upon their demise, Sorche shall inherit the family broach and pass it down within her bloodline.*

"This must be it," I whispered. "The talisman. It's a broach."

Tom nodded. "We keep records of magical families in Ireland, though not all are sanctioned, so it can be difficult to track."

I stared at the page, feeling both closer and further from the answers I sought. My ancestors, the ones that loved each other so deeply they sought out a witch to make their bond unbreakable, so they could always find their way back to each other. They formed the soulmate bond that now affected Nick and me. That moment was surreal, that was the moment that led us to where we were now. "How do we find the descendant of Sorche who has the amulet?"

Tom thought for a moment. "I have a few leads. Let me make some calls and see what I can dig up." We followed Tom back up the steps, slowly feeling the warmth seeping back into the air as we ascended back to the ground level where natural light soaked the room.

Nick and I waited in a large studying room, surrounded by reading lamps and tables in redwoods. The warmth was a stark contrast to the cold of the cavern below. I was shivering, still chilled from the adventure into the depths. Nick slid over beside me, pulling me close, rubbing my arm, his warmth immediately soothed me, at the same time it sent shivers down my spine, not because I was cold then, but because his touch did something to my body. *My traitorous body kept reacting to him, I really needed to have a talk with her about that. We're supposed to be on a fact finding mission to get rid of the magic, not falling for the man who's too perfect for me.*

"He spelled the book," Nick said softly. "That's why it translated for you. Tom's got a gift for that."

I smiled slightly, wondering once again if Nick could somehow hear my thoughts. It was unsettling how often he answered my unspoken questions. I made a note to myself to keep my thoughts pg. rated just in case.

"What's your gift? Do you have any? I mean you have to right? To be a part of all this?"

He chuckled, "I don't have anything as cool as gold tornados. Mine is much more subtle, my dad and I shared the same gift…" Before he could finish Tom returned with a grin on his face. My brain kept wondering what Nick's gift was. I had so many options running through my mind, but Tom pulled my attention to him and the task at hand. "Well, I've found a name: Margaret Wallace. She was the last to have the amulet after your family immigrated to the States. You may need to track her down. We don't have any records of your family after that. I'm really sorry. I hope this can help point you in the right direction at least."

Margaret Wallace. The name was familiar but distant. My mother had mentioned her before, but the details were hazy. There had been a falling out, one no one in my family talked about. I would have to dig deeper.

"I can call my mom and see if she knows anything," I said, feeling the weight of this new lead.

Tom nodded, hugging me once more before whispering something into Nick's ear. I shot Nick a curious glance, but he only smiled back at me, refusing to explain. We made our way back outside, where the car was already waiting for us. Another surprise, no doubt.

I had no idea what lay ahead, but with every step, I felt closer to the answers I desperately needed. I held on to that hope and Nick's steady presence by my side.

Chapter 10

As we left the library, the weight of everything that had happened over the past few days pressed down on me again. I didn't like the unknown. I didn't know what the next steps were, I didn't know how any of this would play out. I needed to get a game plan to make sense in my mind.

"What's the plan now? Is there anything else for us to do here in Ireland, or are we heading back?" I asked, still trying to shake off the surrealness of my situation.

Nick's eyes twinkled as he looked at me. "I thought we could grab a bite to eat and then maybe do some sightseeing. I'd hate for you to miss out on all the beauty Ireland has to offer. But if you'd prefer, we can head straight back. Up to you."

His suggestion took me by surprise. Between the magical discoveries, ancient curses, and soul-searching, I hadn't even thought about enjoying the place we were in. But he was right. I was in Ireland, one of the most beautiful places in the world. I needed to take a moment to breathe and live in the present.

"Food sounds great! And sightseeing sounds even better," I said, my stomach already growling at the thought.

We pulled up to a cozy Irish pub, and I could feel the warmth even before stepping inside. The smell of hearty food greeted me, drawing me in more. Nick smiled as we sat down at a small wooden table in the corner, the low hum of conversation and clinking glasses creating a comforting atmosphere. When the waiter arrived, I let Nick order for me, hoping I wouldn't regret the trust I was placing in him.

"Don't worry," he said with a grin. "It's nothing too exotic. I promise no blood sausage or brains." I was glad he said that because my mind went to all the odd meals I knew other countries were accustomed to. I prided myself on being adventurous with food but eating blood or organs wasn't my cup of tea.

The waiter brought us beers on tap while we waited for our meals, and I took a long sip, feeling the crisp drink ease some of my tension. The past few days had been overwhelming, to say the least. Magic, curses, family secrets, it was all so much to process. A part of me was still in shock that all of it was real.

As I set my glass down, Nick's bright green eyes were fixed on me, a look of concern mixed with something deeper. "When we're done here, do you want to do some sightseeing? I don't want to wear you out," he asked, his voice soft, thoughtful.

The thought of rest was tempting, but I knew that taking my mind off the heaviness of everything would do me more good. "Sightseeing sounds perfect," I replied with a smile. "Is it possible for me to call my family when we get back to the, uh, castle?" It felt weird to say castle out loud. "I don't want them to worry. I... can't remember their phone numbers, though." I blushed, feeling a little foolish for not knowing them by heart.

Nick nodded without hesitation, his eyes never leaving mine. "We can arrange that. I'll have a phone brought to your room with all the numbers you need." He tapped his phone for a moment, then slipped it back into his pocket. "It'll be waiting for you when we get back."

He smiled, that reassuring look again. "Is there anyone in particular you'd like me to add to the list?" he asked, his tone careful, almost too casual, as if he were probing whether I had someone special to call like a boyfriend.

"Just my mom, work, and Axel my best friend," I said, emphasizing Axel's role as my best friend a bit too much, as if to make sure Nick understood. Not that it mattered. Nick and I came from such different worlds that I couldn't imagine us fitting into each other's lives beyond this bizarre adventure.

Nick seemed satisfied with my answer. "Not a problem. My team can handle that. Is there anything else you need? Clothes, personal items?"

I giggled at the thought of asking for anything remotely personal from his team. "No, I'm all set, thanks to the fantastic packing your team did."

Then a question popped into my mind, and I couldn't help but ask, "Is this like Fight Club, where we can't talk about it? I mean, magic?"

Nick let out a hearty laugh, a real belly laugh that made me smile despite myself. "No, you can talk about it. Though, most people just won't believe you. Sometimes, it's easier to leave out the details unless absolutely necessary."

I nodded, thinking about how my great-aunt had been treated when she tried to share her magical abilities. "Yeah, I think I'll keep that to myself for now." I hated lying to the people I love but there were just some things I couldn't explain, and I wasn't planning on keeping my magic anyway so no sense in telling them all to make it go away.

When the food arrived, I was delighted. Fish and chips, a classic, was delicious. The best I'd ever had. I was stuffed by the time we finished, and Nick, as usual, paid the bill without a second thought. I tried not to add up all these costs that were accumulating.

Trying to shake the thought, I broke the silence. "So, do you do this often?" I instantly regretted it, my voice sounding awkward in the stillness.

Nick, of course, took it in stride. He leaned back on one arm, his usual smirk in place. "You mean, do I bring women out to the Irish countryside" he teased. "No. In fact, you're the first."

I raised an eyebrow, unsure if he was being serious or just his usual flirtatious self.

"I'm not lying," he added with a chuckle that always made a part of me spark to life. "The only woman I've ever brought here was my mom. We used to come to the castle every spring when I was younger."

"Oh yeah?" I replied, laughing lightly. "Sounds like a much different childhood than mine. My family's vacations were more like cross-country road trips, tents, campgrounds, and hoping the showers worked."

He smiled warmly. "We definitely had different lifestyles, but I bet both our parents did what they could. My parents worked a lot, so I spent most of my time in the factory just to see them."

We both sat quietly for a moment, letting the conversation settle. Then, Nick turned to me, his expression serious but open. "What about your future? What are your goals?"

It was a loaded question, one I wasn't sure I had the answer to. Before my divorce, I had the typical dream of a house, kids, a dog, and a white picket fence. But now, I wasn't sure what I wanted anymore. I wondered if part of me would miss having magic if I chose to give it up. Would I feel like I was missing something? I didn't want to allow myself to worry about that because I was determined to get back to my life, *what can I say, I was stubborn.*

"I'm just taking life one day at a time," I admitted. "I'd like to open a gallery of my own someday. But for now, I'm content just working in a gallery and showing my work sometimes."

Nick nodded thoughtfully, not pushing me to say more than I was ready to. "I get that. I'm kind of in the same boat, just trying to figure out how to run the family business and see where life takes me."

For a moment, I wondered if he'd left marriage and kids out of his answer because I had. What if that's what he truly wanted? I didn't know if I could give that to him. But that was a bridge we'd cross when we got there, if we ever got there.

"So," I began cautiously, "you said you're an open book. Can I ask what favor you did for Tom that made him go so far out of his way to help us?"

Nick's grin returned. "Are you sure you want to know? I thought you wanted a break from all this magical talk."

I was secretly hoping it wasn't magic-related, but I had a feeling everything Nick did had a bit of magic running through it. "No, I want to know."

"Well, Tom is a Patupaiarehe," he said as if it were the most natural thing in the world. "He needed help escaping his tribe during a territory dispute. It got dangerous, so I helped him find a new place to live. He's been running an underground railroad for magical beings ever since, helping others out of bad situations too."

"A… what?" I asked, my mouth slightly open.

"A Patupaiarehe is a type of fairy. They're territorial, that's why there was a drey war between the neighboring groups, a drey is a group of them, they are always pushing for more territory. They are a unique group that can't be in sunlight for long, but they can live a long time, Tom's over 250 years old."

I blinked, absorbing this new information. "So… are there a lot of magical creatures I don't know about? The people at your factory they're not human, are they? I mean, the iridescent skin should've tipped me off."

Nick chuckled. "You're incredibly accepting, you know that? You never asked about them. Yes, most of them aren't human. But you didn't judge them, you just treated them like anyone else."

I felt a strange warmth at his words, like he saw something in me that I didn't often see in myself. "Okay, so here's the deal: from now on, assume I don't know what any creature is and explain it to me. I want to learn."

He smiled. "I will. But if you break the curse, you won't remember any of it. The spell erases all traces of magic from your memory."

"What? Why would my memory need to be erased?" I asked, confused.

"For safety. The knowledge of magical beings could put them in danger if it got out. Humanity doesn't react well to things it doesn't understand. It's better for everyone to not know."

I nodded, understanding but saddened. I'd forget all the people I'd met, everything I'd experienced. Did I really want to give that up? Give all of them up? Including Nick? As much as I tried to resist him, he was growing on me. He just got me. He didn't make fun of me when I tripped or did something wrong. He seemed to legitimately like me…all of me. If I gave it up, I'd be alone again. I'd have my friends and Axel, but with Nick I felt different. He seemed to fill a gap in my life I didn't know I had.

"You ready to go for a drive?"

"Ready," I had no idea where we were headed, but I was at the point where I'd follow Nick just about anywhere.

The drive took us through the winding roads of Ireland's countryside, the endless green fields rolling out in front of us like a living postcard. The shades of green were almost hypnotic, as though the land itself held some ancient magic that called to anyone who passed through. I must've drifted off, lulled by the soft hum of the car and the peaceful view, because when I blinked back awake, we were parked near a cliff-side ruin. The air was different here, cleaner, crisper, like it had never been touched by anything but nature.

The sunset over the rocky coastline was remarkable. It is almost too beautiful to describe. Oranges, reds and yellows mix like watercolor and danced across the ocean horizon. The small reflections of the sunset bouncing off the waves in the ocean. I could stare at that for hours; the sunset didn't last nearly long enough. As Nick drove, I soaked in the views, I spun around in my seat as fast as I could so I could take in the sights all around me. Nick chuckled at me as I continuously turned in my seat, making the smooth leather squeak under me. I didn't want to miss a second of the ruins that dotted the hills and the houses with thatched roofs that took over the old lands where history seeped into it.

Inside the car was dark, I couldn't see anything inside except the dim light off the dash instruments. It showed just glimpses of Nick's perfect feature profile. He was handsome. Would this beautiful man, inside and out, ever really want me? I'm unremarkable, unsophisticated, and to be honest, kind of a mess. Nick had some mellow instrumental music playing, it wasn't my style, but it was beginning to grow on me, like Nick was.

As we drove back to the castle, I couldn't help but feel grateful for the brief moment of normalcy. It was as if we were just two people enjoying each other's company without the weight of magic and curses hanging over us. When we finally pulled up to the castle, I sighed slightly, disappointed we couldn't drive around Ireland forever, just soaking in all the history. The small staff greeted us and handed us cups of hot cocoa. It was a simple gesture, but it warmed me inside and out. We sat by the fireplace, letting the warmth of the flames chase away the evening chill.

I kicked off my boots and propped my feet near the fire, feeling content and a little sleepy. Nick stood, grabbing a blanket and draping it over my lap before sitting beside me.

He patted his lap. "Want me to rub them?"

I didn't hesitate. I swung my feet toward him, and his warm hands began to knead the tension from them. His touch was firm yet gentle, and I couldn't help but let out a small, involuntary moan of relief. I'd regret that later, but right now, I was too tired to care.

"How did you learn to do that so well?" I asked, my voice barely above a whisper.

He smiled, not missing a beat. "My mom taught me reflexology. She believed in natural remedies, so I'd rub her feet after the holiday season. It was the least I could do for her."

"So, a mama's boy, huh?" I teased, trying to keep my mind from wandering into dangerous territory.

"Not really," he said with a chuckle. "But my parents taught me to respect women. It's one of the most important things they ever taught me."

That wasn't something you heard every day. "You *are* quite the ladies' man, though. Does your girlfriend feel okay with you spending so much time with another woman?"

Nick laughed, shaking his head. "No girlfriend. I've met some nice women, but none that felt… right. And most didn't understand my long hours I have to keep during the holiday season. It's not fair to them."

"You've mentioned the holidays here and there, but not really in detail. So are you like Santa or something." I asked jokingly.

He shrugged and smiled, "something like that. It's our busiest time. We deliver a lot of toys around that time, so we spend most of the year prepping for that delivery. My dad loved making children of the world happy. It brought him such joy. I can still hear his deep belly laugh of pride after the deliveries were made. I miss him deeply, but I'm glad I'm able to carry on his legacy. And mom, she's the one who helped so many people. She changed a lot of lives."

I knew he wouldn't continue that conversation much more, but I had to try. "What did you admire about your mom? You mentioned she was a hard worker, and was natural-minded with health, what else?" I prodded deeper to try and get to know Nick better. I knew surface-level Nick, but I wanted to get to know him inside and out. I needed to see the good and the bad if I had to make a decision to choose him and magic. He finally opened up about his dad. I'd love to hear about his mom too, he seemed close to his mom so it may share more insights about him.

He sunk deeper into the couch to be able to lean his head back while he talked and rubbed my feet. "Her and my dad were an inspiration to so many, she helped people without expecting anything in return. She just saw the best in everybody and wanted to give everyone a chance. Many of the workers of the K Complex were brought in as people she was helping, and she gave them a chance, a career, a life that they could be safe in. I hope to make my mark on people like that someday."

"It sounds like you are highly respected everywhere you go; I don't think it'll be hard to make your own mark."

"They respect me because of my family, last name and money. I often wonder if they would like me if I didn't have any of those things?"

"You do have those things though, so use them for good. So many people I deal with in the art community want to just coast by on their money and give nothing back to society. You have a chance to make a big difference. I know you are helping make a difference in my life. I don't know what I would have done without your help through this whole process." I reached forward to put my hand on his, I wanted him to really understand how much he's helped me and how much I appreciate it.

We sat in silence, gently smiling at each other every few minutes in front of the warm fire crackling and popping embers into the air like popcorn. It was peaceful, and I felt a warmth spread through me that had nothing to do with the fire or Nick's touch. It was just… comfort. Pure and simple. After a bit, I thanked him for the amazing day and the foot rub. As much as I enjoyed having time to relax and talk with him, I needed to make some phone calls, so my family didn't start calling the FBI.

When I got back to my room, there was a phone waiting for me, just as Nick had promised. Neatly written on a notepad with a scrolled K at the top were the phone numbers I'd asked for. I sat on the bed, staring at the list, trying to figure out how to explain everything that had happened well, a version of everything.

I decided to call my job first, knowing that would be the easiest. Jodi, my manager at the gallery, picked up after a few rings, and I launched into an explanation about a "medical emergency." Surprisingly, she wasn't too harsh and even offered me more time if I needed it. A wave of relief washed over me, at least I still had a job when I returned.

Next, I dialed my mom's number. My parents had likely been worried sick. The phone rang twice before my mom's familiar voice came through.

"Hello?" she answered with a question, her voice filled with concern.

"Hey, Mom, it's me," I said, trying to keep my voice light.

"Oh baby, where have you been? We've been trying to call you, but it kept going to voicemail!" she said, the worry evident in her tone.

"I'm okay, Mom. I had to leave for a last-minute work trip, and I lost my phone along the way," I explained, hoping she wouldn't pry too much.

"Are you sure you're alright? How's the weather there?" she asked, subtly slipping in our code question, checking if I was in danger.

I smiled at her protectiveness. "The weather's fantastic, Mom. Don't worry." with my safe code response.

"Ooookay" she replied with a tone of uncertainty.

I smiled at her, I loved that my mom was so protective.

"Where are you? When are you coming home? Do you need us to send you anything?"

"I'm actually in Ireland," I admitted, knowing she'd be both excited and suspicious. "I'll be back in a few days, and I'll tell you all about it."

Her voice softened. "Ireland? That sounds incredible. You have to tell me all about your trip when you get home. When are you coming home?"

"I actually was wondering if it was okay if I swung by soon? I miss you guys" it wasn't a lie, I did miss them, but I had ulterior motives, I needed to find information about Margrett.

"Oh honey, you don't have to ask, come anytime."

"Thank mom. I didn't want to surprise you in case you've been walking around the house naked, enjoying your empty nest." She laughed.

After a few more reassurances, I hung up, relieved, that call had gone smoother than expected.

The last call was to Axel, my best friend. As soon as he picked up, he bombarded me with questions, his concern laced with his usual teasing tone. I assured him I was fine, giving him a vague outline of what had happened, though I left out most of the craziness of magic, the Wiijigoo that was trying to find, the search for an ancient family broach that contained magic… *you know, the completely normal things that happen to me now.* Axel was more perceptive than my parents and would likely suspect I was holding something back. But for now, he accepted my explanation, and I promised to call him with all the details when I returned. He'd hold me to that.

With the phone calls behind me, I felt a little more grounded, but the questions still spun in my mind. What was I going to do about the magic? Could I go back to my normal life, or was that life gone forever? Would my family and friends even believe me if I told them the truth? I know I wouldn't believe me. The mounting pressure of possibly being able to get rid of the magic weighed on me. The closer I got to answers, the harder the decision felt.

I sighed and lay down, staring at the dead moose head mounted above the fireplace. The absurdity of it all made me chuckle. Magic, curses, secret libraries, and now I was lying in a castle, being hunted by dark forces. How was I supposed to cope with all of this?

As I drifted into thought, Nick's face lingered in my mind. There was a connection between us, something I couldn't deny. But was that connection real, or was it just the pressure of the situation? I wasn't sure I was ready to find out.

Chapter 11

Our trip to Ireland was a grand success. I learned the painful story about my family's past, the spell and how it started. I even got Nick to open up a little more. Not to mention the stunning Irish views, food, and castles. But we had a task to complete now.

I think that it's something I needed to talk to my mom in person about. So, I asked Nick if there was any way I could get back home. He insisted on going with me to help shield me, after all, I had only tried it a few times and needed more practice. I couldn't risk the safety of my family, so I agreed. I hadn't thought of how extravagant Nick did everything, that may be an issue. My family is homely and would ask a lot of questions. So, after flying into the airport on his private jet, I insisted on a basic rental sedan. It wouldn't draw as many questions with my family. He reluctantly agreed.

"We need to figure out what I am going to tell my mother about you and our great aunt"

Nick grinned, "I could be your international lover".

I laughed so hard I almost spit out the coffee I was drinking. My family would never believe that. I wasn't exactly the world-traveling, societal type. "Hm, you could never pass for a coworker, maybe a boss?"

"Can I just be your friend? That way it's not a lie. We're friends, right?" He grinned boyishly at me.

"Fine, friend it is. But you cannot mention magic here. My family would not understand that they'd think you were crazy."

"Mums the word. I'll follow your lead."

Nick drove, I called out directions because he refused to use the GPS, must be a guy thing. We arrived at my parents', both of their cars were home, so I knew they'd be there. I was secretly hoping they wouldn't be here, but the conversation needed to happen eventually, so might as well get it over with. I used the spare key they always kept hidden under the garden gnome.

My mom peeked her head from around the corner to see who walked in, "Oh my dear, you scared the living daylights out of me!" She turned her head the other direction and yelled "Everett! Aoife's here! Come down!" My dad must have been upstairs. I heard loud footsteps hurrying down the stairs. They both bolted up to give me a group hug.

"I thought you were in Ireland! When did you get back? How was it? And who is this" she said, trying to wink subtly but not very well. Nick saw and started to chuckle under his breath. My mom wasn't very good at subtle. "I'm Josephine but you can call me Jo", she said, reaching out to shake Nick's hand.

"It's a pleasure to meet you, Jo. Your daughter is quite amazing, I can see where she gets it from" kissing her knuckles instead of a handshake, that made my mom blush, she was a sucker for flattery.

"Mom, we'll have time to talk. Give Nick some space. He's just a friend; he was in Ireland with me and offered to tag along to say hi"

She turned towards me "Friend huh? He's the cutest 'friend' you've ever brought over" With a big smile on her face she was reading more into the situation that there was. I ignored her comments. "Come, let's sit in the living room. Would anyone like coffee or tea? Aoife, I know you'll want coffee right?"

My mom knew me too well, "yes please" I gave her puppy eyes making her laugh.

"I'd love a coffee if it's made already Mrs. Wheeler, but I don't want you going out of your way for me, I'll take whatever you have handy"

"What accent is that, Nick? I haven't heard one like that before." My mom was prodding for information already, but I was secretly glad she did because I always wondered too.

"Oh, the village I'm from in Canada has this unique accent."

"Canada, eh?" my dad said as his typical bad dad joke.

Nick just chuckled; I think he's figured out what my mother was doing. There's no detective as skilled as a mother trying to protect her child. My mom was a great mom, she was always supportive and understanding of my choices. She never made me feel bad about the situation with Josh, she never tried to make me stay when I needed to leave to get away from him. I knew she wouldn't judge me for dating Nick, which I wasn't, or for pursuing a different life path, but she probably wouldn't understand that we had real magic in our family and that I could create portals with mine.

I wanted to share this new part of my life with her. It broke my heart a bit knowing I couldn't. I had to protect her though. I didn't want to expose her to the danger the new world exposed her to. I took a deep breath, holding back the tears that threatened to overflow from my conscience angry at me lying to her.

Trying to change subjects to avoid too many questions we just couldn't answer, I said "So mom, we're really here because when I was in Ireland, I found out we had a family heirloom in the family that I've never seen. A broach of some sort. Have you ever seen it? I'd love to see some of our family history".

"Wow, how did you even hear about that ugly thing? I haven't seen it in ages" Mom said with a disgusted face… seemingly she wasn't fond of it.

"It was mentioned a few times in our family history over there. So, you have seen it? Who had it last?" I asked, trying to not sound too impatient in this fact-finding mission but I needed that information. Without it I would be stuck with magic, learning how to survive with creatures trying to kill me to get to my magic. I needed her to focus and give me answers.

"Last I saw it, your great aunt Margaret had it. Your dad and I haven't talked to her in years though. She never had any kids so I'm not sure who she'd leave it to when she passes."

"Do you think she'd mind if I got a hold of her? I'd love to see it."

"I have no idea honey, you can try, but she isn't all there anymore… or ever was really." Mom looked at dad as if she couldn't say what she wanted.

He took the queue and chimed in finally, he was a man of few words, "Aunt Maggy had a rough time growing up. Her family was murdered when she was younger, she bounced from foster home to foster home until she was 18 and got her own place. We don't know much about her other than she liked to travel when she was younger, always bringing home weird artifacts."

"Oh no, that's horrible! I'm glad she was okay, but I could see how that would make anyone have… issues. Did they catch who did it?" I said pushing to find out more.

"No, they never caught the people, there were no clues to follow either. The neighbors saw dark figures in the house, but it was like they just disappeared" Dad continued.

I looked over at Nick, he was looking at me as if he was trying to tell me something, he just nodded. Oh crap, I knew this had magic involved. Was it the same figures who tried to catch me? I didn't know enough about the new magical world to tell if it was the same creature or not. I realize how little I truly knew about Nick's world.

"Do you know where Great Aunt Maggy lives now?"

"She actually lives just a few hours north. But to warn you, she's a little coo coo for cocoa puffs. She believes in some weird stuff. I wouldn't expect too much from her. I can give you her address though, or at least the last one I have for her, I doubt she'd ever move though"

We chatted and sipped on our coffee for a bit with my folks, then Nick and I excused ourselves so we could go meet this mysterious Great Aunt Maggy. Was she a kook or did she have magic and was just misunderstood her whole life?

"Don't be a stranger Nick" my mom said while hugging him a little too tightly. He smiled and kissed the top of her hand, causing her to immediately blush. Her fair skin tone couldn't hide her emotions either.

My mom then turned to me and hugged me too and whispered in my ear, "I like this one Aoife, bring him around more often, he seems good for you". My mom didn't like anyone I ever brought home, though she'd never say it to my face, she simply would never say she liked them, so I knew what it meant if she was silent. So, her saying she liked him was a good sign.

I felt good leaving them, they didn't find out about magic so I hoped that would keep them safe from all the unknown dangers in the new world I was thrown into. Nick seemed to have a handle on the magical aspect of the broach, and I would get to meet another person in my family that had magic, or at least probably knew about magic. It was the closest link to my family magic I had.

My parents waved embracing each other in their doorway as we got in the rental car and drove away. I wanted a relationship like theirs. They have been through so much yet never giving up on their love.

Nick didn't plug the address into the GPS, so I asked him "Want me to do it so we didn't get lost."

"I don't get lost… ever" he said. Well then, maybe he was a typical man refusing to get directions.

I just looked at him with an unsure look until he said "No, really, I don't get lost. It is just a skill I have. I am good with directions."

I laughed under my breath… "ooookay" I said, not convinced.

"Remember how I said I have a gift? Well, that's it. I'm really good with directions and maps. I can find my way anywhere in the world."

"You cannot." I joked with him.

He smiled at me, "I can. I'm not your average man just refusing to ask for directions. My dad was the same way."

"Huh. That's pretty cool actually. My dad gets lost in campgrounds" I joked.

"Well, it's not golden tornados, but it's all I got."

"I like it. Now I can sleep while you drive without worrying about getting lost."

He laughed, "You can be my passenger princess anytime. You can take a nap if you want. You've had a long, stressful day." Strangely, I trusted him. I felt comfortable resting while he drove, that was a big step for me.

Chapter 12

I blinked slowly as I tried to orient myself, taking in the dark Victorian house before us. It looked like something out of a horror movie, all dark tones of brown, black, and deep reds. The house loomed with an unsettling presence, and every intricate detail seemed designed to evoke unease rather than charm. The air outside was still and quiet, almost too quiet. Great Aunt Maggy's house looked exactly how you'd expect the home of someone described as "a little coo coo for cocoa puffs" to look; chipped paint, an overgrown garden, and a rickety wooden porch that seemed to sag under the weight of time.

I turned to Nick, uncertainty filling my voice. "This is the house? Are you sure?" He said he never got lost but I was holding onto hope that this wasn't the right house.

He gave me a reassuring nod, but even he looked a little wary.

Nick parked the car and gave me a soft smile, the kind that seemed to say, *whatever happens, we'll figure it out.* I appreciated that more than he knew. This wasn't just about finding the amulet. It was about uncovering parts of my family's history that had been shrouded in mystery, and possibly magic.

"You okay?" he asked, noticing the slight tension in my expression.

"Yeah, just… not sure what we'll find here," I admitted, taking a deep breath and unbuckling my seat belt.

"Well, no matter what we find, you're not alone in this," he said, his tone warm and reassuring. There it was again that calm certainty that Nick always seemed to carry with him. For all the mysteries and magical uncertainties swirling around us, his presence grounded me.

I could see a figure moving slightly in the shadows of the entryway. The deck boards creaked with each little movement giving the figure's position away. It slowly came out into view, the sunlight causing shadowing on the sunken, pale face. It was a thin, frail woman, wearing a black, heavily beaded skirt that you could hear jingle with every step, a Victorian-styled black shirt with poofy shoulders and a lace neckline that elongated her thin neck. Her gray hair was wrapped up in a loose bun on top of her head, wisps of uncontrolled curls escaped the loose bun and cascaded down her thin face. She was beautiful in an unconventional way. As an artist I soaked in this moment, as a person, it terrified me.

"You must be Aoife," she said, her voice raspy but steady. "I wondered when you'd come looking for me."

I blinked, caught off guard by her knowing tone. "Yes, I'm Aoife. And you must be Aunt Maggy?"

"That's what they call me, but I know what you're here for," she said, opening the door wider to let us in. She was holding a little broom that looked like it was handmade out of grass and sticks. She motioned for us to follow her. She slowly turned and shuffled her tiny frame and jingling skirt inside the house.

Nick and I exchanged a glance before stepping inside. The air in the house was thick, musty, and it smelled faintly of herbs and something else I couldn't quite place. It reminded me of the shops I used to visit as a kid, the ones filled with incense and strange trinkets that always felt just a little bit… magical.

Nick went in first, I followed, his hand still tight around mine. He was urging me to stay behind him still, so I followed his lead. He seemed like he knew best in situations like this. After all, we didn't know if Aunt Maggy was good, or bad yet or even what she was. As we walked through the doorway, I noticed Nick step over a line of what looked like salt that was on the floor. He made it a point to not slow down and to not step on it, so I did the same. Aunt Maggy was observing us, as if to see what would happen. She sighed a sound of relief and turned around to continue walking to her formal sitting room which looked like no one had cleaned it in years. A fine layer of dust coated everything and made a small visual pouf as she sat down in one of the old chairs with ornately carved wooden arms. The room was decorated in faded photographs, and shelves crammed with books and jars filled with dried herbs and flowers. It felt like stepping into a time capsule, where everything had been frozen in place decades ago.

The front door slammed shut after we walked through it, maybe it was the wind… but I didn't feel any wind in the house, and I think wind would have swept up some of the dust covering everything in the house. That was an uneasy feeling adding to my list of things to be afraid of.

Nick led me to a room off the hallway, it was dark, lit by a single wall sconce that flicked as if it threatened to burn out like all the others. He proceeded to a long couch opposite the chair Aunt Maggy, the couch style mirrored the style of the chair she was sitting in. It was covered in a dated floral print that I could barely make out through all the dust and grime coating it. I sat close to the edge to not get too dirty, Nick sat like usual, with his legs crossed and looking relaxed.

Trinkets and masks from what looked like a lifetime of world travel lined the walls. Every wall, every surface was covered in them. I couldn't help but ask, "You must have done a lot of traveling. These are beautiful."

Aunt Maggy nodded, her eyes distant. "Yes, I traveled for many years, searching for answers." I froze, unsure how to respond.

Nick filled the silence. "I recognize some of these symbols," he said, pointing to a few of the masks. "That one is Mayan, and that one… Celtic?"

Aunt Maggy's lips curled into a faint smile, the wrinkles on her face deepening. "You know your history," she said, her tone softening slightly. "These are for protection from… things most people don't want to believe exist. But I know you aren't here to talk about my travels, you're here for the amulet." Most people kept souvenirs from fun vacations, but Aunt Maggy kept things to protect her from the creatures of this new world. The masks reminded me just how dangerous it was and how little I knew about it. The pit in my stomach grew, I did not like the unknown.

"I do want to hear all your stories though, eventually. But yes, we are here today about the broach." I explained, hoping to get closer to her, not to get the broach that had our magic, but to let her know she wasn't alone, that I believed her, even when the world turned their back on her.

Aunt Maggy leaned back in her chair, her fingers tapping rhythmically against the armrest. "It's been in our family for generations. That broach carries a weight most people wouldn't understand." She glanced at Nick, her eyes narrowing slightly, as if she could sense more than she let on.

Nick remained calm and composed, nodding politely but staying quiet. This was my family business, and he was letting me take the lead. I swallowed, my curiosity battling with a sudden unease. "What do you mean by 'a weight'?"

Aunt Maggy chuckled, a low, knowing sound that sent shivers down my spine. "Breaking a curse is no simple matter. It requires more than just a trinket, it requires sacrifice."

"Sacrifice?" I echoed, my voice barely above a whisper. I could feel the gravity of what she was saying, but I didn't fully understand. What kind of sacrifice? Would I have to find a goat or something worse to get rid of the magic? I didn't know if I was prepared to choose someone else's life over mine.

Aunt Maggy looked at me, her gaze softening just a little. "Yes, child. Something must be given up for something else to be freed. The magic doesn't just let go because you ask it to. There's a balance to keep."

I could feel the tension rising in the room as she continued, her voice carrying a weight of years spent chasing shadows. She leaned forward slightly, her pale eyes locking onto mine. "But before I give you what you want, I have one condition." I didn't expect her to just hand it over because I asked nicely, but I didn't expect her to have ulterior motives. My mind reeled at the possibilities of what she could ask for.

Nick, ever the diplomat, asked calmly, "What is your condition?" I was glad he was calm because I was not. I was stuck on the word *sacrifice.*

Her face became deadly serious. "You must find the demon who killed my parents and vanquish him."

The words hung in the air like a death sentence, but Aunt Maggy said them as if we were discussing the weather. She lived with the death of her parents for a lifetime, I wondered if she truly was in her right mind. That was the first time I heard the word 'demon' in this world. I knew about other magical creatures, but now demons? Bile rose in my throat at the thought.

I couldn't contain myself any longer. "Do you have magic?" The question tumbled out before I could stop it. I didn't want to be alone, a family that didn't understand magic, I was sure I'd be the next one to be committed. It would be nice to have someone to talk to about all of it.

Nick shot me a disapproving glance, but Aunt Maggy didn't seem offended. Instead, she nodded slowly. "Yes child, I have the gift of foresight. It's how I knew you'd come today. But it's not always a gift. I foresaw my parents' death, but I was too young to understand how to stop it." she paused, as if collecting her emotions, "My dreams haunted me, and after they were killed, no one believed me. I was labeled crazy, spent years in and out of foster homes… even a mental institution."

Her story sent chills down my spine. "I'm so sorry," I whispered. I couldn't imagine. Having this 'gift' that made you witness your own parents being murdered, as a child? I didn't know how anyone's mental health could survive that. She was all alone. No one to help guide her through life with magic. I was an adult learning how to navigate this magical world, I couldn't imagine being a child, all alone doing it. My heart shattered into a million pieces for her.

Nick leaned forward, his tone sincere. "I wish we could have helped sooner. I just didn't know. I'm so sorry." The pain in Nick's eyes was evident.

"You're here now," she said, waving off his apology. "I've accepted my fate long ago."

I swallowed, gathering the courage to ask, "Who killed them?" Scared of the answer I may hear, I gripped Nick's hand tightly, bracing for impact.

Her eyes darkened. "A demon named Fenriz."

Nick stiffened beside me, his face hardening. The name meant nothing to me, but Nick's reaction was evident he knew exactly who she was talking about. "Fenriz, the son of Loki?"

Aunt Maggy nodded. "He's been hiding for years, but I know where he is. I can feel him in my dreams, always there, lurking. I want him gone. I don't want anyone else to get hurt by him. I've seen too many of his victims. All I can do is watch him ravage their bodies, over and over again."

Nick turned to me, "Fenriz is a soul stealer. He can shift forms but in the dimension I think he's probably hiding out in, he's his true self. The dimension was created for him so he surrounds himself with creatures he can control. He's like a god there. We have quite a bit of knowledge collected from that dimension so we're not blind going into it." he patted my hand reassuringly as he explained what we were getting into. But all that information didn't make me feel better. I know knowledge is power, but I just felt powerless in this new world.

I looked at Nick, feeling the weight of her request settle heavily on my shoulders. "How do we stop him?" I wanted desperately to help her, but this new world was out of my wheelhouse. I didn't know how to help her, or even if I was capable of helping her.

Nick answered before Aunt Maggy could. "There's only one way to vanquish a demon like Fenriz. You need purified blood, applied to him on hallowed ground. This won't be easy," he added, turning back to Aunt Maggy. "But we'll do it." He didn't wait for me to answer, Nick was feeling the same need to help her as I was. A piece of my heart melted at Nick's response. Slowly he was showing me who he really was, and I was beginning to like what I saw.

Aunt Maggy's hands trembled as she set down her teacup, a sigh of relief escaping her lips. "Thank you," she whispered. "I've waited so long for this." Her voice cracked slightly, the years of waiting, of hopelessness, finally catching up with her. "Once it's done, the broach is yours. I'm sorry for holding it hostage like this. I just…have no one else. I need this peace."

My heart ached for her. Having to live with this all these years and not being able to do anything about it. I wanted to help her, I needed to help her.

It wasn't just about the amulet anymore, I wanted to help her and get to know her. She spent too many years alone.

We stayed for a while longer, discussing the details of Fenriz's location and the preparations we'd need to make. The more she explained, the more surreal it all felt. A demon, a cursed brooch, and now a quest to vanquish a creature from another dimension.

I have been so focused on my own survival that I never imagined helping other people. I know that sounds selfish but as a domestic abuse survivor, it's difficult to get out of your own PTSD to see other people struggling too. I wasn't sure I had the strength to help anyone else, I felt like I was barely surviving this new world. But I had faith in Nick. He seemed sure we could help. This was his world, if he felt confident we could do it, I believed him.

The porch groaned under our weight as we hugged Great Aunt Maggy goodbye. Her features looked softer, more pleasant, perhaps some of the weight from her past had been lifted by us offering to take on the task she was no longer able to do. I wanted to, no I had to do this for her, even if I had no idea what I was getting into.

As we left the house, the front door slammed shut behind us with a bang, startling me again. Nick's hand rested on my lower back as he led me to the car, his touch grounding me in the midst of all the chaos swirling in my mind.

"We're really going to do this, aren't we?" I asked as we got back into the car, my voice tinged with disbelief. "Nick, I don't know anything about this world. How are we supposed to vanquish a demon?" My breath was coming out so quickly, my heart was racing, I felt like the world was spinning.

Nick started the engine and looked over at me, his expression calm but serious. "It'll be okay. I've vanquished demons before. If you aren't ready, I can do it for you."

"You, you'd do that for me?" I stammered out. Trying to slow my breathing.

He nodded and squeezed my hand. "Darlin, I told you, I'd do anything for you."

A small smile tried to reach my lips, but I knew deep down that this was my task, my family trauma I had to heal from. I shook my head, resolute. "No. I need to do this. For Aunt Maggy, for my family… and for myself."

I glanced at Nick, feeling the pull of his presence next to me.

Nick's hand was warm and steady on mine, a quiet reassurance as the reality of what lay ahead started to sink in. The thought of facing a demon, *a real demon*, was both terrifying and surreal. I leaned my head against the window, watching the landscape blur by. But no matter how hard I tried to distract myself, my mind kept circling back to the weight of the task in front of us.

"Everything's going to be okay," Nick said softly, almost as if he could hear the racing thoughts in my head. His voice was steady, grounding, the kind of voice you'd want next to you when facing the unknown. I wondered if he ever got nervous doing things like this? He always seemed so calm and collected, but deep down, I wondered if he really was. He'd probably never reveal that because he knows I need him to be strong for me. I hated that, I hated that I needed him to be brave and I felt so helpless.

I nodded, the knot in my stomach tightened. "I know, I lied". There was something about this whole mission that made me feel like we were only just beginning to peel back layers of something far bigger than a single cursed piece of jewelry. "It's just... There's so much we don't know. So many risks."

Nick squeezed my hand gently, his thumb brushing lightly over my knuckles. "We'll face those risks together. We've got this, Aoife. We'll make sure you're safe and we'll help your aunt get the peace she deserves." His confidence seeped into me, giving me a bit of my own.

I took a deep breath, letting his words sink in. Despite the danger, the uncertainty, there was something comforting about knowing I wasn't alone in this. Nick had been by my side through all of this craziness, and even though we came from entirely different worlds, somehow, we made sense together.

"Thanks," I said, offering him a genuine smile this time. "For everything. I wouldn't have gotten this far without you."

His eyes flicked over to me, a small grin tugging at the corners of his lips. "You give yourself too little credit. You would have done just fine without me, but I'm happy I can help. I'll always be by your side, as long as you'll let me that is." He gave me a weak smile.

I let the compliment hang in the air between us, unsure how to respond.

Nick's confidence in me felt both reassuring and intimidating at the same time. Was I really as strong as he thought I was? Or was I just holding on by sheer willpower, afraid to let everything crash down around me?

The silence between us grew comfortable. The nervous energy that had been buzzing through me finally started to fade, replaced by a quiet resolve. I had made up my mind there was no backing down now. I wanted to be free of this curse, but more than that, I wanted to give Aunt Maggy the peace she'd been waiting for her whole life.

"We're here," he said quietly, as if breaking the silence would shatter the calm I'd finally managed to find.

I nodded, taking a deep breath and sitting up straighter in my seat. "Ready when you are."

The moment my feet hit the ground, I felt a strange surge of energy, a reminder that we were standing on the precipice of something much larger than ourselves. The next steps we took would determine everything: the success of our mission, Aunt Maggy's peace, and the fate of the magic coursing through my veins.

Nick came around to my side and squeezed my hand with reassurance, walking next to me toward the entrance of the building. Inside, the atmosphere felt charged, the usual hum of activity replaced by a tense anticipation. It was as if everyone in the building knew something monumental was about to happen. Good or bad, I was in it with them.

Chapter 13

I crawled into bed, but no matter how much I tossed and turned, my mind refused to quiet down. Between Nick and the crazy journey ahead, I wasn't sure how I was going to get any sleep. I tossed and turned for a while, trying to push away the whirlwind of thoughts racing through my head, until a soft knock echoed through the room.

Nick stood at the door, holding a glass of milk in one hand and a plate of cookies. "I thought you could use something to help you sleep. If you're anything like me with the job tomorrow, your mind won't relax."

I smiled and waved him into the room. He sat at the edge of the bed while I propped myself up against the pillows, pulling the blankets over me.

"Cookies and milk were always my mom's go-to for when my mind wouldn't settle."

"That's very thoughtful," I said, taking the plate from him. "I was having a hard time falling asleep."

"Me too. But we need our rest for tomorrow. It's going to be a long day. And… intra-dimensional travel can really drain you, especially the first time.

Don't be alarmed if you come back and crash hard. We'll have the best doctors and the coven watching us at all times, so try not to worry."

"Easier said than done." I nervously joked.

He chuckled, shaking his head. "Just trying to be honest with you. I want you to know what you're getting into; what to expect."

"I appreciate that. Really, I do. I… trust you. I trust that you wouldn't put me in danger." I took a bite of the cookie, savoring its soft texture and the hint of lavender.

Nick's face softened. "He really hurt you, didn't he? I'm sorry he didn't see your worth."

I blinked, surprised at his sudden shift. "Who?"

"Your ex… I didn't mean to bring him up, but… yeah."

My chest tightened for a moment, the old memories resurfacing. "Yeah, he left a lot of damage in his wake." It was an odd feeling fully trusting Nick. I had no hesitation putting my life in his hands.

Nick's gaze stayed steady on mine, his voice low and sincere. "I'm not him. I promise. I know it's hard for you to let someone else in, even if it's just as friends. But I want you to be happy, and safe. That's what matters to me." I knew he wanted to be more than friends, but I was glad he didn't push me on it.

The warmth in his words and the honesty behind them made my heart skip a beat. I reached out and laid my hand on his. "Thank you. I appreciate that…and I appreciate you."

For a few moments, we sat in a comfortable silence, just holding hands. There was no pressure, no expectations, just an unspoken understanding between us. Then, in true Nick fashion, he broke the silence by sneaking one of my cookies and shoving it into his mouth with exaggerated triumph.

I gasped, pretending to be outraged, and nearly fell off the bed laughing. "You thief!" I managed between fits of giggles.

Nick was laughing too, his infectious joy filling the room. We flopped back on the bed, gasping for breath, our faces flushed, our cheeks aching from the fun.

After we contained our joy, I turned my head to find Nick already looking at me, his smile soft and genuine. At that moment, I couldn't help but wonder if there was more to this connection between us. He seemed to get me, my limits, my fears, my humor. Maybe there was something to this "fated lovers" idea. Maybe… he really might be my "perfect" someone.

Nick broke the moment with a grin. "Well, I think I've caused enough trouble for one night. You should get some sleep. Eat those cookies though, they've got lavender in them. Helps with relaxation."

He stood up and walked backward toward the door, giving me a playful bow before disappearing into the hallway.

As the door clicked shut, I sat back against the pillows, feeling a little lighter. The air still buzzed with his presence, but my heart felt steady. I nibbled on another cookie, hoping for a peaceful night of sleep, despite the whirlwind of thoughts still tumbling in my head.

The morning brought a mix of hope and dread. It was the day that would bring me closer to my freedom. If I still wanted out of magic that is. My mind constantly weighing the pros and cons of keeping magic and giving it up and going back to my normal, stable life.

I needed to get out of my room, or my mind would never stop the torture of indecisiveness. The whole place was abuzz with people helping us with this mission. Huyen, as expected, was at the reservation desk, greeting me with her usual warm smile. She came out to give me a hug but what I saw made me freeze in place. She looked… part snake. Where there should be legs, there was a large, thick tail. Dark red and brown scales in intricate diamond designs slid under her in smooth motions. My reaction must have been obvious because her expression instantly dimmed with sadness.

"I'm so sorry," she said quietly. "I thought you knew. I assumed Nick told you about everyone here." She pulled away from her attempted hug.

I shook my head, feeling ashamed of how I reacted, I had just never seen her full body, she was always behind the desk. "No, no. I'm sorry for reacting like that. Nick did tell me a bit, just… not in detail about everyone. I just wasn't expecting it. It's beautiful. You're beautiful". I felt so bad that I made her self-conscience of how she looked. I had to fix it.

She kept looking down as if she was embarrassed. I need to break the silence, "Legs or no legs, it doesn't matter to me Huyen. You're still your awesome self." I paused, thinking of how to change the subject, "So, how did you come to work here?" That was all I could think of at the second, my mind was just thinking… *she has a tail.* I don't know why it was such a surprise to me that she was… unique, it seemed like everyone around there was. I just didn't expect it. I took a few deep breaths and thought, she's still the same Huyen, the woman that has been there for me since I arrived, the person who kept me sane during this whole adventure. She was no different. I thought of myself as accepting of people's differences, this was just a bigger difference than I was used to. But I reminded myself we're all different in our own way, it just added more uniqueness to her.

She gave me a small smile, softer than her usual one, but reassuring. "Nick rescued my family when I was little. We were in a bad situation, and he brought us here. I grew up in this place, and my parents worked here until they passed. This is home for me, so I've never wanted to go anywhere else. Helping out here feels like my way of repaying Nick for everything he's done."

"Nick seems like he's helped a lot of people here," I said, feeling a new level of respect for him. "And I'm really sorry about your parents."

Huyen nodded. "Thank you. Nick is a genuinely good man. His parents would be proud of him, he's following right in their footsteps. To me, he's like a brother." I thought about how she acted around Nick, I never got flirtation from her, she was just helpful Huyen. I never saw them do anything to set off my alarm bells, I just assumed Nick flirted with everyone, but maybe he was just friendly, and I read into it. "And, Aoife, I can tell you this, he's been happier since you got here. You make him happy."

I blinked, surprised. "I don't know about that. I feel like I've caused him a lot of trouble since I've been here." I've taken him away from his business for trips to help me figure out my magical lineage, I felt bad I'd taken so much of his time up.

She laughed softly. "Are you kidding? He thrives on helping people. But it's more than that, he's different with you around. More… alive."

It was a relief to hear I wasn't just a burden to him. And the part about them being like siblings? That eased my mind. I had wondered if there was something more between them, but it seemed like she mentioned that specifically to clear up any misunderstanding.

Huyen smiled but added a small warning. "Njeri is… different too. I know you're pretty open-minded about us non-humans, but she can be sensitive about how people react to her. I just wanted to give you a heads-up." I sensed I had hurt her feelings more than she showed, I had to show her that I valued her as a friend, no matter what she looked like.

I nodded. "Sure, can I ask what to expect? Is she part snake too?"

Huyen laughed. "No, no, she's not like me. She's a satyr, so she has goat legs. She likes to hide them most days but on mission days she embraces her whole self."

"Oh, okay," I responded, though I wasn't exactly sure how to prepare for that. I tried imaging goat legs on her and it actually fit, the baggy pants were a distraction. I bet she looked great with her goat legs, just like Huyen did as a part snake. These were my friends, it didn't matter to me what they looked like. They had proven their worth over and over again to me. It was my turn to earn their trust.

"Don't worry, she's not as intimidating as she seems in training. That's just her tough exterior to keep people in line. It's more of a facade."

I smiled, relaxing a little. "Got it. Thanks for the heads-up."

As if right on cue, Njeri strode up to the desk with her hooves clacking on the smooth tiles, her presence commanding attention. She smiled and gave Huyen a high five, then slapped each other's butts or where a butt should be on snake, some sort of secret handshake I guessed. They laughed like they knew some sort of inside joke I wasn't privy to.

Njeri turned to me and grinned. "So, how have you been doing on your own? Been practicing your magic? Or just having fun with our Nicky?" she teased, winking at me. I did my best to not look at her hoofs and extremely hair legs that were most definitely not human.

I laughed. "Well, no, not like *that*," I said, trying to keep it light. "It has been fun, but honestly, I haven't practiced much. Nick's been helping me with the amulet, so I haven't had to." I felt guilty for not practicing my magic more. I made a mental note: start practicing more.

The mood shifted, and they both went quiet for a moment. "So, you're really thinking about giving up your magic? And... Nick?" Huyen asked gently.

I sighed, "I don't know yet. I thought I wanted it gone, but all of this feels weirdly natural now. I know I'd miss you guys, and Nick. But I still want the choice to be mine, you know?"

They both nodded, but I could tell they were sad about it, even if they understood my feelings.

"Well," Huyen said after a moment, "we'd miss you and so would Nick. We haven't seen him this happy in a long time, since before his parents passed. He hasn't stopped smiling since you showed up."

I blushed, "Has he said anything about me?" I asked, trying to sound casual, though I was suddenly nervous.

They giggled like two teenagers before Njeri spoke. "You're *all* he talks about now. He's really smitten, even if he's trying not to push you. He wants you to make the decision for yourself. If you stay, he wants it to be because *you* want to, not because of him. But between you and me, he really wants you to stay."

Feeling the weight of that statement. "No pressure, right?" I joked uncomfortably.

"We just want you to know we support you, no matter what. But yeah, we'd miss you," Huyen said softly.

Njeri thankfully changed the subject, though not to a lighter subject. "How are you feeling about this whole thing with Fenriz and traveling through dimensions?"

"Honestly, I'm freaking out. But if I want a real choice, if I want to help Aunt Maggy find peace after all these years, it's something I have to do."

Huyen smiled warmly. "You have such a big heart, Aoife. You *do* belong here, you know."

I blushed again, feeling awkward. "I'm just not sure what to expect."

"Don't worry," Njeri said, her tone comforting. "We'll go over all the details. Nick would never let you go into this blind."

We continued chatting for a few moments before Huyen and Njeri led the way to the conference room where Nick went. I followed behind, trying not to stare too much at their hooves or tail as it moved gracefully along the floor. It would take some getting used to, but I didn't want them to feel uncomfortable around me, they really were beautiful, exactly how they were.

Nick greeted me with a big smile from across the room full of people, though his eyes held more weary thoughts behind them. I took his cue and wove through the groups of people chatting over large stacks of old books to get to him. He held out his hand, uncurling his fingers revealing a small box.

I stared at the purple gift in Nick's hand, my heart skipping a beat. His thoughtfulness always caught me off guard, especially when I was least expecting it. It felt like he had a knack for knowing exactly what I needed before I even realized it myself.

"Nick, seriously, I…" I trailed off, at a loss for words. I didn't feel like I deserved something else, not with everything he'd already done for me.

He gave me that half-smile I'd come to associate with his quiet determination. "Open it," he said softly, holding the box out closer to me.

With a hesitant hand, I took the box from him and slowly lifted the lid. Inside, nestled in a soft velvet lining, was a simple silver bracelet. It was delicate but sturdy, with a single charm hanging from it, a small tornado. It shimmered slightly in the dim conference room lighting, I could feel a faint warmth emanating from it.

"It's… beautiful," I said, my voice barely above a whisper.

Nick reached over and gently took the bracelet from the box, holding it up so I could see it more clearly. "I thought you'd like it but also it's spelled for protection," he explained. "Pauwau helped me with it. If you ever feel like you're in danger or need a little extra strength, just touch the charm. It won't do anything too obvious, no fireworks or anything but it'll give you a bit of a boost, help steady your nerves."

I blinked, feeling my throat tighten with emotion. "Nick, I don't even know what to say…"

"You don't have to say anything," he said softly, taking my wrist and fastening the bracelet around it. His fingers brushed against my skin, sending a shiver down my arm. "Just know that no matter what happens, you're never truly alone. Even when we're apart, this will remind you of that."

I looked down at the bracelet, its tiny whirlwind resting just below my wrist. It was more than just a trinket, it was a promise. A promise that Nick would always be there for me, even in the darkest of times.

"Thank you," I whispered, my voice barely holding steady. "It's perfect."

Nick smiled, his eyes softening as he looked at me. "You're welcome."

We sat there for a moment, the chaos of the room around us fading into the background. I fingered the charm on the bracelet, feeling a sense of calm wash over me. Maybe it was the spell working, or maybe it was just the thought that Nick had put into it, but either way, it helped.

A large man with a crew cut and thick Russian accent whistled to get everyone's attention. The room went silent. He went over the logistics of traveling to a different dimension in great detail. I was overwhelmed at all the information so I made mental notes of what I thought was important, hoping I wouldn't forget and get someone hurt by my lack of memorization.

Nick stood and spoke next, "This is everything we know about the Frenix dimension," Nick explained, his tone serious but calm. "It's incredibly dark there, so we'll need a lot of light sources. The place is crawling with poisonous plants and wildlife, don't touch *anything*. The creature we're hunting likes to hide underground, so locator spells are a must. And we need a way to trap him and bring him back. That's the tricky part. So, keep looking for ways we can keep him contained. We'll reconvene shortly. Thanks, team."

The groups nodded and separated again to continue their research. After a few minutes, Pauwau approached us, interrupting the quiet moment with a warm smile. "Ready for your crash course?" she asked, her voice gentle but purposeful.

I nodded, feeling a mix of nerves and determination bubbling inside me. "Yeah. Ready as I'll ever be."

Nick stood up, offering me his hand. I took it, his steady grip grounding me as I rose to my feet. "You've got this," he said, squeezing my hand one more time before letting go.

Pauwau led us to a smaller side room, filled with all sorts of magical items, bottles of glowing liquids, ancient scrolls, and strange crystals. It looked like a scene from a fantasy novel, and yet it felt oddly familiar now. I was no longer the girl who had stumbled into this world by accident. I was a part of it, whether I liked it or not.

"Alright," Pauwau began, picking up a small vial filled with a glowing blue liquid. "This is the tracking spell. Like Viktor mentioned earlier, all you have to do is break this on the ground, and it will create a trail that only you and Nick can see. Fenriz won't have any clue that you're on his trail, but the key is to follow it closely. The path can be tricky, and if you lose it, it might take you somewhere… less pleasant."

I nodded, taking the vial from her carefully. "Got it. Follow the blue trail, don't get lost."

Pauwau smiled. "Exactly. Now, as for the snare…" She picked up a coil of what looked like silver thread. "This is a bit more complicated. Once you find Fenriz, you'll need to throw this around him and say the incantation written here." She handed me a small scroll. "The snare will bind him, but only temporarily. You'll need to act fast to transport him to the location you arrived at, and you'll be transported back. Do not, I repeat, *do not* delay."

Nick glanced at the snare, his expression serious. "How long will it hold him?"

"Not long," Pauwau replied. "Maybe five minutes, ten at most. He'll fight it, but the magic is strong enough to give you the window you need to get him out of Frenix. Once he's out of that dimension, he'll weaken a little. He'll still be strong, but the net will hold him longer once he's out of there."

I swallowed hard, the reality of what we were about to do sinking in. This wasn't just some magical adventure, it was life or death. "Okay. And the protection spell?"

Pauwau handed me a small leather pouch. "Inside here is the dust you'll need to activate the protection cast. Sprinkle it in a circle around you and Nick as soon as you arrive in Frenix. It won't make you invisible, but it'll keep most of the creatures at bay and make the environment more hospitable for you."

I nodded again, my hand gripping the pouch tightly. "Thanks, Pauwau. For everything."

She gave me a kind smile, her dark eyes warm with understanding. "You're strong, Aoife. Trust yourself, and trust Nick. You'll get through this."

I looked over at Nick, who gave me a reassuring nod. "We'll be fine," he said softly, his voice full of quiet confidence. "Just stay close to me."

Taking a deep breath, I felt a mix of fear and resolve settle into my bones. This was it. There was no turning back now.

"Let's do this," I said, though my voice sounded a little shakier than I'd hoped. Nick led the way, we stepped into a laboratory looking room with a large silver metal ring in the center with grated floors surrounding it. Lights flashing from large machines around the room drew my attention. People wearing white coats were running from machine to machine, pushing buttons and checking gauges, making random beeping noises as they hit buttons. It was much more than I thought.

Nick gave me a soft smile, one that was meant to ground me, but all it did was send my mind spiraling again. What if something went wrong? What if I couldn't handle it? My hand instinctively moved to the tornado charm on my bracelet, rubbing it for comfort.

"You'll be fine," Nick said, clearly sensing my thoughts. "I'm right here, and we've trained for this."

"Trained," I scoffed lightly. "You've been training for this your whole life. I've had, what, a crash course?"

Nick chuckled softly, the sound almost swallowed by the hum of the portal in front of us. "You're tough, Aoife. Think of all the stuff you've been through already, you've already proven how strong you are. Now you just need to believe it."

I tried to hold on to his words as the swirling gold curtain in the center of the round metal structure shimmered, growing brighter and more stable by the second. The lab had fallen into a tense silence, everyone watching us with hopeful eyes. No pressure, right?

The scientist wearing a white coat and large goggles that covered most of his face cleared his throat to grab out attention, "The portal's ready. The coordinates are locked. You'll be sent directly to the last known location. Once you arrive, remember the steps, activate the protection spell *first*"

I nodded, the weight of his words sitting heavy on my shoulders. One wrong move, and everything could fall apart.

"Remember," Nick said, his voice low as he stepped closer to the portal, "we're a team. No matter what happens, we stick together."

I looked up at him, feeling a surge of gratitude. "Thank you," I whispered. "For everything."

His eyes softened, and for a brief moment, it felt like there was no one else in the room but the two of us. The hum of the machines faded, the tension in the air dissipated, and all I could feel was the warmth of Nick's presence beside me. "You don't have to thank me," he said, his voice almost a whisper.

Before I could respond, the portal shimmered even brighter, casting golden light across the room. The time had come. My pulse quickened, the reality of what we were about to do crashing down on me all at once.

"We should go," Nick said, his voice pulling me back to the present. He gave my hand one last squeeze before gently letting go and stepping through to the unknown.

Chapter 14

We stepped forward together, the golden light of the portal was so bright it was almost blinding. As we crossed the threshold, the air around us shimmered, and pulsated, making it hard to breathe. The familiar world of Nick's lab faded from view. My heart raced, the sensation of weightlessness taking over as the portal enveloped us. My arms and legs floated leaving me feeling out of control of my own body. I began to panic, my breath came out in small bursts, I couldn't focus on anything, there was nothing to focus on, just bright gold around us.

Then, with a whoosh that made my ears pop from the force, everything went dark. It was darker than I ever experienced. There was no light, no sound, no air. It was the absence of everything. I couldn't tell if my eyes were open or closed, my ears were ringing from the loud sound when the light disappeared. My body didn't know what to do, so it did the only thing it could, panic!

Streaks of light showed up in my vision, I couldn't focus on them, it was as if we were spinning. I blinked trying to clear my head. I was disoriented.

My feet felt solidness beneath them but my legs had no power to stand up, I collapsed on all fours. The air felt thick and heavy, like it was weighing me down. I couldn't breathe, my lungs refused to accept the new heavy air. Eventually, they gave in and let me take a breath in slightly, I gasped and coughed, trying ferociously to catch my breath. I was on the ground, heaving with effort. I focused on the feeling of the ground beneath my hands and knees felt soft, almost spongy. It had a hum like it had hives of bees living beneath it. The sky, if you could even call it that, was dark, swirling black with streaks of purple and green, like an endless aurora borealis, with no stars visible.

After I caught my breath enough I asked, "Is this… Frenix?", my voice barely audible in the oppressive silence.

Nick nodded, already reaching for the pouch that held the protection dust. "Yeah. Welcome to Fenriz's dimension. Stay close."

The air here felt… wrong. It was hard to describe, like the atmosphere was dense and heavy, making every breath feel like a chore, but the faint lingering scent of decay took over my senses. I glanced around, trying to take in my surroundings, but everything seemed to blend together in the darkness.

"First things first," Nick said, pulling me closer to him. "The protection spell."

He knelt down closer to the spongy ground, carefully spreading the dust in a circle around us, murmuring the incantation Pauwau had drilled into us earlier. The moment the circle was complete, I felt a shift in the air-like a barrier had formed around us, making the oppressive weight of the dimension just a little more bearable.

"That should keep most of the creatures at bay," Nick said, standing up and brushing the dust from his hands. "For now, at least."

I nodded, trying to focus on the task at hand. My heart was still racing, but at least I didn't feel like I was going to pass out anymore. *One step at a time, Aoife,* I tried to talk sense into myself. My mind wasn't prepared for what I saw, what I smelled, what I felt, dread set deep into my bones.

"Next," Nick continued, pulling the vial of tracking liquid from his pocket, "we find Fenriz."

He handed the vial to me, and I stared at the glowing blue liquid inside. "You're sure this will work?"

Nick smiled. "It'll work. Just smash it on the ground, and it'll show us the way."

With a deep breath, I didn't know if it would break on the soft ground so, I took the vial and threw it towards a black rock near us. Watching as the glass shattered and the glowing blue liquid seeped into the ground. For a moment, nothing happened. Then, slowly, a faint blue trail began to appear, snaking its way through the strange terrain in front of us.

"Alright," Nick said, his voice calm and steady. "Let's go."

In the deafening quiet of that place, my mind wandered to my past. I was blindly following a man I'd only known for a few days, into a dimension where everything wanted to unalive me. He vowed to keep me safe, and I believed him. If you'd asked me before arriving in Canada if I'd ever even believe a man I hardly knew, I'd say no. Now here I was holding Nick's hand, trusting him with my life. *My how quickly things can change.*

We followed the trail, the eerie silence of Frenix hanging over us like a thick fog. The ground beneath our feet squelched with each step, and I had to constantly remind myself not to touch anything, not to stray too far from Nick's side. Every now and then, I'd catch a glimpse of movement out of the corner of my eye, something shifting in the shadows, lurking just beyond the reach of the blue trail. My hand instinctively went to the bracelet charm, rubbing it for comfort and the calm it was supposed to give me.

"Don't worry," Nick said, his voice low and reassuring. "We're almost there."

We tried to walk as silently as we could the rest of the way. Glancing back and forth, scanning, every few seconds to keep a lookout. Nick pulled on my hand to make me stop walking. I could feel him tense up, which made me start looking all around, getting a not-so-good feeling. I finally saw what Nick spotted, red glowing eyes tucked in the shadows. I felt Nick moving his other arm, he was reaching in his pocket for another vile. I had to trust he knew what he was doing, because I had no idea.

It felt like my heart was going to explode from my chest! My adrenaline was pumping so hard that I had to fight the urge to run. The red glowing eyes started to get larger, the creature seemed to be getting closer to us, but we still didn't move. Nick gave my hand a squeeze like he did when I was worried, it did little to settle me then. I heard a deep rumbling growing as the creature came closer. It was close enough that I could make out what it looked like now. I couldn't believe what my eyes were seeing. It was all black like everything else there but it looked like a wolf of some sort. It had long sharp spiny quills that stood up instead of hair on its back and tapered to shorter needle-like hairs on the rest of its body. Its tail had the thicker quills, looking more like a porcupine than a wolf that way. Its lips were curled up revealing two extremely long sharp yellowing teeth jutting out. Something seemed to be dripping from the teeth, falling in thick gloopy drops as it overflowed the creature's mouth.

I was pulling on Nick's arm out of instinct to run away from the danger. Nick ignored my request to run, instead holding me in place, letting it get closer. My body was trembling, from the adrenaline coursing through my system. Finally Nick reacted, quietly he said a few words in Latin then he threw a small vial at the creature. It shattered upon impact with the creature's spikes. The wolf-porcupine creature was still trying to growl and bare its teeth to us but it started to sneeze uncontrollably. It was trying to use its paw to wipe its face as if it had something on it. After a few seconds, it retreated, unable to contain its sneezes. It backed away, sinking back into the shadows, leaving an uneasy feeling, now that I knew what kind of creatures lurked in the darkness.

Nick leaned over and whispered so calmly, "that was a Fenrir, they are evil creatures who kill everything they see, even their own young. Don't let it bite you, its poison is deadly." I had no plans of being bitten. It slightly annoyed me how calm Nick was about that whole situation. I mean I'm glad he was able to remain composed because I sure failed at that. But Why did he always have to be so damn good at everything? I brushed that feeling aside and focused on just getting out of that situation first, then I'd allow myself to be annoyed at him.

Nick squeezed my hand again and pulled me forward since my feet apparently refused to move on their own. It wasn't just my brain freaking out about what just happened. My body was also trying to tell me to run away. I had to trust Nick to know what to do, because I felt utterly useless.

He led me the way, following the blue lit path through large trees that had branches like needles, they seemed to try and reach down towards us as we walked under and past them. Dripping a dark tar-like substance from the knots in them; as it met the ground the liquid sizzled. They didn't have leaves like anything I'd ever seen. They seem to float above the branches instead of being attached to them. They weren't leaves, they looked more like small embers or flames, dancing around and moving as if the wind was pushing them, but the air was still. It was Erie.

The light illuminated patches of what looked like should be grass, instead it resembled more like shards of black glass, sharp and lethal. We tread carefully around them, unsure how our boots would hold up to them. We stuck close together, both scanning the perimeter for potential threats. Our nerves were on high alert at every movement, every slight sound we heard.

The trail of blue led us to the mouth of a large, dark tunnel, the faint sound of something moving inside sending a chill down my spine. I could feel the wind billowing out of it, carrying the stench of death. I fought the urge to bring up my cheese Danish from that morning. Nick got my attention and pulled his neck bandana up over his nose and mouth, I copied him. That helped keep some of the smell out. The trail snaked inside, weaving around big boulders and black shiny, obsidian-looking stalagmites from the floor that looked more like pieces of art than pieces of a cave.

The screeching from the creatures around us reverberated through the dark cave, growing louder with every second. I could feel the weight of the shadows pressing in around us, as if the very darkness was alive, closing in, threatening to swallow us whole. My breath came in ragged gasps as I tread carefully alongside Nick. His hand still tightly gripped mine, anchoring me to the moment; keeping me from spiraling into panic.

The tunnel seemed to stretch on forever, the glowing trail we had left behind flickering faintly in the oppressive blackness. Every corner we turned felt like a gamble, and every footstep felt like it echoed too loudly, betraying our presence to the creatures nearby.

We ended in a large, cavernous room. There were black carved bowls and cups laying out on some of the larger boulders, it looked like it was being used as a makeshift table, on the sides of the 'room'. A small fire burned in the middle. The flame wasn't like any I'd ever seen before. It reminded me of when we camped and we put a copper pipe in an old piece of garden hose in a fire and it morphed into unnatural colors, except it was all like that, there were no natural shades. No hints of red, orange, or yellow. Only purple, green, and blue flames, that made a roaring sound like when a fireplace is first lit, and it starts to rush up the chimney. It felt very unnatural.

Nick elbowed me gently to get my attention again, he had his vial made of red glass in his hand, I quickly searched in my pocket for mine, but before I could grab it out, something rammed me hard from behind, sending me rolling on the ground, gasping for air. Thankfully, the protective bubble around us was still intact. Nick was frantically trying to grab the vial that had been knocked from his hand when a black shadowy creature crawled up on top of the bubble and started making a terrible clicking sound that I will forever live in my memory.

Nick managed to grab his vile, repeating the words the witch taught us then, threw it as hard as he could at the shadow creature. The shadow flew off our bubble, shrieking with such pitch it made my ears hurt. It climbed to the ceiling of the cave and was clinging in the corner of the ceiling between two stalactites with its long, razor-sharp talons. The clicking started again and it slowly lost its form, sinking back down to the ground like food coloring in water, flowing down. I shivered.

"Now, throw yours!" Nick screamed, pulling me out of my panicked trance. I found my vile out and said the words and threw it as hard as I could at the creature too. I hit it square in the face, well where the face should be if it had a face. Nick tossed the silver string trap on the ground in its direction.. The string began to weave itself into a net and started to cover the shadow, pinning it to the ground like it weighed hundreds of pounds. It was so thin, it looked like just touching it could make a strand snap, but astonishingly, it seemed to hold the shadow creature in. The net cinched down on the creature, tighter and tighter, condensing it, until it was about the size of a beach ball.

The shadow before was huge, at least 8' if I guessed so I was astonished it seemed so small and insignificant in the net. It was much less intimidating, but the clicking sound still resonated from it, reminding me how dangerous it still was.

Nick looked over at me, panting, out of breath, and gave me a smile of accomplishment. I smiled back at him, we had done it. I began to sink into a sense of relief when I caught movement out of the corner of my eye. Something small. It wiggled past us in a blur. Before I could say anything to warn Nick, it dug into the ground with its mouth full of teeth and disappeared. I jumped up out of instinct, hoping it was gone. Nick didn't see the creature, I was trying to get the words out to warn him when Nick's eyes widened. A look of terror, an expression I'd never seen on his face before. I knew something was terribly wrong.

He reached a hand up to me, I rushed to grab it. But when I got to him it went slack. His sparkly green eyes no longer had life in them, his eyes rolled back as his lids closed. I rushed to check his body, I knew something was very wrong but I didn't see any signs of injury. I rolled him over to check his back. That's when I saw a small hole in his shirt with a little blood dripping out of it. Nick was beginning to gasp for air. I didn't know what to do. Panicking, I dug through my pockets and trying to remember what all vials did, my brain went blank in the moment. I didn't remember them giving me anything for a toothy worm invasion anyway.

In a fit of terror, I clicked the screen on my armband, it came to life with a beeping noise. Immediately a voice came through, recognizing the scientist's voice on the other end, "I'm here, what happened? Nick's vitals are dropping by the second."

"I uh, I don't know. I didn't see what it did, I don't know if it was Fenriz or not, but I did see a weird worm with teeth before he… I don't know what happened, something happened to Nick, there's blood on his shirt. He's having trouble breathing I think. What do I do?" It rushed out in a panic.

There was silence for a second, it felt too long, I almost started to repeat what I said in case they didn't hear me, but the voice came back, "it sounds like a Death Worm. There's a vile of green liquid in the first aid pack. Thrust the needle into his chest and push the plunger down. It will help slow the toxin until you get him back."

I rustled through the pack to find the syringe, with unease and fear I slammed it down into Nick's chest, it felt all wrong, I should not be having to put a needle into his chest! As soon as the syringe went into his body, his eyes shot open, black was seeping into the sides of his eyes where red veins should be. My heart shattered. This was not how this was supposed to go.

"It's done. Now what. He doesn't look good. I don't know what to do."

"You have to get him back here ASAP. Follow the trail back. Aoife, hurry." His tone made me realize how bad this could be.

I turned to Nick after packing all the syringes back in the bag and got out the bag Pauwau gave me to put Fenriz in after he was captured. I wondered at the time how that huge shadow creature would fit in such a small bag, but now I knew. I carefully lifted the net by the string at the end, set it in the bag and pulled the drawstring as tight as I could. I tied the bag to my belt and went to collect Nick who was moaning quietly in pain, was dripping in sweat by the time I got back to him.

"Come on big guy, let's get you out of here." I told him as I carefully lifted his large arm over my shoulder to help him stand. He tried his hardest to stand, but it was evident he was getting weaker by the second. We didn't have any time to lose. I forced him to start taking steps, my legs were shaking with every movement, struggling to hold his weight. He grunted with force as he tripped, shuffled and drug his feet along the cave floor.

Our bubble had broken at some point after capturing Fenriz, maybe it was the worm. I hoped we wouldn't run into any more creatures because we didn't have the bubble anymore to protect us, it was just me and I doubted my kickboxing would be any match for any of these toothy creatures. I was thankful for at least the glowing trail marking our way back.

Following the trail into the woods without the protective bubble left a more terrifying feeling. Red eyes dotted the forest, watching us move. I did my best to keep an eye on them, on the treacherous path, and watching Nick, his strength seemed to be fading with every step. My heart sank into my stomach seeing Nick like that. He looked so fragile, teetering between life and death.

I couldn't let him die because of my selfish thinking. I wanted to be free of my magic so bad that I allowed Nick to put himself in harm's way for me. He had to be okay, I had to get him back so they could heal him.

I glanced back instinctively, even though I knew I shouldn't. My pulse quickened. The red eyes were no longer just watching us from a distance. They were moving now, coming closer, gaining on us, surrounding us. Shadows twisted and merged into grotesque forms, some with wings, others slithering like snakes, all of them with glowing red eyes fixed on us.

"Nick!" I gasped, the fear in my voice rising. "We have to move faster! I know you're tired but you can't give up on me."

We pushed harder, My feet pounding against the uneven ground, Nick lost his balance easily, causing him to drag his feet along the soft earth. I felt the heat of the creatures' presence like fire licking at the back of my neck. We had no time to waste.

A loud, piercing shriek echoed through the dark woods, so close that it sent a jolt of terror straight through me. My legs burned, but the primal fear kept me moving. There was no stopping, not if I wanted to live. I had to get myself and Nick to safety.

By some miracle, we made it back, without an attack. Nick was getting weaker and heavier on me by the second, I wasn't sure how much longer I could hold him up. We were almost back to the portal, I spotted red glowing eyes no longer just watching from a distance, but rushing up to us. I instinctively pushed Nick forward, forcing him to fall through the portal. I was knocked down by the wolf creature again, scrambling to get out from under it. It's mouth snapping with yellow teeth just inches from my face. I kicked it in the only place that I thought it didn't have those spikes, its stomach. I must have knocked the wind out of it because it was heaving and coughing. I used the second distraction to dive into the portal as fast as I could.

Rolling onto the metal platform in the science lab room, I saw people scrambling to help Nick up. I glanced back at the golden portal and could see the glowing red eyes peering at us, but not coming through. The scientist hit the red button hard with his palm and the machine's whirring noise tapered off to silence. I sat there in a daze for a second until I realized someone was trying to make me stand up. A few white coat-wearing people were grabbing me by the arms and helping guide me to a rolling bed, both saying things I couldn't understand.

I was so out of it, but I felt the pinprick of electricity still on my leg from the net that contained Fenriz. I did not want to hold this thing on me much longer, "what do I do with it?" I said in a panic, "take it please, take it!" I yelled holding the bag up by the drawstring. Someone ran over and grabbed it from me, and I could see them carrying it off to a shiny metal box that had holes all over the sides of it, with wheels on the bottom. They put the bag in it, closed and locked the door, and wheeled it off and I could breathe again. I frantically wiped at the black thick liquid that dripped onto my face, the smell of death clinging to me.

After a few minutes of laying there in shock, my brain seemed to turn back on and I remembered Nick. He was injured. I had to find him. I looked around and saw him, across the room, lying very still on another rolling bed. I broke free of the doctor's grip pushing them back and ran to Nick's side. He wasn't moaning anymore, which worried me. He felt so clammy and cold. My heart sank. I burst into tears and draped myself over his chest and just kept repeating "I'm sorry, I'm so sorry". The doctors and scientists continued to work around me, I got myself together and pulled away, wiping the tears as I made my way back to give the doctors room to work.

Someone slid a chair up behind me to sit in, I just sat there in a daze as people were scrambling all around Nick, prodding him with needles, taking blood, checking his vitals, attaching pads to monitor him, and repeating phrases in Latin while splashing an oily liquid on him. Huyen was by my side, patting my arm and hugging my shoulder from the side. It did little to comfort me but I am glad she was there.

Guilt gnawed at me. I got Nick hurt. He could die because of me. Because I was afraid of my magic. Because I was selfish and wanted a life that I chose, because I was so stubborn about having a soulmate. That was it. Realization hit me. I was afraid that I had someone that was perfect for me. I didn't have a choice in it, fate decided Nick was what I needed. The thought that I didn't get to choose who I spent my life with scared the crap out of me. I used all sorts of excuses, the magic, Aunt Maggy, a regular life, but in reality, I was afraid that I had someone that would turn the world I created for myself, the boring, uneventful life, on its head.

Chapter 15

After what felt like an eternity, they said his vitals were stable and they were moving him to a private room. They wheeled him out of the room still on the same bed, his eyes still closed and body still limp. I was in a daze as Huyen guided me by the arm to my room and helped me get in the shower. I peeled the shirt off my body, with Nick's dried blood, stiff and stuck to my skin. I threw it in the trash, I didn't need a reminder of what happened. I let the water run over me, washing away my tears, Nick's blood, and my guilt. Well it didn't wash away my guilt but that's because I couldn't let that go yet.

When I finally mustered up the energy to shut the shower off and go back into reality, Huyen had my favorite clothes laid out for me, leggings and a baggy t-shirt. She brushed my hair while we just sat in a silent daze.

She eventually broke the silence, "It's not your fault you know?"

"If we didn't go, he wouldn't have gotten hurt. It is my fault. If I could have just accepted my fate and not fought it, he would be fine." I said as tears started streaming down my face again.

She handed me a wad of tissues, "Honey, this is what he does. He lives to help people, even if that means putting himself in danger. He wouldn't be happy living any other way."

That didn't make me feel better, but I appreciated her trying. She let me cry on her shoulder for a while. I lost control of my emotions once again.

"I need to see him Huyen."

"Okay Hun, let's get you down there, first wipe your nose, you have snot everywhere." That made me laugh a little which made more snot come out. I was a mess. She helped me wash my face and clean up a little, then we headed back down to find Nick. My stomach started to flip-flops, threatening to bring up my cheese Danish again.

I was grateful for Huyen, she was quickly wiggling her way into my heart, no pun intended. She had been there since day one for me. She seemed to know what I needed before I even did. Without her support, the whole magical journey would have been overwhelming. Nick was great but there was a special place in my heart for friends.

Huyen led me to a white hospital area and slid a curtain to the side. Nick laid on a hospital bed, his cheeks were missing the pink tint they usually carried. White sheets covered his legs and hips, his bare, tattoo-covered chest had a large bandage around it. He had tubes coming out of his mouth and wires attached to his head and chest, machines beeped and whirled all around us. He looked so fragile, not like the resilient, sassy Nick I first met.

She slid a chair up next to the head of his bed and waved for me to sit. I slowly sank into the cold plastic. I grabbed Nick's hand, giving it a squeeze like he always did for me when I was worried. He didn't return the gesture, his hand laid limp in mine. I wished he'd squeeze my hand now.

A woman wearing a white coat came in, my eyes were blurry from tears filling in them. I had to take a second look because she had short spotted fur on her face and long whiskers jutting out from her cheeks. With human hands also coated in fur. She grabbed the metal clipboard, flipping through the pages for a few minutes making small "hm" and "oh" sounds that made my stomach sink with every noise. She sighed and finally came up toward the head of Nick's bed and laid a hand on his shoulder and looked over to me,

"He's in a coma but stable. His body is fighting the venom from the Death Worm, there's cytotoxins and hemorrhaging in his body. We have him on antivenom, and the witches have placed a cast on him so no more damage will happen, now we must wait for his body to heal. I'm not sure how long he'll be like this. But he's responding well to treatment so far, so I think he'll be okay. He's a tough one, I have every hope he'll pull through."

I wiped my eyes and nose again with the tissues Huyen made me bring, glad she did. I just nodded to the doctor unable to speak yet. I felt like my throat was closing up along with his. I felt such guilt. The doctor reached over and laid her hand on top of mine and he smiled at me, small points of her top teeth poked out from under her lip.

I couldn't make myself get up. I stayed at his side, sleeping, laying my head on his bed, never letting go of his hand, squeezing it every few minutes hoping one of those times he'd squeeze it back.

Huyen brought me a tray of food. I picked at the noodles, moving them around on the plate but not being able to eat for fear I wouldn't be able to keep them down. My stomach was a ball of knots and threatened to deny anything I ate. How could I eat when Nick was lying here like that? If he was wasting away, so should I. The nurses tried to get me to leave and take a break, take a walk, anything, but I couldn't. I wouldn't.

I don't know how long we were there, Nick lying lifeless, me ignoring everyone and never letting go of his hand, squeezing it every few minutes. I felt the familiar squeeze of his hand. I thought I was dreaming so I squeezed it back. He squeezed it again, I gasped awake from my sleep to feel another squeeze. Was he doing it on purpose or was it involuntary like a seizure or muscle spasm? I didn't want to get my hopes up.

I yelled for a doctor and the cat-doctor came running over, flashlight in hand already. Lifting his eyelids to look at his beautiful green eyes. Nick squeezed my hand again. The doctor looked at me and gave me an authentic toothy smile and a nod, that was a very good sign. She backed up to give us space but stayed close in case we needed her. I stood up and leaned over Nick, with my other hand I gently stroked his cheek and brushed his hair back the way he liked it.

Seeing those beautiful green eyes staring back at me was the best sight ever. They were bloodshot and he had dark circles under his eyes, signs of how hard his body was fighting the toxins, but he was back. He came back to me. I burst into tears and threw myself on him again, this time he hugged me back, weakly, but it was the best feeling. I couldn't get off him yet, we just laid there for a while. Him rubbing my back, me crying all over his bare shoulders, trying to avoid his bandages the best I could.

I finally collected myself enough to get up, wiping my face with my t-shirt since I used up all my tissues. He probably wished he was still in a coma instead of seeing me look like this, I laughed to myself. I couldn't believe he was awake. He gave me a weak smile and squeezed my hand again. The doctor came back up and started checking his vitals, taking tubes out of him and checking his bandages.

"Well Nick, looks like you'll be back to torturing us all again very soon. Just keep resting, your body is still healing." Nick didn't say anything out loud, he just shook his head, he understood. Then she walked away again, I swear I heard her purr.

"Do you need anything? Are you cold? Do you hurt anywhere?" I was back to my rapid-fire questions I did when I was nervous, he just smiled and again and shook his head no. He patted the bed next to him where I was sitting before, quietly asking me to comfort him again, or maybe he knew I needed the comfort just as much. I sat back down and continued rubbing his hand until he fell back asleep, I joined him in dreamland.

I woke up to Huyen rubbing my arm slowly trying to not startle me. "Hey Honey, they're going to take Nick to his room to recover there. Why don't you take a shower and get something to eat while they get him all situated." I turned and looked at him still sleeping, and smelled myself, I did need a shower. "He'll be okay, he's doing better or they wouldn't move him. He's in good hands Aoife, promise."

"Okay, but I won't be long, I'll take a quick shower then I'll be there."

"Okay Hun, no rush though, it'll take them a while to transport and get him settled. There's not much for us to help with while they do that". I kissed his cheek, and told him I'd be back soon.

I took longer in the shower than I wanted to, but I couldn't stop myself from crying. I wept until I had no tears left to cry so hopefully, I wouldn't cry in front of Nick. It was my fault Nick was hurt. I'd never forgive myself for that. I turned the water cold, hoping it would relieve the puffiness I knew was pooling around my eyes, letting it run down my face. I wasn't one for vanity, but I didn't want to look like a complete mess either.

I found the comfiest sweatpants and baggy shirt I could find, because days like that were meant for comfort, not looking cute for a man who was unconscious most of the time…*because of me.* I didn't even bother with a comb in my hair, I just threw it up while still wet in a messy bun to keep it out of my face. This was as good as it was going to get, puffy red eyed, messy hair, baggy clothes. My typical melt down attire.

I slowly walked down the hall to Nick's room, the door was propped open, I could hear talking inside but it didn't sound like Nick's voice.I hadn't realized how much I hoped it would be his voice, my heart sank a bit. There were lots of doctors and nurses, a witch cleansing the space with sage and another placing crystals around Nick. I didn't know where to stand, there were so many people, so I stood by the door for a while. The kind cat lady doctor noticed me and waved me over to her, the nurse she was talking to excused herself.

The doctor grabbed my hands, her fur was so soft, I ignored the urge to pet her. She said, "he's doing great, healing much quicker than we even expected. Studies have shown people heal much quicker when they're in their own home, so we wanted to get him moved as soon as he was well enough. Keep talking to him and touching him, it'll help him heal too, touch is important to brain healing." She gave my hands one last squeeze and left the room.

A nurse put a chair next to Nick's bed and patted it for me to sit down. "If you need anything at all, for you or him, just call us", and she handed me a card with different phone numbers. "He'll be okay", she said as she walked by me and patted my shoulder.

The room cleared out and I sat down, I hesitated to grab his hand. I almost felt like I shouldn't be allowed in there because of what I did. I slowly grabbed his hand, it was warm. Thank goodness it wasn't cold and clammy anymore, he felt more like himself again.

I laid my head on the bed and said "I'm so sorry Nick. This is all my fault. I should have just let good enough alone and been happy with what I had. I had magic, this place, these amazing new friends, and you. If I lose you, I never deserved any of this. I wouldn't blame you if you hated me forever after this. I just want you to come back to us. You can banish me or hate me, whatever you want as long as you come back."

I laid there in silence. The last room was noisy, full of people and beeping noises. The silence was almost deafening, I focused on his breathing, the calm, steady breaths gave me comfort. I gave his hand another squeeze, he squeezed it back, I stood up, startled, Nick's eyes were open, and he had a small grin on his face. I leaned in, crying again of course, touched our foreheads together. Nick reached up and wrapped his arms around my back and pulled me into him. I tried to resist out of fear of hurting him, but his strength surprised me as he pulled me onto him. We laid there, crying for what felt like a long time. I finally controlled myself enough to wipe my face then I leaned up and looked at him. His arms still wrapped around me, not letting me fully get up.

"It. Is. Not. Your. Fault." He said sternly. "I knew what I was getting into when we went there. It was my choice; you didn't make me do anything. You are not allowed to blame yourself; you hear me?"

I couldn't talk, I just nodded as I sniffled, fighting back the tears again. He pulled me back down onto him. I intertwined my legs with his, laying my head on his chest, avoiding the bandaged side. I'd hurt him enough, I was trying to avoid hurting him more.

The morning came, the nurses were changing out his IV, I slid off him, with a little shy smile, I could feel my cheeks getting warm. I wasn't used to PDA but especially that much after only knowing someone a few days. The nurse ignored us and just did what she came in to do. Nick looked over at me and smiled. He held out his hand, I put mine in his and he squeezed it. That one simple gesture made my heart so happy it thought it would burst. I spent the rest of the day there with him. They brought us both food and Nick managed to eat a little, that was a good step. It probably helped that it was nothing like hospital food. This was delicious restaurant food. I felt less guilty about eating so I nibbled on a few bites too.

They brought us some books and magazines to read so he picked out what he wanted, while I sat at the opposite end of the bed, my legs propped up on his bed. He gently rubbed the bottom of my feet, drawing shapes on them while I read to him. I was getting more comfortable with his touch, as the fear of losing him eased. The doctors and nurses worked around us, it felt like they weren't even there, it was just us two.

"Will you come lay with me please? I can't fall asleep without you". He was feeling better, using my guilt to gain some affection. I let him, he wasn't manipulating me like Josh did. He knew if I didn't want to, I wouldn't. He respected me.

"Are you sure? I don't want to hurt you."

"You could never hurt me, Aoife." He said tapping his chest where he wanted my head to be.

I carefully as I could crawled up onto his bed, as he lifted the blanket for me to slide under with him. I snuggled in, he rolled over to spoon me, I liked being the little spoon. His hand wrapped around me, rubbing my arm, it felt nice.

Sometime during the night, I heard Nick say something, I couldn't understand what he was saying though. I turned and looked at him, his eyes were closed but he was mumbling something in a panic. He had to be having a nightmare, I rubbed his cheek and called his name, hoping it would pull him out of it. He calmed down after a few minutes, and unintentionally pulled me down to lay on top of him and was rubbing my lower back. Not that I minded that, but he was unconscious. It felt like I was taking advantage of him. I tried to slide off to the side again but he slid his hand down to rub the back of my thigh, pulling my leg up on him higher. Um, sleepy Nick was frisky. That can't happen, it would be like taking advantage of an unconscious person. I would not take someone's free will away. If he didn't fully consent, then it's a no from me.

Eventually, I was able to slip out from under his heavy arms and return back to our spooning position. He nuzzled his face into my hair and took a deep breath then fell calmly back into sleeping. I wondered if he'd remember that tomorrow or if I should tell him. I thought I'd pretend like nothing happened, I mean nothing did happen but could have pretty easily if I didn't have so much stubbornness to me. I have found that moving fast was never good, at least in my experience. So I wanted to do it right if we were to do anything that is.

The light flicked on, and the hospital team came into the room. I slipped off the bed and out from under Nick's arm. Waking him up on accident. He was rubbing his eyes to adjust them to the bright light. "So, doc, am I going to turn into spiderman?" The doctors and nurses all burst out laughing, it was nice seeing him back to his joking self.

"No fortunately but you will have quite the scar from this one."

"Chicks dig scars I hear" he said winking at me.

I laughed. I shook my head at him. I turned to the doctors and asked, "so really though, how is he doing?"

"He's doing great, the venom is out of his system now, just has to heal his wound now. We will have Pauwau come later and help heal it a bit more. By tomorrow he should be up and running again, but at a slower speed for a bit until it's fully healed." She said looking from me to Nick.

After everyone left, Nick patted the bed for me to sit next to him. I hope this wasn't going to be an awkward conversation about the prior night's cuddle-fest. "I need you to know…" he paused, making me very nervous for some reason. Was it going to be something bad? "…that I really like you, Aoife. I know it's soon and I was trying to give you time and space to decide and not say how I felt because I didn't want to force you into anything unless you really wanted it. But I was scared I wouldn't have the chance to tell you and I promised myself I would as soon as I was better. And you are not allowed to pity party about me getting hurt, it wasn't your fault, and you are worth it; worth everything life can throw at me. You don't have to say anything back. I didn't say it to convince you of anything or force you to do anything you aren't ready for. You're worth the wait, I'd wait forever if I had too, to get just five minutes with you. You're worth it all".

Tears were streaming down my face again, I didn't know what to say. That was literally the sweetest thing anyone's ever said to me. He tapped his chest again and I fell back into his embrace. It felt safe, comfortable, right. But was I ready to give up my whole life? I've only known about this world for a few days, could I give up everything I knew before? Those were heavy thoughts.

I was quiet while we laid there, then luckily Pauwau came in to help heal his wound, so I excused myself to get a break. I was a little overwhelmed, I didn't know what to say to Nick, I didn't want to hurt him by ignoring what he said but I wasn't ready to say anything back yet. I did like him, but I still felt torn between my old life and this new one still.

I ran into Huyen on my way to grab coffee from the restaurant and stretch my legs. "You two are the talk of the building right now. Heard you two were getting pretty… comfortable." she joked.

"Ugh, so everyones talking about me again? Great. Nick needed someone, and I was there, that's all." I tried to downplay it but we both knew it was growing into something more.

Njeri snuck into our conversation. "Not what I heard," said Njeri under her breath, giggling with Huyen.

"We slept in the same bed, fully clothed, well I was fully clothed, he didn't have a shirt on. But nothing happened, some hand holding maybe. The dude was on death's doorstep!"

"Nothing wrong with 'comforting' someone when they're in need," Njeri said, winking at me.

"Oh goodness, seriously you two. I don't know what to do. He said he likes me, and I didn't say it back." I burst out, unable to hold it in any longer.

"So, do you? Like him I mean" Huyen asked.

"We're supposed to be soul mates, and I do feel drawn to him and comfortable around him, but I don't know if I'm ready to say anything that serious. It feels like if I do, I'd be giving up my old life, and I love my old life."

"Honey, you don't have to choose. It's not us or them kind of thing. You can be in our world and theirs, er, yours. You know what I mean. We have lots of people in our community that do both, they work and live normal lives, but if they need help or want to help, they let us know." Huyen added.

"Yeah, the first few years I only came here to train Nick one week out of the month, I lived my normal life in Colorado, working in a bike shop. I didn't mind it at all", Njeri said.

"Why did you decide to give it up? If you don't mind me asking".I was curious.

"Oh, I was in a relationship with the owner of the bike shop and she, uh, decided to date someone else, while we were still together. I needed a change after that, so Nick welcomed me here. Been here, buggin him ever since"

"Ugh, I'm so sorry Njeri. How has it been being here?"

"Everyone has been so amazing here, Nick fixed me up with a job that I love, a place to stay, I've been on some amazing adventures and made some great friends" she said looking at us, with tears welling in her eyes making her statements hit even harder.

Huyen and I looked at each other and nodded like we were on the same wavelength. We went over to her and enveloped her a group hug. She even let us for a few minutes, then said "alright, alright, alright. I already have a girlfriend to make out with, you two have your own men", we all burst out laughing. Our old Njeri was back.

"So, how's it going with Theo?" Njeri asked, leaning a shoulder into Huyen and batting her eyes at her. I had to hold in a giggle.

"Theo is… going well." She said with a huge grin.

"I saw you two together before we… left," I said trying to not sound too sad at the memory of getting Nick hurt, "you two look cute together"

"He's so tall!" she said looking up. "I have to stand on the tip of my tail if I want to even be close to his height" she said stretching her neck up trying to get taller, making us laugh. "But I do love his skin, did you know when you push on it shimmers different colors? My favorite thing to do is draw shapes and designs on his skin, making it shimmer and leave a line like sparklers in the dark. It's really cool"

Njeri got a look on her face then asked, "Wonder if *everything* glows?"

Of course she went there. I was worried that I would give up my old life and I'd have to start all over in a new place again, but Njeri and Huyen had made their way into my heart so quickly, I didn't even have to consider it. They were automatically a big part of my life. They made life in this new world feel more like home. I had a dreaded feeling that something was about to blow up the life I was just starting to settle into. I pushed those feelings down and tried to ignore them, but they edged their way back up.

Chapter 16

I t was nice to get a break from worrying and crying. I almost felt like it was a normal day. Then I remembered; I was fighting a magical family curse in a magical building, with a demon locked up in the basement somewhere. I snapped out of my happy moment. Realization hit me that I was still in K Corp.

I must have fallen asleep while I was overthinking everything that's happened and things I had yet to do. I woke up in a panic. Dread chewed at me from the inside. I had a horrible feeling that something had happened. My adrenaline spiked, unable to calm my mind. I needed to talk to someone. I needed to check and make sure everyone was safe.

I darted into Nick's room yelling "Nick! Nick!" my heart raced like it was going to win the Indy 500.

"Aoife? Are you okay?" I heard yelling from the bathroom,

I ran over and squeezed him so tight, he rubbed my back and put his chin on my head like he did before. After I calmed down a bit, still not letting go I choked out, "I thought, I thought he got you."

"I'm right here, I'm fine Aoife. He's locked up and I promise he can't get out. And I'm not going anywhere" he said, still rubbing my back.

"I'm sorry, I had a horrible dream earlier and I guess the fear stuck with me."

"Don't ever apologize, the fact that you cared enough to even worry means a lot to me." He was validating my fears, not dismissing them. Something I wasn't used to. I didn't quite know how to handle that, It sounds weird that being respected was a new territory for me.

I had to tell him how I felt, in case something did happen to him. He needed to know. My feelings had grown for him. "I more than just care about you Nick. I was so scared I was going to lose you. The thought of that scares me more than anything. I'm so glad you're safe."

I could feel his cheeks pull his lips into a smile. He didn't say anything, just stood there, towel wrapped around his waist, rubbing my back.

Then it hit me, he only had a towel on. Barely covering parts of himself that I tried to not think about. "Oh goodness, you're naked!" I covered my eyes, and backed away from him, feeling for the doorway to get out of the bathroom. "I'm sorry to barge in on you. I'll let you finish; whatever it was you were doing in here."

He laughed a deep belly laugh, "I was just trying to clean up, the doc gave me the 'all clear' to shower but then she said I'd have to redress my wound. I was having trouble reaching my back, I'm still pretty sore. Do you think you could help me?" He looked at me with big dough eyes, how could anyone say no to that? He must have been a spoiled kid who looks like that. He mastered that face.

I wasn't sure it was a good idea to be that close to him. I needed a clear head to make a decision later. I worried if we got too close it may muddle my thoughts. But he was injured because of me. The guilt still ate at me, I owed him more than I could ever repay. I decided I could keep a clear head and just help him wash up. *What was the worst that could happen?* "Um, sure," I hesitantly said. "Just tell me what you need me to do."

He handed me a large soft sea sponge and sat down on the stool in his shower, leaving his towel on for me. He felt my unease at his nakedness, not that I didn't want to see him naked, I did, just not at that moment in time. The water streamed down his back splashed onto me, soaking my shirt. I was hesitant to touch him, his red angry wound was healing but I was nervous I'd hurt him… more than I already had. Nick asked for my help, I'm sure he had nurses that would gladly volunteer for the job of sponge bathing him, but he chose me.

I laid one hand on his thick muscular back and the other gently slid the sponge across his angry looking jagged healing wound on his back. He winced, "sorry" I gritted my teeth.

He reached back with a hand and touched my leg, "you're doing fine".

His touch calmed me, I focused on his warm hand, strong and comforting on my leg. I tried to be more gentle with the wound, carefully swiping it until the water ran clear from it. Nick was rubbing my leg, his touch made me crave more from him, to feel every part of him. I was so conflicted, my head screamed to stop, to keep distance. But my heart… that bitch said to dive in head first, to grab him and never let go.

I was deep in thought, battling with myself when he grabbed my arm and pulled me into the shower with him. Water ran over my hair and clothes, fully soaking me. I didn't even care at that moment. He wrapped his large hands around my waist, guiding me to stand between his legs. I was so shocked, I didn't know what to do, I just stood there, processing the deceive action. He wrapped his arms around my thighs, making me move even closer to him, he rested his cheek on my stomach. I could feel his heart pounding in his chest that was pressing against my thighs.

He sat there hugging and soaking me in for a few minutes. I of course was overthinking the situation. He needed comfort, he almost died, he chose me to seek comfort with. But a small piece of me still was unsure if I wanted to stay in that world. I didn't want to get attached if I was going to leave.

My heart eventually won, he deserved to have someone comfort him. Afterall I did it to him. The least I could do was comfort him. I never had caring interactions with my ex, that was new territory for me. Hesitantly, I ran my fingers through his hair. His breathing became deep and slow, but his pulse was racing. My body reacted to his touch, my heart was trying to catch up to him.

My hands began to wander down his neck, tracing his strong shoulders. He let out a small gravelly growl of excitement. My heart ignored my brain once again and my fingers made their way further down his back, feeling his strong, well defined muscles, being careful to avoid his tender wound.

The water ran over us as if we were one. Our bodies, so close, soaking in every feeling. He put a hand on the back of each of my thighs and pulled them apart as he lifted me up and sat me on his lap, still covered by a towel, thank goodness.

He put his hands on the sides of my face, making me look at him. I'd never been looked at the way Nick looked at me, like he was peering into my soul. It was like he truly seen me, all of me and he didn't care about any of my flaws. He pulled my face closer to his and kissed me, a deep sensual kiss. His lips, soft and full tugged gently on my lower lip. I'd never felt passion like that. He moved his kisses down my neck, sliding my t-shirt neckline off the side to gain access to my collar bone.

I got lost in the moment, my brain shut off, allowing only my heart to make the decisions. My body happily followed. His fingers danced down the back of my thighs, making me wish they'd move a little further up than he allowed them. He had more self control than I did in that moment, I was glad for that.

My brain started to kick back on, pulling me out of the moment. I slowly pulled away,careful to not make him feel rejected; because in no way was I rejecting him, or what we'd just done. But I wanted to take things slowly, well kind of slow, I guess. I looked him in the eyes, admiring all the shades of green and little flecks of gold in them. I kissed each eyelid.

"Can we take this slow?" I said, proud of my brain for finally joining the situation.

He sighed clearly trying to compose himself, and said "as slow as you want, I'm sorry about this, I just… missed your touch; I wasn't thinking clearly." I always saw him as so perfect, never struggling with anything, but in that moment I realized he's just as human as I was. He just hid his struggles better than I did.

I shook my head, "no, I didn't mean I didn't want to. I wouldn't have done it if I didn't want to. But if we are going to go anywhere, I need it to develop slowly and naturally. You just had a traumatic event happen and I worry that we're not making the best decisions right now."

"You're right. I'm sorry. I won't push it, I will let you take the lead when you're ready." he steeled his breath.

I nodded my head and took my finger and gently traced his lips. He looked up at me, smiling, but I saw the tension behind it. I smiled back then stood up with dripping wet clothes and hair half out of my bun. He just snickered at me as I grabbed a towel off the rack and tried whipping him with the tail of it. That made him full belly laugh leaving him wincing from pain. I felt bad for making him hurt himself but I was trying to break the tension that had built when I backed away from him.

I attempted to dry off but it was futile, I was thoroughly soaked. I decided to just take off the T-shirt and jeans, plopping them in a soggy pile on the floor. He sat in the shower, watching me, now in my underwear. I felt so exposed but also empowered, I knew he would respect me, so it was fun testing the newfound power I had. I never felt empowered with Josh, he just made me feel small. Nick did the opposite, I felt like I held the power. He wanted me to consent, to fully give myself wholly over to him. He let me explore this new feeling in my own time.

He smirked, got up and started taking off his soaking wet towel. He was testing me as well, seeing how much willpower I had in that moment. I quickly turned around to give him some privacy, though I will admit that I snuck a little peek from the mirror, the view was nice from behind. I waited for him to put the new dry towel on then he walked past me with swagger and confidence. He went to a dresser and grabbed a few things out of it and tossed them my way.

I caught the pile of clothes, a shirt and sweatpants that would be much too large for me but better than walking around in my underwear or just a towel. I slipped them on, Nick still hadn't taken his eyes off me. He watched me with a naughty little grin on his face, leaning against the door frame of the bathroom.

"Thanks, I'll get them back to you."

"Don't worry about it, you look better in them than I do" he said with a wink.

"Okay well, now that I know you're feeling better, I'm um, going to go back to my room and change." I could feel the redness starting to show on my cheeks, my moment of empowerment had passed, doubt and confusion began to creep back in.

"If you must." He said pouting. He was insufferable. "Hey, we'll be having a meeting in the conference room to go over the mission and plan the vanquish. If you're up to it that is. I know it's taken a toll on you."

"No, um, I can make it, just let me know what time."

"I'll have Huyen let you know the plan. You two seem to be getting close, nice to see her happy and you too obviously."

"Yeah, she's great. I really like her." I said with a smile. He just smiled back, and I awkwardly tried finding the door handle, while facing backwards; trying to hold up the baggy sweatpants with one hand in the front. Pretty sure if I let go, they'd just fall to the floor. I finally found it and backed out of the room, quietly shutting the door behind me. Closing my eyes and taking a deep breath to contain myself.

I opened my eyes to see Huyen was there, with a cheeky grin on her face and hand on her hip.

"Soooo, what have you been up to?"

I shook my head and laughed, "I was just helping Nick get washed up."

"I bet you were," she said with a wink. Goddess help me, I was never going to get rumors to stop here. "Hey, I don't judge, I'm just glad he's found someone finally. And I'm really glad it's you. You're good for him, his eyes sparkle again."

If I wasn't blushing before I definitely was after that. I thought of running back to my room out of embarrassment but I remembered, "Hey, Nick said something about a meeting, do you know what time?"

"Yeah, hold on" she said as she pulled out her phone and tapped the screen a few times, "3pm"

"Kay, thanks! I'm, um going to go change now."

"Uh huh, you do that. Is it safe to go talk to Nick or should I wait a few minutes?" Clearly trying to poke fun at the situation again. She probably thinks more happened that actually did, I didn't have the strength to correct her.

Giggling out of nervousness, "We, um, I mean he just got out of the shower so should be dressed by now maybe?" I said with a shrug. "Bye," I said quickly before she could ask anything else and hurried off to my room.

I closed the door behind me and leaned against it to catch my breath, from everything that just happened. I could almost feel his big strong hands on my thighs lifting me up still. I started smiling to myself at the thought. *Get it together Aoife, you can't fall this hard this fast for him, it's lust not love.* The feeling will fade like it does with all the others; but I'd never felt like that before. Yes, I was attracted to them and there may have been a few nights of passion but nothing in comparison to what I felt with Nick.

Chapter 17

I was sitting in the conference room, in one of the rolling chairs surrounded the table, waiting for one of the people to start the meeting. Nick walked in the room, everyone stood up and started hugging him or shook his hand as he walked by, saying sweet words of encouragement. He was making a great recovery and everyone was relieved. I stayed in my seat, trying to not look at him because I knew my face would instantly flush. I kept fidgeting with the papers in front of me trying to distract myself.

He of course came and sat in the chair next to mine. I spun around, not looking at his face and said, "hey". Trying to sound nonchalant and slightly uninterested, trying to ignore the feelings brewing in me.

"Hey" he said back, I could hear the smile on his face. "How are you?" he asked leaning toward me, I could feel his breath on my shoulder, it sent shivers down my whole body.

"I'm, um, good, I'm good. How are you? You get all bandaged up again?" *God, I hated how awkward I was. Why couldn't I be the confident one?*

"Yup" he said with a grin, lifting up his T-shirt, showing off his abs, tattoos and bandage at the same time. He knew what he was doing. Taunting me.

I knew I was a vibrant shade of red. I shook my head at him and turned back around, doing my best to look uninterested in him. He crossed his leg and used it to spin me around in my chair. I glanced back at him and rolled my eyes, making him laugh. He knew he was cute and he had gotten under my skin.

The military looking guy from the last prep session, Viktor walked us through everything before the mission walked up to the front again. Everyone stopped talking and waited for him to start. "So, we have a lot to discuss today. Thanks for joining us. Let's jump right into it. The mission was successful, Nick and Aoife captured Fenriz, and he's locked away in a containment unit."

Nick cleared his throat, "um, actually Aoife, captured Fenriz" great I was red cheeked again. He stated it so proudly, taking none of the credit for himself. He truly was selfless. Chip, chip chip, the wall I had built around my heart was beginning to get smaller.

"Yes, she did, thanks Nick. Aoife captured Fenriz ", the man said, and the room clapped for me that time. It made me really uncomfortable to be center of attention. I didn't want recognition for that anyway, it's how Nick got hurt. I let him get hurt. Images from the cave and the wolf flooded back into my mind. My anxiety began to kick up, somehow Nick sensed it, reaching a hand around my chair to grab my arm. His warm touch brought me back to the present. I didn't know how Nick knew I needed him to do that, but I was grateful for it.

Viktor continued, "As you all know Nick was injured during the mission by a Death Worm. Aoife administered the antivenom and got him back here in time, so he's on the mend now but will be out of commission for a few more days. The medical team and coven have been attending to his wounds, so take it easy on him the next few days okay. Don't let him talk you into rock climbing or a duel or anything." He said with a small chuckle at the end.

He went on, "Once Nick is healed up, he and Aoife will commence the vanquishing. The coven has the location already planned out, and they are working on some spells and bindings of protection for them to take with them. We'll sit down with you two and finalize the vanquishing plan. Until then we'll keep working on logistics and safeguards needed. Get your rest, it will take a lot out of you to vanquish this one. He's extremely powerful. We want you to be at your best, so mistakes don't happen." We both nodded at him. We'll see if Nick would let me rest, he did say he'd let me make the next move so maybe he'd be a little more chill now. We'll see…

With that, the room started to clear out, as people were talking to each other about the mission as they walked out the door. It did seem like Nick had a good team of people here. They did a lot more in this building than make toys, that's for sure. The pressure of having to handle Fenriz again felt like too much. We barely captured him before, and Nick got hurt. We had to do it all over again, what if he got hurt worse than before? Now that we had him, I felt like we had to follow through with the plan. I couldn't allow him to hurt anyone else, and Aunt Maggy deserves to know he can't hurt anyone else.

Nick snapped me out of my worrying cyclone by taking his leg and spinning me around to face him again. I let out a little 'yip', that made him smile. I was worrying about the possible things that could go wrong, but we had him, it would be easier the next time… I hoped.

"So, what are you up to the rest of the day?" he asked like he sensed I would just sit in my room and overthink the situation again. He seemed to always know what I needed before I did.

"I'm not sure yet, I don't have anything planned. How about you?" I knew I should keep my distance, to keep my mind off of him and prepare for the vanquishing but Nick had a way at weakening my resolve.

He smiled a big, playful grin, "Nothing planned, yet, wanna do nothing with me?"

I put my hands on my hips, glaring at him. "I thought you were supposed to take it easy until you're healed."

"Well, I was going to invite you rock-climbing but since I'm not allowed to have any fun because I might break, I guess I won't. I don't know, I just want to hang out with you, if you want to that is. We happen to have a theater room… if you'd like to watch a movie tonight?"

I didn't trust myself to be alone with Nick after our shower session so I had to think quickly, "What about a group date…er gathering." I wasn't ready to call it a date. "Njeri and Huyen are kind of dating people, it would be fun to have them get together too." That seems like a logical thing to suggest, and it wasn't a lie, it would be fun for them.

He lost a bit of his excitement when I said 'group' but he still had the sparkle in his eyes so I knew he was okay with it, "That sounds great. I'll give chef a heads up that we'll probably be wanting snacks later" He still seemed excited about the idea. It made me feel better about avoiding alone time with him.

I found Huyen and Njeri at the desk, they were ecstatic about the idea of movie night. Njeri called her girlfriend Clara right away and Huyen slithered at warp speed to the breakroom to talk to Theo. Everything was set! A regular night, I was looking forward to it. Well as regular a night can be in a magical building with mythological creatures and a rich kind of boyfriend. The more I thought about it, the weirder it felt.

Nick led me to the theater. It was so much more than I expected, but I can't say I was surprised at the extravagant furnishings knowing Nick. Overfilled red leather reclining chairs dotted the angled floor. The couples quickly grabbed a blanket from the basket by the door and ran to claim their seats. Nick and I couldn't stop laughing as they fought over the front spots. He handed me a fuzzy purple blanket and let me choose our spot. I was half tempted to sit where he couldn't sit next to me because I didn't trust myself but knew that would cause issues and I honestly didn't want to sit far away from him, just far enough to be safe.

We settled into our seats as the movie started. The large white screen lit up and began playing previews of an upcoming movie that I wanted to see but didn't think was out yet.

Nick leaned over, "I may or may not have asked Axel what kind of movies you liked. I had a friend fly this in for you a few days ago. I hope you like it." He said with a huge grin, feeling proud of himself.

"I'm gonna kill Axel, that little snitch" I joked. "Wait, a few days ago?"

"Yeah, I had hoped we could get to know each other and have some down time, but some things got in the way of my plan." By 'thing' he meant I almost got him killed, my stomach sank. I tried to not let it affect my mood, he didn't mean it like I took it.

I smiled at him, unable to respond out of fear that I'd start crying. He took my cue and turned to watch the screen. As the previews ended and the movie came on, I squealed when I figured out what movie it was. I reached over and slapped his arm, "No! I don't know how you do this but I'm so excited!" No longer able to be upset at things that had happened, I let the good times outweigh the bad and enjoyed the moment.

His smile reached his eyes as he leaned over, draping his arm over my shoulders and laid a gentle kiss on my temple. "I'm glad you like it." I slid closer to him, careful to not bump his bandaged area, welcoming the warmth and safety of his arm.

I wanted to enjoy the movie, but my mind was traveling to so many different places, "Hey, can I ask you a question?"

"Anything"

"Not that it matters or is any of my business but did you and the waitress from downstairs ever date?"

He chuckled quietly, shook his head, "absolutely not. She's been here for a few years and has recently taken a liking to me, I think. She's not my type though. We never dated; I've tried to be very blunt about me not having interest."

"Psht, Nick, that girl has always been tryn' to get in ya pants." Njeri shouted from the rows ahead of us.

"Maybe I am completely oblivious to everyone's feelings around here," he said as he sunk his whole body into the chair.

Njeri shouted over to Huyen and Theo, "Nick thought Cami just recently started liking him"

Huyen and Theo both burst out laughing and shook their heads. Huyen said, "Oh Hun, she's been on a mission to get with you since she got here. You just recently noticed."

Now it was Nick's turn to turn red from embarrassment. He was chuckling and shaking his head. "I promise, I want nothing to do with Cami. It's only you I want. I will do a better job at making sure Cami knows that."

"Don't hurt her feelings though, no one deserves that."

"Promise. She needs to realize that *we* are together" he waved between us and paused, "even if you choose to leave later, she and I will never be together."

Njeri spoke up, breaking up the awkward moment, "anyone want to order food?"

"Not if Cami's still working," Huyen said laughing. I had to agree with her, Cami rubbed me the wrong way, practically throwing herself at Nick. She screamed desperate. We all just laughed.

Nick typed on his phone for a second then gave me a smile. A little later Cami came strolling in, scanning the room for Nick and locking eyes on him right away. She took her time laying the food out in front of us.

"Thanks Cami." Nick said as he took my hand and kissed the top of it while making direct eye contact with me making my insides melt. Cami got the hint then and huffed off. The group laughed more, not at her, but at the situation. The woman couldn't read signs for anything.

Looking around at all the happy couples, I couldn't help but smile. Nick noticed, "What are you smiling about?"

"Everyone looks so happy. I didn't think I could ever feel comfortable here, but it's starting to feel like …home. It's nice having friends here, I sure miss mine from home, but Huyen and Njeri have been amazing to me. I'm grateful for them. And you, grateful for you."

"Well, you're amazing Aoife."

I laughed, "no I'm not, I'm no one special."

"Aoife, when are you going to realize how truly amazing you are? You are like gravity; everyone wants to be near you. You have something about you that I can't describe but it is truly something special."

My face must have been sad because Nick said, "hey, you okay?"

I looked up realizing I spaced out, "yeah, I'm um great. It's been a great night. Thank you again for everything here."

"Then why does your face look like someone just took your puppy?"

"I was thinking about when I have to go home. We've been so busy I haven't really had time to think about, after"

"No pressure, really, I'm just curious, do you know what you'll do yet, about your magic?"

"I can't imagine not seeing you all again. I love this world, you all are so great. But I do have a life that I worked hard to build. Would I even be able to go back to my normal life knowing about all this. But if I choose to remove my magic, would I be the same person as before or would I feel like something is missing?"

"I can't answer those questions for you Aoife. But I can tell you, if you choose to keep your magic, you don't have to give up your life. We'll be here. Whenever you need us. Just a 22-hour flight, less if you let me fly you on our jet. Or you could always portal to me whenever you want me, I mean need anything." He said with a wink at the end.

"It's so much pressure. I have been trying to put it out of my mind but the more we all do together, and I get to know you all, the more I want to stay here. You have built such an amazing thing up here. The world is better with you in it."

"You'd be a great addition to our team if you ever wanted. Your talent of materializing could help a lot of people but also your empathy for others helps make you special too. I often think very business-like, you feel so much and so deeply, we could use that kind touch around here. But I also understand if that's not something you'd be interested in."He seems to always leave me an out, so I didn't feel pressured.

"I'm honestly not sure what I want to do yet. I've only been in this world for a few days and have almost died 2 times, and almost got you killed once, that was too close to the other side than I'm okay with. The most pressure I usually have is trying to make sure I sell enough art to pay my rent."

"I get it. I grew up in this, but I did go to college and travel a lot before, my parents… It was hard coming back to this and having a lot of pressure from everyone depending on you. But you would have a team, the pressure won't be solely on you, and we do our absolute very best to keep everyone, even our teams out of harm's way."

"I think I still need time."

"No pressure on deciding, but I should tell you that tomorrow we may have the best time to vanquish Fenriz, it's a waning moon which the witches say is the best time to vanquish something. He will be at his weakest and our spells at our strongest. I really don't want to put pressure on you, but some of our best ideas come to us in times of need."

I sighed. "Great. Looking forward to it." I felt like the weight of the world was on my shoulders.

He spun in his lounging chair to look at my face, "you'll figure it out. Either way you decide, I'm so glad we met, I don't regret anything."

I needed his grounding touch, the gravity of what was going to happen was hitting hard. His arms wrapped around me, pulling me into his body. My attention was on him, the warmth of his body, the steady rhythm of his heartbeat, the gentle circles he was drawing with his finger on my leg. I felt so utterly comfortable in his arms, I dozed off.

I woke up to Nick pulling the blanket over me like he was tucking me in, I realized I was no longer in the theater chair but my bed. He turned to leave when I caught his hand. Facing towards me he nodded as if he knew what I needed, and he slid into the other side of the bed. Wrapping my body around his, entwining our legs and arms until we couldn't tell whose body limbs were who's. We just laid there in silence and fell asleep. I didn't have any dreams that night. It was the most peaceful sleep I've had since I got there.

Waking up next to someone again was a weird feeling. But waking up next to Nick, I felt different… right. With my ex I had to walk on eggshells, I couldn't be myself. I felt the exact opposite with Nick. I felt like I only had to be myself, as messy and chaotic as that can be, I felt comfortable showing it.

I opened my eyes to see Nick staring at me, hands resting behind his head, little grin on his face. "Good morning sleeping beauty."

"Morning, how long have you been staring at me?"

He laughed, "not very long but long enough to spot constellations in your freckles."

"Um that seems like it would take a while…" I said making a face at him.

"I don't think I could ever look at you enough."

"Is that code for 'I think you're beautiful'"

"I don't need a code to tell you that."

"So, handsome, what's the plan for the day?" I had silently hoped it would be a normal day, no danger, no magic, no vanquishing; I knew it wasn't the case but a girl can dream.

"Well, First I thought we'd get the stressful part out of the way and figure out what we want to order for breakfast. Try to eat all of said breakfast, then both take showers, together or separately, it's up to you; but we try to encourage saving water here at the K Corp." he ended with a wink and a chuckle.

"Someones back to their old self, huh." I liked knowing he was feeling better, it eased my guilt a little. And I was beginning to miss Nick's flirting, *never thought I'd say that.*

"I feel 100%", as he rolled up to rest on his elbow getting closer to me. "So, what do you feel like for breakfast?"

"Hm, I feel like I need to brush my teeth before you get that close to my morning breath," I laughed, as I tried to push him away, but he didn't move at all. "I'm feeling like eggs benedict sounds pretty good this morning. Do you think they have pineapple juice?"

He laughed, "they literally have everything or at least can get it. Not even kidding. Magic has its upsides too. Oh, and your morning breath smells like heaven." he leaned closer towards me and took a deep breath in.

I couldn't contain my laughter. That man was incorrigible. "Okay then, I'll take that. Maybe a cup of coffee too, I have a feeling I'll need the caffeine today."

"You got it" he said and leaned across me to grab the phone off the side table, pressing into me with his chest intentionally. He placed our order, laid back down next to me so I crawled up to lay on his shoulder. My hair must have been getting in his face because he tried blowing it out of the way, apparently that failed, he had to use his hand to smooth it down. The hair issues would be something he'd have to get used to if he wanted me around.

We snuggled in silence until there was a knock at the door. He hopped up, still wearing his clothes from yesterday. It gave me reassurance he was being a good boy. I pulled the sheets up higher on me as the food cart rolled in and the young pointy eared waiter gave me a shy smile.

I've never had breakfast in bed except when I was in a depression mode after my divorce and Axel brought me a box of donuts to eat in bed with me.

Nick took his spot next to me. We both devoured our breakfast, preparing for the exhausting day we both knew we had ahead of us.

Once we were pleasantly stuffed I broke the silence, "So, what now boss?"

"Well, I'm not your boss, even if you chose to stay here, you'd be your own boss. You'd set your own hours and do your own thing. Just so you know. Your life is and will be yours to run as you see fit. But as for today, the witches said it the best time of day to vanquish Fenriz is dusk. So if you're up to it, we should probably do that."

"I can't say that I really want to do that but he's dangerous and needs to be dealt with before he can hurt anyone else. Might as well get it done and not drag it out." I let out a defeated sigh as I flopped back on the bed, half tempted to cover up with blankets and never come back out.

"Sounds like a plan. So, whenever you're up and around, wanna meet me in the conference room? The witches will go over what we have to do."

"Sure, let me take a quick shower then I'll be down."

"No real rush, you can take your time. So, that was a no to saving water then?" he winked.

"I help the earth in other ways, thanks Nick." I said and kissed the air as he waved goodbye and walked out the door.

This feels so unreal, like a dream. The very good parts and the horribly scary parts too. I laid there for a few minutes, took a few cleansing breaths to gather my confidence, deciding I had to get up and vanquish a demon. It would change my future forever. I took a very hot and long shower, glad Nick wasn't in there with me because of course I had another good cry. I'm not usually emotional but the thought of Nick doing anything that could hurt him again made me sick to my stomach.

Chapter 18

I took a deep breath as I stood before the mirror, trying to pull myself together. It was mission day which meant; no-makeup, a messy-bun, cargo pants, and boots. I hated that I knew that outfit meant shit was about to go down. I closed my eyes for a moment, inhaling deeply, steadying myself. *I can do this. I have to do this. For Aunt Maggy.*

When I walked into the conference room, it wasn't as bustling as usual. Only about half a dozen women and Nick were gathered around the table, a mix of ages. Ancient-looking books were scattered across the table, along with small bottles filled with colorful liquids, each capped with corks. Nick saw me come in and waved me over to him. I took a seat beside him.

The oldest looking woman in the room, her long white hair braided down her back, was the first to speak. Her voice was clear and commanding. "This is the most auspicious time to vanquish this evil. Fenriz is at his weakest, and the waning moon gives us the advantage. But make no mistake this will not be easy. He remains strong, and you must not relent until he is completely gone."

My stomach sank, I knew that day would come and I thought I'd be ready for it, but now that it was happening, I felt doubt creep into my body. I was just a regular person a few days ago, no I was getting ready to do the most dangerous thing I'd ever done. Could I really vanquish a demon?

My thoughts were cut off when another woman began to speak. She was a tall, willowy woman with striking black hair, so dark it was almost blue. "You will need to transport Fenriz to hallowed ground. We've identified the strongest ley lines connected to the Shadowlands, and they intersect in Salem, Massachusetts. There, the veil will be thinnest, and opening the connection will be easiest. It will give you the best chance of success."

"Salem?" I whispered to Nick. Of course, it would be Salem. He gave me a reassuring nod. The unease in my stomach grew as the situation became more real.

Then, Pauwau, who I recognized from our previous mission, stepped forward and took over. She handed me a small, ornately engraved blade. "Aoife, you must use this blessed blade. At least six drops of your blood must fall on Fenriz before you begin. Then, you and Nick must hold hands around him and repeat the incantation continuously until he is vanquished. You will then have to recite this incantation to open the gateway and vanquish Fenriz:

'By the power of the sun and the forces of the moon, become one in our quest to open the doors to the Shadowlands. Let our light illuminate the eternal night and leave no corner untouched, so that we may vanquish our enemies from the darkness that hides them from our sight.'

"How will we know when it works?" I asked, unsure if it was a stupid question.

The eldest woman let out a soft chuckle. "Oh, child, you'll know," she said, the confidence in her voice leaving no room for doubt.

A curvy, round-faced woman, who hadn't spoken yet, gestured to the table, picking up a couple of the small bottles. "We've prepared a few protective spells for you both. When you arrive, drink this first," she said, holding up a vial filled with a glowing liquid. "It will deepen your connection to the land and to the spirits around you."

She then held up a round, glass orb. "This one is crucial. Set it on the ground next to you when you begin the spell. It will light up, but do not, under any circumstances, look directly at it. Its light will do more than protect you; it will ward off any darkness that tries to interfere."

Nick and I exchanged a glance again. This was happening, for real. We were about to face down a creature from another realm with nothing but ancient spells, a dagger, and hope. For Aunt Maggy. For me. For all of us.

I nodded, my heart pounding but steady. *I'm ready.*

Pauwau spoke again, "You'll need all your strength for this, he will try to struggle and drain you. You are very strong but not as practiced as most that attempt this so do it fast. You'll have a short window, at dusk, when light meets night. Don't let go of eachother and stay strong. Your bond is unlike any I've seen. With you both there, you can do this." She said as she reached over and touched mine and Nick's hand.

"We'll create a portal for you to get there without haste. The longer he's in the net, the less effective it is so we need to limit his time in it." She handed us a few papers with the spell written on it and another with another spell tied around another small decorative glass bottle. "This is your backup plan in case he breaks free, or any other demons attempt to help him break free." I hadn't even considered they may be helping him more. "Just read the incantation and throw the bottle at the ground in front of him or them. Make sure it breaks. Then we'll portal you back and regroup to try again. But hopefully it won't be needed."

Nick spoke up luckily because I was still processing all this, "Thank you so much for all your help and hard work on this. Your help with our coven is greatly appreciated around here."

The coven witches and Pauwau nodded once at Nick and single file, hands behind their backs clasped, walked out in unison. Leaving Nick and I alone to process everything we'd been told. A pile of assorted small glass vials on the table in front of us. Let's hope I don't almost get Nick killed again.

"Okay, we know the game plan, just before dusk they'll transport us to Salem. Then you prick yourself with the knife, but don't go too deep, okay, we only need six drops, not your whole hand", he said with a wink. "Then we say the incantation together. I'll be on the lookout for his buddies that think they can help him. Then we come home, unwind in the hot tub, and have a boring day tomorrow. Deal?"

I just gave a tight-lipped smile and nodded. I was afraid if I said anything out loud, I'd chicken out or do something embarrassing, like cry. But I was beginning to think after my horrible ex, I just shut off my emotions, I wasn't being brave, I was numb, pretending to be brave.

The team was working together on a large station with a ton of buttons that made a roaring noise so loud that I had to cover my ears. While they were busy I snuck out to think. *I might not make it back from this.* I decided I needed some closure in case the worst scenario happened and I didn't come back. I grabbed the phone Nick gave me and called my mom. I slid down the wall in the hallway and sat with my legs curled into me on the cold tile floor.

"Hi mom."

"Honey, I've been waiting to hear from you, if you didn't call by tomorrow, I was going to call you, but I didn't want to bug you while you were, uh, working." Clearly, she thought I wasn't just working.

"Sorry I haven't called sooner, we've, um, I've been busy. How have you guys been?"

"We're good Hun. Same old, same old. How about you Aoife? How are you, really? You sound like you've been crying. Everything okay?"

She knew me all too well. "I'm okay mom, just a stressful day is all, well a couple stressful days really."

"If this job is causing you too much stress, it's okay to quit honey. Your dad and I will help you out as much as we can until you find a new one. You sound very unhappy, my love."

"Not unhappy, I've actually been the happiest I've ever been in a long time, there's just some stressful things going on right now, hopefully they'll be gone tomorrow."

"Is it Nick? Is he the stress?"

I laughed and a little cry, "No, Nick's… great. He's helping me sort out the stress actually. I think I'm causing him more stress."

"Well honey, I can tell you, if he really likes you, any amount of hurt he goes through for you, he's okay with it. He chose you honey. I could see it from the first minute you came over together. You're his person and he's yours."

I was crying again. "Mom, I don't know what to do, someone could get hurt if I do what I should, but If I don't someone will definitely get hurt. I feel like I'm damned if I do and damned if I don't."

"You can't let fear run your life. Remember after Josh when you didn't leave your apartment for months because you were afraid of seeing him again. You don't want to go back to living in fear. That's not living. You have to face whatever it is that you're afraid of."

I sighed, "your right mom. I just…"

"You love him, don't you?"

"I think I do. I am trying to fight it, we are so different, it could never work."

"Why do you think opposites attract? Because they balance us out. They're our other half, they aren't supposed to be exactly like you. Maybe he is exactly what you need honey."

"I don't want to need anyone, mom." Tears streaming down my face..

"Oh honey, none of us do, but reality is, life alone is okay, but it's better when we have someone to share it with. It doesn't mean giving up part of yourself or changing yourself. It means adding more goodness, more laughter, more love to your life. Fear is good too, listen to that gut feeling but don't let it control you. You control it."

"Thanks mom. That actually helped a lot. I miss you guys."

"When you're done with your project, come for a visit. We'll go blueberry picking and make that quilt."

"I will, thanks. I love you and tell dad I love him."

"Will do Hun. We love you too. You take care." With that we hung up.

I thought leaving my abusive ex and finally getting divorced from him was hard and scary, that made this look like a piece of cake. Although, both did try to kill me so maybe about even, but the divorce I only had lawyers to protect me, now I had Magic and Nick on my side. Aunt Maggy deserved peace before she died too. It's not fair what she went through just because she has a gift. Time to put on my big girl panties and woman-up!

I dried my tears and walked back in the lab to see if they made any progress. The scientist's voice broke through my thoughts. "Alright, you two, take your places on the stage in front of the portal. It'll be over in a few seconds. Fight through the discomfort this time it should be easier since you're not traveling as far." That was a relief. The last journey through the portal was rough, to say the least.

The scientist handed Nick the silver-threaded leash that held Fenriz, now a swirling black mass in a containment field. Nick carefully wrapped the cord around his fist several times, making sure he had a firm grip and lifted it out of the box. I was grateful he was the one holding Fenriz that time. Even with Nick's presence and bracelet to help keep me calm, the sight of that dark energy made my skin crawl.

Nick reached for my hand, I instinctively slipped my hand in his. He turned to me with a quick smile and squeezed my hand, silently telling me everything was going to be okay. I nodded back, drawing strength from his confidence.

The portal machine whirred to life behind us, and the familiar golden shimmer filled the metal frame. It looked like liquid gold, rippling as if touched by an invisible wind, beckoning us forward. Too bad every cell in my body wanted to rebel against the pull. I had to force myself to take one step closer to it, then another and another until my body moved through it on its own accord.

Instantly, I felt the strange sensation of weightlessness. My limbs floated without any gravity to hold them down. I attempted to take a breath but air felt like it was being pulled from my lungs. It wasn't as suffocating as the first time, but it was virtually impossible to take a deep breath.

I panted, gasping for air, dizziness washed over me. I shut my eyes without realizing it. A firm squeeze of my hand brought me back to reality. I opened my eyes, blinking to clear the haze. My breath finally came in easier, allowing my lungs to fill with air again.

I checked Nick over to make sure he arrived safely, my anxiety still running on high after the outcome of the last adventure. He stood tall, he still had the silver-threaded leash wrapped tightly around his hand. Fenriz's swirling darkness pulsed within the net, reminding me just how dangerous the trip was.

One obstacle down, we had made it to Salem. We stood in a forest, the scent of damp earth and rotting leaves thick in the air. Ahead of us was an old, weathered building, an abandoned church, silvered with age and crowned by a tall, narrow steeple. The graveyard surrounding it was ancient, with broken headstones covered in moss and lichen, some cracked, others leaning precariously. Everything about the place felt forgotten, a relic of a different time.

Now, it was time to face the real danger. My adrenaline picked up, heart racing, tension building in my shoulders. "Aoife, drink the potion," Nick's voice took me through the steps. I was in a daze, my mind whirling as I searched for the vial in my pocket. My hands shook as I pulled the cork out with my teeth and spat it onto the ground. Tilting my head back, I swallowed the bitter liquid, grimacing as the cold liquid hit my throat and then quickly warmed. It tasted awful, like something medicinal and earthy, but I could feel its effects almost immediately. I felt the magic deep inside me growing, warming me, filling me, threatening to overflow. The pull of the ley lines was so strong, my magic wanted to connect with it.

Nick's voice broke through again. "You ready?"

I nodded, still unable to trust my voice, and followed his lead. A rhythmic, low clicking started, emanating from the black ball of danger that hung from Nick's hand. The ground beneath us began to vibrate, the sound traveling through the earth, rattling the fragile headstones until bits of dirt and stone crumbled away. Nick knelt, laid the glowing ball down on the shaking ground, the movements eased slightly, as if it was soothing it. The area around us glowed so brightly that every blade of grass seemed to shimmer, every insect in the surrounding graveyard visible in sharp detail. The headstones cast long, thin shadows. The clicking noise that had haunted my dreams seemed to fade, pushed away by the brilliance of the light. It was working at least, for now.

"We can't wait any longer," Nick said urgently. "The longer he's here, the more the others will sense him and come. Do it now!"

I swallowed the lump in my throat and took the blade from my pocket. My hand trembled, but I forced myself to focus. Holding my palm over Fenriz's swirling black mass, I made a shallow cut, wincing as the sharp edge split my skin. Blood welled up immediately, I squeezed my fist, letting the drops fall onto him. Each drop sizzled as it made contact, like water hitting a hot surface. The ball began to vibrate more violently, rolling slightly in its place, a visible representation of the anger contained within it.

The vibrations grew stronger with each passing second, making it difficult to remain standing. Dust and dirt slid from the nearby headstones, some of them crumbling further as the ground seemed to pulse with Fenriz's energy. He was getting stronger, feeding off the environment, even while trapped.

"Now," Nick said, gripping my hand tightly. Together, we stood on opposite sides of the black sphere that was Fenriz, our hands clasped above him. The sky was shifting, the bright orange hues of dusk slowly giving way to the deep purple of night. This was the moment we had prepared for, whether I felt ready or not. *When light meets night*, the witches' words stuck in my head.

As we began the incantation, I felt it immediately, the draining sensation. It was like being pulled from the inside out.

"By the power of the sun, and forces of the moon, become one in our quest to open the doors to the Shadowlands. Let our light illuminate the eternal night and leave no corner untouched so that we may vanquish our enemies from the darkness that hides them."

My limbs grew heavier, my body slumping as if gravity had doubled its force. Fenriz was drawing our energy, trying to weaken us. Every movement, every word I spoke felt like a struggle. It was as though the air itself was getting thicker, harder to breathe, harder to think.

Nick squeezed my hand, bringing me back to the moment. I focused on his warmth, and forced myself to keep going. We had to finish it before Fenriz could break free. We could not let him get free, I wouldn't let him.

The world around us continued to tremble, but we didn't stop. Together, we chanted the spell louder, firmer, holding on to each other and pushing through the suffocating fear.

The wind picked up speed around us, causing my hair to escape from its knot on top of my head. I could hardly see through the mess of red curls. More clicking sounds, not the same familiar tone we were used to. It was a new sound, not coming from Fenriz, my stomach sank. It was coming from behind me and another behind Nick. He was looking around in a panic too. It didn't instill confidence in me when Nick looked worried.

The moment the last word left our lips, a brilliant explosion of light erupted between us. The force of it was staggering, it threw both Nick and me several yards away from each other. I hit the ground hard, my ears ringing, my body paralyzed for a moment. I lay there coughing, trying to catch my breath as the world spun around me.

I could see what looked like black smoke, Fenriz, slithered out of the silver-threaded sphere as a swirling, black void appeared in the sky. It was like a vortex, pulling the shadowy mass toward it like water draining through a funnel. It was terrifying and mesmerizing all at once. I watched in stunned silence as Fenriz was sucked into it, his form disappearing into the abyss. Then, there was a final, deafening explosion, louder than anything I'd ever heard. It felt like my eardrums were shattered. My already ringing head and now my painful ears made me sick to my stomach with pain.

I remained on the ground, gasping for air, trying to function through the pain, trying to process what had just happened. My body still felt heavy from the lingering effects of Fenriz's draining, but I forced myself to move. I sat up slowly, blinking through the pain in my eyes. My ears were still ringing, and the world felt distant and muted.

"Nick?" I croaked, my voice barely a whisper. I could hear no response.

Crawling on all fours, I fumbled through the grass, feeling pieces of broken headstones beneath my palms. The light from the glowing sphere still worked, casting harsh, blinding rays over the scene, but I could barely see anything. I continued to crawl, my senses disoriented and scattered.

Suddenly, a hand grabbed my arm, startling me. Instinctively, I screamed and lashed out with my elbow. I heard a grunt and the sound of something, or someone, falling.

"Nick?" I managed to blink through my haze and saw Nick lying on the ground, blood pouring from his nose. His hands were raised in surrender, and his eyes, though pained, were full of understanding.

I scrambled toward him, horrified. "Oh my goodness, Nick! I'm so sorry!" I cupped his face, checking the damage. His nose wasn't broken, but the blood was pouring steadily. Guilt washed over me as I kissed his face, tasting the metallic tang of his blood.

"Aoife, we have to go!" Nick pulled away urgently, his voice cracking through the lingering fog in my mind. "There are more coming! We don't have enough supplies to deal with them all." I looked around and saw black shadows dancing around in the woods, gathering density as if they were combining and getting larger. Their clicking echoed off the trees making it hard to tell how many were there.

Nick grabbed my hand and pulled me to my feet. The ground was treacherous, littered with broken headstones and uneven patches of grass, and I kept stumbling, barely managing to stay upright. His urgency fueled my panic, the echoing clicks around us getting louder, growing closer.

"Aoife, my armband is broken, you have to use yours to summon the portal!" Nick's voice was edged with desperation.

Frantically, I pushed buttons on my armband but nothing happened "It's broken!" I yelled, panic gripping me tighter as I saw the concern flash across Nick's face.

"Then you have to use your magic, Aoife! You have to take us home!" His voice cut through the rising dread. The clicking noises were now all around us, getting closer. It felt like we were surrounded.

"I can't!" I shouted back, terror choking me. "I don't know how!"

"You *can* do it, Aoife," Nick urged, his voice pleading. "You can save us."

No pressure.

I tried to remember what Njeri had taught me about focusing my magic. I took a deep breath. I had to stop the fear. I touched the tornado bracelet charm Nick had given me. Closing my eyes, I focused on the sensation of the charm against my skin, on the warmth of Nick's hand still holding mine. I pictured the feeling of being safe, of being back in the room, Nick's reassuring presence beside me.

I let the warmth that called to me from deep inside free. I let it flow over me like a tidal wave. I lifted my arms out in front of me, gold dust floated from my hand, forming into a large tornado in front of me. Its winds were so strong I had to widen my stance to keep upright. The magic was so strong there, unlike anything I'd ever felt. It consumed me. Nick grabbed onto my arm, waking me from my trance. I almost got lost in the magic, we needed to get home. I yelled "home!" and let the magic take over, hoping it would obey my command. The gold vortex enveloped us.

And then the world disappeared.

Suddenly, I woke to cold water enveloping me, my lungs screaming for air as panic set in. Everything was blue. My eyes stung as I tried to make sense of where I was. I swam upward, or at least what I thought was up. The weightlessness of the water disoriented me. Finally, I broke the surface and gasped, sweet air filling my lungs.

I looked around, realizing we were in the K Corp pool. That's where I brought us, but where was Nick? My chest tightened in fear, but before I could panic, I saw him swimming toward me, blood trailing from his nose. Relief washed over me. He reached me, his strong hands cupping my face, scanning me for injuries.

Without warning, Nick pulled me into a firm, passionate kiss, our legs kicking under the water to stay afloat. After what felt like minutes, we pulled away, both of us smiling, and then, the tension of the past few days broke, and we burst out laughing. We floated there for a while, just soaking in the absurdity of it all, alive, together, and safe.

The door to the pool area flung open, and in came a rush of people, scientists, doctors, and witches, all filing in hurriedly. The lead scientist, out of breath, reached the edge of the pool. "We tracked you in the building! But... you didn't use the portal. How did you get back?"

Nick helped me out of the water, wrapping an arm around my waist. "Aoife saved us," he said with a grin, looking at me with pride. My cheeks burned with a mix of embarrassment and relief.

"I didn't know you could do that," the scientist said, astonished.

"Honestly, I didn't either," I admitted, chuckling at the sheer craziness of it all.

Nick gave my hand a reassuring squeeze. "I knew she could." Then, laughing, he added, "But why the pool?"

I couldn't help but laugh too. "I don't know. I just imagined a place where I felt safe and comfortable. I guess the pool won."

A few people jumped into the pool to help us out, handing us towels as the doctors rushed in, checking us over with blood pressure cuffs and quick inspections. They handed Nick a wad of gauze to press under his nose, the bruise already starting to form under his eye.

"Let's get you two to the infirmary," one of the doctors said. "You're not in bad shape, but we need to check for any deeper injuries."

We were both sat down in wheelchairs and rolled to the infirmary. The same room where Nick had recovered before. I couldn't help but feel the flood of memories from the last time I sat in this room, but this time, Nick was okay, just banged up, a little worse for wear, but still very much alive.

He was still holding the gauze to his nose, his bruised face making me feel a pang of guilt. All that because of me. I tried not to think about it too much, but the guilt gnawed at me, no matter how much I pushed it down. I looked at Nick and said, "I seem to have a habit of hurting you. You sure you want to room next to me?"

Nick gave me a warm smile, "You're worth everything and more, Aoife. This? It's nothing." He reached for my hand. "Honestly, it makes me feel better knowing you can defend yourself. That was a solid hit."

I laughed nervously, shrugging. "I didn't even think about it, it just... happened."

Nick leaned back, a thoughtful look crossing his face. "I'm thinking we should implement self-defense training around here. With all the dangers, it might be necessary."

"Do you think people would want that?"

He grinned. "There are perks to being in charge. Some things won't be optional. While I believe in choice, knowing how to defend yourself is a basic survival skill. I don't know why we haven't thought of this sooner. Maybe we relied too much on magic and our guards."

"I think it's a great idea," I said, nodding. "It was really empowering to know I could defend myself. Even if I didn't need it... this time." I chuckled. "Still, you're right, better to be prepared."

Suddenly, Njeri pushed back the curtain and sauntered into the room, a wide grin on her face. "So, is this what you two call pillow talk?" she teased, bursting into laughter.

I could feel my cheeks burning, blotchy with embarrassment. I shook my head, speechless but laughing along with her.

Njeri glanced at Nick. "So, boss, what's the verdict? Will you two live?"

"We're fine. Just looks worse than it is," I said, while Nick nodded, giving a thumbs-up.

Nick's nose had stopped bleeding but under his eyes were turning a deeper shade of red by the minute. I grimaced at the sight. That bruise was going to look nasty.

Without Nick next to me, everything felt empty and unsettling, like a piece of myself had been torn away. I tossed and turned, every ache from the explosion a sharp reminder of all that had happened, and yet, my mind wouldn't quiet. Now that Fenriz was gone, a different kind of battle had started within me. Aunt Maggy planned to pass on the amulet holding our family's magic, and with it, the weight of a decision I wasn't sure I was ready to make. Should I go back to my old life, or should I stay here, with him?

Conflicting thoughts clawed at my mind, tearing me apart. I felt lost, desperate for some grounding. A walk around the building seemed like the only thing that might clear my head. As I stepped out of the elevator, I practically ran into Nick. Before I could even apologize, he wrapped his arms around me, pulling me close, and I melted into his warmth.

"How's your, uh, nose?" I asked awkwardly as my face was pushed into his chest. I winced as I looked up at the deep bruise blossoming around his eyes.

"Oh, I'm fine. This is nothing," he said, dismissing it with a shrug.

I bit my lip, feeling guilty. "Sorry again about… you know," I waved my hand vaguely toward his face as he released me from his embrace.

"Really, it's fine. I'm just glad you know how to protect yourself. That was a solid move," he said, trying to reassure me, his eyes warm with pride. "Can't sleep either?"

"No, my mind is all over the place. Every time I close my eyes, it's like everything starts replaying, and I can't escape it."

He tilted his head, understanding flashing in his eyes. "I was going to make some cookies from my mom's recipe. Want to join me? Maybe a little distraction will help." He gave me a playful wink, and somehow, it made me feel a bit lighter.

"You… make cookies?" I thought he couldn't get more perfect, I was wrong.

"Yeah, I am not a great cook but I can bake some mean desserts." He pretended to shine his fingernails on his shirt.

I laughed. He knew how to lighten the mood.

"So?" he pushed for an answer.

"Sure, why not?" I followed him through the quiet restaurant, feeling a sense of peace settle over me as we passed the double doors into the industrial kitchen. He flicked on the lights, and the cold metal counters gleamed under the fluorescent glow, casting a strange warmth over the space. He started gathering ingredients, and I couldn't help but watch him, the ease in his movements, the quiet strength he carried in every step.

He handed me a small glass jar, cracking the lid open and lifting it toward me. "Smell this," he said softly. I leaned in, and the scent of lavender surrounded me, sweet and delicate. It instantly took me back to childhood, to my grandmother's warm hands and the bubble baths she'd run for me, where the whole room would fill with that same comforting scent. I could almost hear her voice, feel her presence, just as real as if she'd been standing beside me.

I opened my eyes to find Nick watching me, his face soft with an expression I couldn't quite name. "What?" I asked, my cheeks flushing under his gaze.

"Nothing," he murmured, his eyes never leaving mine. "I just love watching you. You experience things so deeply. It's like you bring the world to life just by being in it." His voice was filled with something raw and honest, and it made my heart ache in the best way.

I looked down, suddenly shy. "It reminded me of my grandmother. Lavender was her favorite. The scent brings back so many good memories." My voice caught, and I took a steadying breath, the ache of loss mixing with the warmth of the memory.

Nick reached out, brushing a strand of hair behind my ear. "I hope these past few days won't scare you away. It's not usually like this," he said, his voice low and soothing. "Life here is usually much quieter. The most excitement we have is arguing over the last bite of a new dish the chef tries out. I promise, there's beauty in the calm."

He looked at me with such tenderness, it felt like a promise of its own, something I could hold onto. In that moment, I knew I wasn't alone in it. It was a world filled with magic and danger, yes, but it was also filled with people like him, people who made it all worth it.

I couldn't help but laugh. Maybe I hadn't given that place a fair chance. It had been a whirlwind of stress, but once everything settled, maybe it could calm down. Maybe I could have a semi-normal life there. But then again, what if more things happened, pulling me into new problems? Would it ever really end if Nick and the others were always saving people? It was a lot to think about. For now, I just focused on watching Nick put on an apron. Only he could make an apron look sexy.

He slipped another apron over my head, pulling the strings around my waist and tying them at my back. His hands lingered as he finished, fingertips grazing my sides. My breath caught, I closed my eyes, inhaling the familiar cinnamon-spiced scent that always seemed to cling to him. I tried to imprint it in my memory, in case I had to leave that life behind, leave him behind. I hoped his scent would always remind me of that moment, of him. The thought of life without love felt hollow, but this life of unknowns scared me too.

I cleared my throat, trying to shake the feeling off. Nick turned back to cracking eggs and measuring out flour, sending little clouds of it into the air with each scoop. Every so often, he'd give me that grin, his green eyes crinkling in a way that made my heart race. I could feel the heat rising in my cheeks as I grabbed a handful of flour and flung it his way. "Stop it," I said, feigning annoyance.

"Stop what? I'm just baking," he replied innocently.

"You know what you're doing. Stop looking at me like that."

"This is just my face. You'll get used to it." He shot me a wink and flicked a bit of flour back at me. I gasped.

"Oh no, you didn't!" I yelled, laughing.

"Oh, I did. What are you going to do about it?" he teased, daring me with a raised eyebrow.

That was it. A full-on flour war erupted! We flung handfuls of flour at each other, coating the counters, the floors, everything. I jumped toward him, rubbing flour into his perfectly styled hair. He gasped, then burst into laughter as flour spilled off him with each chuckle, his hair now a messy halo of white. He looked so carefree, laughing like that, and it made my heart swell with joy.

In that moment, with flour everywhere and laughter echoing through the kitchen, I let myself forget all the doubts and worries. Right there, with him, that was all that mattered.

In true Aoife fashion, my foot slipped out from under me, and I went down, arms and legs flailing as I desperately tried to grab onto anything close. Unfortunately for Nick, he was the nearest thing. I latched onto his arm, throwing him off balance as he tried to pull me up. But he overcorrected, and we both went down, crashing in the opposite direction. He landed on the floor with a thud, and I found myself sprawled on top of him. My hair fell over his face, blocking his view. He used one hand to gently sweep it aside so he could see me.

His tan skin was speckled with flour, creating a playful constellation of reverse freckles across his face. I couldn't help but burst out laughing, breaking the soft silence that had settled over us. We laid there, laughing together, his arms wrapped tightly around me as I felt the deep, warm rumble of his laughter in his chest. I hated how effortlessly he made me happy. I wanted to resist him, to feel nothing for him or that place, but there I was, tangled up in him, starting to see that chaotic, unpredictable life as home.

We reluctantly climbed off each other, both of us making half-hearted attempts to brush off the flour that clung to our clothes. "We should probably finish these cookies if we have any hope of sleeping tonight," I said, still catching my breath.

"Yeah, you're right, as usual," he replied with a grin. "If you want, I can bring a plate up to your room once they're done, if you'd like to get cleaned up."

"I think I will," I nodded, loosening the apron strings. "I seem to make a mess of things every time I'm around, anyway."

"I like messy," he replied, his tone softening. I couldn't help but smile as I turned to leave. He liked my messy, and that feeling that I could just be myself with him, felt better than I wanted to admit.

After I showered the pound of flour out of my hair and slipped into clean pajamas, there was a knock at the door. I opened it to find Nick, his hair still dusted with flour, holding a plate of cookies. I closed my eyes and took a deep breath, savoring the sweet, comforting scent.

"I know I smell amazing, but don't ignore the cookies, they're the main event," he teased.

I laughed and lightly slapped his chest before stepping back to let him in. "I won't stay," he said, his gaze softening. "I know it's been a long day. I just thought I'd drop these off. And, uh, I was thinking, maybe tomorrow we could visit your Aunt Maggy and give her the news. I thought you'd like to share it with her."

"That sounds perfect. She deserves peace as soon as possible." I nodded, taking the warm plate from his hands, grateful for this thoughtful gesture.

He paused, his eyes lingering on mine. "Good night, Aoife."

"Night, Nick." I watched as he slipped quietly out, closing the door softly behind him.

Tomorrow, I'd finally tell Aunt Maggy that the creature who murdered her parents was caught and vanquished. It felt surreal even to think about, those words seemed like they belonged to someone else's story. My long lost aunt now had closure. I was so proud I was able to help her get that.

Giving her the news of the vanquish would be rewarding, but it would also lead to more confusion. I'd leave her home with our family's amulet, the one that held generations of magic, my magic. I could finally free myself of it, if I chose to. The weight of what was to come felt just as heavy as the vanquishing we just accomplished.

What would it be like to return to my old life? I wouldn't know anything about this world, these people. I wouldn't know that Nick was my soulmate, or that I'd chosen to leave him behind. Would I feel the loss, somehow? Would there always be an emptiness, a subtle ache that told me my life wasn't quite as it should be?

The cookies did little to soothe the knots in my chest, though they did calm my mind enough for my heavy eyes to finally close. Confused, I Struggled to understand where I was. It looked like Aunt Maggy's house, but her home was alive with color, more vibrant than I remembered, every intricate wood detail seemed to shimmer in the sunlight. Aunt Maggy herself looked radiant, a floral dress flowing around her as she walked. She was waiting for me at the edge of the driveway, waving me over with a bright smile. I ran to her, she wrapped me in a warm embrace, smoothing my hair down to comfort me.

"Child, I know what you did," she said, her voice soft but filled with emotion. "You did well. Thank you for bringing me peace after all these years. I feel like I've missed so much of life, but you've brought a spark of it back to me."

I pulled away, confused. I hadn't even told her about Fenriz yet. How could she have known? I took a good look at her then, really looked. Her face was softer, her cheeks fuller and tinged with pink, and her bright blue eyes sparkled with a carefree light I hadn't seen before. She was beautiful but not in the way I remembered her. She looked younger, transformed into the vibrant woman I'd only ever seen in old photographs. The Aunt Maggy who had faced years of grief and loss was gone, replaced by this version, untouched by pain.

I reached out, tentative, unsure of whether this was real. She seemed to glow, almost ethereal, her happiness radiating like sunshine. The warmth of it filled me with an overwhelming sense of comfort, but it also made me acutely aware of everything I would be giving up. If I left this world, I might lose not only my magic but this piece of my aunt as well.

"The amulet is yours. I had it sent to you before…. Do with it what you wish, but remember, magic isn't a curse. The magic in our bloodline was born from love, a love that longed to be found and fiercely needed to be kept. Don't let such a gift go to waste. I wasn't as lucky in life or in love, but you, child, have the chance to fulfill what our ancestors had. True love. My wish is simply that you find happiness, whatever you choose." She smiled, her eyes warm and full of the wisdom of ages.

Tears poured down my face in rivers I couldn't control. She looked so carefree now, no longer the frail, lonely woman I had known. She was radiant, full of life and love. Words escaped me. I could only nod, overcome with emotion.

"I'll try to visit you in your dreams now and then. I'll be watching, so be good, and do good." She hugged me once more, patting my back gently as she began to fade, her form turning translucent, then scattering like dust caught in a gentle breeze. The house, too, dissolved, each piece disappearing until only darkness surrounded me. I stood alone, in a void so quiet and empty that it felt as if the world itself had ceased to exist.

The ringing of my phone jolted me awake. I rarely received calls, especially at this hour. "Hello?" I answered, my voice thick with sleep and tears.

"Aoife, I just got a call. I'm so sorry. Your great Aunt Maggy has passed away," came Nick's voice, gentle but tinged with sorrow.

"I know," I whispered, feeling my face still wet with real tears. The dream had felt so real, as if she had truly been with me.

"Are you okay? Do you want me to come up?"

I swallowed, the ache in my chest pressing tighter. "No, I'm. I'm okay. She visited me in my dream. She looked beautiful, Nick, young again, and so alive. She seemed at peace."

There was a pause, as if he was taking in what I had just said. "That sounds like a beautiful dream. I'm glad you got that moment with her. Truly."

"Me too," I replied, a fragile smile breaking through my grief. "Thank you for helping bring her that peace, Nick. I couldn't have done it without you."

"It was my pleasure," he replied softly. "I'll always be here for you, if you want me."

His words wrapped around me like a comforting embrace, a reminder that I wasn't alone. "I know. I'll see you in the morning. Thanks, Nick."

"Anytime, Aoife. See you in the morning."

As I hung up, I closed my eyes and let myself feel the weight of everything, grief, gratitude, and love, all intertwined in a way that left me both heavy and free. The ache was there, but so was the warmth of Maggy's final embrace and the quiet strength in Nick's words. I wasn't sure where my path would lead, but in that moment, I knew I'd carry their love with me, wherever I went.

I contemplated what had just occurred. None of it seemed real; Aunt Maggy was finally at peace, the creature that had killed her parents was vanquished, and now the family amulet was mine. I had longed for this, for the freedom to choose my future. But now that it was here, I didn't know which path I wanted anymore. My mind wrestled with the weight of the decision until I finally fell into a dreamless sleep, my body too exhausted to think any longer.

The morning felt lighter, as though the world had shifted. The air was fresher, the sun brighter. Aunt Maggy was finally free, and with her release came a sense of hope for my own future. I dressed quickly and made my way down to reception to check in with Huyen, eager to see what the day would bring, after grabbing a much-needed coffee, of course.

With coffee in hand, I approached her desk. "Good morning, Huyen."

She glanced up, a little surprised by my upbeat tone. "Well, aren't you chipper this morning? Did they make that coffee extra strong for you?"

I laughed, feeling lighter than I had in days. "No, I just had a good night. Hey, did anything come for me by chance?"

Huyen glanced at the small pile of mail beside her. "The mail just came in, but I haven't had a chance to go through it yet. Are you expecting something?"

"I'm hoping the family amulet is here."

Her eyes widened with understanding. "Oh, *the* amulet? Really? I thought you had to go see your aunt to get it."

My voice softened as I replied, "She passed away last night."

"I'm so sorry," Huyen said gently, placing a comforting hand on mine.

"It's okay," I said with a small smile. "She found peace. I'm just grateful she had that before she died."

Huyen nodded solemnly, rifling through the letters and packages. Finally, she straightened her tail so she was upright, holding a small box wrapped in gold foil. She handed it to me with a reverence that made my breath catch. This was it, the amulet. The weight of my family's history lay in my hands. Aunt Maggy held onto it, hoping to find love, but her path took a dark detour after her family was murdered. She never found love. It felt like a betrayal to her to even consider giving it up because I'm scared. But she also said she wanted me to be happy, if that meant giving up my magic and Nick then I hope she'd accept that decision.

Just as I was about to ask Huyen for her opinion on if I should open the package or not, I felt a kiss on my cheek. Nick had come up behind me, his presence both grounding and electric. Huyen smiled knowingly as she watched us.

"Is that…?" Nick gestured to the box in my hands.

"I think so," I whispered, my voice barely holding steady. "Should I open it?"

"It's up to you," he said softly. "No matter what you decide, this is a part of you. It's been in your family for generations. Think of the history it holds."

"I have to open it, at least. I don't have to decide right now, do I?" My fingers traced the edges of the box as I spoke.

Nick smiled gently. "No, of course not."

Taking a deep breath, I nodded. "Then I should open it. I've been dying to see what it looks like."

I slowly lifted the lid, revealing an oval gold stone, its surface dulled with age and surrounded by thick, swirling bands of gold. It wasn't as ugly as my mom had described, but it wasn't something I'd wear every day, either. It looked ancient, worn and cared for by many generations. I pictured my ancestors wearing it with pride, carrying the honor and love that filled our family line.

I picked up the heavy brooch, feeling its surprising warmth and the faint buzz of energy pulsing through it. It felt alive, almost as if it recognized me. The weight of it was more than physical; it felt like the weight of my future resting in my palm.

Nick broke the silence, laying a gentle hand on my shoulder. "Are you okay?"

His touch grounded me, pulling me back from the swirling thoughts in my head. His eyes searched mine with genuine concern.

"I'm fine," I replied, still somewhat dazed. "It's… warm." I let out a breath, trying to wrap my mind around this unexpected moment.

He nodded, understanding. "There's a lot of magic in that piece. It's not surprising you'd feel it. Do you need anything? Can I help in any way?"

I shook my head. "No, I just need to decide." I looked at him and Huyen, grateful for their support but knowing this was a choice only I could make. "For now, I think I'd like to be alone."

Nick and Huyen both nodded, silent and understanding, as I turned and walked back to my room. I sat there, alone with the amulet in my hands, my mind racing with possibilities and consequences. Aunt Maggy's words echoed in my mind, her belief in love, despite all she had endured. Even with the pain magic had brought her, she still saw it as a gift, something worth cherishing. I didn't want to dishonor that by rushing to a decision.

Time seemed to blur as I sat there, lost in thought. The staff brought up food and quietly removed empty plates, but I was too absorbed to notice much. I needed more time, and I wasn't ready to face anyone's questions or opinions. I needed space to decide what this amulet, and this life would mean for me.

Chapter 20

A familiar voice hollered at me through the door, "E, you better not be naked with someone in there."

There was more pounding. "Aoife! Open up already!"

I had to take a second to make sure I wasn't dreaming, nope I was awake. And that voice yelling through the door sure sounded like Axel, but that was impossible. He couldn't be there, in front of my door.

I cracked open the door and peeked out to see if I was going crazy. Sure enough, there he was, his stupid grinning face staring back at me. Before I could process it, he burst through the door and swooped me into his arms, swinging me back and forth like I was a ragdoll.

Tears welled up again. "How are you even here?"

"Nick called," Axel said, squeezing me tight. "He said you were going through some things and could use a friend."

"Oh, my goddess! I can't believe it!" I pulled back just enough to look at his face,scruffy and unkempt face, tears streaming down my own. "You're really here!"

"I can't believe your new guy has his own private jet!" Axel said with a laugh. "Honestly, E, I'm impressed!"

I laughed, too. Of course, that's what he would focus on. "Wait, what exactly did Nick tell you?" I was suddenly nervous about how much Axel might know.

"Not much, just that you've had a rough few days and that me showing up might help. What's going on, E? This place is insane! No wonder you haven't come home yet!" He spun around like 'The Sound Has Music'. "Girl, you're a hot mess. Clean yourself up, we have tea to spill!"

"It's not that I don't want to come home," I said, wiping my eyes. "I miss you guys so much. But I have some… work here that I need to finish before I can leave."

"Work?" Axel raised an eyebrow, skeptical. "What kind of emergency does an artist have?"

I hesitated, wondering how much I should tell him. Could I even begin to explain it without sounding totally crazy? I decided to give him the truth, well, most of it, anyway. "Nick's helping me with something. It's… some family history stuff, to help Aunt Maggy. Well, helped" I corrected myself, as she was no longer here.

Axel's eyes widened in disbelief. "The batshit crazy aunt? That Maggy?"

I nodded. "Yup, that one. Turns out she wasn't crazy, though. Our family just didn't understand her."

"Did you say *was?*"

"Yeah, she passed last night."

"I'm sorry E, I didn't realize you guys were close." noticing how solemn I was.

"We weren't really, we just met the other day, but she made a big impact on me. We were helping each other with something. She was really sweet and she deserved so much more than life gave her. I was hoping I'd have more time to get to know her."

"Uh… E, she was literally in a mental institution."

"Yeah, because nobody in the family understood what was going on with her."

"Understood what, exactly?" Axel's voice was cautious now, he knew I wasn't telling him everything. He should have worked in the FBI because he was like a human lie detector.

I took a deep breath. "She's psychic. I know it sounds insane, but she's not crazy. And it turns out, some of our family members have… gifts."

Axel stared at me, unsure whether to laugh or be concerned. "Uh-huh… and you believe this?"

"I don't just believe it, I know it's true. But I don't want you to think I'm crazy, too."

He raised an eyebrow. "Right now, you're sounding a little nuts. Has Nick brainwashed you?"

I couldn't help but laugh. "No! Nick's been helping me through this whole thing. He's shown me things or I wouldn't have believed me either."

Axel crossed his arms. "Shown you what, exactly?"

I sighed, realizing the only way to convince him was to show him. "Okay, let me just show you, but you have to promise not to freak out."

"Oooookay." His tone was full of doubt.

"Hand me your wallet."

Axel narrowed his eyes, then laughed. "If you need money, just let me know how much you need."

"No, butthead, just give me the wallet. I'll give it back, I promise."

Still looking at me like I was nuts, Axel reluctantly handed over his wallet. I took it, and then pointed to a chair across the room.

"Go sit down over there, hold out your hand." I didn't want him to faint or fall over, so better safe than sorry. He raised an eyebrow but did as I asked, looking at me with growing curiosity.

"Okay, here goes nothing," I whispered to myself. I closed my eyes, focusing on the technique Njeri had taught me. I could feel the familiar pull of energy, and then, whoosh. A mini whirlwind whipped through the room, ruffling my hair as the wallet vanished from my hands.

When I opened my eyes, I saw Axel's expression. His eyes were wide, mouth hanging open in complete shock seeing the wallet in his hand. "What. The. Hell. Was. That?"

"That's my gift, apparently," I said, trying to stay casual, though my heart was racing.

Axel just stared at me for what felt like forever. Finally, he managed to speak. "Why the hell did you hide this from me for so long?"

"I didn't hide anything. This just started," I said, waving my hands around like a crazy person. "I didn't even know about any of this until a few days ago! I still don't completely believe it, but I've seen too much to ignore it. Magic is real, Axel. There's a whole other world that, uh, humans have no idea about."

"Wait, what?" His eyes widened. "There's more than… whatever *that* was?" He rubbed his forehead. "My head is going to explode."

"Trust me, I get it. It's a lot. I don't know how much you *want* to know, but from personal experience, I suggest taking it slow. It's overwhelming, to say the least. I didn't have that option. I got thrown into it, and I'm still trying to wrap my head around it."

He looked around like the walls might be hiding something else weird. "D-Does your family know you're… magic?"

"No," I said, shaking my head, stifling a laugh. "They don't know anything about magic, or me, or Aunt Maggy. Apparently, it's some hidden gene from a long-lost family member. Nick's been helping me trace our lineage to find out more. That's why we went to Ireland."

Axel's eyebrows shot up. "So… why are you still here, E?"

"Nick's helping me with something else, too. Something… complicated."

"More complicated than a hidden gene of magic and gold freaking tornadoes?" He crossed his arms.

I blushed. "Uh, yeah."

"So you're not going to tell me?"

"I just don't know how."

"I think I'm taking this pretty good so far, try me." he said with a smug gin, leaning back in the chair trying to look confident but i knew he was freaking out inside.

"I get to decide if I want to keep my magic, or give it up."

"Well I'd think that would be easy. Give it up and let's go home E." he grabbed my hand and tried pulling me towards the door.

Laughing, I punched him in the ribs gently, "It's not that easy Axel. If I give up my magic, I also… give up my soulmate." I whispered out the last part.

"Exsqueeze me?" he put his hand on his chest exaggeratedly, with a gaping mouth.

"Complicated, I told ya."

"So you have a 'soul mate'?"

"Yeah, apparently it's… Nick." I covered my face.

"Nick?! Why him?"

"I don't know, Axel. It just is what it is. This whole thing has thrown me for a loop, too. And I don't know if I want to give up the idea of a 'one true love.' I've never believed in that kind of thing, but I do feel… different around him."

Axel rolled his eyes. "E, that's because he's rich."

I scowled. "No, it's not. You know me better than that. I don't care about his money. I feel… safe with him. Like I don't have to hide who I am or pretend to be someone else."

"But has he seen you cry yet?" Axel asked with a grin. "Because, girl, you are *not* a pretty crier. I love you, but it's true. Snot everywhere, puffy eyes, the whole nine yards."

I burst out laughing because, of course, Axel was right. "Yes! He has seen me cry, more than once, actually."

"And he didn't run the other direction?" Axel looked impressed. "Marry that handsome hunk of man meat right now!"

"Let's not get ahead of ourselves, okay? But yeah, I do really like him, and I've been trying to take things slow. I don't know what to do. I want to go back to my normal life, but also this is starting to feel kind of normal to me too. It's not so bad here. And I wouldn't have to stay here, I could learn how to protect myself and I could go back to my life in Michigan. I'd still have to figure out the whole soulmate thing though. He runs this place, and I think he has a lot more responsibilities than he's told me. He can't move to Michigan."

"Hm, so you learn some more karate moves," he pretended to roundhouse the air, "Then you come home and date Nick, long distance relationships don't seem so bad."

"I don't know if I could do that. Having Nick near me feels like I can breathe better. The world just makes sense when he's close. It's like he's my leaf spring to my bumpy road. It just makes life smoother." I tried to throw a car pun in there for him.

He laughed, "So, basically you either stay here and fall madly in love or you come home and are still you."

I flopped down on the bed, "I would forget all about this place and the people I've met. Would I know I was missing something? Would I always feel like there was a hole in me that no one else could fill?"

"Has he been pushing you into anything you're not ready for?"

"No! Not at all. He's been a complete gentleman, Axel. He's left the pace up to me, he's been patient, never rushing. And he hasn't bugged me about the decision to keep or give up my magic, even though it affects him, too."

Axel leaned forward. "How does your decision affect him exactly?"

I took a deep breath. "We're soulmates, Axel. If I give up my magic, I also give him up. That means we both lose our one true love, forever. We'd have to settle for something… adequate. It's not fair that the choice is mine alone, but he's leaving it up to me."

Axel was quiet for a long moment. Then he said, "So, you'd have an okay life? I mean, you could probably grow to love someone else eventually, but at least you wouldn't have to deal with all this crazy magic. You could come back home and live a normal life, right?"

"What if I can't settle for 'okay' anymore?" I asked, my voice trembling. "What if I want a true love?"

Axel sighed. "Look, E, I know Josh hurt you, but you can't just assume the first guy you date after him is your true love. It's called a rebound."

I laughed. "This is not a rebound, and Nick isn't the first person I've dated since… him."

Now he was laughing too. "One date doesn't make it 'dating,' Aoife!" He rolled his eyes.

"I've gone on a few dates with other guys before," I defended. "But there wasn't a… spark. This isn't a spark, it's full-blown fireworks. It's an atomic bomb kind of feeling. It's unlike anything I've ever felt, Axel."

He looked at me thoughtfully. "I want to believe you, but I've never felt anything like that, so I can't say I understand. But I'll support you, whatever you decide. Seriously though, are you ever coming home? I miss you, and our Taco Tuesdays."

I burst out laughing. Of course, Axel would be worried about our Taco Tuesdays, he couldn't cook to save his life, and he loved tacos more than anyone I knew. "We'll still make time for each other, even if I stay here. It might not be every Tuesday, but I'll do my best."

"Is that why Nick brought me here? You're worried about what to decide?"

I nodded. "Yeah, I think he knew I could use a friend from my old life. I don't know what to do." I regretted saying 'old life', I noticed Axel cringe as I said it. It sounded like I had already given up my life.

"Okay," he said, his voice soft and sad. "So, what do you need from me? I can't make your decision for you, but I'm here, however I can help. Nick seems like a pretty stand-up guy, especially bringing me in. He had to know I'd try to convince you to give up magic and come home. I think he genuinely cares about you and wants the decision to be fully yours. The dude has confidence, I'll give him that."

"Ugh, I don't know what to do." I rubbed my face with my hands, trying to block out the decision.

"You need to decide tonight? Because I have an idea that may help you sort out your feelings" Axel's ideas were either amazing or utterly ridiculous. It could go either way.

"No. There's no rush. I just feel like I need to decide and not draw this out. The longer I stay the more connected I feel to the people here. I don't want them getting hurt either. I just don't know if I'm a good fit for this place. Everyone seems like they have their shit together, and I'm just a messy artist. I don't know if I'm worthy of being here."

"With Josh, you always blamed yourself for making him mad, thinking you did something wrong or feeling like you weren't enough. Don't do that with Nick. You, Aoife Wheeler, are perfect. You deserve someone who treats you the way you deserve. You are worthy of it, Aoife." Axel leaned in for a hug, and I was crying again, ugly crying, as he would kindly point out.

"I'm glad you think so."

"I do. I see the real you, and you're perfect just the way you are. It seems like Nick sees it too. Anyone who doesn't? They're an idiot."

"Thanks, Axel. I love you, butthead," I said, punching his shoulder lightly.

"OW! Dang, E, you've gotten stronger! That hurt!" He rubbed his arm dramatically.

I smiled. "Don't be such a baby. You'd love Njeri, she's been my trainer. If you think I'm tough, you'd flip over her."

"Ooh, is she single?" He bumped my elbow with a mischievous grin.

Through my laughter, I said, "Nope! She's got a girlfriend… well, almost."

He snapped his fingers like a disappointed old man. "Any other hot single, straight females around here?"

"I thought you wanted me to leave, and now you're trying to date someone here?"

"Nobody said anything about dating." He winked.

"Ugh, Axel. You're so gross."

"Nah, I just like to have fun."

"You have a lot of fun. Some might say too much."

"There's no such thing," he said, grinning. "But seriously, any other options?"

"I only know two women, and both are dating someone. Though, there is one you *definitely* shouldn't date."

"Ooh, spill the tea girl" he said in his best gay boy voice that always cracked me up, "I love good gossip." He crossed his legs and pretended to sip tea with his pinky up.

I rolled my eyes but gave in. "There's this waitress who's been trying to get with Nick for years, and she's not subtle about it."

"Ugh, what trash! Did they ever date?"

"Nick says no. He shuts her down pretty quickly, so I believe him."

"Well, that's good. But still, ew. Who does that?"

"Yeah, it's awkward. But I've got more important things to worry about than being jealous right now."

"You have no reason to be jealous, it seems like he chose you. I can't think on an empty stomach, is there any place to eat around here?"

"You always want to eat," I teased. "But yes, I could go for some food. They've got a pretty nice restaurant here. I'm just not sure if we need a reservation."

"No problem, let's head down. If the wait is too long, we'll kill time. If it's booked, we can find somewhere else… if there is anywhere else in this barren ice town. Should I change, or is this okay? I wasn't exactly prepared for all *this*." he spun around the large room again.

"You're perfect." I said. It was so nice to have Axel there. He made the world make sense. I hoped I wouldn't lose him if I decided to stay…

We both smiled and linked hands, swinging our arms back and forth as we skipped, looking ridiculous I'm sure. As we passed through the lobby, I saw Huyen at the front desk and waved to her. She looked a bit shocked but waved back. Axel and I slipped into a conversation about his latest dates and how work had been going, just like old times.

It felt good to have him there.

We walked into the restaurant and stopped at the greeting stand. I gave the hostess a hopeful smile. "We don't have a reservation. Do you have any tables available?"

She didn't even bother to look up, her tone colder than necessary. "Name?"

"Aoife Wheeler," I said, a bit unsure. The greeter snapped her head up immediately, eyes wide for a second.

"Oh, Aoife! Yes, we have a table available for you and guests," she said, dragging out "guest" with an unmistakable hint of disdain. "Please follow me." She turned on her heel and started speed-walking away.

"Well, that was… weird," Axel muttered, eyebrows raised.

"Definitely. Wonder what all that was about?" I replied, following the hostess.

We arrived at the table, and the hostess gestured stiffly. "Right here, Ms. Wheeler. Your waitress will be right over. Have a pleasant evening."

Axel chuckled. "That was awkward."

I nodded, feeling a little off-balance, but before I could figure it out, I heard the sound of someone approaching. Axel smiled up at them, but when I heard her voice, my stomach dropped.

"I heard Nick ordered us to hold a table for you just in case you decided to show your face." It was Cami, and her tone was cold. "What can I get you?"

she clearly did not want to serve us.

Axel, oblivious, smiled. "Hi! I'd like a local beer, brown ale if you have it. If not, surprise me."

I nudged him, shaking my head furiously. But it was too late.

"Oh, you're *her*!" Axel almost shouted in sudden realization, making the situation ten times worse. My face flushed immediately.

"Excuse me?" Cami snapped, narrowing her eyes at him.

"Oh, nothing," Axel said, trying to recover, but he was too blunt to stop. "I've just heard about how close you and Nick are."

"We were getting close… until *she* showed up," Cami replied, rolling her eyes as if I were invisible.

"Honey, she can't take what was never yours," Axel shot back with a snarky grin.

Cami huffed and stormed away, leaving us in awkward silence.

"I don't think we'll be getting those drink orders now," Axel said, pouting like a child. I laughed despite myself, feeling a mix of embarrassment and relief that Axel had stuck up for me. Still, I hoped we wouldn't get kicked out.

A few minutes passed, and we were chatting when the chef himself walked out. He beamed when he saw me, bending down for a hug.

"I am so happy you came back! That means you liked my food! I will make you something special tonight. For you and your friend," he said, glancing at Axel with a twinkle in his eye.

"This is Axel, my best friend from home," I said, and Axel's face lit up when I introduced him.

"Oh, how nice to have visitors! I will make you both something special." he said with a wink.

"Oh, we don't need anything fancy," I tried to protest, laughing. "A couple of burgers would be more than enough. We don't need much."

"Nonsense! You need great food to be great!" the chef declared before rushing off.

I saw Cami and the hostess talking in the corner of the room, their hands flailing around as if they were having a very heated conversation, they'd glance at me every few seconds. Axel followed my gaze to the corner to see what was taking my attention off of him. "Ignore those b-ee-otches." He always knew how to make me laugh.

A moment later, a different waitress appeared, smiling warmly. "Hello, what can I get you two to drink?"

"I'll still take that brown ale," Axel said, grinning.

"And I'll take a green smoothie, or lemonade if you can't make that," I added, still slightly embarrassed from the earlier encounter.

"We can make everything! I'll be right back," she said brightly before heading off. I still wasn't used to them being able to make literally anything.

"Well, she's nice at least," Axel joked, and we both burst out laughing, releasing some of the tension.

A few minutes later, our new waitress returned with a green smoothie for me and a dark brown ale for Axel. He took a sip, nodded approvingly, and grinned.

"I like it here," he said, leaning back in his chair. I smiled back, feeling a warmth spread over me. Having Axel here really did make it feel a little more like home.

We fell into familiar conversation, talking about his latest dates and his chaotic work schedule. For a few minutes, it felt like we were back home, just enjoying a normal day. And for the first time in a while, I felt a bit more at peace.

The waitress came back with a bright smile and set down two covered plates in front of us. "The chef made something special for both of you. He sends his regards, there's a staff emergency, so he couldn't come out personally." She lifted the covers, revealing Axel's burger first. It was stacked sky-high with multiple patties of meat, topped with thin, breaded onion fries, and slathered with a deep red sauce between toasted onion buns. Mine was a beautifully seared salmon filet over a bed of fried rice, with a side of perfectly roasted vegetables. I smiled, wondering if the chef remembered my love for seafood or if Nick had mentioned it. Either way, it was a welcomed surprise.

Axel clapped his hands together in excitement, grinning as he took a massive bite. Judging by the silence that followed and the sauce dripping down his chin, it must have been incredible. Axel never stopped talking, so the fact that he couldn't even form words meant the burger was doing its job.

I was grateful for the quiet. The salmon was delicious, the crispy skin blending perfectly with the richness of the fried rice. For those few minutes, I could just focus on the food and push all my worries out of my head.

As we finished up, we sipped on refills, the conversation drifting to life back home, his new job, the mess he called his love life, and even how Taco Tuesday wasn't the same without me. For this moment life was great. It was uncomplicated, just good food and good company.

Axel and I hauled our overly full selves back to my room. We flopped on my bed and stared at the ceiling when there was a knock at the door. Axel jumped up, rubbing his hand like he did when he was up to something.

A young man with antlers rolled in a cart with boxes of craft supplies and a giant easel with a poster board on it. He smiled at Axel and left.

"This is your project," he posed with his arms displaying the board.

"I don't get it."

"E, art is how you work out your emotions. You are struggling because you haven't made any art here!" I was skeptical but he did know me pretty well so I was willing to go with it.

"So, go through these magazines and cut out images that speak to you. We're doing art therapy! I googled it, and apparently it's a thing, who knew?" he said laughing.

"You're ridiculous."

"Possibly but just do what you're told for once."

It looked like a craft store exploded. A rainbow of feathers scattered in a bowl on the table, bottles, bottles of glitter scattered around it. It was a crafter's version of a charcuterie board. My little artist's heart jumped to life. He was right, it had been too long since I'd made any art. I didn't understand it but art helped me sort out the feeling that I didn't know how to deal with.

Axel grinned, clearly proud of himself. "We're going to help you find yourself again! You've been through a lot, but I know deep down you're still the same Aoife. So, we're making a vision board! Like we used to do back when you first moved here and you felt lost, and needed to work through stuff, remember?"

"Oh, I remember." I laughed, rolling my eyes. "But how is a vision board going to help me now?"

Axel crossed his arms, refusing to back down. "You've been feeling lost, right? Maybe this will help you visualize what you want. What's the harm in trying? That weird little artist brain is chaotic, art is how things make sense in there." he said knocking on my head. I slapped his stomach, making him grunt.

I sighed, knowing he wasn't going to let it go. "Fine, let's give it a shot."

Axel's face brightened again, and he clapped his hands together. "Great! While you're cutting out pictures that speak to your weird little heart, I thought we could make an old-fashioned Venn diagram!"

I couldn't help but laugh. "You're really going all in on this, huh?"

"You bet I am!" He drew two wobbly circles on a poster board. "Alright, let's start with option one: removing your magic. What's the plus side to that?"

"Well, no more magic, obviously," I began, sitting down on the bed and crossing my legs. "And I wouldn't have to deal with magical creatures coming after me."

"E, you're a woman. Unfortunately, whatever you do, there are always predators out to hurt women."

"Dark Axel, very dark."

"But true. Tell me I'm wrong. How many times have you been abused, scared, threatened, or stalked by men?"

I hung my head, he was right, again. "Too many to count."

"You'll be safe from one threat but will always have another other. The Aoife I knew wouldn't make a huge decision like this out of fear, you're not a runner, you're a fighter.

"I just don't know if I have enough fight left in me. I'm tired of fighting." I said as I rolled on my stomach, propping a pillow under my chest.

"What else you got?"

"I could go back to my regular life," I added, though the words felt hollow as I said them.

Axel looked up at me, his expression softening. "Yeah, but would you really be happy with that? You've always been destined for more, Aoife. You've outgrown that life."

I thought about it for a moment. "I guess... I could settle for it. I mean, it's safe."

"Sure, but you don't settle. That's not who you are," Axel said, his voice serious now. "The Aoife I know would never give up just because something's hard. Where's that Aoife?"

I flopped back onto the bed, staring up at the ceiling. "I don't know, Axel. I feel like I've lost that part of myself."

Axel sat next to me on the bed, nudging my leg. "You're still in there. I know it. We just have to find her again."

"Plus side of keeping magic is I'd get to live here if I wanted and have this amazing community of friends."

"There you go", as he wrote it on the board in red. "What else?"

"I would have to lie to people about magic if I kept it."

"Is there a rule about not telling people?"

"Not really, but my family would have me committed if I said I had magic. Remember my Aunt Maggy?"

"True."

"I would be able to help people here, Nick's already talking about adding a self defense class for the employees." That made him smile. He knows how empowering the self-defense courses were for me.

"How about Nick? You're just going to skate around the subject?"

I pursed my lips at him, "Fine, I'd also get to keep having him in my life if I stayed too."

"He is your supposed true love after all. Would you really want to give that up?"

"I've lived just fine without true love so far."

"Yeah, but it hasn't been great, and now you know what it feels like. Could you give that up?"

"I guess they erase every memory of magic if I give up my powers so I probably wouldn't even remember him or what I feel like."

"Want to know what I think?" I knew he was going to tell me anyway, so I nodded. "I think you'd know something was missing, someone was missing"

Deep down I felt like he was right. It has crossed my mind before. "I think I could settle for an okay love"

"It would be 'like', not love Aoife. And no, you couldn't. You aren't the business transaction kind of person. You have to do things out of how it makes you feel. You have an artist's soul. You need passion to be happy. How have you felt being here?" he asked me.

"Scared, excited, worried, and comfortable. I somehow feel comfortable here."

"And what did you feel at home?"

I sighed, I saw where he was going with this. "Stable, content, bored"

"Now, what do you really want for the rest of your life? To be 'stable' or to feel like you belong. Because let's face it, you've outgrown our community back home long ago."

I plopped my face down on the pillow and released a muffled scream.

"Better?" he asked.

"A little" I sighed again. "I think I'd always feel something was missing and I think it would drive me nuts. I don't want content, because I wouldn't stay content, I'd get bored."

"Okay now that you've finally accepted who you are and what you want, let's get to the vision board!" he said with pizazz and doing spirit fingers.

"Oh lord" I said with an eye roll

"Where would you like to start? Let's start with some words, it may help get you started." He said pretending to be a teacher at the front of the room with a ruler.

"I know how to make art, Axel."

"Huh" he said as he waved his arms around the room, "because you've been here almost a week and yet I see no art you've made since you've been here".

"I've been... busy".

"Uh huh. Aoife, you work out your feelings through your art. No wonder you're so confused right now. Now get to cutting woman!" I laughed.

Flipping through the pages, I cut out pictures that called to me. I don't know why they jumped out at me, it's like my heart chooses things without my brain knowing why. I put them in a pile next to me then tossed the magazines on the floor when I was through with it. Axel handed me another. By the time I got through the huge stack of magazines, I had quite a mountain of pictures and words in varying sizes cut out. None of them made any sense, just random words, letters, and pictures. This was a trust the process situation as most art is.

"Great! Now for the fun part! Make some magic!" We both laughed at his unintended pun.

I got on the floor and spread the pictures out around me so I could see them all. I started grabbing one by one as they jumped out at me and glued them onto the empty board. Without thinking, I was placing them how it felt right. It's hard to explain, it's something that isn't thought about or planned out, it just flowed from me. When I began painting, I didn't know what I'd paint, I didn't go into it with any plan. It just happened. My heart takes over and my body listens and it shows me how I'm feeling or it makes a beautiful picture that makes me happy. It didn't always make sense at the time but once it was finished, it always blew me away how much my art knew me, healed me,

My mountain of pictures began to dwindle, and the board became fuller. I tilted my head to the side and tilted my head to the side, trying to make out what all the pieces formed.

Axel broke the silence first, "Well, that's… something." His voice was a mix of amusement and surprise. "You see what I see right?" Axel asked, startling me. I had been in the art zone so much I had forgotten he was there. But I saw it.

All the images and words were the outline of a head, to be exact, Nick's head. His beard was formed from words that hung vertically. Small pictures of lakes and planets pieced together formed his green eyes. I stepped back more until I felt the bed at the back of my knees and sat on it. We both sat there in silence for a while, I don't know how long, I zoned out with my mind racing.

I just stared at the collage, my mind trying to make sense of what I'd created. I didn't go into it with a plan, I wasn't even thinking about Nick. Yet somehow that beautiful man's face showed up on my canvas. In the past, I trusted my art to help me through hard times, I needed to do the same now. It didn't give me answers, but it helped point me in the right direction. I wanted it so badly to make things easier, instead, it showed what I had been trying to ignore the whole time.

"What do you think it means?" Axel asked, leaning forward and examining the board with a smirk. He knew what it meant.

I sighed, ". I guess it's obvious, though, isn't it?" I waved my hand in the direction of the collage. "He's… he's important to me. That much is clear."

Axel nodded, giving me a serious look. "Aoife, I think it's more than that. This guy is in your head, in your heart. You didn't just choose random pictures, this is how you see him, how he fits into your life."

"Maybe," I whispered, almost scared to admit it. I hadn't been ready to face the reality of how deeply Nick had affected me in such a short time. But now, it was staring back at me, literally.

"Do you love him?" Axel asked bluntly, the kind of direct question only a best friend could ask.

I hesitated, my heart racing. Love? Was it too soon? Could I really know? "I don't know," I said quietly, looking down at my hands. "I'm not sure if I'm ready to know. But… he makes me feel safe, like I can be myself. I haven't had that in a long time."

Axel smiled softly, resting a hand on my shoulder. "That's not something you should ignore. Feeling safe with someone is huge, especially after everything you've been through. You deserve that."

I let his words sink in, glancing back at the college. Nick's face, made up of all the things that called to me, strength, beauty, mystery, connection. It was more than just a random art project. It was a reflection of something I wasn't sure I was ready to acknowledge but knew deep down was true.

"I'm scared, Axel," I admitted finally. "I'm scared of what all this means. Of what choosing this life could mean."

He pulled me into a hug, squeezing me tight. "I know. But you're strong. You've already faced so much. Don't let fear stop you from living the life you're meant to have."

Tears pricked the corners of my eyes, and I buried my face in his shoulder, grateful for his unwavering support. "Thank you, Axel. I don't know what I'd do without you."

"Lucky for you, you'll never have to find out," he said, pulling away just enough to smile at me and hand me tissues. "Wipe your face, woman."

We both looked at the collage again, the weight of the moment settling between us. I didn't have all the answers yet, but at least I knew one thing for certain, I wasn't alone in this. Not with Axel by my side, and maybe, just maybe, with Nick too.

For now, that was enough.

Chapter 21

I woke up with feathers stuck to my face and arms, Axel was beside me, covered in scraps of magazine paper. I couldn't hold back my laughter. We must have fallen asleep right after our art project, and now the room was a chaotic display of our creative frenzy.

My laughter stirred Axel awake. He rubbed his face, dislodging bits of paper as he moved his hand down. He opened his eyes, looked at me, and joined in my laughter. With a playful grin, he grabbed a handful of feathers that had been under me and tossed them in my direction, sending them floating around us like confetti.

In the spirit of the moment, I cupped my hands and summoned a small golden tornado. It whirled to life, drawing in the feathers and swirling them in a mesmerizing dance. I expanded the tornado, letting it grow larger before gradually shutting off the flow of magic from within me. The feathers scattered gracefully in the air, drifting down like autumn leaves, leaving us surrounded by the soft remnants of the morning's magic.

"Show off" Axel said with a huff.

"Don't be jealous, you have a talent too." He looked at me questionably, "yeah, you have the power to clear a room after you eat dairy."

"Har har. I see you're feeling better."

"Yeah, I actually do. I think you were right." I whispered the end.

He cupped his ear and leaned closer to me, "What? I didn't quite hear you. What did you say?"

I sighed, "I said you…were…right."

He smiled, showing me all of his teeth, and patted himself on his back.

"You're such a weirdo. Close your mouth, you have morning breath!" I waved in front of my face.

He blew his breath in my face then, making me cough and wiggle trying to find fresh air. "Go brush your teeth, then let's go get breakfast." I pushed him towards the bathroom.

"Can we order in? Do they have room service here? I'm feeling lazy." he flopped on the bed.

I laughed, "yeah, let me text them and they'll bring food up. Don't get too used to this, you do have to go home at some point."

"And you seem pretty at home here…" he said. I sighed knowing he was right, again. It did feel like home to me.

A knock on the door, I thought it was too soon for the food to be done, but then again, the place was magical. Not much surprised me anymore.

Cami stood at the door, clearly agitated. She couldn't stand still, she fidgeted with her clothing and kept glancing down.

"Oh, hey Cami. What's up?" I tried my best to not sound irritated. I saw Axel peek around the corner, trying to be nosey.

"I um, need to tell you something." I tipped my head to the side wondering what she could possibly tell me. *That her and Nick had a secret affair? That she poisoned our food?* The options running through my mind were endless.

"Okay." I paused, not wanting to invite her in.

She kept looking over her shoulder as if she was afraid someone was watching her. "Can… can I come in? It's not safe to talk out here."

"Um, okay I guess." I hesitantly opened the door wider for her to slip in. Axel stood up as if to show his presence in the room so she wouldn't try anything.

"Is everything okay Cami?"

I sat on the unmade bed while she stood, switching her weight from foot to foot.

"I know something. Something bad is going to happen but I was warned to not tell anyone. I could get in serious trouble if they find out but I don't feel right keeping it a secret."

"Okay, is this something you should be telling Nick?"

"It involves you." My stomach dropped.

She started pacing the room. Speed walking from the door to the window, stopping once only briefly to look at the art project that ended up looking like Nick. She quickly went back to wearing out the carpet in the room.

I tried to pull her attention back to talking, "Just tell me Cami, I don't have the energy for this."

She wrung her hands nervously, "Well, I'm a banshee." She shifted her weight several times again, " A little bit ago I had a coainheadh." She paused like I was supposed to know what that meant.

"Cami, I don't know what that means."

"I sense death, either to people near me or people close to them. The coven warned me to not get involved… to not tell you. But I couldn't keep quiet any longer. I can't keep just letting people die." she rushed out almost incoherently to me. Her expression looked tortured, like she truly was in pain knowing all that information. I almost blew her off but her expression told me that she was struggling with this.

"Talk faster Cami" I was getting impatient at her lack of urgency once she mentioned 'death'.

"What?" The relief that I wasn't the one in danger didn't last long, I was quickly going over the list of people who could be after that.

" I think someone close to you is going to die." She chewed on her bottom lip, clearly nervous. "I'm not supposed to say anything though. They warned me that there'd be consequences if I broke my silence. I know we aren't friends or anything and I don't even know if you believe me, but I had to tell you. I hope you do believe me because I can't feel another death. I feel everything they do, it's just too much." She hugged her arms around herself in an attempt to self soothe.

"We'll talk about all that later, right now let's pretend I believe you. What did you see in this vision?" I urged her on, desperate for a name or clue.

"It was a parking lot," she said, her eyes narrowing in concentration. "There weren't many people around, but there were cars. The building nearby was black, with a mural of a bird on it. There was a woman, heavier set with a brown bob and a man with dark blonde hair, he had a… a mole above his eyebrow. The sun was high, around noon, maybe." she rushed out the details.

My heart sank. I knew that mural, ripping off my pajamas as fast as I could and grabbing the first clothes I could find. Axel looked at me in a panic, he knew the mural too. That painting was a commission piece Susan wanted me to paint for her. "That's Susan's photography studio. " My head was thinking about too many bad scenarios as I grabbed my jacket and shoes, dressing quickly as I listened to Cami's description of the scene. Her words were clipped, and she avoided my gaze as she recounted the details, but I was focused on the information.

"Aoife, do you need me to come? What can I do to help?" Axel asked, clearly worried.

"I…I think I need Nick to go with me. In case it's not normal stuff, ya know." meaning magical. I didn't want Axel to get caught up in that world.

Cami stepped back as I moved toward the door.

"Thanks for telling me." I shouted to her as I ran by. I'd give her a better than you once I got back, hopefully before Susan was hurt. But now, I had to get there ASAP.

I left Axel and Cami without waiting for a response. There was no time for explanations or reassurance. I had to find Susan, and I had to do it fast. I ran out the door, leaving Axel and my nemesis behind, together. It wasn't ideal, knowing they were in the same room made my stomach twist, but I couldn't dwell on that. Susan needed me. Every second felt like it mattered more than the last, so I didn't have time to call Nick. I could only hope he was in his room; if not, I'd leave without him.

When I reached his door, I started pounding on it, my hands shaking as I knocked harder than I intended. The door flew open, and there he was, his eyes wide with confusion and concern. I could barely catch my breath as I began spilling everything I knew, my words a frantic rush.

"Cami told me that Josh is going to kill Susan. We have to go now. We have to save her."

He didn't hesitate. He grabbed my hand, "let's go. The quickest way would be for you to portal us. Can you do that?"

"I um, can try."

"Do you know where?"

"Yeah, she described the parking lot outside of Susan's studio."

"Okay, do your best, the closer you can get us, the better it'll be."

As Nick and I stood there, hands clasped, my pulse raced with such force that I could almost hear it echoing. I squeezed his hands, grounding myself as adrenaline coursed through me. I looked up, meeting his steady gaze, and that was all the reassurance I needed. I took a deep breath, closing my eyes and reaching deep within, letting the magic inside me break free. I imagined it locked away, behind some unseen door, and with a surge of determination, I flung it open.

Warmth spread through me, radiating outwards as I felt the familiar, tingling sensation rise up, flooding every corner of my being. The whirlwind formed around us almost instantly, swirling faster and faster until the world around us was a blur of motion. And then, just like that, we were gone.

When my feet hit solid ground again, I blinked, adjusting to the sudden change. We were there, Susan's building loomed in front of us, its silhouette sharp against the sky. I barely paused to catch my breath before grabbing Nick's hand, pulling him forward, into the parking lot, past rows of cars. My heart raced even faster with dread.

Ahead, I saw him, a man with dirty blonde hair, a familiar figure, hunched as he kicked something on the ground. Someone, not something. I couldn't see who it was from where I stood, but I felt the ice in my veins as reality hit me. Nick didn't wait; he bolted ahead of me, running straight at the man and tackling him to the ground with force. They hit the asphalt hard, rolling as they fought, Nick's strength matching the other man's fury.

I reached the figure on the ground, dropping to my knees beside her. It was Susan. My stomach clenched as I took in her battered face. Blood trickled from the corner of her mouth, a fresh cut above her eye was bleeding heavily, and the swelling had already started. She was curled up, clutching her stomach, her whole body tense with pain. I fought the wave of nausea threatening to overtake me. How could he do that to her?

"Susan," I whispered, reaching out to touch her shoulder gently, trying to reassure her, to let her know she wasn't alone. I felt my anger rise, a hot, consuming fire that made my hands tremble. At that moment, nothing else mattered. I would protect her with everything I had.

"I'm here, Susan. I'm here. I'm so sorry," I whispered, rubbing her arm gently. She blinked her eyes open, her tears mixing with mascara streaked down her cheeks.

"Oh, honey," she managed, her voice soft but full of relief.

A harsh voice cut through the moment. "So, you're the whore's new toy, huh?" Josh sneered, his words dripping with malice.

"Don't talk about her like that," Nick spat, his voice full of controlled fury.

Josh's eyes were wild, a twisted grin on his face. "I'll talk about that little bitch however I want. She ruined me. So, I'm gonna ruin everyone she knows. I will make her suffer!"

The sound of their fight filled the air, the scuffle of shoes on asphalt and the thud of fists landing with bone-jarring impact. I watched, my heart pounded, as Nick landed blow after blow, his face set in fierce determination. But then, with a brutal swing, Josh caught him across the temple. Nick staggered, his eyes unfocused, and for a moment, I saw the vulnerability there, just a split second, but enough to make me afraid.

Josh's face twisted with a sickening grin, eyes gleaming with anticipation as he moved to strike again. My body reacted before my mind could catch up. With adrenaline surging through my veins, I leapt forward, channeling every ounce of anger and fear into action. I swung my leg around in a roundhouse kick, striking Josh hard in the kidney, taking him by surprise. He gasped, his whole body recoiling as he doubled over, clutching his side.

Not giving him a second to recover, I threw a quick jab into his stomach, feeling the resistance of muscle and flesh as he jerked forward, groaning in pain. I followed through with a swift uppercut to his chin, the force of the blow snapping his head back. His eyes rolled up, and he crumpled to the ground, limp and unconscious.

I stood there, breathing hard, watching him lie motionless on the ground. Every muscle in my body was tense, ready for him to get up again, but he stayed down. I felt the fight drain out of me all at once, leaving a hollow ache behind. I glanced over at Nick, his eyes meeting mine with a look that was equal parts relief and respect.

Nick shook his head, trying to clear the dizziness as he got back up. I rushed to him, checking his face for injuries. "Are you okay?"

He nodded, still slightly dazed. "Go to her," he urged.

I turned back to Susan, who was watching the fight with wide eyes, her hands still cradling her stomach. "You did it, honey. You got him," she whispered, a small smile breaking through her pain.

As I knelt beside Susan, I felt a surge of emotions rise up, threatening to spill over, but I swallowed them down, trying to stay strong for her. I helped her sit up slowly, whispering apologies that tumbled out in a rush, each one a little louder than the last. "I'm so sorry, Susan. I never wanted you to get hurt. This is all my fault."

She reached for my hand, squeezing it weakly but firmly. "Stop it," she murmured, the warmth of her voice betraying the pain in her eyes. "You didn't do this. I'm so proud of you, Aoife. You're stronger than you know."

Nick was already on the phone with the police, his tone steady, his gaze fixed on Josh, who lay unconscious on the asphalt. When the distant wail of sirens cut through the still night air, relief washed over me, but it did nothing to ease the heavy guilt that had settled in my chest. I felt as though the weight of it might crush me. If I hadn't pulled her into my world, maybe she wouldn't be lying there, bruised and bleeding. I couldn't shake the feeling that I'd let her down, that was all on me.

Soon, flashing lights flooded the parking lot, painting the scene in red and blue. The paramedics were efficient but gentle as they lifted Susan onto a stretcher, all while she continued to murmur words of reassurance, refusing to let me shoulder any of the blame. Yet, as they took her away, her hand slipping from mine, I felt the loss keenly, the sting of knowing I'd have to live with this, carry it with me like a scar I'd never fully heal from.

Josh regained consciousness just as the police arrived, his shouts piercing through the night as he struggled against the officers, cursing at me with the venom of a man who had lost everything. I watched as he was cuffed and roughly pushed into the back of the squad car. His face was smeared with blood from the cuts he sustained; a thick trickle seeping from the gash above his eye, dripping into mouth. He spat blood in my direction but the squad car had its windows up, the blood splattered across it, distorting my view of him, he truly looked like the monster he was.

He glared at me with a hatred that was cold and unyielding. As I met his eyes, I realized I felt nothing for him. No fear, no sympathy, no regret, not even the lingering love that had once held me captive. Whatever hold he had over me was gone. In that moment, I knew that he could no longer hurt me. He was powerless, caged by his own rage, and I was free.

I turned away from him, taking a deep breath as the weight began to lift. For the first time, I felt whole. He had taken so much from me, stolen parts of myself I thought I'd never get back, but standing there, I realized that I'd reclaimed every bit of it. I had my power back. And for that, I was finally at peace.

Nick pulled me into a tight, almost crushing hug as soon as the paramedics had finished examining him. His warmth seeped into me, steadying the tremor that had lingered in my bones. I squeezed him back, drawing strength from his presence, relieved that his injuries amounted to only a mild concussion and a few bruises. He would be fine, but it did little to quell the swirling guilt in my mind about Susan. The list of people that got hurt because of me grew.

We decided to take a taxi to the hospital, avoiding the attention that magic could bring. During the ride, the city lights passed by in a blur, my thoughts racing just as quickly. I kept replaying everything over and over, wondering how it could have gone differently. If we got there later, Susan may have not made it out alive. If we'd gotten there sooner it could have all been prevented.

The bright lights of the hospital parking lot woke me out of my worrying spiral. At the hospital, we sat in a cold, sterile waiting room while the doctors looked after Susan. When they finally came out, I held my breath, bracing for the worst. But their words were reassuring. Susan had a fractured rib, a small cut on her forehead, and some bruises, but no internal bleeding. She'd recover in time, and they seemed optimistic about her healing process.

Relief washed over me, yet it was tinged with bitterness. It shouldn't have happened at all. If I'd been stronger back then, if I'd pressed charges against Josh, if I'd called him out when I had the chance, maybe he would have been locked up; unable to hurt anyone else. But he had hidden his true self so well, cloaked himself in lies and charm that made it impossible for others to see the monster beneath. Back then, no one would have believed me. No one ever saw what he really was.

Sitting there, I realized there was no point in looking back, no point in wondering "what if." Those days were gone. The only thing I could do was move forward, to be stronger and never let someone like him have that kind of power again, not over me, not over anyone. I took a deep breath, hoping that the past would finally release its grip and let me step into the future, one where I could protect those I loved and let go of the shadows that once held me captive.

I insisted on covering Susan's medical bills, believing this was all my fault. Of course, Nick stepped in and refused to let me pay for anything. " I feel so guilty."

Nick's grip tightened, holding me together when my emotions wanted to fall apart. "You can't control what other people do. But you *did* control what you could. You got her out of there. You stopped him. That counts for something. I'm so sorry this happened," he said, his voice tinged with frustration. "If Cami had told us sooner, we could've gotten here before the attack."

I cut him off. "It's not Cami's fault," surprising even myself. "She wanted to tell you. It was the coven that told her not to get involved. They thought that because Susan is human, it wasn't their concern. Cami could have paid a high price for defying them, but she did the right thing by coming to me. If it weren't for her, we might have been too late."

Nick nodded, though he still looked tense. I realized that maybe I'd misjudged Cami. She had taken a risk to save Susan, and that counted for something.

"You're right. I'm sorry, I'm just so angry, and I need someone to blame. The coven kept a secret, and it nearly cost someone their life. Human or magical, all lives are precious."

"So, what are you going to do about it?" I asked, crossing my arms.

"I… I don't know what I can do. The coven operates separately from K Corp. They support us in a lot of ways, and I'm not sure we can afford to lose them."

"So you're okay with them ignoring danger and letting people get killed just because they're human? How far will this go? Who else will get hurt because of their vendetta against people? You have the power to change things, Nick. You literally run the company! Do something about it."

He was silent, deep in thought I presumed. I pressed him further. "Either you make changes there, or I'll make them myself. I can't be around people or businesses that think so little of humans. I refuse to be associated with that kind of hatred. I haven't decided if I'll keep my magic or give it up, but either way, if you don't make changes to protect people, I won't be around."

He looked taken aback by my ultimatum. "I need time to figure this out, Aoife. Please, just give me some time. I know you had a big night and I have no right to tell you how to feel but I also can't tell the coven how to conduct their business."

"I don't know how it all works. What I do know is that if you run this company that's supposed to help creatures, yet refuse to help humans, then you're a hypocrite. If you aren't going to step up and actually run the company, you might as well just hand it over to the coven. Then they can do whatever they want, they do that anyway." He looked shocked that I said that. I was shocked I said that. I'd never spoken to anyone like that. It felt good to finally speak my mind. "I have been pushed around, bullied, and coerced by Josh for years. I refuse to go through that again with the coven calling the shots. It's time for you to figure out what kind of leader you want to be Nick. When you decide, let me know."

I was frustrated at his lack of urgency, but I knew change wouldn't happen overnight. I had to admit, I didn't fully understand what it was like to run a massive business. I decided I'd give him a little time to work things out. I gave Susan a kiss on the cheek, a promise that I'd be back.

"I'm going to take you back to K Corp," I said, sighing. "But I think I'm going to pack my bags and leave for now. I… need some time away. I need space to think."

We walked to the back alley behind the hospital silently. I held out my hand for him to take. He didn't grab it with his usual confidence; his touch was hesitant, almost cautious. I let my magic rise, it wasn't hard; it seemed to simmer close to the surface when I was upset. The warmth surged, and in a whirl of gold. As we arrived back at K Corp, the swirling golden light of my magic faded, and I quickly pulled my hand from Nick's, turning away without a word. There was a tension lingering between us now, thick and unspoken. I needed space, to escape from the suffocating weight that had built up from the night's events. The building seemed to close in on me, walls heavy with every moment that had just unraveled, so much devastation, all of it avoidable.

I hurried to my room, where I found Axel waiting, worry etched deep into his face. Before I could say a word, he reached out, his eyes scanning over me, piecing together the blood on my clothes, the mess I must've looked. I managed to mutter, "It's not my blood," my voice barely more than a whisper.

He guided me over to the bed, his hand firm but gentle on my shoulder as I sank down. "Whose blood is it, Aoife?" he asked, his voice tight with concern.

"It's Susan's," I admitted, and then, almost as an afterthought, "and maybe some of Josh's." There was a flicker of pride in me that I couldn't quite extinguish, but it was buried beneath layers of exhaustion and guilt.

"What? E, you've got to give me more than that. What happened?"

"Josh was attacking Susan…because of me." The words slipped out, laced with shame that I could no longer hold back. I was the reason she was hurt, and that knowledge weighed heavily on me.

He sat down beside me, the worry in his eyes softening as he absorbed my words. "Oh, E. Is she okay?"

"She will be. She's still in the hospital, but she'll be alright." I rubbed at my temples, trying to block out the memory of seeing her blood, of knowing it was Josh who'd done it because of the way I had unwittingly provoked him. "I can't leave her there alone," I said, almost to myself, the thought of returning to her making my stomach twist. "I still can't believe this happened because of me."

Axel placed a steadying hand on my shoulder. "This wasn't your doing, E. Josh attacked her because he's a weak man with a twisted mind. You didn't make him do anything."

"He said I ruined his life," I whispered, my throat tightening as tears began to fall. "He blames me for everything."

Axel's grip tightened, a reassuring presence. "Josh brought this all on himself. His life is in shambles because of his own choices. Don't let him twist this around to make it your fault. You've fought too hard to let him drag you back down with him. Remember your strength, E. Don't let him gaslight you again."

I nodded, the ache in my chest easing just enough to allow me to take a deep breath. His words reminded me of all I had overcome, how much I had grown since breaking free from Josh's hold. And I knew Axel was right. I had to stay strong, not just for Susan, but for myself. I was no longer the person Josh could control or manipulate, and I wouldn't let him have that power over me again.

I started packing a bag to leave. Axel didn't ask what I was doing, he knew better. He let me work through my emotions in my own way.

I wanted to feel like the confident woman who escaped an abusive relationship and carved her own path but at that second, I felt like the person that I was before. I needed to not let Josh determine my fate. I straightened my shoulders, "You're right. I can't let Josh control me anymore. I made my life what it is. I am a good person. I deserve good people in my life that support me." Josh was just one of my obstacles, the coven also had a hand in Susan getting hurt. Josh will be punished by the law, but what consequences will the coven have? Will they do it again, how many more people will get hurt because of them?

There was a gentle knock at the door, Axel opened the door for Huyen. She smiled at him as she rushed past to hug me. "I heard what happened. Are you okay?"

"I'm fine, but my friend isn't. We stopped him before he hurt her too badly but she could have died because the coven refused to say anything. That's not right." I shook my head, still reeling.

Axel knew it was girl time so he evacuated to the bathroom to give us space to talk. He was the smartest man I knew when it came to what women need.

"I know, Aoife. But she'll be okay. You got there in time. The coven is set in the old ways. They still think the human and magical worlds should remain separate."

"Are you really defending them right now?" I felt the anger rising in my voice.

"No, I'm not," she said quickly. "What they did was wrong. I just meant… this is how things have been since the beginning of magic. When people ridiculed us for being different, they hunted some of us to extinction. It's a lot of years of hurt to overcome."

"I understand hurt. But letting people get hurt because of some ancient feud is just wrong. All they had to do was make one phone call. They didn't even have to get involved! One call could've saved her from all this." I resumed packing, shaking my head. "I can't stay here if humans are seen as disposable. Their lives are just as worthy."

"You're right. I'm so sorry you got caught up in all this."

"It's not your fault. It's the coven's. And Nick can change things. But I can't stay here until he does. I hope you understand."

"I do," she replied, her voice thick with emotion. "I'll miss you so much. You'll keep in touch, no matter where you go, right?"

"I will." I tried to smile, grateful for her support. "Thanks for always being there. This place was overwhelming, but you made it feel… almost like home." I barely whispered the last words, feeling the weight of them settle in. It almost felt like home, until I didn't feel safe anymore. I didn't know where I fit in after that.

Axel came out of the bathroom when he knew Huyen left and the coast was clear. He was a guy but a smart one, he knew when to not speak. He helped me pack a bag. My hands were shaking from adrenaline, he patted my hands and took over packing for me.

Once I calmed down, we sat on the bed to talk before I left. "Axel, I'm sorry you just got here and now I have to leave. I can drop you back off at home if you want but I have to go be with Susan."

"I get it E. and don't be mad at me for saying this, but I think you should give Cami a chance. We uh, talked while you were gone," I sure hope he meant actually talked and not 'talk'. "She has had a really rough life, Nick rescued her so she felt drawn to him, but she doesn't love him. She knows you two are soulmates. Can't blame a girl for trying to get that man. Heck if I was a girl, I'd probably try to get him too!"

I slapped his arm, cry-laughing. He handed me a wad of tissues. "I know, I was jealous at first, but I think I've misjudged her too. She didn't have to tell me about the vision or the coven. She did, knowing she could be punished for speaking the truth. That shows a lot of character. I just can't deal with that right now. Susan is my focus. I have to make sure she'll be okay."

"Agreed. I am glad she's OK, or will be. You did good, E. I hope you can look back at this and see how strong you were, how strong you are."

"Thanks. I mean it, I really appreciate you being here. I'm sure this wasn't the vacation you imagined."

"I mean, I got to see my bestie, eat the best damn burger I've ever had, I flew on a private jet, aaaand I got a girl's number."

I was supportive of him until that last part, "Um, what?" You've been here a few hours, whose number did you get?"

"Don't be mad E, after you left we started talking and we just hit it off."

"You mean Cami?" I almost couldn't believe what I just heard. Never in a million years did I expect that. It felt like I had a knife stuck in my back.

"Yeah, she's not what we thought. We're not getting married or anything, but she's cool E. And she knows about cars! Do you know how rare that is?"

"I know about cars!"I said defensively.

"Only because I make you watch "Garage Wars" with me."

"So how does she know about cars?" Probing to see how much he actually knew about her.

"Well, that's a long story, and I don't want you to judge her for her past. Like you, she was in a bad situation and couldn't get out." I nodded, letting him know I'd hear him out, "her family ran a chop shop. She was forced to help scrap the cars as a kid." So that was what Nick rescued her from, a family of criminals. She was just trying to survive, and she was a child, it's not like she could say no. I did think I judged her too quickly.

"Okay, I hear you. I will give her a chance. Is she done hitting on Nick though?"

"Well, she has me now." He put his arms up like Vanna White, displaying his body. I couldn't help but laugh.

"I guess." I said making a face.

"I'm offended" he clutched his pretend pearl necklace. "Thanks E. It means a lot. Someday when we get married, I want you to be my best wo-man" He was such an idiot, and the best friend anyone could ever ask for.

As we held hands, our bags looped over our arms, I let the warmth overtake me. The gold swirled, getting faster and faster until I felt weightless. I opened my eyes to see Axel, his expression was the best thing I've ever seen. I didn't think his eyes could get any larger than they were then, his mouth dropped open in awe and wonder. I closed my eyes again, imagining being in his room.

I felt my feet hit the ground. When I opened them again, we were in a dark blue room, with an unmade bed and clothes thrown over every inch of it.

"The wind, tornado thingy must have uh, thrown my clothes all over. What a mess it made!" I laughed, knowing damn well Axel made that mess.

"You did not just blame your messy room on my magic!"

He shrugged, "It was worth a try".

"You forget that I know you."

"Too good it seems. Maybe Cami loves cleaning and wants nothing more than to stay at home and clean up after me, while making me tacos? A guy can dream".

"Did you really just go all misogynistic on me? Axel Adams Miller, you know better!"

"I do, I'm sorry. You've been gone for so long, I slipped up without you keeping me in check."

"I've been gone for a few days."

He held up three fingers, "I swear I will not turn into a douchebag man who doesn't respect women. I solemnly swear to listen to them and to uphold their beautiful, soft, curvy, warm bodies as often as I have the chance. Against a wall, on the table,…"

I cut him off before he could list off more places, "Ew. Seriously, did you just make up that disgusting oath?"

"Yes, yes I did. I thought it was pretty good."

"You would. Alright, I have to go. Be careful okay, I don't know if I can handle another friend getting hurt. And clean up this room, it smells like a locker room."

"Yes mother. You be careful too. And give that place a chance. Give *him* a chance. I see how you've changed. You're growing E, don't run from your future because you're scared of change." Change didn't scare me then to be honest, the thought of Nick not making the changes needed scared me more.

"I could save so much money and stop going to therapy and just talk to you."

"Oh, I am not cheap Ms. Wheeler, You couldn't afford me."

We hugged, and did a fist bump, slap and wiggled our fingers, our handshake for each other. I left him in his messy room, while being whisked off by my magic to make sure my friend was safe.

Chapter 22

Sitting in a cold, uncomfortable chair at the hospital, I watched over Susan, guilt gnawing at my soul. I picked my nails until they were raw and there was nothing left to torture myself with. She had been attacked by my ex-husband, all because he was angry with me. An innocent bystander, she had simply tried to help. How could I stand by and let other innocent people get hurt? The surge of empathy and the drive to stop this injustice swelled within me.

"Hi, honey," she squeaked out, her voice hoarse.

I jumped to attention. "Oh my goodness, Susan! You're awake! How are you feeling? Do you need me to get your doctor?" I rattled off the questions, unsure of what to do.

"No, no, honey. I'm fine. You've been here the whole time?"

"Well, I had an errand to run, but I came right back. I needed to make sure you were okay and to apologize."

"You have nothing to apologize for, you hear me? Nothing! Josh was bound to hit rock bottom and take it out on someone. I was just an easy target. This is not your fault."

Tears streamed down my face. "If you hadn't helped me, he wouldn't have gotten to you."

"You can't think like that. Him snapping was inevitable with a fragile man like that. They got him, right? He's in jail?" She asked with hopeful eyes.

"They did. He's in custody. They assured me he wouldn't be getting out anytime soon. The police are waiting to talk to you about your side of it." I wasn't sure how much she'd seen, and I hoped she hadn't witnessed my little magic trick, so I kept that part to myself.

"I don't remember much, just Josh waiting for me to come to my car. I didn't realize who he was at first. He started yelling at me for stealing you away from him. He tried attacking me, I tried to get the pepper spray from my purse but he ripped it away from me, I fell at some point and hit my head." She felt her head, the wound now bandaged up, and winced as she touched it. "I just remember those ugly loafers he liked to wear coming at me. He kicked me so hard in the stomach, I couldn't breathe."

I tried to maintain a steady, calm face for her, but knew it was slipping. As she recalled the details of the attack, I had flashbacks of my own. Night when he'd throw things at me when he was upset, but he never actually attacked me. What he did to Susan, it was beyond what I thought he was capable of.

She continued after a few deep breaths, "I must have gotten a bad bump on my head because I swear I saw a puff of gold, then there you were. I must have been hallucinating." She paused, her eyes searching mine. "How did you get there so fast? I thought you were away working?"

I hated lying to her, but I had to keep her out of the magical world, for her own safety. "I, um, was in the neighborhood and was going to check in and say hi. It was just good timing." She had been nothing but good to me, but I had already put her in danger from the 'normal' world. A shiver ran down my spine at the thought of the dangers the magical one could bring her.

"Well, aren't I the lucky one?" she said with a painful smile.

"I'll tell the police you're awake. I kept holding them off; they tried to wake you up, but I wouldn't let them."

"Hey, I don't want you to let this affect you. You shouldn't live in fear because of what happened to me. I saw how you took care of that dirtbag. You kicked his ass! You're not the scared woman I met years ago. You've reclaimed your power. Don't you dare go back to living in fear, you hear me?"

"I hear you," I choked out, the words feeling unconvincing as they left my lips.

"I might have hit my head, but I know what I saw. You're magic, baby." I gasped. Had she seen my magical entrance? "I mean it! I saw how you beat him up and then helped your...who was that handsome man with you, by the way? Aoife, you haven't told me about him!"

I sighed in relief; she hadn't seen my magic but now I had to try and explain Nick to her. "Oh, that's Nick. He's been helping me with something. He's great, but..." I trailed off.

"But what, honey?"

"There's something I need him to do, to change. He could help keep a lot of people safe, but I think he's scared to make the change."

"Change is hard. You know this firsthand," she said, giving me a knowing look. That reality checked me a bit. I did know how difficult change could be. Maybe I needed to give Nick some grace as he figured out how to handle the situation. Susan was ever the wealth of knowledge. I appreciated her so much.

"You may be right," I conceded, contemplating how I could better support him in this transition.

"He's cute, by the way," she said with a wink.

"Oh, not you too! My mom did the same thing, and he's not that cute." I rolled my eyes, trying to convince myself that he wasn't that handsome...even though he really was.

"Ooookay." She knew I was lying to myself.

"I'll go get that policewoman now so you can make your report. You seem to be doing much better, sassy pants." I joked, making her laugh.

I took a moment to call Nick back while Susan was making her police report. I felt bad ignoring him, but I wasn't ready to let go of my anger yet. Still, Susan had talked some sense into me. I was being too hard on him.

My heart raced as I pushed the 'call' button. "Aoife," he answered in an unsure tone.

"Hi Nick."

"I'm glad you called. I, uh, I'm sorry I didn't respond better to the situation. But I have a plan now. Would you be willing to come back, just for a bit? Then you can leave again if you want. I'd like you to be here when I announce the changes to how K Corp will work."

He had a plan, which meant he'd thought about what I said and was willing to listen, even if it took him a while to get there. Josh would have never considered that he was even doing anything wrong or listened to my input. I had to at least give Nick a chance.

"I'll come back, just to hear you out. I can't promise anything."

I heard an audible sigh over the line. "Thank you, Aoife. Thank you. How is Susan doing?"

"She's… good. She's good. The doctors say she'll heal up fast."

"We can send the coven to speed up the healing if you'd like." He paused, knowing I wouldn't be comfortable with that after what they just did. They put her in this situation; why would I let them anywhere near her? "I'm sorry, I wasn't thinking."

"Nick, I know you're trying to change things, but I won't trust them until I hear the changes and see them follow through."

"I understand."

"I'll come back in a little bit," I said, feeling defeated. I had to hang up or I would just get mad at him for talking. When I returned to Susan's room, the police had just finished and were giving her the case information before they left.

"You okay?" I asked her.

"I'm okay, honey. How are you? Was that Nick?"

I sighed. "Yes, it was. He wants me to come back so he can share the changes he wants to make there."

"You need to go, honey. I know you don't want to, but you need to hear him out. He's not Josh. He cares about your opinion and is willing to change for you. That's not something to snub your nose at."

That cut deep. She knew I was being stubborn. "I know. I will listen to him.

I can't guarantee it'll be enough, though."

"Good for you, Hun. Listen to your gut about this. Just don't go into it with rage in your heart; give him a chance."

"I will. Promise."

"Go, go. I'm fine. I'm in good hands here."

"Are you sure?"

"I know you're just trying to avoid going there, but I won't be your scapegoat. Go. Sort this out."

"I'll be back to check on you. Don't go eloping with any of the cute male nurses, okay?"

"Can't guarantee that one." She winked. I hugged her and left her with a kiss on the cheek.

Chapter 23

I walked out to the back alley behind the hospital, imagining K Corp, the front reception area with its large Christmas tree, wreaths adorning the walls, and Huyen standing behind the desk, always there when anyone needed her. I let the warmth take over, surrendering to its pull. The gold enveloped me.

The white walls of K Corp materialized. I made it. A sigh of unease escaped my lips. I didn't know how it was going to play out. So many unanswered questions loomed over me, and countless ways it could end. I tried not to predict what Nick would do; I didn't want to set myself up for disappointment.

Huyen glided up to me, squeezing me tightly from behind, surprising me, until it was difficult to breathe. I grasped her arms, holding on for dear life as my tears broke loose again. She spun me around and hugged me deeper, tucking a handful of tissues into my hand as I cried, laughter bubbling up between my sobs.

She whispered in my ear, "I had a feeling you'd be back, and I wanted to be ready."

"You're too good to me," I murmured into her shoulder.

"I'm so glad you're here. Nick won't tell anyone what he's planning, but the coven is all unsettled over him changing things. He's been waiting for you. He was afraid you wouldn't come back. Thank you for giving him a chance to make this right."

I pulled away, wiping my tears. "I can't guarantee how I'll react or that I will stay, but I promise to give him… well, it's a chance." I couldn't guarantee I'd forgive Nick, but I was open to hearing what changes he'd make, then maybe depending on the outcome, maybe he'd get a chance too.

Right on cue, Nick walked into the reception area, pausing to brush back his hair with his hand, clearly nervous. He froze. Huyen smiled at me as I approached him.

"You're here," he said with a sigh of relief.

"I am." I said shortly. "I, uh, wanted to thank you for bringing Axel here for me. It was a great surprise and it helped a lot."

"It was no problem, I imagine people get homesick when they first come here. I wanted you to know that you didn't give up your other life."

"It was…overwhelming. It was very thoughtful." I said, trying to soften my tone.

"Thank you for giving me a chance."

"Yup. So when will all this start?" I was at the end of my emotional rope, I had no more time for fake conversations.

He stumbled over his words. "R… right now, if you want."

I nodded, holding on to my anger. He motioned for me to follow him down the hallway behind the reception area, toward the conference room. I knew it well by then. I didn't wait for him; I walked in and took the closest seat. Nick pushed a button on his phone, and alerts began beeping on multiple people's devices, indicating a mass text. People started filing into the room, filling chairs until it was packed, with several others standing deep into the hallway. I had never seen that many people there before. Though I used the term "people" loosely, there were plenty of horns, whiskers, and floppy ears present.

Nick motioned for the coven to stand near the front of the room. Their faces were cold, showing no emotion, but their tight shoulders and clenched jaws betrayed their anger.

Nick began, "We're discussing how to prevent a future issue like the one we faced yesterday. The coven made a decision that affected the whole community, minus Pauwau, she is independent from the coven." His tone was firm and commanding. Pauwau nodded at him in response.

"We have told you; we do what's best for the entire community," one coven member spoke up rudely.

"So, because Susan wasn't in your community, she wasn't worth saving? She was in *my* community. She is my friend and a good person who didn't deserve what happened to her. What you did to her…" It exploded out of me. I couldn't stop it.

"You're new here. Our community has been persecuted for centuries. We have to protect our own."

"If you see someone as expendable just because they aren't magical, I can't be here. I don't trust that kind of thinking. Everyone deserves protection." I began to push myself up to stand, and Nick hadn't said anything else yet. Maybe he was letting me vent, or maybe he was just a coward. I hadn't decided yet.

"Aoife is right," he finally said. "If you don't believe everyone is worth saving, you're doing more harm than good."

"We protect our community," they repeated in unison.

"Aoife trusted us to keep her and her loved ones safe. You knew about the danger yet refused to tell anyone. You didn't keep them safe. *I* didn't keep them safe. You put me in a bad situation." He paused. "Things will be changing around here. Either you sign a new oath to protect everyone you can, human and magical alike, or you will be cast out of K Corp and the network forever."

I felt my eyes widen. He was actually doing something. Would he follow through? That was my new question.

"You wouldn't dare. You need us," they hissed.

"We will be just fine, and I can bet there's another coven willing to support our cause who would be happy to help and enjoy all the benefits that come along with it," he said, gesturing toward the walls of the building.

The coven leaned in toward each other, whispering among themselves. The oldest member spoke up, "We won't go against our community."

"And I'm not asking you to. I'm asking you to view everyone as equally important, human and magical. Every life is precious and deserves to be treated as such."

They sat in silence for a while, and then the oldest one said, "We agree to your terms."

"I want you to promise that there will be no retaliation against Cami for helping us either."

The old one looked upset at Nick's demand regarding Cami. Maybe she already had something planned.

Nick spoke first. "Cami and anyone who shares knowledge of your misdoings in the past or future will never be harmed. Agreed." This time, it wasn't a question or a suggestion; it was a demand. Strong and confident looked good on Nick.

She sighed, "Agreed."

"There are no more second chances with this coven. Follow these rules, and we'll get along just fine. But go against our agreement, and you'll be cast out. We won't be quiet about it. I know how much the witches cherish their position in the corporation; it wouldn't be smart to be the ones to lose that privilege."

He laid out a large sheet of tan, thick paper, on it had scrolled letters with detailed rulings on the new laws. There was a large space at the bottom of it for signatures, Nick reached for the pen and in his usually fancy handwriting, wrote his name. He laid the pen down and gestured to the coven to follow his lead. They huffed as they each picked up the pen and signed their names.

With that, he stood up and lent me a hand to pull me up too. "Thank you. I look forward to starting a new, better future together at K Corp. Good day," he said with a nod as he walked out. That was it. I was a little in shock. I hadn't seen him assert himself like that before.

Once we got out of the hallway and past the front desk, he picked me up and swung me around with a big smile on his face. I was confused but liked seeing him happy. I wasn't ready to let go of my anger. He showed me he could accept change, but so much had happened, I was cautious.

"That felt great! I should have done that a long time ago! Thank you for giving me the courage."

"I didn't do anything, but I'm happy to help, I guess." I said a little unsure how to act. I was torn between anger and hope, not ready to fully give into either at that moment.

"Are you kidding? You were so strong! You spoke your truth and did it with grace. I value you. I value your opinion. We… I need you here."

There was a pause, I didn't know what to say to that.

"Would you consider staying and taking on a leadership role? By my side," he added.

I looked away so I could think; I couldn't focus clearly while looking at his beautiful face. I grabbed hold of my broach I attached to a necklace. The tingle of magic flowed through me, making me feel more anxious. He took it as a sign I was saying 'no.'

"It's okay. I understand. You have a regular life to get back to."

"That's not it. I'm not saying no. I just… I'm not sure I'm ready for that kind of stress yet. I'm pretty overwhelmed with life at the moment."

"Of course. You can take all the time you need to think about it. Whenever you're ready, let me know either way. I won't be upset, I promise." And he left it at that.

As I watched him walk away, I felt a mixture of gratitude and confusion swirling inside me. I knew he meant it, and it stirred something within me. Perhaps there was a place for me there after all, but the thought of taking on more responsibility felt daunting. I turned back toward the reception area, taking a deep breath as I tried to gather my thoughts.

As he was walking away, he added, "What's mine is yours here. If you need anything at all, let me know or Huyen, she'll get you whatever you need." He gave me space, and I was glad. I couldn't think with him around. My heart was screaming to run and jump into his arms, but my brain wanted me to slow down and think rationally.

I sat in the restaurant for a while, sipping coffee. A concerned looking chef brought me out a slice of tiramisu. I picked at it for a bit, not really having much of an appetite but it was a kind gesture.

It was nice to know things were working out for the most part. I just had to wait and see how the new rules played out, if people in the company would follow through and protect humans too. He was trying to keep everyone safe and figuring out his role as the new head of this company. I knew there would be growing pains with the change, so I didn't expect it to shift immediately. I just hoped no one else would get hurt while everyone adjusted. I wanted to pick Huyen's brain on this one. I could use a friend to vent to.

I headed down to the front desk to find Huyen.

"Hi, Aoife. What can I do for you?" She propped her chin up on her arm, resting on the marble countertop.

"I want to know what you think about today. Do you think the coven will follow the new rules?"

She laughed a little. "They'd be stupid not to. This place is a prize for any coven; they'd be shunned in the community if they got banned from here."

"This place is thought of that highly?"

"Oh yes. The work Nick's family has done for the magical community is massive. They're pretty big in the magical community. Creatures would kill for a chance to help out here."

While that was impressive that they had such a great reputation, I wondered how they'd take it, dealing with humans now too. "Do you think they'll protect humans?"

"Nick sent out the oath to all of the K Corp branches worldwide and interdimensional. I guarantee they'll be signed and honored. No one would dare go against K Corp."

That made me feel better. "Thanks, Huyen. I appreciate your candor. I wanted to believe Nick, but I worry he'd just say or do something to impress me. I wanted the honest truth."

"Nick is many things, but a liar isn't one of them. He is a man of his word. You can trust him. Give him time. I know you haven't had a great track record with men treating you well, but Nick, he's a different breed."

Her words settled in my mind, a quiet reassurance that flickered like a candle in the dark. Maybe she was right; perhaps Nick was the kind of person I could trust. But the weight of my past lingered, casting shadows on my hope.

"Do you think I'm overthinking this?" I asked, my voice barely above a whisper.

"No," she replied firmly. "You're just being cautious, and that's okay. Trust takes time, especially after what you've been through. Just take it one step at a time. And remember, you're not alone in this. You have a whole community backing you now."

I smiled at her encouragement, feeling a warmth spread in my chest. "You're right. I need to give myself permission to take it slow."

"Exactly. Now, go enjoy that tiramisu I saw chef brought out to you. It's one of his best creations," she winked.

I went back and took another bite, savoring the rich flavors. With Huyen's support and Nick's determination, maybe I could start to believe in the possibility of something new and better, for both myself and the people I cared about.

After I ate a little of the dessert, I needed to have a conversation with Nick. I couldn't have uncertainty hanging in the air between us. I found Huyen at the desk, "Have you seen him by any chance?"

"He's in the workshop again."

"He's been working a lot lately, huh?"

"Yeah, he tends to do that when he gets stressed. I think it's a place he feels he can control the outcome."

"Well, that's very perceptive of you."

She shrugged. "I just pay attention."

"Thanks, Huyen." I headed toward the workshop. There were a lot of workers scattered around the machines, moving in a grid pattern from the storage bins to the center conveyor area. I found Nick at the last machine, covered in soot.

"Everything okay?" I asked him. He must not have seen me walk up; I had never seen him jump before.

"Um, yeah, fine. Just needed to give her a tune-up. She's one of our more...

temperamental machines, but she's also our biggest producing one. Some things just need a little more attention than others." He said this with a little half-grin at the end, a spark of the old Nick. "What brings you all the way down here?"

"Well, I wanted to check on you."

"I'm fine; I should be the one checking up on you."

"I'm fine, or I will be at least. Susan wants me to not live in anger. I promised her I'd try to give this place a chance." I didn't want him to think I was still giving him a chance, maybe I was, but I hadn't had time to decide with everything going on.

"Hey, Nick?" I asked as he bent back under the machine.

He poked his head out. "Yeah?"

"You wanna watch a movie or something tonight? If you have time, that is. I see you're busy with things here, so it's okay if you can't. Don't feel obligated." I wanted to make sure he had an out if he didn't want to. I wouldn't blame him; I hadn't been the easiest to deal with.

His smile reached his eyes, making them crinkle at the corners ever so slightly. "I'd love to. She's pretty much all patched up anyway." he slid out, holding a dirty rag in his hands attempting to wipe them off.

"You want to get cleaned up first?" I asked, wiping some soot off his cheek.

"What? You don't like my new look?" he said, striking a pose with a playful smirk.

"I like all your looks, but I like when I can see your beautiful face best." I turned to walk away, giving him a wink.

"Wait!" he called after me, and I glanced back, heart racing.

He hesitated for a moment, his expression shifting to something more serious. "I appreciate you coming down here. It means a lot to me, really."

I nodded, feeling warmth spread through my chest. "Just trying to be a good friend."

"Friend, huh?" He leaned against the machine, arms crossed, a teasing glint in his eyes. "Is that all I am?"

"For now, yes," I shot back with a grin, but I could feel my cheeks warm under his gaze.

"Alright then. I'll see you tonight." He turned back to his machine, but not before I caught a glimpse of that hopeful smile lingering on his face.

As I walked away, I couldn't shake the feeling that it could be something special. There was still so much uncertainty between us, but perhaps it was time to explore our connection. I took a deep breath, ready to face whatever came next.

"Hey, Aoife?" he called after me.

"Yeah, Nick?" I turned around to look at him, curious about what he might say next.

"Thanks."

"For what?" I asked, genuinely confused.

"Just for being… you."

"It's all I can be." I shrugged, chuckled, and headed out. Butterflies started to take over my stomach. Why was I so nervous? I'd hung out with Nick before. Was it because I was still mad at him? No, I thought he dealt with that tough situation very well. My flip-flopping stomach made it hard to think.

Huyen smiled as I walked back out of the break room. "I see it must have gone well?"

"We are going to watch a movie tonight and just… be."

"Oh, a movie, huh?" She raised an eyebrow and winked.

"Yes, just a movie. I thought it would be good for Nick and me to get comfortable with each other again."

"Shall I give the chef a heads-up that you two may be ordering food?"

I thought about it; after the horrible hospital food, the restaurant food did sound nice. "Sure, why not? Might as well take advantage of the benefits of this place while I can." That comment made her think I may not be staying, so I added, "I haven't made up my mind yet. We'll see how things go with Nick, I guess." She visibly relaxed at that.

"Okay, good. Glad you're giving it a chance."

Just then, Nick walked out of the break room, wiping his hands on a cloth, the rest of him covered in black grease.

Huyen laughed, "You're gonna need more than a cloth for that mess, boss."

He looked down, assessing the damage. Laughing, he said, "Yeah, I think

I'll take a shower before our date… er, movie." He corrected himself quickly while swiping his hand through his hair, inadvertently wiping more grease into his silver-streaked locks. Huyen and I laughed at his awkwardness.

"Yeah, you do that. I'll wait in the theater for you." I told him. He walked away, giving me a finger gun and then cringing at his own gesture. I wasn't used to him being so embarrassed; it was almost endearing. He must really be stressed. I wondered if I was the cause or if it was the situation with the coven.

As I stood there, a mix of excitement and anxiety bubbling inside me, I realized this was a turning point. Nick was trying to change, and I was trying to change, too. Maybe this movie night could help us both breathe a little easier and navigate the uncertainty that lay ahead. I smiled, feeling a glimmer of hope for what was to come.

He listened to my concerns, he was willing to make changes, big changes not only for himself but also his business. He showed me that he truly cared about me and what I think. I tried so hard to put up a wall, to protect myself from getting hurt by another man, but Nick, he took a wrecking ball to that wall and annihilated it.

I chose the same comfortable chair I had last time, memories flooding back of happier, carefree times before the coven's deceit. I attempted to count the folds in the curtains covering the walls to kill the time while I waited for Nick, but boredom quickly set in. As I picked at the fuzz on my sweater, Cami walked in, rolling a cart full of popcorn and snacks. She froze, staring at me wide-eyed.

"Oh, I uh, didn't know you were here. I can get a different staff to help you if you'd like." She turned to walk away without waiting for my answer.

The leather seat squeaked as I slipped out of it, walking over to her and catching her by the arm. She stood silently, looking at me for my response. I pulled her in for a hug. I wasn't much of a hugger, but she saved Susan's life. I owed her so much. I needed to let go of the past.

"Thank you," I spoke through her hair.

She patted my back awkwardly before returning my hug without saying anything.

"You saved my friend. You didn't have to do that. Thank you." I pulled away from her, the hug lasting a bit longer than I intended.

"I'm just so tired of knowing people are going to get hurt and not being able to do anything about it."

"I don't mean to pry, but how do you know these things?"

"I'm a banshee," she shrugged. "I just sense upcoming death from people around me or people close to them." She paused, looking into my eyes. "I wish I didn't. It's… it's horrible. I feel how they're going to die. I… I felt my best friend die. She was human. The coven wouldn't let me do anything to stop it. I felt every agonizing second of her death, unable to help. It's a feeling that will always haunt me. I couldn't let you go through the same thing I did." I could tell it was difficult for her to tell me that story. I reached a hand over and laid it gently on hers, trying to comfort her. "I'm sorry; I shouldn't have told you all that, especially with your friend being hurt and all."

"No, I asked. I'm glad you told me. I am sorry you have to experience that. It sounds like a nightmare."

"It is. I'm just glad your friend is going to be okay. And thanks for having my back with the coven. They have such power around here; I was scared to go against them. I'm sorry I didn't say something sooner. I, I'm a coward."

"Nick won't let anything happen to you for telling the truth, or anyone. I know he'll follow through with his word. The coven holds great power here, I could see how they'd be intimidated to go against. I'm glad you did say something, otherwise my friend may have died. So thank you." She gave me a weak smile. She looked like she wanted to say something else but was holding back. "Axel told me how you two talked."

"Oh, he did?" She looked surprised.

"Yeah, he told me about your past, don't judge him for not keeping that from me, he shared it out of compassion and so I could understand where you were coming from. I wont tell anyone."

"It's not really a secret around here, it's just not something I'm proud of."

"I am sorry I judged you so harshly without knowing the full story."

"I didn't give you any reason to trust me. I won't lie, I did like Nick, it was more infatuation than love though. I don't know what a healthy relationship looks like. My family wasn't exactly great role models ya know."

"Relationships aren't my strong suit either." I confessed.

"I can tell Nick and you belong together. You balance each other out. I'm glad you're here for him. He's happy now."

"Thanks Cami. That means a lot. And I can tell you that Axel is a good guy, he's a little rough around the edges, okay very rough around the edges but he has a good heart. He's funny and loves adventure. And it takes a lot to scare him, if there's ever someone to be able to handle your 'gifts' it's him."

That must have struck a chord because put her hands over her face and wept. "I'm sorry, I didn't mean to make you upset."

"No, I'm not upset, I've just never imagined anyone could really handle my life. I thought I'd be alone forever."

"Well, I'm not saying Axel is forever but he is a good guy. And at the very least, a great friend to have in your corner."

"Thanks Aoife." She said sniffling. She was a much prettier crier than I was, I tried not to be jealous of that. Axel would most definitely be rubbing that in my face when he figured it out later. Something to look forward to. I laughed to myself.

"I've never seen Nick like he is now. He looks genuinely happy. That's because of you. He's been different since you came. I see it now. I recognize that we weren't meant to be together. He's happy. Happy *with* you. I'm glad you two found each other; life is hard going through it alone." Her eyes welled with tears, threatening to overflow.

"Cami, I see that I misjudged you. I am sorry for that. I hope we can start fresh and maybe become friends after all." We embraced each other, recognizing our loneliness and misunderstanding and a hope for a better future for both of us.

"Does that mean you're staying?"

I paused, "I haven't decided yet," reaching for the amulet on my necklace. It rested heavy and warm in my hand.

"It's a big decision. I don't know if I'd choose to keep my 'gift' if I had the choice. I try not to, but I do wonder what my life could have been like if I were normal."

"I'm so sorry. That sounds rough. I know my ability isn't so bad compared to others."

"They're all a burden in one way or another. But you have Nick to help you through it. He's special, you know. He makes everything better, or tries to. He has a big heart. I hope you know how amazing he is. Don't take him for granted."

"I know. It's just not the life I imagined for myself, not the life I worked so hard to get. I feel like it was all for nothing if I stay here."

"You don't have to give up your old life. But this one does have its perks, too. Just look at all the friends you've made here so quickly and how you've already changed the company to be safer. I just got an email about a required self-defense class the company is starting. I assume that was because of you, too. You and Nick could be great together." She left me to my thoughts, my mind a little lighter.

Her words hung in the air, settling over me like a warm blanket. I considered everything I had experienced since I arrived at K Corp. The fear, the uncertainty, and now the glimmer of friendship with Cami. There was still so much I didn't know about this place, about Nick, and about myself. But maybe, just maybe, there was room for growth and healing.

"Thanks, Cami," I said softly, feeling a newfound sense of hope. "I think I'm ready to try."

She left me with a lot to think about. If my nemesis saw the good I could do, maybe it was true. Nick didn't make me wait much longer, his hair still damp, pieces falling from their usual place into his forehead. I liked messy Nick. I liked all the sides of him, really. He grabbed a bowl of popcorn as he walked past the cart and slowly sank into the seat next to me. I could tell he was hesitant to say anything.

So I started, "Thanks for the movie night. It sounded relaxing, and I think we could use a little more of that right now. How are you doing with everything?"

"I feel… good. I feel like you gave me the push I needed to make this place into something that represents me, to leave my mark. I was so scared to change how my parents did things that I was afraid to go against it. It felt like losing a piece of them. But now I see they wanted me to make this place into something I'm proud of too. I think we're heading in the right direction now. All thanks to you."

"You did this, Nick. You found your voice, and you made the changes. I didn't know your parents, but I do think they'd be proud of you."

He reached over and squeezed my hand. I felt warmth radiate from the connection, grounding me. I reached over and stole the popcorn bowl from his lap. The deep, sexy rumble of his chuckle left his chest, sending vibrations through parts of me I didn't want to think about right then, I needed to think with my head, not my…

Things were feeling back to normal, whatever normal was in that place. But for that moment, everything felt right. I hadn't made up my mind if I was going to keep my magic or not, but that was a worry for another day. For now, I was there with Nick, and maybe that was enough.

As the movie began, I settled into the comfort of his presence. The flickering light of the screen cast shadows across his face, highlighting the determination in his eyes. I couldn't help but feel a growing sense of hope, a possibility of building something beautiful, even amidst chaos. I took a deep breath, letting the moment wash over me, ready to embrace whatever came next.

I was started out of my sleep. "Hello?" I answered my phone, still half asleep.

"E, are you still sleeping? It's 8:00"

I blinked at the clock to clear my sleepy vision, "It's 6:00 here man."

He laughed, "oh sorry, forgot there was a time difference. You didn't call me last night. I've been dying to hear about what Nick did"

I sat up in bed, clearly he wasn't going to let me go back to sleep. "Oh" I cleared my throat, trying to wake up more. "He made a new rule that human lives are just as important as magical ones. The coven threw a big fit about it but finally gave in and agreed."

"Man, I can't believe I just heard that sentence. This is so weird. But good. I'm glad that Nick found his balls and is stepping up to the plate. How are you feeling?"

"I'm" I had to think about it for a second, "I'm good. Nick seems to be willing to change, I need to follow my own advice and be open to the idea of change too. And I talked to a certain leggy blonde here."

"Oh yeah?"

"Yeah, she seems to be smitten by you."

"I have that effect on people."

"Axel, don't hurt her, okay. She's been through enough."

"Look at you, sticking up for her now! Why Miss Aoife, I do believe you have changed. But I promise to treat her well, you can't see my hand but I'm doing the scouts honor finger sign thing."

"You were never a boy scout. And you better treat her good man or you'll have me to deal with." I laughed. "I know where you live and now I can show up whenever I want… magic" I said drawing it out to be funny. "So you better."

"But can you please not show up when I'm nakies," I'd hate for Nick to get jealous. I'm wiggling my pinky finger." he narrated himself.

I couldn't contain my laughter. "Stop! You're disgusting. And I've seen you naked before, remember when you streaked at Mikki's party, I had to squint to see it." I poked fun back at him.

He gasped, "Ugh, I'm wounded!"

"Okay let's stop talking about Axel Jr. now.

"If you want, fine. But I am glad things seem to be working out there for you. Did you decide what you're going to do about your magic?"

I sighed, "No. I am so torn. I don't feel like there's one right decision here yet."

"It's a big one to make. Don't rush into it. I'm not going anywhere, and I'll check on Susan for you. Did you know she's let me help out on some of her shoots? She appreciates the female form almost as much as I do."

"Don't be a creeper. But thanks for checking up on her and helping her out. It means a lot that you two like each other. Oh but she doesn't know about magic, so let's keep that between us, and well, now Cami apparently."

"Got it, I'll keep it on the D.L. I'm here whenever you need to talk or escape."

"I appreciate you, but can you be here a little later in the morning though?"

"Ugh, yes."

"Love you butthead."

"Love you too whirlwind."

I cringed, "whirlwind?"

"Just trying out new nicknames for you," he joked. "That one didn't feel right, I'll keep trying."

Axel was the best, I was a lucky person to have him as a best friend. Now that I was awake, I needed to start sorting out my future. I strapped on my new roller skates that Nick made for me and took a roll down the halls, I spun and twirled on them, clearing my head for what the new day might hold. I was going down the hallway backwards, doing bubbles, I hit something hard.

I went flying to the floor, landing hard on my hip. Wincing through the pain I saw the 'what' I crashed into. It was a 'who'. Nick specifically. He landed on his butt. He looked so casual, holding himself up by his arms like he was on a beach somewhere relaxing. How did he always look so effortless? He stood up first, grabbing my forearms, helping me back upright..

He bent down to grab a stack of papers that had fallen. "Sorry, I didn't see you, I was reading and not watching where I was going."

"Well, I wasn't watching either, it was just as much my fault."

'I'm glad I ran into you though. Pun not intended." he said with a smile. "I wanted to know if you'd sit down with me and a few others to help make new guidelines. We had everyone sign the new oath, but now we need specific steps to follow in case the situation arises again."

"Uh, sure."

"I have a meeting coming up with some creatures that can sense danger or death, so we can work together. We need to use everyone's ability to our advantage so we can save more creatures and humans."

"I had no idea there were more things out there that did that." I said a little stunned. I had seen a lot of creatures since I'd been there, and even in different dimensions but I never really thought about how many more there could be.

"Yeah, there's a lot actually. This world is fairly new to you so you'll be getting a crash course. You okay with that?"

"Nick, I, I haven't decided if I'm going to keep my magic or not though. I don't want you going into this thinking I decided to stay."

He nodded, "Whatever you decide, I support your decision. I think your unique human viewpoint will help us all tough."

"Okay."

"Great, Njeri is setting it all up, so I'll have her let you know when it is."

"Okay." was all I could say again. I was a little stunned at his request. I wasn't even a part of the building but he valued my opinion. It felt… good.

He left me with a smile, a fine view of his butt in his tight slacks, walking like nothing ever happened. While I was sure mine would be badly bruised. It was time to hang up the skates for the day. I was walking down the hall in my socks, skates slung over my shoulder when none other than Njeri came strolling down with her hooves clacking and echoing around her.

"I was just coming to look for you." she said.

"I just keep running into everyone today, must be serendipitous."

She gave me a questioning look but ignored it, "Nick wanted me to fill you in on the meeting for the guidelines later. It's set for dusk, around 6:30. These aren't your average creatures. One of our guests is strictly nocturnal, they only come out at dusk. And the meeting is by the pool because, well, some of our attendees need to be near the water. Let's just say… staying on the pool deck might be the safest bet for you. Some of them aren't too fond of humans, even those with magical abilities."

I could feel the hairs on the back of my neck start to rise, the weight of her warning settling in. "So… who exactly are we talking about here?" I asked, curiosity mingling with apprehension.

"They're all beings who deal with death in some form or another," she explained. "Some of them sense when it's going to happen, some guide souls afterward, and, well… some even cause it. That's why I thought you'd want to stay out of the water. It's a safer vantage point, and you can observe without getting too close."

I took a steadying breath, absorbing what she'd said. "Right, got it. Watch from the sidelines. Anything else I should know?"

She tilted her head, considering her response. "Just keep your wits about you. This isn't a crowd that takes kindly to disrespect, and some of them are… ancient. They play by a different set of rules."

"Understood," I replied, mentally steeling myself. "I'll be on my best behavior. This will be interesting huh."

"Yeah, you're really getting thrown into the deep end of the pool with this one. Hope you can swim!" She yelled laughing maniacally after as she left.

My stomach sank as I stepped into the pool area, a wave of unease tightening my chest. Maybe I really was in over my head. But I had to trust Nick; he wouldn't let anything happen to me, right? I caught Njeri's eye as she entered the room behind me, and for a split second, I swore I saw a glint of amusement in her expression. She had a way of enjoying other people's discomfort, but I doubted she'd let things get out of hand. Still, there was a sliver of doubt lingering, a whisper in my gut telling me I wasn't entirely safe.

Thankfully, it was almost time for the meeting to start. The more I stood here waiting, the more my mind ran wild with nightmarish scenarios of what could happen. But nothing I imagined could have prepared me for what I walked into.

The pool room was transformed into a space straight out of a dark fantasy novel, crawling with beings that would haunt anyone's nightmares. I froze as I scanned the scene, my heart beating louder in my chest. Several tall poles were anchored into the tiled floor, and perched on them were what I could only describe as… bird-like creatures. One in particular caught my attention, it clung to a long branch with its talons, looking down at me with a mix of curiosity and disdain. The feathers on its body were patchy, revealing patches of pale, human-like skin beneath. Its large beak gleamed in the light, but its eyes, human and unsettling, bore into me with an unnerving intensity.

"That's a Siren," Njeri whispered into my ear, her voice almost gleeful.

I blinked, confused. "I thought Sirens were mermaids," I murmured, pointing toward the pool where another creature lounged, half-submerged in the water. This one fit the mermaid description: her lower half was covered in gleaming blue-green scales that shimmered as she moved. Her upper half, though human, exuded a dangerous beauty. Dark skin and thick, natural hair adorned with seashells and pieces of coral gave her an ethereal appearance, except for her smile, which revealed sharp, predatory teeth. It wasn't a welcoming smile. No, this one looked like she was considering me as her next meal.

She quickly pushed my hand back down and slapped my hand gently, shaming me for pointing. I blushed at the action. I barely stepped in and I was already getting in trouble. "Nope, myths often get things wrong. That's a Jengu." She corrected me.

I was confident I didn't know what any of the creatures were then, "so what's that one", motioning with my head to a short creature with wart and mole covered skin that hung off its stocky body.

"That's a squonk, try to not make eye contact with that one, he's a little skittish and if it gets scared it turns into a puddle of tears and it takes a very long time for him to return to form. I'd like to not be here all night."

I'm pretty sure I made a face as she said that.

"And don't make that face at anyone. I'd hate for you to be eaten tonight."

"Oookay. Noted." I quickly changed my expression. Axel always said I had resting bitch face so I made a mental note to always look 'happy' during the meeting. Hoping to not offend anyone with my regular face.

"Since I know you're going to ask about them all. That one over there is a wraith. It's like a ghost, but it can prevent death or choose to kill creatures in any dimension. That one over there playing the fiddle is a Fusse Grim. Depending on how he plays he can heal or kill people." I was stuck staring at the Fusse Grim, with its large nose and unkempt hair in knots down its face, partially covering its eyes. It played the fiddle with webbed fingers, I just hoped it was playing a song that wouldn't kill me.

"I know that one, it's a reaper right?"

"You got it. So don't piss it off, its scythe is very sharp, he comes in hand at birthday parties though when there's packages to open." I couldn't tell if she was joking or not.

As I stood frozen, trying not to lock eyes with any of the creatures, a naked man with brownish-green skin lumbered past me. I couldn't help but stare, even as my mind screamed at me to look away. His skin was mottled with patches of moss and dirt, and a thick, solid beard of moss clung to his round face, partially obscuring his features. His sneer, though, was unmistakable, like he knew I didn't belong. He grunted in my direction, his sneer lingering just long enough to send a chill up my spine.

Thankfully, his large potbelly hung low, covering parts of him I definitely didn't want to see. Without acknowledging me any further, he slipped into the pool, settling himself next to the mermaid-like Jengu, and began making strange clicking noises. I assumed it was some form of communication, though the sound felt sharp and jarring in my ears. The Jengu turned to him, responding with her own series of clicks, and for a moment, they seemed locked in a language I couldn't understand.

I focused on not starting, but it was nearly impossible. This wasn't just another odd crowd in an art gallery, this was something entirely different. The people watching were on a whole other level.

I tried to breathe slowly, reminding myself that Nick wouldn't let anything happen to me. Still, standing in the midst of so many beings with little regard for human life made me feel like I was walking a tightrope between fascination and fear.

Nick walked in last, and his entrance was magnetic. It wasn't just his impeccable style, dark blue button-up, printed slacks, brown leather shoes, and those signature red suspenders that somehow made him look both professional and rugged, it was the way he commanded the room. I swallowed hard, pushing down the wave of attraction that hit me. This wasn't the time for distractions, not when we were surrounded by creatures that could very well devour me if I made the wrong move.

Njeri motioned toward a row of chairs lining the wall, and I followed her lead, trying to project a confidence I didn't feel. My heart was pounding in my chest, but I hoped none of it showed. As I settled into the chair next to her, she handed me a pen and paper. Nick's handwriting scrawled across the page, likely his speaking points for tonight. I clutched it, grateful for something to focus on besides the intense atmosphere in the room.

Nick cleared his throat, and just like that, the room went completely silent. The strange clicks and murmurs stopped, the gentle movement of the water seemed to still. The creatures were listening. He sat down in a high-backed chair, clipboard in hand, radiating authority.

"Thank you all for coming tonight," he began, his voice clear and calm. "The coven has now spelled the room so that we can all communicate together.

Please don't be offended that I chose English for this gathering. I respect all of your cultures; it was not chosen out of favoritism."

I noticed a ripple of nods and slight gestures of agreement from the gathered creatures. They came from so many different realms and backgrounds. I was relieved that Nick had made sure I could understand, but more than that, I marveled at how easily he handled this delicate situation. This room was filled with beings who, in their own right, commanded immense power, and yet Nick seemed to know exactly how to balance authority with respect.

Nick's voice filled the room, resonating with authority. "Let me start off by saying I'm glad you've chosen to align your communities with our network. We are striving to help as many magical beings as possible, and as of tonight, humans as well."

I tried to distract myself, doodling on the paper in front of me to keep my eyes busy. The creatures in the room were far more fascinating, and terrifying, than I'd imagined. Drawing them made it easier not to stare, especially when the disapproving grunts echoed across the room at the mention of humans. I tried not to flinch.

Nick, however, remained calm, unfazed by their reactions. "I know you may not have the best record with humans," he continued, "but the world is changing. We must change with it."

The grunts grew louder, more impatient, but Nick pressed on. "Recently, we had a situation where a human almost lost their life because the coven failed to notify me of a potential danger. We got lucky that Aoife here," he waved a hand toward me, and suddenly all eyes were on me. My heart pounded as I felt their gazes burning into me. I forced a small, awkward smile, hoping they couldn't sense the fear crawling up my spine.

"Aoife was able to create a portal, and we arrived in time to stop the attack," Nick continued. "But not before it had already begun. That should have never happened. So, from now on, I'd like to propose a truce with humans, at least those connected to the magical world."

Murmurs rippled through the room, some still doubtful, others intrigued. Nick leaned forward, his eyes scanning the crowd. "If you or your kind hear of any danger to someone in or connected to our network, please tell someone who can help. We cannot afford more lives lost."

I could feel the tension in the air, a mixture of curiosity, skepticism, and silent debate among the creatures. Nick was trying to bridge a gap centuries old, and I wasn't sure how well it would go. But in that moment, I realized how much he believed in what he was doing, and in me. It was a weight I hadn't expected, but somehow, it felt right.

The creatures' expressions varied, some narrowing their eyes at me, others shifting in contemplation. I held my breath, unsure of what would come next, but one thing was clear: Nick wasn't just fighting for humans; he was fighting for a world where we could all survive, together.

The Siren was the first to break the silence, her voice rising in harmonized layers, a strange, melodic chorus of sound. "Why should we do this? They've always portrayed us as monsters, creatures who lure them to their deaths. Why would we want to save them now?" Her sharp, ocean-blue eyes locked onto me, a challenge behind her musical words.

I felt the weight of the room shift as all eyes turned to me. My heart hammered in my chest, but I knew I had to speak up. I swallowed the knot of fear tightening in my throat. "My friend was put in danger because of me", I began, my voice steady but edged with emotion. "I have magic. If I'd been with her, she wouldn't have gotten hurt. Instead, I was here, helping others, helping creatures like you. She shouldn't have been in danger because of something I am, something I had no choice in. We were warned about the attack but not until it was almost too late. It could have been completely avoided if we'd known sooner."

The Jengu, her sea-green skin shimmering as she swam lazily in the pool, tilted her head toward me, her dark eyes studying my face. "But you do have a choice, do you not, Aoife?" Her voice was soft but carried a weight of knowledge that made my skin prickle. She knew. Somehow, she knew I could give up my magic. I hadn't told anyone about that yet. A hush fell over the room as all the creatures waited for my response.

I took a breath. "Yes, I do," I admitted, the honesty feeling like a stone in my chest. "I have the choice to give up my magic and return to a regular life. I haven't decided what the ending will be yet." I glanced over at Nick, his face unreadable but supportive. "But I know I feel a deep connection to this world, the magical world. I'm still very new to it, but I empathize with how you've been portrayed and punished. It's not right. People fear what they don't understand."

The room seemed to hold its breath as I continued. "I've seen it happen to someone in my own family. They were cast out, misunderstood because they didn't fit into the mold. I don't have the right to tell you what to do, but I want to share the other side. I've lived in both worlds, human and magical, and I've seen the beauty and the struggle in both. Each has its own form of magic, its own dangers, and its own wonder. But change has to start somewhere."

There was a murmur among the creatures, some nodding slightly, others still skeptical. I couldn't tell if I had swayed them, but I knew I had spoken my truth. We were standing on the edge of something new, something that could shift the balance between humans and magical beings forever. And I was part of that change, whether I wanted to be or not.

The translucent wraith, hovering in the air with its misty form, spoke next. Its voice was a chilling rasp, like wind through a cracked window. "What if a human tries to harm us? Are we allowed to protect ourselves without repercussions from K Corp?"

Nick answered before I could. His tone was calm, but firm. "Of course. You all have the right to defend yourselves, and you won't be punished for it. What I'm asking is that we don't go out of our way to attack, taunt, or harm humans for sport. If they're a threat, protect yourself. But let's not be the aggressors." He glanced around the room, his gaze steady, earning more nods from the crowd.

"Some of you," Nick continued, "are blessed with gifts of healing. If you can use those abilities to help humans, I encourage you to do so. By showing that we're not always a threat, we can start to bridge the gap and bring about the change we all need."

The Fosse grim, a tall, skeletal figure with long, mossy hair, raised his fiddle in solidarity. His dark eyes glistened with agreement, and Nick gave him an appreciative nod. The tension in the room was beginning to ease, and I felt a small flicker of hope.

Nick scanned the room. "Any questions or concerns?"

Silence. The quiet was not hostile but reflective, as if the creatures were digesting what had been said. Finally, Nick smiled. "Good! Our chef has prepared a feast in honor of this momentous occasion! Eat, dance, and enjoy this day!"

The atmosphere shifted instantly. Large tables, overflowing with platters of fish, both raw and grilled, cheese, bread, exotic fruits, and nuts, were rolled in by staff dressed in crisp white shirts. Floating tables glided over the pool's surface, laden with seafood delicacies I didn't even recognize.

The Fosse grim began playing a lively, upbeat tune on his fiddle, the melody filling the room with infectious energy. The floating wraith and the reaper-like figure, once menacing, spun in circles, moving gracefully with the music. Around me, creatures of all kinds joined in, swaying, dancing, and feasting. Laughter echoed through the room, transforming the once intimidating gathering into something filled with joy and celebration.

For the first time, I felt the weight of tension lift. What had begun as a potentially volatile meeting now had a sense of unity and hope, a flicker of change in a world that so often felt divided. And even though the future was uncertain, in that moment, there was a glimmer of peace.

I sat, still processing everything, watching the creatures interact, laughing, eating, sharing stories in languages I didn't understand. The mountain of food was steadily being devoured, and the air was filled with music and joy. Then Nick stepped in front of me, blocking my view. His smile was wide, genuine, and it reached his eyes. He looked proud, truly happy.

"You did it," I said, returning his smile, feeling a warmth bloom in my chest.

He shook his head slightly. "We did it. You started this revolution, Aoife. Your caring heart and determination made this happen."

I was caught off guard. I had never seen myself as someone who could spark change, someone capable of leading or making a difference on this scale. But standing there, among those beings who once viewed humans as enemies, I realized something had shifted in me. Maybe that place was showing me who I was meant to be, someone stronger and more capable than I ever thought. Or maybe it was Nick, giving me the space and support to discover that side of myself. Either way, I was grateful.

"Thank you," I said, my voice quieter, more sincere. "For even considering this… for making it happen. I know it couldn't have been easy to convince them," I paused, catching myself. I didn't know what to call these magical creatures. "These different groups to agree to something like this."

Nick's smile softened, and his gaze held mine. "It wasn't easy, but they're starting to see what I see. That things need to change. That it's time for something bigger."

I nodded, feeling the weight of it all. "Your parents would be so proud of this. I'm sure of it."

Nick's eyes flickered with emotion, and he glanced away for a moment, composing himself. When he looked back at me, his expression was softer, more vulnerable. "Thank you," he whispered. "That means more than you know."

For a brief moment, the chaos of the world outside faded. There was no danger, no fear, just this quiet understanding between us. It felt like the beginning of something new, something bigger than both of us.

Nick took the paper from my hands, glancing at the sketches I had doodled during the meeting. "You know," he began, his voice thoughtful, "we could use your other skills around here."

I raised an eyebrow, intrigued. "What do you mean?"

"Well," he said, turning the paper so I could see, "most magical beings have been misrepresented in human stories and lore. They've been made into villains to fit human narratives. You could help change that."

I still wasn't following. "I'm not sure I get it. How would I help change that?"

"You could paint them," he said, his eyes locking onto mine, a spark of excitement there. "In their true likeness. Spread awareness of what they really are, not what the myths say. Your art could bridge that gap. If your paintings are anything like these sketches, it would be a huge step for the magical community."

Before I could respond, the reaper, who had been floating nearby, hovered over us, his dark hood covering the space where his face should be. His skeletal hand pointed at my sketch of him.

"I do look good in this," he said in a deep, unnatural voice that made my spine tingle. "You got my good side too."

I froze, unsure how to react, but then he let out a deep, raspy laugh that sounded like rocks tumbling down a cliff. Nick joined in, clearly amused. Meanwhile, I stood there, wide-eyed, not quite sure if I should laugh along or stay quiet. The reaper floated off towards the food table, still chuckling to himself.

I turned to Nick, my voice uncertain. "He was kidding, right?"

Nick chuckled again, nodding. "Yes, he's a real hoot when you get to know him."

I stared after the reaper in disbelief. *A hoot? The reaper?* This world was turning upside down. I had no idea the grim reaper could have a sense of humor. I'd clearly underestimated how little I knew about the magical community.

Still, the idea of staying there… of being surrounded by those creatures every day… It felt surreal. And yet, there was a part of me, a part I wasn't ready to fully acknowledge, that was warming to the idea. *If* I stayed. That was still the big question looming over everything. Could I really live there? And more importantly, did I want to? I could still paint, help the creatures be seen as less of the villains and more of the saviors, I could also help with the self defense courses, who knows what else. I was only beginning to understand my magic, maybe I'd feel comfortable doing something with that at some point too. I was willing to let in the possibilities of staying, what it could look like.

Nick didn't leave my side for the rest of the night as we wandered through the crowd of creatures, talking about potential portraits. The night had taken on a surreal, almost magical quality as each being shared how they wanted to be seen, how they wanted the world to know them. As the conversations flowed, it seemed that the project could really turn into something important, something transformative.

The last creature we spoke with was the Squonk. Its saggy, wrinkled skin made it difficult to gauge its emotions. It looked like its own sadness had worn it down over time. "Could you paint me from when I was younger?" it asked, its voice shaky. "I'd like to be represented like that instead of… this."

I chuckled, thinking it was making a lighthearted joke. But the moment the laugh left my lips, I realized I had misjudged the situation. Nick gasped, his hand squeezing mine, and before I could stammer out an apology, the Squonk's tears started to fall, streaming down its bumpy, wart-covered skin. The tears kept coming, faster and faster, until its whole body was consumed, dissolving into a puddle of murky water on the floor.

I froze. My heart sank. I had insulted one of Nick's guests. I didn't mean to, how could I have known?

Before I could react, I heard the rhythmic clicking of hooves behind me. Njeri rushed up, sighing as she assessed the situation. "Great," she muttered. "Now we'll be here all night. Girl, I told you not to scare him."

"I didn't mean to!" I said, my voice shaky with guilt. "What can I do to help?"

She exhaled in frustration. "Nothing. He'll reform eventually, but I'll get a bucket so no one steps on him."

As Njeri trudged off, looking defeated, I felt the weight of my mistake pressing down on me. My heart raced with regret. *How could I have been so careless?*

"I am sorry about the whole water thing."

Nick chuckled, the sound warm and reassuring. "Don't feel too bad. They're sensitive creatures. Once, I sneezed and turned their entire village into puddles. I spent days trying to help them reform safely," he said, laughing at the memory. His lightheartedness made me feel a little better.

"Thanks for that," I replied with a soft smile. "Apart from the water incident, it was a good night. Definitely strange at first, but Njeri helped explain who everyone was. I think it's pretty neat. It's like we're part of a secret world, a special club."

Nick grinned, his eyes lighting up. "We should get jackets made," he joked, but then his expression softened. "But really, Aoife, you're doing amazing. You're a natural. I wish my parents could've met you. They would have loved you. Instantly." He paused, looking deep into my eyes, he said, "I know I did."

I gasped, caught off guard. "Nick…" His confession felt like a lot to handle, especially after everything that had happened. He knew I needed time, yet here he was, opening up completely.

He held up a hand before I could respond further. "You don't have to say anything back. Even if you decide to leave, I'll always love you. You've changed me, and this place, for the better."

I felt my chest tighten. I couldn't reciprocate those words, not yet. "I… I can't say it back. I'm just not there, Nick. I'm sorry."

"Don't be sorry," he said softly, his voice full of understanding. He didn't seem hurt, just patient, like he was willing to wait for me to figure things out at my own pace.

The weight of the moment made me feel awkward again. I shifted on my feet and rubbed my arms. "I think I'm going to head back to my room now. I'm really tired. It's been a weird day."

Nick's expression turned more serious, his brows knitting slightly with concern. "Are you okay? Really?"

I gave him a small nod. "Yeah, I'm fine. Just tired, like I said. It's been a lot to take in."

He hesitated for a moment, then smiled gently. "Alright, Aoife. Sleep well. I'll see you tomorrow."

I nodded, my voice barely above a whisper. "Goodnight, Nick."

As I walked away, my heart felt heavy with a mix of emotions I wasn't ready to confront yet. I could feel Nick's gaze on me as I disappeared down the hallway, unsure of what tomorrow would bring.

I sat on the edge of my bed, glancing at the now spotless room. The art supplies were neatly tucked away, but the easel stood there, front and center, with Nick's face staring back at me. I couldn't help but smirk, imagining the confusion on the staff's faces when they walked in on my half-finished portrait of him. They probably thought I was a bit unhinged, an artist obsessing over the man who'd upended her life. But then again, everyone already knew our relationship was… complicated. That just added another layer of weirdness.

I chuckled softly, brushing a stray curl behind my ear. "It is what it is," I muttered to myself, shaking my head. If the staff hadn't already gotten used to the strange dynamics between Nick and me, that definitely wouldn't help. But then, I wasn't sure *I* fully understood our dynamic either.

The quiet of the room was almost suffocating. After everything that had happened tonight, the creatures, the intense conversations, Nick's unexpected confession, I felt like I was swimming in uncharted waters. And there was his face on the canvas, staring at me like it held the answers I couldn't seem to find.

I sighed, pulling my knees up to my chest and wrapping my arms around them. "What am I doing?" I whispered into the silence.

Chapter 25

It felt strange being back in the room that had begun to feel like home. The only company I had was the painting of Nick, his face staring at me from across the room. His eyes held that same intense gaze, the one that made me wonder what secrets he was keeping and whether I would ever be able to discover them. The room felt emptier than usual, and though I'd spent countless hours there, it felt different, hollow, as if something was missing.

Sliding into the warm bed, I let the blankets wrap around me, offering a small sense of comfort. With Nick's painted eyes watching over me, I felt a strange sense of safety, even though it was just a canvas version of him. The darkness of the room pressed in, and I squinted into the shadows, trying to focus on anything other than my swirling thoughts. Slowly, a face began to emerge, blurry at first but then sharpening into view.

Aunt Maggy. Her long hair was tied up in a bun, just as I remembered, and her familiar knowing eyes locked onto mine. The same eyes that had given me the choice to decide my fate. But there was something different now, something off. She didn't move, didn't speak, just watched me silently, her face illuminated in the dark.

I tried to walk toward her, but every step I took only seemed to push her farther away. It was as if the space between us stretched endlessly, no matter how hard I pushed forward. My body trembled with effort, straining to close the gap. Panic bubbled inside me, why couldn't I reach her? What was happening?

Suddenly, a piercing shriek shattered the silence, so sharp and disorienting that I couldn't tell where it was coming from. I spun around, heart pounding in my chest, searching the shadows for the source of the scream, but all I saw was Aunt Maggy. Her expression had changed, no longer calm, her face was etched with worry. The lines on her face deepened, and her once-wise eyes were filled with fear, staring at something I couldn't see.

A bony hand reached out to me through the shadows, unnaturally long, stretching from the darkness that surrounded Aunt Maggy. My heart raced. Was it truly her, or some twisted trick? The grip that closed around my wrist was startlingly strong, yanking me toward her with a force that stole the breath from my lungs. I couldn't stop the yelp that escaped my lips as my body was dragged forward so fast, my head whipped down before I could steady myself. By the time I looked up, Aunt Maggy's face was inches from mine, her deep-set eyes, usually so warm and full of wisdom, now shone with an urgency that chilled me.

She raised a thin finger to her lips, her eyes darting cautiously to the side. "Shh," she whispered softly, the sound barely audible, but the weight of her caution was palpable. Her gaze swept the darkness around us, searching, waiting, as if she expected someone, or something, to appear. I followed her eyes, straining to see what she could, but all I saw was an endless void of shadows pressing in on us.

Then, Aunt Maggy looked straight into my eyes, her voice dropping to a near inaudible whisper, "I've heard whispers. Whispers of happenings in other dimensions. There's a Wiijigoo, one with a vendetta against you." My blood ran cold. She continued, her voice tight with warning, "They know where you are, they've found a way in. Someone will betray you, Aoife."

My heart thudded painfully against my chest, I could barely breathe as she went on, "They're trying to wait until the ceremony, until the moment you decide to give up your magic. But they want it before you give it away… to kill you and take it for themselves."

She hesitated, her face tightening, as if recalling something horrible. "He wasn't shy about what he would do to you once inside. You mustn't let him get the magic. Even if you choose to give it up, don't trust the safety of the building." Her eyes bore into mine, filled with both desperation and care. "Be cautious, my dear. I had to warn you. Tell Nick, only Nick. Trust no one else."

Her words lingered in the air, thick and suffocating, before she smiled sadly. The wrinkles around her eyes deepened, and for a brief moment, she looked like the aunt I once knew, soft and kind. Then, as quickly as she had appeared, she began to fade. The grip of her hand loosened, her form dissipating like smoke into the dark, leaving me standing alone, her final warning reverberating in my mind.

The shadows crept closer around me, the warmth of her presence gone. But her words, those remained, echoing in my chest, as I realized the weight of what I now carried. I had to tell Nick, and I had to figure out who I could trust before it was too late.

I shot up in bed, gasping for breath, my chest heaving as though I had just run a marathon. My arm burned, and as I looked down, I saw the distinct red imprint of fingers, Aunt Maggy's fingers. The dream, if it even was a dream, felt far too real. I rubbed my arm, the sensation too vivid to dismiss. Did she actually reach out to warn me? The whispers of danger from the Wiijigoo rang through my mind. I had almost forgotten about the creature since arriving here, too secure in the comforts and protections of K Corp. But Aunt Maggy said the building wasn't safe, that someone would betray me, and them.

I sat, frozen, replaying every moment of the strange, haunting encounter. I couldn't shake her words, or the cold certainty that something terrible was coming. Who could possibly betray me? My mind raced as I mentally ran through a list of people. There weren't many who had a reason to dislike me, or were there?

Cami used to be on that list, but she and I had reached an uneasy truce. I no longer felt the old tension between us. Njeri crossed my mind briefly, but I couldn't seriously believe she'd do anything to endanger me or the building. She was tough, but not malicious. Still, the new creatures who had come in for the oath-taking ceremony could be harboring resentment. Many of them had suffered because of humans, what if one of them decided to act on that?

And then there was the coven. I had definitely rubbed them the wrong way. Their dislike for me had been palpable ever since I challenged their authority and forced Nick to change things. Would they go so far as to betray us all? I couldn't be sure, but I had no time to overthink it.

Aunt Maggy's voice echoed in my mind, *Tell Nick, trust no one else.* I had to talk to him. He was the only person I could rely on, and I needed someone in my corner. Someone I could trust before everything spiraled out of control.

It was early, too early, but there was no way I could wait until later. I quickly brushed my teeth, telling myself Nick didn't deserve to deal with my morning breath on top of everything else, and steeled myself as I walked to his room. My knuckles hovered over the door, my heart pounding as adrenaline coursed through me. I knocked, the sound too loud in the stillness of the early morning.

He opened the door with groggy eyes. "Aoife, what's wrong?" It was beginning to become a pattern of me waking him up with emergencies apparently.

"Aunt Maggy came to me again, with a warning. Someone has been talking where she's at. Someone is after my magic and they found a way in the building. She said someone would betray us here. It was real, it wasn't a dream, she grabbed my arm Nick, she looked scared. Can it happen? Could someone get in?"

Nick's eyes snapped fully open, the sleepy haze instantly vanishing as my words sank in. He studied the red imprint on my arm with an intensity I hadn't seen before. His jaw clenched, and I could almost see his brain working, trying to piece together what I had just told him.

He moved closer to me, his expression serious now. "It's possible, Aoife," he said, his voice low and steady, no longer burdened by sleep. "The wards protect us from outside threats, but they rely on everyone inside upholding the magic. If someone on the inside betrays us, they could weaken the wards or let something through, especially if they know the right rituals."

I shivered, feeling the weight of Aunt Maggy's warning settle deeper into my chest. "So, what she said, it could happen. Someone could bring a Wiijigoo in to attack me while I'm vulnerable?"

Nick nodded grimly, his hand reaching out to gently rest on my shoulder. The warmth from his touch radiated through me, grounding me in the moment. "If she warned you about this, we have to take it seriously. We need to figure out who would want to betray you, and why." His eyes searched mine, his concern unmistakable. "But I won't let that happen. You won't be alone when the time comes. We'll figure this out."

I took a deep breath, trying to steady myself. Nick's reassurance was comforting, but the fear still gnawed at me. Someone here, in this building, someone we trusted, might be planning to let in a monster bent on killing me. It was almost too much to wrap my head around.

I sank into the nearest chair, my legs suddenly feeling too weak to hold me up. "How do we figure out who's behind this?" I asked, looking up at him, desperate for answers.

Nick's expression hardened. "We start by looking at those who might have something to gain from your magic, or from your death. We'll need to be careful, keep this quiet. We can't trust just anyone. But you can trust me, Aoife. I'll make sure nothing happens to you."

His words were resolute, and I wanted to believe him with every fiber of my being. But the nagging doubt remained, how could we stop an enemy we couldn't see, someone lurking in the shadows, waiting for the perfect moment to strike?

I couldn't respond to Nick's words. All I could do was nod as my heart pounded in my chest. He grabbed some clothes from his dresser and went to the bathroom to change. The door didn't close all the way, and I caught a glimpse of him pulling his sweats down, but I quickly turned away. Now was not the time for distractions. Later, I'd probably regret not looking, but right now, survival was my priority.

Nick rushed out of the bathroom, fully dressed in a fitted black t-shirt and jeans. His expression was serious as he came over, gently grabbing my face in his hands and bending down to kiss my forehead. It was a small gesture, but the weight behind it made my heart ache. When I looked up at him, he seemed… afraid.

That unsettled me even more.

"I should be scared, right?" I asked, my voice barely above a whisper.

He sighed heavily. " I won't let anything happen to you, Aoife. You need to stay put. Don't go anywhere, don't answer the door unless it's Huyen, Njeri, or me. You hear me?"

His tone was firm, leaving no room for debate. But I still couldn't shake my own paranoia. "Nick, you don't think Njeri would do something like this, do you? I mean, she seemed pretty upset last night… about the Squonk."

Nick's eyes softened for a moment. "No, she wouldn't. She gets irritated, sure, but she loves her role here. And she doesn't have the kind of power to pull something like this off." He paused, then added, "Don't feel bad for asking. We need to be cautious about everyone."

I nodded, feeling a little relief, though not much. "Okay. I'm sorry I even suggested it. Please don't tell her… I don't want to ruin what little trust we've built."

He smiled, though it didn't reach his eyes. "It's good to be wary. Better safe than sorry. But promise me you won't open the door for anyone but me, Huyen, or Njeri."

"I promise," I said softly. "Just… please be careful, Nick. I can't stand the thought of you getting hurt because of my mess."

Nick's expression softened, and he squeezed my hand. "I told you before and it's still true; you're worth everything life can throw at me." His smile was pained, a reflection of the worry we both shared, but then he turned and left, leaving me in the heavy silence of his room.

As soon as the door clicked shut, I felt the weight of the situation settle deeper on my chest. I lowered myself slowly onto his unmade bed, the lingering warmth of his body still wrapped in the sheets. How had my life gotten that chaotic? Was that what my future held if I decided to stay?

An eternity seemed to pass as I sat in the room, my worry eating away at me. Every creak of the building, every faint sound made me jump. Then, a knock echoed from the door, and my heart leapt into my throat. I froze, terrified to move, just like when I was a kid, hiding from imaginary monsters. But, the monsters were real now. I tiptoed toward the door and peeked through the tiny hole. It was Huyen, but her usual bright smile was nowhere to be seen. Nick had told me I could trust her, but my instincts screamed to not let anyone in.

Still, I opened the door, and she walked in quickly, not wasting any time. I shut the door immediately, fighting the childish urge to jump back onto the bed like I used to. Like it would somehow keep the monsters from grabbing me.

"What's going on?" I asked, trying to mask the urgency in my voice but failing miserably.

"Nicks holding all the guests in the pool room until we clear them. He's looking for any connections to the Wiijigoo. So far, nothing's come up. We knew they wouldn't make it easy," Huyen said, her tone serious.

I felt a surge of frustration and helplessness wash over me. "What can I do to help? I can't just sit here while everyone's doing something. They're here because of me, after all."

"Nothing," she said firmly. "Your job is to stay here and stay safe. If Nick has to worry about you, then he's vulnerable, and we need him to focus. But he thought you could use this," she added, handing me my replacement phone and a small sketch pad with a pack of Prismacolor pencils. Even in the middle of a crisis, Nick knew exactly what I needed to keep my mind from spiraling.

"Thanks, Huyen. And thank Nick for me, too. I appreciate the update. Please, be careful out there."

She gave me a small smile. "I will. Remember, only open the door for me, Njeri, or Nick. He wanted me to remind you, of course." She rolled her eyes playfully. Nick really was a worrier.

I saluted her, trying to lighten the mood. We exchanged a quick hug before she left, leaving me alone in the room again. This time, though, I had my phone and some art supplies. It wasn't much, but it was something to help keep my mind from imploding.

I filled up pages with sketches of the creatures I'd seen at K Corp, almost like a Grimm's fairy tale gone wild. Yet, as I looked at the faces of these supposed "monsters," I realized most of them weren't monsters at all. They were kind and caring, nothing like the frightening legends humans had created about them. I couldn't help but wonder, if I showed people my sketchbook and told them these beings were real, would anyone believe me? Probably not. I mean, I wouldn't have believed it myself if someone had told me just weeks ago.

I was mid-sketch, drawing another one of the unique creatures I'd encountered, when my phone rang. I glanced at the screen. *Cami?* Why in the world would she be calling me? Sure, we'd started to make amends, but we weren't at the "let's chat" phase yet. My heart skipped a beat. Something had to be wrong.

"Hello?" I answered cautiously, unsure of what to expect.

"Aoife! Aoife!" Cami's voice came through in a panicked rush. "I'm so glad you answered. I wasn't sure if you would. I need to talk to you."

"What's wrong? Is Nick okay?" My heart raced, fearing the worst.

"Yeah, yeah, he's fine," she said, but her voice was shaky. "But... I had another caoineadh."

Her words hit me like a punch to the gut. My stomach twisted in knots. "What? Who? Who's going to get hurt?" I couldn't bring myself to say the word **die.**

Cami hesitated, and I could hear her struggling to find the right words. "Um, I... I don't know how to say this."

"Cami, this is serious," I pressed, my voice trembling. "Just tell me. Right now!"

She took a deep breath, and then the words tumbled out. "You are going to kill Nick."

My world froze. "Wh, what? No. That can't be true." I could barely form the words. There's no way I would ever hurt Nick. Ever.

"I'm just telling you what I saw," she said, her voice strained. I could tell she was upset too, but I couldn't wrap my head around it. How could she even say that?

"Cami, there's no way that's true," I repeated, my voice shaky, trying to convince myself as much as I was trying to convince her.

"I don't know… it's just what I saw. I have to go." Her words rushed out, and before I could say another word, the line went dead.

I sat there, stunned, my mind racing. *Kill Nick? Me?* It didn't make any sense. I would never hurt him. There had to be a mistake. Cami had to be wrong. I couldn't believe it. I wouldn't believe it.

But no matter how hard I tried to dismiss it, Cami's vision haunted me. I rocked back and forth on the edge of the bed, trying to make sense of it all, trying to block out the rising panic in my chest. There was *no way* I could ever do that to Nick. There was **no way** I could hurt him, let alone kill him. I repeated that to myself over and over, hoping it would drown out the fear threatening to consume me.

Suddenly, a knock at the door broke through my spiraling thoughts. My heart jumped, half-expecting to see Huyen again. But when I opened the door, it wasn't her.

It was Nick.

He looked fine. He didn't look hurt or stressed. Just normal Nick, with his easy smile and calm presence. But seeing him standing there, alive and well, after what Cami had just said, only made my anxiety spike higher. I had no idea how to even begin explaining what I'd just been told.

I turned the handle to open it for him, he pushed past me in a hurry. That wasn't like him, he'd never do that to me.

"Why didn't you just come in?" I asked. Something was off.

He was looking around the room, then turned to face me when he said, "Oh, yeah, the lock must be broken or something."

I tipped my head to the side, questioningly, it's a biolock, it opens with people preprogrammed genetics, it wasn't mechanical so I doubted it was broken. He walked up to me, closely. Too close, his breath was hot against my skin, I leaned in slightly to breathe in his scent, he smelled like bar soap. He never smelled like bar soap. Ever. I had a bad feeling.

I quickly took a step back and tried to move to the bed, where my phone was in the blankets where I'd been. His eyes tracked me as I moved. I did my best to act normal, I was not known for being a good actress though. It would be the role of a lifetime.

He stood at the foot of the bed, watching me silently. I sat on the bed and climbed in the blankets to try and hide my plan. I slowly felt around to find my phone hidden somewhere in the sheets. I got it! "So, Nick, what's up? Everything okay?" I tried to keep him talking and his attention off what my hands were doing in the sheets.

I held onto the phone tightly under the blanket pushing buttons, hoping I hit the right one that called Nick, praying he'd actually pick up. My voice had to remain steady, no matter how terrified I felt. I couldn't let this imposter know I was onto him.

"Yes. I just wanted to… check up on you" he looked agitated.

"Check up on me? That's sweet," I forced a small smile, hoping it looked natural. My heart was racing, and I could feel my palms sweating. His eyes stayed glued on me, watching my every move.

"Yes," he said, his tone still wrong, "I wanted to make sure you're safe. You know… with everything going on."

I fought the urge to shudder. Nick never spoke like this, so stiff, so forced. The real Nick was warm and comforting, this… this was all wrong. I needed to buy more time. My fingers tightened around the phone, praying Nick was hearing everything on the other end.

"I appreciate that," I said, trying to keep my voice casual, "but how did you get away from the search so fast? I thought you'd still be with the others."

He paused for a second, his eyes narrowing ever so slightly. "I… I got a break," he replied, almost too quickly. "I wanted to see you first."

I swallowed, my throat dry. There was no way the real Nick would leave something so important to "take a break." I needed to keep stalling, keep him talking.

"That's nice of you so, uh… any leads on the Wiijigoo? Did you find anything new?"

His jaw tightened. "Not yet," he muttered, his eyes shifting to the side for a brief second. His gaze snapped back to me. "Don't worry about that, Aoife," he said, stepping closer again. His tone was unsettling, like he was trying too hard to sound reassuring.

I nodded, my heart racing faster. "You're right," I said softly, keeping my hand steady as I spoke into the phone hidden in the blankets, hoping Nick could hear me clearly. "I'll trust you to handle it. I know you always protect me. Always have."

There was a long pause before he replied. "Yes," he said slowly. "I always will."

The temperature in the room seemed to drop. My hand, still clutching the phone, was trembling now. I couldn't keep this up much longer. I needed Nick, the real Nick, to show up, and fast.

The imposter moved closer, his eyes darkening, a strange smile creeping across his face. "So, what were you drawing?" he asked, his voice lower now, as if trying to steer the conversation away from anything that might expose him.

My mind raced. "Oh, just… sketches. You know how I love to draw." I tried to keep my tone light, but the tension between us was suffocating. He was standing so close now, too close, and I could feel the danger lurking behind his forced words.

I took a deep breath, hoping the real Nick was listening, ready to save me. Because this wasn't going to end well.

"I'm, I'm scared Nick" I said louder than my normal volume, hoping the phone being under the blankets would pick up my voice. I had no idea if Nick even answered or if I dialed correctly.

"What are you scared of?" he asked, tipping his head and showing his teeth in an odd way.

"Well, I'm scared of people getting hurt because of me, Nick. I don't want anyone else to get caught in the crossfire. They didn't deserve it."

He let out a small deep rumble, that gargled, not Nick's deep sexy rumble that did things to my body, this version made me recoil and wince.

"Nick, do you promise me that no one will get hurt?" I hoped Kept saying his name so that he'd appear. Then it dawned on me, if I could create portals to send things to Nick, I wondered if I could create portals that would bring Nick to me. But how would I do it without drawing attention to myself?

"Hey, Nick?" The thing was looking around the room, that drew his attention back to me. "I uh, need to go to the restroom. Give me just a sec."

His lips curled into a small snarl, clearly not happy with me leaving proximity to him.

"Yes. Hurry." He said in a borderline threatening tone.

"Don't worry, I'll be right back." I walked far around *that thing*, not wanting to get too close. I didn't know what he'd do.

I shut the door as quietly as possible, but every instinct in me screamed to slam it and lock it tight. I didn't know what the imposter was capable of, and I couldn't risk setting it off. Once inside, I let out a shaky breath and focused, opening the door inside me where my magic was stored. I let it flow freely, warmth surging through my body, bringing me a strange sense of comfort. I pictured Nick, his sharp, beautiful face, his strong hands, his eyes that always seemed to hold the answers. I called out to him with every ounce of my being.

The golden tornado rushed through the room with incredible force. Gold flecks whirled around me, moving so fast it was hard to focus. Then, through the flurry, I saw a hand, a strong, familiar hand, tattooed in tribal patterns. It was him.

Nick reached out blindly, his hand searching through the magic-laden air, trying to find me. I held my breath, watching as he pushed through the golden storm. Once I was sure he had arrived, I began to close the magical door. Before the tornado fully died down, Nick's hand found mine. He grabbed it with an intensity that made my heart race.

Without hesitating, he pulled me into his arms, his grip firm yet gentle. His other hand cupped my face, pulling me close. Then, his lips crashed into mine in a deep, passionate kiss. Everything else faded away, my fears, my doubts, the danger waiting just outside the door. All I could feel was Nick. His touch drained every last bit of my resolve, making me forget, even for just a moment, the reality we faced.

But the sharp, sudden knock on the door shattered the moment. The imposter Nick was still out there. "Time to come out my little rosebud." Nick never had nicknames or pet names for me, that one, coming from *him* made me want to vomit though.

Nick's grip on me tightened, possessive and protective. I could see the tension in his jaw, the burning desire to break down the door and confront whoever, or whatever, was on the other side. His breath was warm against my ear as he whispered, his lips grazing my skin, sending a shiver down my spine. "I got your call. I was trying so hard to get up to you. You never cease to amaze me."

His words, soft as they were, made my heart race, but there wasn't time to enjoy the moment. "As much as I love the compliments, can we save them until after we figure out how to deal with this Nick imposter?" I whispered, trying to keep my voice steady. "Cami said I'd kill you, Nick. Do you think she was talking about the fake you? There's no way I could ever hurt you."

Nick's eyes darkened as he mulled it over. "Caoineadh are glimpses of possible futures, not certainties. They can change depending on the choices we make. Let's hope she was seeing the imposter, not me." He tried to laugh, but it fell flat, his own tension too high. "Do you think you can transport us again? Move us all to the practice arena? I'll text security and the coven to meet us there."

I hesitated, unsure of myself. "I, I don't know," I admitted, my voice shaky. Moving three people, including a dangerous imposter, was more than I'd ever tried before. But I had to do this. For everyone. "But I'll try."

Nick's grin, sexy and full of confidence, made me feel stronger than I thought I could be. "That's my girl. Here's the plan. You step out there, buy a few seconds, and then unleash your magic. Move us all to the arena as quickly as you can. Don't hesitate. I'll jump in right before you take off. I'll be in front of you, and he won't be able to touch you without going through me first."

Before I could respond, another heavy bang shook the door. I jumped. "I'm coming! Sorry, uh… girl problems," I called out, trying to sound casual. My heart pounded as I slowly opened the door just wide enough to slip through, squeezing past Nick, who stayed hidden behind it.

Once outside, I slid past the imposter's towering frame and perched myself on the bed, doing my best to appear calm. "So, what are we going to do?" I asked, trying to mask the panic churning inside me.

"Do?" he repeated, his voice too sharp, too cold.

"Yeah, how are we going to catch the Wiijigoo that's after me?" I tried to sound casual, even playful, as if I wasn't fully aware that something was wrong. Every fiber of my being was screaming at me to run.

The imposter's eyes darkened, and a twisted grin spread across his face. "Oh, I wouldn't worry about that. I'll take care of you."

A sick feeling settled in my stomach. Time was running out.

That didn't sound like "take care of" in the nurturing sense, more like "you'll be sleeping with the fishes." I could feel the bile rising in my throat as dread crept over me. I'd kept the imposter talking long enough, it was time to act. I couldn't hold back any longer. Summoning every ounce of strength and fear, I ripped the door off the imaginary magical box inside me.

The force was too much for me to handle quietly, I screamed as the magic burst out of me, no time to release it with grace. The gold winds filled the room in a blinding rush, swirling wildly. Fake Nick shielded his eyes, momentarily disoriented, and that gave me the split second I needed.

"Now, Nick!" I screamed, knowing the real Nick was just behind the bathroom door.

The door flew open with a bang. The real Nick barreled through, immediately positioning himself between the imposter and me. Without a second to waste, I pictured the training room in my mind with every detail I could muster, and with a herculean effort, I wished us all there.

The ground beneath my feet changed, and I took off running, darting behind the line of guards with shields that had already formed a protective circle around me. Nick and his double remained at the center of the windstorm as it began to die down, leaving the two men facing each other.

The real Nick's voice cut through the tense air like a blade. "You come into my building, and try to hurt someone I love? Unacceptable!" His voice was low, dangerous. I could feel the raw anger radiating from him.

Fake Nick's bravado started to crumble. His eyes darted around, searching for an escape, but the circle of armed guards had him trapped. Still, he tried to maintain a front, shrugging nonchalantly. "I'm just visiting. Aoife and I have a score to settle." His eyes met mine, and they shifted, from Nick's familiar green to a sickening, unnatural yellow.

"We have no score, nothing in common, you monster," I spat, my voice dripping with disgust.

He laughed, a deep, savage sound that made me want to retch. "Monster? Oh, you have no idea, little rosebud. But don't worry, you won't have to concern yourself with it much longer."

"Stop calling me that!" I yelled, my voice trembling with fury. "You don't get to call me anything!"

Nick, ever composed in the face of chaos, stepped forward, his fists clenched. "What do we call you, though?" His voice was steady, but there was a sharp edge to it.

The imposter tipped his head back and laughed again, his teeth, now long and pointed, gleaming under the lights. "You should know me, Nick. We met a few years ago. You don't remember?" His tone was teasing, relishing the tension.

Nick's face shifted, his brow furrowing as he thought deeply. And then the imposter's features began to morph. The smooth, attractive facade melted away, leaving behind black thick swirls of shadows, sharp teeth and red eyes. My heart sank, this was the creature that followed me that night in the alley, the one that changed everything for me.

Nick's breath caught. "I remember you now," he whispered, his voice tight with rage. "Your voice, you were the one who requested an appointment with my parents," his voice broke slightly, "the night they died."

A slow, malevolent smile crept across the imposter's face. "Ah, you do remember. Wonderful. I do love when things come full circle."

Nick's fists trembled at his sides, his fury barely contained. And in that moment, I saw something terrifying pass between them, old history, unfinished business, and a desire for vengeance. "Did you kill them, shapeshifter? Or should I say demon? Which do you prefer?" Nick spat out.

"I take pride in all that I am, you may call me any of those names. But I am not yet ready to answer questions about your dear sweet parents" He ran a thin snake-like tongue over his sharp teeth.

"Too bad I knew that you weren't Nick right away and spoiled your plan huh?" I screamed at him.

"No one else did though, I walked through the entire building and not a soul noticed I was different. Your security could use some work Nick." He said, smirking at Nick.

"I noticed, that's what matters." I gave him a proud smile.

"Too bad you didn't have the power to do anything about it. All you have is magical wind? What is that anyway? Pathetic." He spat on the floor in my direction.

"It was enough to get you here."

Nick walked over to me and whispered, "Do you think you could send him to a different dimension?"

"Nick, I have no idea. I've never done anything like that and I've only gone to that one dimension once."

"You've never done a lot until you tried but you've succeeded at everything you've attempted."

He was kind of right. Maybe I didn't know the depth of my power. It wouldn't hurt to try though… I think. "I can try. What dimension do I send him to?"

"It's called the Mystic Abyss. It's nothing, has no one to imitate, no one to trick, no one at all. He'll be utterly alone forever."

"Sounds like a place where he belongs. How do I do it?"

"Picture layers above earth, picture blackness, alone. Then say 'Mystic Abyss' and it should send him. I think."

"Okay, I'll try." Nick squeezed my hand and gave a small smile. I could tell he was still struggling with lack of answers from the shapeshifter demon about his parents.

Nick walked back to the center and faced the creature. "If you want to tell me about my parents, tell us your name."

He tipped his head and bared his teeth, "I do not have a name, I belong to the shadows, I hide in the voids where only fear lives."

"Very well darkness, any last words? Or confessions you'd like to get off your chest? Clear your conscience maybe."

"I have no conscience. I live only to suit myself." The shapeshifter laughed, revealing his teeth again, "It's not too late Nick, I could owe *you* a favor if you help me. I am a great demon to have on your side. She can't be that good in bed anyway, though after I'm done with her, she'll be ruined for the next so if you wanted one more time, I'd do it now."

He paused and smiled at me like he wanted to eat me, not in the fun way, more in the Hannibal Lector kind of way, then looked back at Nick and laughed, tossing his head back. "You haven't even had her yet! Tsk tsk Nick. You've wasted your opportunity. Guess you'll never know now. Unless… you wanted to take her right here; give us a show." He raised his eyebrows and licked his thin lips.

I saw Nick slightly glance with his peripherals at me. My heart threatened to beat out of my chest. What did that mean, *pass me onto the next*? How had he known that Nick and I haven't… been together? And now he wanted to watch us? It made bile rise in my throat. I fought the urge to send him to the Mystic Abyss right then and there but I knew Nick hoped to get answers about his parents. He deserved answers but drawing this encounter out was proving unhelpful if not harmful for us.

"That kind of talk will not be tolerated here. I don't know how you got in here but now that you're here, we require everyone to follow a strict code of respect. You are not following that code so I hereby banish you from this building. You will not be joining us back here again." Nick looked composed and cool. Like the boss he was. I was so proud of him coming into his own as a leader.

"You don't have the power to banish me! You're just a little helper that delivers toys. You're nothing" he laughed maniacally.

"You're right, I may not have the power but she does." he pointed proudly at me. I stepped through the line of people who surrounded them, trying to look as powerful as Nick said I was. That was a big role to live up to. I had to make it work, I couldn't make a liar out of Nick.

The demon laughed again, "the little rosebud? She has no power over me!"

"I was powerful enough to bring you here." I smirked, holding out my arms to display all the people that encircled him.

"I was caught by surprise. I was told you didn't have much power. I hadn't planned for this. It won't happen again." He said with such confidence. Little did he know I'd done so much more and I was determined to finish this with him.

"Well, I think it's time for one more surprise then!" I opened my magic, Nick ran behind me, past the gold tornado that spun around the evil creature. The gold was so thick I could only make out small parts of him, his face didn't look smug anymore, it was full of fear, and it brought me pure joy. I took a deep breath, drawing on the warmth of my magic. I pictured the layers Nick had told me about, the ones I barely understood. Layers above the earth, places where no one else existed, where there was only darkness and silence. The Mystic Abyss, a void where even a shapeshifter demon would have no tricks left to play.

Closing my eyes, I whispered, "Mystic Abyss."

Suddenly, the air shifted. A strange, eerie quiet filled the room, and the golden wind I'd summoned before began to stir again, stronger this time, wrapping around the demon in spiraling waves. His eyes widened slightly, when he realized it was too late.

"Wait!" His voice wavered, but it was too late. The vortex of magic encircled him, pulling him upward as though the very air itself swallowed him whole.

He screamed, but it was cut off as the golden light flickered and he vanished, gone. The room erupted into cheers and celebration!.

I stood there, shaking, my breath coming in short gasps. I had done it. I had actually done it.

Nick crossed the room in an instant, pulling me into his arms, holding me tightly against his chest. "You did it," he whispered, his voice thick with emotion. "You really did it."

I exhaled a breath I didn't realize I was holding, sinking into the warmth and comfort of his embrace. I had accomplished my biggest feat yet. I doubted myself but Nick, he knew I had the ability to pull that off. I needed to start believing in myself the way he did "Is it over?"

"Yes," he murmured, his chin resting on top of my head. "He won't be bothering anyone again." He pulled back, just enough to look at me, his green eyes filled with a mix of pride and something deeper. "You were amazing, Aoife."

Magic was beginning to feel so natural to me. While I didn't love all the danger that came along with it, I loved all the strength it gave me when I succeeded.

"We still need to find out who let him in the building." I whispered to Nick, wishing we could stay in this joyous moment forever but knowing we weren't done yet.

"I have a feeling I already know", he said as he sat me down on my feet. His smile faded as he spoke.

I looked questionably at him, waiting for him to elaborate.

"Right before you whisked me away to your bathroom earlier, I ran into Njeri, she was checking on me because she saw me with the doc. I was confused because I hadn't even seen him today. I knew something was off. The Doc has had a few run-ins with bad creatures before, he wasn't good at paying off his debts. I had my security hold him and question him while we did our part." He tapped his ear revealing a transmitter. "They've been filling me in on the progress as we've been working here. He had a gambling debt before he came here, I paid them off for him so he'd be in the clear but apparently, old habits followed him. He owed the Wiijigoo a favor. He claimed he didn't know it was coming to hurt you. He told him that he just wanted information. I don't know if I fully believe him but either way, he's violated our code and he can't stay here." he said with a sad hearted sigh.

The little round doctor that greeted me so warmly was responsible for all of it? I couldn't believe it. He was so sweet, how could he betray Nick like this, and me? I didn't know him that well but this situation made me so uneasy. He's supposed to do no harm. I reminded myself that he had an illness, he was an addict and his actions reflected that. He needed help, not punishment.

"Nick, I don't want harm coming to him. Can we send him to a facility that can help with his addiction? I don't want him back here, he's ruined his chance but he's sick Nick. He needs help, not maltreatment." I pleaded with him.

He stood still for a few seconds, mulling it over, "I see your point. I think

It's a fine idea. I'll find a place that can help him. You truly are one of a kind Aoife."

My cheeks got hot, "I can only be me. You've taught me it's safe for that here."

He nodded in agreement and pride and drew me into him with one arm around my waist. "All I've ever wanted is you."

His words melted me, "Oh Nick," I fought back the tears, my ugly crying would not ruin the moment. "But what about finding out about your parents? Do you think it's the same Wiijigoo?"

He shrugged. "I don't know. I'm beginning to realize that finding the answers wont make my life any happier. Adding you to it will though. My parents only wanted me to be happy. I want to do right by them and not continue this pursuit for vengeance. I choose peace and happiness."

"You're such a good man Nick." I hugged him so tight, he was my weight or I'd float off into space because I was so full of happiness. "I um, have something I wanted to tell you. Well two actually."

"Is this good news/bad news situation?" He tipped his head in question.

I smiled, "it's more of a good new, better news situation." I leaned in for a kiss, pouring all my love into it. He must have liked it because he let out a little growl that made me want to be his prey. "I whispered into his ear, I love you." His body went still, but I could feel his heartbeat picking up pace where our chest touched.

"That is good news, I don't know how anything could top that, but what's second?"

I held my hand out between us and made a small golden cyclone in my palm, I let it grow until it enveloped us and we couldn't see anyone else. "I'm keeping my magic. I couldn't imagine life without it now. It's part of me, always has been, I just didn't know myself enough to be open to it. I feel… whole."

"That is better news. I'm so happy that you're happy." He looked the happiest I'd ever seen him. Knowing I was the cause made my heart want to explode.

Njeri called out from a group of guards, "Hey boss, What do you say about giving us the night off after all this?"

Nick started to say something but Njeri cut him off, "Yeah, I was talking to her," she pointed at me.

I smiled at Nick and said, "You may have the night off my friend. If you need us… don't." She smiled and winked at us as she walked away clearly proud of how the situation ended.

Nick had a mix of shock and pride on his face, then leaned in to kiss me so deeply, there were no walls inside me now, just openness that welcomed him. We embraced, letting our bodies become familiar with each other. Without the doubt of losing them. We had no fear, no worries, only us in that minute.

"Let's go upstairs," I said, my breath coming in deep, quick bursts. Nick swooped me into his arms, I breathed in his comforting scent as he carried me.

"I can speed this up". I smiled and summoned another tornado and delivered us into my room. He smiled like a kid on Christmas morning as he laid me gently on the bed and stepped back, his gaze fixed on me with an intensity that made my cheeks flush pink.

"What?" I finally asked, curiosity piqued.

"Nothing," he replied, a soft smile playing on his lips. "Just taking in my soulmate, my gift from the universe. I can't wait to look at you every day. I've been sneaking glances at you when you weren't looking, trying to memorize every freckle and curve in case you decided not to stay."

I playfully waved my finger in a 'come here' motion, and he crawled over my body with a deliberate slowness, kissing his way up from my feet, past my legs, and finally to my stomach. When his lips met mine, it was a spark, passionate and electric. Our tongues danced together, exploring each other in a rhythm that felt both new and ancient. He nibbled on my lips, while our hands roamed over each other, discovering every inch that we hadn't yet dared to explore.

In that moment, our bodies melted into one another, as if we were crafted from the same essence. I soaked up every caress, every kiss, and every heartbeat that resonated against my skin.

This is what it feels like to be whole, I thought. How could I have almost given it all up? I would have regretted so much. I looked forward to every stolen glance from across the room, every brush of fingers as we passed each other in the halls, and every night we would spend together for the rest of our lives. I was where I was meant to be. I was ready for any adventure life throws at me. With Nick at my side, I could tackle anything.

…this was the start of a beautiful life together, one I could never have imagined.

About the Author

Teysha W.L. is a fantasy romance author with a passion for storytelling that weaves magic, adventure, and unforgettable characters. Her debut novel invites readers into a world where the fantastical and the romantic collide, creating a tale that will enchant fans of fantasy and romance alike.

When she's not dreaming up new worlds, Teysha channels her creativity into crafting, sewing, and drawing, infusing her imaginative spirit into every project. She also writes for a non-profit organization she founded and volunteers with, sharing stories that inspire change and connection. Teysha lives by the belief that magic can be found in the everyday—and she strives to capture that magic in every story she tells.

You can connect with me on:

🌐 https://teyshawlauthor.my.canva.site

🔗 https://linktr.ee/TeyshaWL

Subscribe to my newsletter:

✉ https://forms.gle/eHJWe5cJbdN7ZEYR6

www.ingramcontent.com/pod-product-compliance
Lightning Source LLC
Chambersburg PA
CBHW072100300726
48975CB00003B/642